MW01452434

DATE DUE

MY 16 '93			
JE 18 '93			
JUL 12 '93			
JUL 30 '93			
AUG 6 '93			
SEP 7 '93			
SEP 26 '93			
OCT 27 '93			
NOV 9 '93			

F
LIO

Liotta, P. H.
Diamond's compass

DEMCO

Diamond's Compass

P.H. Liotta

Diamond's Compass

a novel

ALGONQUIN BOOKS OF CHAPEL HILL   1993

This is a work of fiction. While, as in all fiction, the literary perceptions and insights are based in part on experience, all names, characters, places, and incidents are either products of the author's imagination or, as in the case of some historical figures and events, are used fictitiously. No reference to the life of any real person, living or dead, is intended or should be inferred.

Published by
Algonquin Books of Chapel Hill
Post Office Box 2225
Chapel Hill, North Carolina 27515-2225

a division of
Workman Publishing Company, Inc.
708 Broadway
New York, New York 10003

© 1993 by P. H. Liotta. All rights reserved.
Printed in the United States of America.
Interior design by Deborah Wong.

Library of Congress Cataloging-in-Publication Data
Liotta, P. H.
   Diamond's Compass: a novel / by P.H. Liotta. — 1st ed.
     p. cm.
   ISBN 0-945575-74-2
   I. Title.
PS3562.I568D4   1993
813'.54—dc20   92-33371
                                           CIP

1 2 3 4 5 6 7 8 9 10
FIRST EDITION

Contents

PART ONE: Hejira 1

PART TWO: The Shadow of God 39

PART THREE: Sháh-Námé 101

PART FOUR: The *Ghazal* of Memory 131

PART FIVE: Kooh Damávand 183

PART SIX: Zabán 225

PART SEVEN: Dead Reckonings 251

Author's Note 265

Glossary 267

For my mother and for my father

Sáyeh ye shomá kam, nashavád
May your shadow never grow less

The past is a foreign country:

they do things differently there.

—*L. P. Hartley*

Diamond's Compass

Part One

Hejira

هجره

It is said that when the Prophet Mohammed, he whose name is to be thanked, fled on his great Hejira, he was uncertain of the surest means to escape from Mecca. He and his disciples had suffered for the faith of their one God, and their lives were in danger. They came to know that he must go north to Yathrib, the place which is today called Medina. There he would find his new disciples; there their faith would spread to the world.

The Prophet was carried out of Mecca on the back of a disciple. He lay still, inside a sack of strong cloth. At the gates of the city, two soldiers stopped the man, and demanded to know what he carried in his sack. "I am carrying the Prophet Mohammed," the man answered truthfully. The soldiers, laughing at this stupid reply, called the man a fool and told him to pass by.

1

Faith,

Tonight the moon is perfectly full, barren and bone. Beneath me, to the west, the fires of Al-Madid burn like eternal flames. They have been burning for years now, dumping their foul fossil excrement into the air. Some days the sky is dark as a new moon.

But tonight, the air is clear. I can focus through the astral tracker and follow the path of moving figures on the ground. A trail of Bedouins across the desert. A single camel carrying a load of stolen cargo, explosives, opium.

The air is clear, and cold. If anyone down there suspected my existence, all he would have to do is look into the stars and see my shadow. See the contrail made by cold heaven. Hear the hushed whine of my almost silent engine. But he would have to know where and how to look.

Shabah—*the Ghost.* That's what we call ourselves. Officially, of course, we do not exist. But we make no secret of our existence. When we move into the Area of Responsibility, or "AOR," we start broadcasting immediately. We speak out for justice and the right of individual choice. We speak of the love of the one God and his prophet. We tell the truth. Especially, we tell how Shápuhr Mareta is no prophet, no leader, how he is less than a man because he speaks from a temple called the Heart of the Kingdom to followers who do not exist.

"The only words that issue from that kingdom," I tell my audience, "are meant for the Peoples of the Lie. Nothing good can come from this."

•

Nothing good has ever come from this.

It took us a while to realize that. But eventually we found out. After all the wars, all the storms of the desert, all the lines in the sand, after the Alliance for Nation-State Securities had determined that the war for this place they call the Paradise was at an end. Still, the violence and agony and suffering continue. Thousands have lost their homes, their ways of life. Misery has lengthened into prolonged despair. This was what Shápuhr Mareta, voice of the *umma*—the community of believers—had predicted would happen. There would be another war, of course, but why should that matter? Had this place known anything other than war for thousands of years? He proclaimed this place would one day be united as the Paradise, and so demanded nothing less than eternal torment before the sweet fruit of victory would be revealed. Harmony and hatred became synthesis. War meant freedom, he declared. Death meant life.

But worst of all, he survived. He could not be removed. He was the thing that haunted Paradise. If he weren't so damned frightening, it would be almost funny the way he controlled us.

"My children," I hear him whisper. "We must return to the Order of God. These dogs cannot remain. Our purity will sustain us. And though they are strong, know that we are many. Know that we can never die.

"Here we will come together as none before us," he commands. "We will live as Moabite and Philistine and Aramaic brothers never could, under terms forbidden by Mosaic law. We will come together in the Paradise we name Behesht."

But it wasn't funny. Shápuhr Mareta was real—and terrifying. It had been years since I had seen anyone or anything hold people's lives in such balance and under such control. That had been in Iran, when that nation still existed. They carried the body of the man some had called the Twelfth Imam to his final plot of earth. I wonder.

Mareta even appears the way Khomeini was. His eyes drill into you through the camera lens, wherever you are.

"Farangi dogs," he will call us. "Unbelievers. You will swim in your own blood."

People's minds—that was the one thing he knew. He knew us better than we knew ourselves. For years he had held us in his grasp. And despite anything the Alliance might claim, he always shifted and slipped through our hands. Like water. He was the ghost that haunted Paradise. The voice that turned our gyros, led all our compass points astray. A ghost—rising from the past. A ghost inside you. A ghost beside you. At night, dreaming in a kind of frenzy, he was the ghost telling you that you would never wake, that you had been dead already for many years. And even as you play with a kind of remove and composure in the waking light of day, you coil back in horror when you think of him, knowing he's out there. Somewhere. In a land that is only desert or dead mountains, he is in every crag and crevice, every level path of sand. At night, when rocks release steam and heat and crack with the cooling

HEJIRA

air of darkness, a place so barren, anything was beautiful and everything meant something, you wondered if it was him or one of his minions in any odd shape that flickered in the shadow or stood watching at the horizon. He could change form. He could become the sand, fire, air, a drop of water. He could pass overhead as you slept. Watching, checking your next move. He was the genie that no one believed really existed until you flew a plane shaped like a giant boomerang twenty miles above the earth. And then you knew. Your mind tumbled like a gyroscope, and then you saw. Flying beside you, in the missing-man slot, cross-legged on his magic carpet. "Be well, my little friend," he would coo. "I will find you. All in good time."

•

We called ourselves Shabah, part of a larger security force to erode his power base, to remove his form of existence. And it was official policy that operations, and in particular psychological operations, would continue at the strategic level until it was over. Perhaps it would never end.

"If you know the enemy and know yourself, you need not fear the result of a hundred battles," Sun Tzu wrote more than twenty-five hundred years ago. That was what we wanted most to do: to know ourselves.

None of us know how many planes there are. We should not know, or need to know. Each of us has a tightly defined role: to broadcast the voice of the Alliance, to speak directly to the people of the Paradise, to convince them, to disrupt the physical and internal messages sent by Shâpuhr Mareta. To be the eye of God.

Faith, you know that once I left this way of life. But I was called back, without a choice. There was a war and I was needed. Now it seems I've been here forever. If a man must leave a place, a place he has lived in and loved and where all his memory is buried, he must leave it with a sense that it has all been lost. That's how it is. There is a certain part of all of us that lives outside of time.

For me, the way it is has turned to hours of flight in the darkness, flight at the speed of my own voice, over a ravaged terrain. I listen and sometimes speak to the darkness, alone but never lonely. I will end up knowing everything about everyone and nothing about who I am.

Deduced reckoning; in other words, your best guess at where you are from where you came. But "dead reckoning" is what we called it. What direction, speed, and winds aloft are telling you—position without observation of the sun or stars. The voices of the dead accounting for those who still remain. To have no eyes, but to see with their eyes. To shrink into the envelope of twilight, fixed like a rock or a tree, or a man when he is dead, above the cold provinces of air, watching your own human shadow dwindle and fade while you rise into the troposphere, ionosphere, and beyond, over the glistening rim of the earth's horizon curving back from you, against the slender edges of the earth itself, until you breathe among the boundless stars.

•

Alone for hours on end, I end up mesmerized: the quiet of my solitary engine; the soft digital glow of my instrument panel; one hand resting on the control stick, which rests by my right thigh; my arm in a brace, giving only my hand the freedom to move; a flicker of thought, a hundredth-of-an-inch movement in my wrist, and the Shabah responds. The genie inside lives.

The soft glow of my altimeter shows my readout: 120,000 feet, straight and level flight. I fly the Great Circle course, along agionic lines and points of least magnetic variation. My Sperry laser-centered artificial horizon shows my drift at six degrees east, and the central nerves of my inertial navigation adjust the flight path. Through the soles of my feet on the rudders, I feel the Shabah pulse and ease through the night, the flex of muscle and response.

The Shabah tells me there is no wind tonight. The night is fine. Time is a function of distance that is a function of relative speed. Speed is the air slipping over my wings. The future and past are somewhere in the universe above my head, a universe I am staring into now—where 90 percent of the stars I see do not exist, a universe where I become a history of other voices, other hands at the controls.

Where the moon is full.
Barren.
Bone.

٢

If there were one day when I could say it all began, when all the clocks unwound and the calendar was new, it would be that one, late spring, 1978. We stood perfectly aligned, as we always were, preparing to march squadron by squadron, rank by rank. We would march, behind our commander. Tall and thin, proud emblems of our nation, arms swinging naturally in a controlled rhythm, hands slightly cupped as if each cradled a roll of quarters in each palm.

I guess it was a strange way for college students to head off to lunch. But then we were heading for Mitchell Hall, the largest dining facility in the world, named for Brigadier General Billy Mitchell—*America's greatest military martyr and don't you ever forget it, Diamond!*—who got himself courtmartialled because no one listened closely enough when he raved about the unlimited potential of airpower: it was the wave of the future.

The cadet wing commander would squeak a tiny order that rolled across the long terrazzo: "Pass-in-Review!" Each commander of each of the forty squadrons would lift his saber to his lips, salute like the knight errant who confronts the Lady of the Lake with Excalibur. Reverent, powerful, submissive.

"Piss in your shoe!" someone in the ranks always muttered.

But it was a beautiful sight. I believe that. All four thousand uniforms melted into one. We surged at the command of "march-turn-eyes right-front!" In those days we were all exceptional. We were the future, and the future's wave.

And I can tell you the two things I remember most from that day. The first was our commander, my roommate and closest friend: Scott Hind. A rude, arrogant, crude, nasty bastard. I really loved him.

"Diamond, you whining, sleazy, miserable sack of shit," he announced. He stood at attention facing us, his saber aligned the length of his wrist to his shoulder, voicing his true opinion of me to the 140 proud first and second and third and fourthclassmen of the 27th Squadron—Goshawks—of the military academy in the Rockies we called simply, "The Zoo." He was speaking basically as he had done every day of the semester that he served as our commander.

He always called me Diamond. In those days everyone else just called me D. Or Diamond's kid.

"Cadet Hind, know that I will always love you," I said from the rear of the formation. I'm fairly tall—six-feet-five—and so I had to stand back there with the basketball players and the geeks.

Funny. He said the same thing nearly every day, and I said nearly the same thing back, and everyone always laughed. It was like that.

After we lost Mitchell James, I became Scott's roommate. I was two years younger than him, and a year behind him, a secondclassman—a junior you'd call it at most schools. I was the Goshawk first sergeant, the highest-ranking secondclassman in the squadron. But I held that rank only because Scott had selected me at the end of last semester. He took a chance. The squadron did well academically, militarily, athletically. We weren't at the top, so we didn't have to satisfy anyone's expectations. But we hovered damn close to it.

Scott would always bark back, "Let's maintain some order around here, goddamn it. This ain't some kindergarten, people." The squadron would laugh again, but keep the laughter down, of course. And the call to attention would be given, the military band would rouse to a single drumbeat booming from the honor court, we would present arms, and then off we would go to lunch.

But that didn't happen that day. Here is the second thing I remember: the flying wing.

Sometimes planes would pass overhead during the noon meal formation. It was motivation, sure. But it was also tradition, the way we understood it. As the youngest sister service of the American military, we always had a complex about stressing tradition. Probably because we didn't have too much of it.

Sometimes the planes would be a flight of Phantoms in the missing man formation, remembering the dead and missing in Southeast Asia. On homecoming weekends, when other schools might be worrying about football games and class reunions, we would stand in formation remembering lost graduates and our one lost war. There would be a roll call for the missing and there would be a reply, "Absent, sir!" thundering across the long terrazzo, and then the Phantoms would pulse overhead leaving a vacant slot for

HEJIRA

the missing pilot. The slot would be behind the lead Phantom, in the place where the best wingman always flew.

The jets would blast over the seventeen-spired chapel: twelve spires for the twelve apostles and five remaining for the chiefs of staff.

One of my favorite memories was of a single U-2, the mysterious high-altitude spy plane—a glider mounted on a rocket engine—passing overhead one grey, dead afternoon in winter. Huge, trailing wings of colorless black, the pilot passed just over our Goshawk formation and tilted his throttles up and jammed the yoke into his lap. The nose of the glider shot straight up and then started climbing, straight for the darkness. Climbing toward the D-horizon, the place where the atmosphere ends and space begins.

I wanted that.

I had the eyes of a hawk: 20/7 vision. And I had the fire for flight. Two summers before, I first felt that fire in a sailplane—solo. I'll never forget the feel of simply reaching over to pull the cable release for the tow plane or the sharp tug as the cable flew back and the tow plane dived left and I banked hard right and up into the sun, searching for thermals. I started screaming. Seventeen years old and I had never been happier.

So quiet. No engine, no instructor telling you your worst faults, no rhythm but the pulse of your own blood rushing as you move stick and rudder. Only the wind grazing the canopy.

All of this is a legacy, of course, that I inherited from my father, Brigadier General Therrien Boyd Diamond. Fighter pilot *extraordinaire*. A good man. Someone everyone knew. Someone I never knew.

From the moment I first dropped my bags at the base of the BRING ME MEN ramp, ready for anything, especially the end of life as I knew it, especially when an unsmiling firstclassman stepped up and barked: "Listen up, gentlemen! We begin with the five things, and I mean the *only* five things you may say during the next year . . ." (which, by the way, were: *yes, sir; no, sir; sir, may I make a statement; sir, may I ask a question;* and, my all-time favorite, being the only response to a why question, *no excuse, sir!*), I heard a voice behind me say, "That's him, that's Diamond's kid."

Chuck Yeager and Karl Richter were legends. So was my father. Yeager went on to make battery commercials and get the reputation he deserved. Richter was killed on his 198th mission over Southeast Asia, after punching out of an F-105 Thunderchief. He couldn't release himself from his parachute harness after touching down; the monsoon took him kicking and screaming into the jungle until his chute finally strangled him. And my father got himself appointed Air Advisor to the court of Mohammed Reza Pahlaví, Imperial Shah of Iran.

When people mentioned him, it was with respect. A strange thing, really, to hear your father's name popped off with admiration, awe, and jealousy so many times—always in the third person. It became natural for me to think of him in this way, even when talking face to face with him, as General Diamond, *veteran of Korea and fighter ace from Vietnam*. At the Zoo, I heard stories he'd never told me: how, after falling asleep in a P-51 Mustang he had opened the canopy to stick his frail, plastic radio transmitter into the slipstream for an Automatic Direction Finder, or ADF, and steer to the nearest airfield because he was so lost; how he punched out of an F-104 Starfighter and was thrown around in the violent fringes of a thunderstorm for an hour and a half before he was thrown clear of the storm and his parachute took him safely back to earth; about launching his aircraft during the deepest part of the night for an air intercept of a Soviet Tu-95 Bear bomber, without informing traffic controllers of his flight plan or his final destination; about the only story he ever told me and then I heard repeated a hundred times: about the head caught in the undercarriage—how his crew chief had puked on the runway when he saw it.

When I saw any plane passing overhead, I thought of him. It's true. I couldn't look at the contrails of a jet high in the atmosphere and not think about T-Boy Diamond.

And that's who I thought of that day. The *real* second thing I remember from that day was just a plane. But the real person I thought of, looking up at the shape pulsing fast over our heads, was my father. I was depressed, a little pissed.

My father had come back to the States on business that week. He was hoping, he said one night on the phone, he could make it out to see me. But the night before he'd called and said it wasn't going to be possible after all. He had a flight scheduled cross-country in a new fighter trainer. There just wasn't time.

But that plane.

It came straight down from Eaglehead Mountain on a flat trajectory, like an incoming warhead. Straight over the terrazzo.

11
HEJIRA

It had no markings. The wings were swept *forward!* The cockpit, cut like a diamond, sloped into the face of the body. I'd never seen anything like it. None of us had. A flying wing, a boomerang out of the sky.

The whole cadet wing erupted in one massive roar.

The pilot, who had to be nuts (they never caught him), pushed the afterburners to the max, and the plane accelerated at a rate that seemed impossible, coming at us so fast we seemed *pulled back* from it.

Go! Go! we were screaming, because we wanted to be up there, to be with him, to be gone from there forever. One hundred feet off the deck and heading straight for the north dormitory.

Somewhere, probably right on top of Doolie Hill, the plane went through the speed of sound. This huge *WHAP!* and the figure of absence where his plane had been, and the sound of his engine rushing in behind his trailing wake.

And then the whole south wall of Mitchell Hall, framed completely in glass, fractured and exploded. A million dollars' worth of windows down the tubes. You could hear the tinkling of glass as the last pieces fell reluctantly from the metal and shattered on the marble pavement.

Scott Hind just smiled, giggled once, and lifted his saber in salute.

One day, I thought, *I'm going to be that pilot.*

٣

Tehran, 21 April 1978

Dear Family,

You may or may not have heard about the trouble in Tabriz. Terrible religious dispute. It may even be possible that some troops fired into the crowds. The workers, groundskeepers, and even Ghossemi, seem nervous about the whole affair. Much has been happening here.

Perhaps it is more harmful than we know, but the truth is we don't know exactly what is going on (or your father ISN'T telling me). We are needed here. We have been happy here. We live comfortably. We have a home.

People are suddenly so quiet on a bus or walking in the streets. Other times we hear shouts and broadcast announcements blaring from speakers in buildings. It's business as usual, and that's the way it should be, but we've been told to make an inventory.

We are not frightened. We can only hope for the best. We'd be happy to live in a bare house if things quiet down a bit. We are sorry about any anxiety our presence here has caused.

Despite all this business, we still think it best that Dante visit this summer. He's had a rather rough year. We need to see him.

Love to all,

Beatrice

ع

That morning, as I stared out my window toward the Rockies, the smog had not yet settled around the ring of Denver. The sky was impossibly blue. And my seat was broken. I couldn't lean back without the backrest falling away. Maybe I'd be able to control myself during taxi, but during the acceleration and takeoff I would be forced back into the seat, crushing the kneecaps of the passenger behind me.

I brought this discrepancy to the attention of the flight attendant. But she couldn't have cared less. Rushed in her preflight, she had time enough only to replace an irritating strand of hair that was falling down her cheek.

"Yes, sir," she said, flashing a smile of ignorance and total sympathy. It was like a tape recorder had flicked on in the back of her mind, ready to deal with idiot passengers who got in her way. "Please insure your safety belt is attached for takeoff," she recited. This was my problem and not hers. Maybe she was right. After all, I was the one stupid enough to fly on *her* airline.

So I looked for the nearest emergency exit, which was three seats aft, and opened the ventilation nozzle above my head, which brought a welcome flood of air moments after engine start. Reaching into the seat pocket in front of me, I found all the travel information I needed. The emergency data card said there were slides available at every exit in the event of an emergency; the attendants were trained professionals, ready to help; and that my seat was a flotation device (in case we were lost at sea). I found the access port to my oxygen mask, preparing myself for the inevitable rapid depressurization at thirty-five thousand feet somewhere over Iowa. I positioned an air sickness bag within easy reach, its bright colored flap waving at me over the airline catalogs and magazines in the seat back in front of me. My carry-on bag, in compliance with FAA regulations, was crammed under the seat. I was ready for anything, except maybe a crash landing seconds after takeoff.

I was heading home, to Tehran, to a place I had never been.

"Is this the first time you've flown?" A woman across the aisle leaned over, touched my arm. I hadn't noticed her before. But I could see, now, that she was amused by my antics, how I searched for the nearest exit.

She was beautiful—perfect white teeth, aquiline nose and coffee-dark eyes. Her veiled head and the vermilion tikka dot between her brows, identified her, I thought, as Hindustani. I smiled shyly and mumbled something. Then, embarrassed, I thought of how she probably thought I was just another dull American, full of wit and slow comment.

She held her smile and settled back to her *New Yorker*. Later I explained to her that I was visiting my mother and father for the first time in Iran.

"And you are the oldest child?" she asked.

"Well, yes," I said. "I am the *only* child."

She laughed. "Still, you are blessed. Have you been to Tehran before?"

"No," I said. "This is the first time. My first time in the Middle East."

"Well, then," she smiled. "You are doubly blessed. A young handsome man like you among an ancient, handsome people. Perhaps you will find a wife, yes?"

My face was burning, red.

During takeoff, I leaned forward, clutching for something to grab onto, trying as humanely as possible to save the life of the fool behind me. The throttles advanced when we took the runway, and my seat responded by wobbling on its railings. If we aborted, my neck would snap, and my face would stuff the seat pocket in front of me. My head was tucked in to my chin, my hands rolled around my thighs, as though I were tumbling. The woman across from me probably thought I was going to puke. My backrest vibrated. The railings trembled.

Never, I thought, never fly Pan Am.

•

Somewhere over the North Atlantic, out through the window, through the boiling stories of clouds, I started to lose hold. My whole life was imagined, was out there, floating. I felt a kind of true and lasting sorrow, sorrow for the world and for myself, for the suffering of all humans. I knew that the

HEJIRA

images dancing by me out the window weren't real. Illusions. Maybe things that never happened. Or happened now the way I must remember them. But even then, at nineteen, I was smart enough to know that what I saw was more real than anything I might ever feel.

I saw myself as a child, four years old. I stood there, buck-ass naked, staring at our Christmas tree. A pair of leather chaps covered my front, but my grandparents had forgotten that I would be so excited by my new cowboy gear I would strip myself of everything I had on and jump into my new outfit on the spot, draw the six-shooters around my middle and lace the holster to my thigh, strap on my boots, and cinch the string of my hat so it wouldn't blow off when I rode my Palomino. *Silver, away!*

And I saw myself at five or six, in a car with my father, cresting the peak of a hill in Maine, and my father yelling "Don't look"—and, of course, I looked: the truck driver sobbing, holding his hands in front of his face; the woman who had passed through the windshield lying on the hood, shrouded in the mist of the scalded radiator; and the driver, blood coursing from his ears, hands splayed across the dash, impaled on the steering column; the deer they had stopped to watch still dumbly grazing. Even then, nearly fifteen years later, I shook at the memory.

I saw myself, how I looked from that window staring into the vast ocean that covered the world. Sad-faced Diamond. A little lost, a lot confused. A seven-year-old boy in Australia, trying to do anything he could to live in his father's shadow, and always failing; a twelve-year-old telling his father he missed him and hoped the war would be over soon, and the boy slipping the cassette tape into an envelope and mailing it to some place named Bien Thieu in Vietnam.

And then a fifteen-year-old, convinced now that the very war his mother and father had told him to believe was right and just was likely wrong; that same boy, watching his father, a young colonel, walk down the street of the neighborhood and up to the front lawn of their home. *How would he look if I did not know him?* the boy wondered. The man stood there. He seemed to tilt his head into the dark, and turn, slightly, as if listening. Uniform crisp and pressed, thumbs resting along the seams of his trousers, left breast crested with medals. Two silver stars. Twelve distinguished flying crosses. The wings of a command pilot. But the man looked broken. The boy's father had returned from telling another family of the loss—almost always the death—of a son. It was a terrible job. His father did what he was ordered to do, not because he was an automaton, but because if he did not do it, someone less than him, someone with less compassion and understanding of what it meant to fight in a war that no one believed in anymore, not even his father, would do it. And someone else could never speak to the agony he always saw in their faces.

He wondered then if his father had ever cried. He didn't know the answer to that question. But the boy cried. He whimpered at first and then he broke into fierce, bitter tears. He wanted to say it then, to whisper it through the curtains to the man in the street: *I love you.* But the boy cried. He would tell no one.

•

I felt sweat tickling my armpit as I thought about having to tell my mother and father I was fairly certain I would leave the academy. And what would I do after that? What if I just told them, signed my papers, packed my bags, and walked out the front gate? I buried my nose against the window, and my breath frosted the plastic. As it cleared, I thought I could see land. But there was nothing down there. When the clouds broke, I saw only whitecaps rolling in absence. I felt the cold chill of the window.

The aisles filled with wandering, happy, loud people. Most looked Indian or Pakistani, and most ignored me. My beautiful companion had left her seat hours before. I took out my passport and studied the dark ink of my visa. I had done this many times already. The swirling mystery of Farsi looked like Cyrillic runes, hieroglyphs I could never decipher. A language neither wholly Arabic nor wholly Persian, forged from the dead languages of Khwarazmian and Pahlaví and Parthian and Khotanese, that, in turn, had forged Kurdish and Tadzhiki, from the Pushtu of Afghanistan. I looked to the faces of the passengers and heard the soft rhythms of their language. *Farangi*—that was how you said it. Foreigner. Barbarian.

I had spent the last three weeks training at Coronado Island, across the water from San Diego, with the Naval Underwater Demolition Team, the Sea-Air-Land team: the SEALs. The experience had convinced me that I wasn't exactly suited for the military. Despite what I had thought, despite everything I had believed I wanted. It was best that I end it now.

I settled back quietly, my face pressed against the window. I drifted

HEJIRA

toward sleep while my feet swelled and my body dehydrated without me, and in the background the soundless shadows of a film flickered on a wall. The plane cruised east from the night, moving toward dawn, and my dreams began in a long vaporous contrail trailing from a wing, away from my imperfect past.

7

My parents didn't force me to go there. They did not argue against it. I was their only child. They wanted me to have a choice. I was, I suppose, lucky at that.

"The academy is a fine place, son." My father said nothing more than that. But that was enough. I suppose.

I didn't go to the Zoo, I think, just to please him, or my mother—but those words, they were just enough. For a while I had a choice. I had the discipline. I loved—and still love—to fly. But I didn't have the desire. I didn't have the guts to do it forever. I lacked the necessary fire.

There were two people who showed me this. One was Scott Hind, my closest friend. He loved this macho crap. Macho—though when he said it, he pronounced the word "mako," like the Mako shark.

"Can't believe they're paying us to do this, Diamond," he said every morning at Coronado. "I'd do it for free."

He was a little crazy—a lot crazy. Like me, he came from a military family—brats, they call us. Unlike me, this was the only way of life Scott Hind could ever imagine. *He* had the necessary fire.

I remember one night at Coronado, the night before our deep-water dive, he just took off till morning. Walked in the door an hour before, ready to *go, go, go!* If he were normal, of course, Scott should have been in a hospital. But he was abnormal. He was exceptional. He got punched in the kidney during the Aqualung Proficiency Drill, and he just ignored the pain.

That morning, just before we left for morning calisthenics, he yelled from the bathroom. "Goddamn, it hurts," he shouted. "Hawaiian Punch."

"Hey, how about closing the door?" I shouted back. "You sound like a friggin' moose." I wondered if I could take that kind of pain and joke about it.

"You could do anything you want, Diamond," he told me once. "You just need direction. A little clarity, my boy. A little clarity. And don't think so goddamned much."

But then anyone who survived the bounce dive and the run to Mexico could survive anything. We felt like we could do anything we wanted.

19
HEJIRA

It was strange, that morning. He must have felt incredible pain, and yet he was yipping with some kind of bizarre joy. "Zippo!" he screamed, running around a room as cramped as the smallest berth on a ship—two beds, a footlocker, one grey upright locker. "We're gonna do it!" he screamed. "Got the world by the balls, now."

It was never difficult for him. On the obstacle course, a great wooden behemoth that sprawled almost a hundred yards down the beach, Scott would always attack it with a kind of insane happiness. Blond, tanned, thickly built—he looked like the Mako he wanted to be—Scott was on fire when he hit the course. The fact that he was also president of the Academy Mountaineering Club didn't hurt of course. But it was more than that. I had gained intermediate ability with climbing and bouldering, but I couldn't keep pace. His face would turn dark. You could hear his thin breaths as he flew through the course. His tongue would stick out a little.

No SEAL could keep pace. Scott went after the obstacle course saying, "This looks as easy as Copper Canyon." He would grab a wooden brace, swing himself up, and be gone. When it was over, he wasn't even winded.

I can see him climb into the blue. Everything about him seemed to say, *This was what I was meant to do.* And I could share in that kind of joy. But I couldn't be him. I couldn't do it forever. I wasn't meant to.

They called us Hummingbirds. There were ten of us there from the Zoo, for three weeks with the navy SEALs: frogmen, special operations. The things you never hear about, or if you do, it's whispers and rumors and half-truths: that's why Scott was there. He wasn't even really a cadet anymore. He had graduated from the Zoo that June, picked up his commission as a second lieutenant and marched straight up to the Commandant of Cadets office and explained to Brigadier General Richards how the Air Force needed him in special operations, and how he needed to go to SEAL training. The commandant said, "OK."

"And you get to be my roommate, Diamond," he said afterward. "You didn't do it right last semester, so let's see if we can do better in the real world. And you better call me 'sir' this time."

•

Scott chose me as a roommate because of Mitchell James. After Mitchell's death, when everyone was afraid to go near me, Scott just grabbed me by the arm and said, "Come on. Let's get your crap. We're roommates." Scott helped me through it. He became my closest friend, after Mitchell. He was born to be in the military.

Mitchell James. The Third. We had roomed together nearly every semester since we fell into the same basic cadet squadron three years before. A quiet guy. He stuttered sometimes. Upperclassmen swallowed him alive that first year. But I should have seen it coming, with Mitchell. The way he came to hate the place. We were friends.

I knew he wanted to leave since, hell, since I'd ever known him. But how was he any different from the rest of us? We *all* wanted to leave. That last semester of the secondclass year, he used to lie in his bed, long after taps and lights out, and mumble. He never slept. I never slept. It took him three years to decide. "If I had the guts," he started saying, "I'd tell them what I really thought." One night I woke to see him standing by the plate glass of our room. He spoke without turning around. "There is something I have to tell you," he said.

But he said nothing. Two days later he was dead.

His father had given him an ivory-handled Colt for a Christmas present. It's true. This isn't some kind of sad joke. It was a .45, I think. It had been in his family for over four generations. And more than four generations of Jameses had attended West Point. It wasn't a question of which university poor Mitchell was going to attend. It was only which service academy.

Mitchell's family didn't want him to leave. Not his sisters, not his mother, not his one older West Point grunt brother. Especially, his father. *You can't change the tradition of this family. This is not open for discussion.* Some classmates in Goshawk told me I should watch out. He'd been acting weird.

That night, I heard a *crack* in my sleep. I woke, thinking it was far off. Getting up from the bed I slipped and fell on the hard tiled floor. "Hell!" I spat out, trying not to wake Mitchell.

I walked to the window, pulled the curtain aside and looked out. There was nothing. The green light from inside the seventeen-spired chapel hummed. I turned and saw something on the floor. I swallowed hard. I switched on the reading light by my desk and saw Mitchell, lying half-under his bed. His mouth was open. It was his blood I had slipped in.

I can still see him. I can still hear his voice. I can still hear him come out with one of his outrageous comments, when he hadn't spoken for days practically. That's what scares me the most. I don't think he knew what he was doing, really. He started to crumble inside. And then it just went.

When we were fourthclassmen I remember walking across the Honor Court together. Happy to be at rest, not having to walk "braced" with eyes forward and greet every upperclassman in existence with a *Good morning, afternoon,* or *evening, sir.* The court was mobbed with tourists. They came to gawk at the cadet chapel and to gawk at us. Two men and a woman confronted us. They looked like college students, the same age as Mitchell and I were. They were angry. They said the war in Southeast Asia made them angry, but I know that standing there on the Honor Court, the unrealness of the Zoo was what made their anger real.

"How can you condone," one young woman pleaded, "the killing of innocent women and children with napalm?"

That was it. A simple question. But who were we to know that answer? We were college freshmen, just students, suffering through an impossible life. I was stunned.

But Mitchell just fired back, "Well, you can't eat 'em raw, can you?"

He was like that. This strange humor. Sometimes, climbing in Seven Mile Canyon, he'd yell up during our second pitch, "Hey D, you think you'll ever learn to do this right?"

No, Mitchell, I guess I won't. I guess I'll never understand what drove me there to the Zoo. But I loved my parents and I was afraid of them. I was afraid to tell them that I wasn't right for all this nonsense. You were the one who showed me that, Mitchell.

Scott, too. He *loved* it. Hawaiian Punch. Christ, I'd be screaming if that happened to me. But he was perfect for that stuff. Like Nesbitt, our SEAL instructor, who saved a buddy that took a Vietcong bullet in the head. The wound was bad. Part of the brain was exposed. Nesbitt carried him on his back while an active patrol chased them through the jungle. They made it to a beach, and Nesbitt swam twenty miles in open ocean until they were rescued. The saltwater apparently cleansed the wound. The SEAL survived. Nesbitt won the Medal of Honor for that. And, a year later, his buddy won it, too.

That's how Scott would be. Consumed by it, all of it, until nothing else existed. "It's not just a job, Diamond." And then he'd stop after he said it. He wouldn't smile. He wouldn't sound like a recruiting slogan. He'd be dead serious. "It's not just a job."

I wanted to be a Hummingbird to see if I could do it. If I could take it. Daily warm-ups of three hundred sit-ups and two hundred leg lifts in the Courtyard, followed by a leisurely sprint up the beach in combat gear, or a five-mile swim in the surf. If the instructor felt cheery that day, we'd run all the twenty miles down to Tijuana. And then came Hell Week: if you made it through, you could make it through anything. If you didn't, then, you didn't. All you had to do was cross the Courtyard and ring the bell, a miniature liberty bell maybe two feet across at its mouth. "It's the longest walk in the world," a recruit once told me. "No one ever speaks to you again."

No physical conditioning prepared you for this training. You broke down. Everyone broke down. The entire week you were allowed no more than four hours sleep—four hours for an entire week. Twenty-minute bursts. You woke drugged and confused, more tired than before. You fell apart.

When I first got there I saw a recruit screaming in pain during morning calisthenics in the Courtyard. Beyond thought. Two instructors just leaned over and screamed back at him. His legs kept rising and falling.

That final day, the day of the surf run to Baja, the locals came to cheer us on. It was the culmination. We were dressed in full combat gear and carrying two life rafts in teams of five each. We ran the whole way. Down there we enjoyed a leisurely box lunch while up to our asses in the Mud Flats.

"As the pastor of the 'Church of What's Happening Now,' I declare this food blessed," said Nesbitt. He stood with his arms crossed, smiling. Sadistic.

"Hind, give us the invocation," said Nesbitt.

"Good food. Good meat. Good God, let's eat," said Scott.

"Make it so," said Nesbitt.

After lunch, we practiced tag-team relays and sprints through mud. All of us ended up puking. For our reward, the instructors ran us back to Coronado, bathed in mud. Every crack, every crevice, every possible orifice, every piece of clothing or equipment. We looked like zombies carrying our recently departed chief on our heads.

The mud began to dry and cake. It burned our skin in the heat. And the crowds grew larger and more wild as we ran. An old woman shouted, "Give 'em hell, boys!" Young girls in bikinis sprinted down the beach and tossed candies in our rafts.

I was always the trailing student at the end of our morning runs, always the victim for instructors who waited at checkpoints—little perches of rock where they could spy our bodies falling down the beach. The instructor running us would pick up the pace to an all-out sprint when we got near. Anyone who couldn't hold the pace, and that meant me, got picked off. I'd be in the surf, head pointing toward Hawaii, and my feet kicking at Nebraska. The surf would wash over me, and an instructor would be bending over, in my face, telling me what a *worthless shit* I was. Which, by that point in my military career, I thought was common knowledge.

Scott, of course, thought it was all great fun. "It's just a joke, anyway," he'd cackle. "These guys are wimps."

When he said things like that, I wondered how we could be friends. I mean he was a little cracked. Weird. But then he threw it all off, like he was joking, like no one could be as crazy as he tried to be. He would shoot me that leering half-grin. "Diamond," he said, "you take all this shit too serious. You'll never save democracy with an attitude like that."

But I thought it all was supposed to be serious, dead serious—as when we spent days in the diving bell so instructors could check our rate of ascent prior to the real dive. The bell itself was maybe thirty feet, but it seemed to go on forever. Exiting the bottom station the surface of the water was years away—only colors and the shape of figures hovering at the surface. I could make out the framework of arches and supports that crossed the ceiling. Bubbles of air tripped from my lungs, and small pockets of gas wriggled up.

A hand would nudge my shoulder and push me upward. Another instructor would pull back into his chamber of trapped air like a moray retracting into its den, the glint of razored teeth shivering in light.

I don't know how long he let me float there, staring at liquid space, before he came out. He pulled me in. "You're taking too long, Diamond," he said. "Don't dawdle down here. Do it for real with tanks and you'll get an embolism in your head. Your friggin' brain will explode."

We never learned to blow up bridges during the program, which was a major disappointment. But three weeks, after all, is a very short period. Our time had just been classroom work, short spurts in the bay with SCUBA gear, constant physical training, and serious attention to the science of diving—hour-long sessions in the decompression chamber, getting ready for our 120-foot bounce dive. I'd had experience with such things before. On my eighteenth birthday the Air Force shipped me off to Lowry to experience the wonder of the altitude chamber. Though they worked on different principles—the increase of atmospheric pressure with depth and the loss of atmospheric pressure with altitude—their purposes were the same: learning how to stay alive. In the altitude chamber we hit rapid depressurization at thirty thousand feet. We learned how long we could maintain consciousness without oxygen at nineteen thousand feet. Seconds before I *lost* consciousness, with my fingernails turning purple and my brain floating on its own high, a voice came over the intercom: *"Gentlemen, remember your personal hypoxia symptoms!"*

Here we learned about nitrogen narcosis. Inside the chamber, I imagined what it would be like. If we hit greater depths, we'd use purged tanks to prevent it. But it still happened. We learned of every form of marine life that was waiting to kill us when we hit the water. Our chances were slim. We experimented with bubbleless tanks and tied ourselves to a companion and navigated through murky channel inlets toward checkpoints, with only a compass and each other to pull us forward. If we reached the checkpoint and were on target when we surfaced, we were thrown in the boat. If we were too far off for an instructor's taste, we were thrown in the boat and invited to demonstrate fifty push-ups with full tanks. The tanks weighed seventy-five pounds.

"You worthless shits!" they'd scream. "How can you expect to save your country when you can't find your own ass in a swimming pool?"

They said that to Scott, of course. He was my navigation partner. They liked him. That's why they screamed at him so much.

Me?

"Not bad," they'd say.

•

Our final test before our deep-sea dive was the Aqualung Proficiency Drill. Even Scott freaked at the APD. I saw bubbles from his tanks suddenly explode. He surfaced, yelling something. An instructor pulled him back under. When it was over, he crawled from the ladder to where I sat, waiting my turn. His face was blue and strained. He could barely breathe.

HEJIRA

"The son of a bitch cut my cord," he said. "You have to take your tanks off, flip 'em over your head . . . wait for them to jump you. I don't believe it. I don't believe it." When my turn came, Scott raised himself on one arm and said, "Dante, listen to me." He actually said my name. I was floored. No one calls me that. I didn't even know he knew my first name.

"You can breathe the air bubbles when they cut the cord," he said.

I broke the water with my tanks, heading in backward, my hand on my face plate, an arc of water separating under me. I dropped, scuttled along the bottom, breathing evenly. I had been told not to look up. Just wait.

I unstrapped my tanks and flipped them off my back and over my head, still breathing. Our instructions were to take off the tanks and try and breathe . . . and just wait. It was a double-hose system, and the air surged as soon as the hoses rose higher than the level of the tanks. I tried to let some of the air out at the edge of my lip, but my cheeks swelled with tight pockets of it. I swallowed most of the gas, breathing as a pilot pressure breathes in a depressurized cabin, my stomach swelling and expanding, like it was going to explode.

I saw a shadow, covering the sun, above the black lane markers. My breaths became short, panicked. I watched the air rip from the tanks. I saw a knife in front of my face. Someone grabbed me from behind. Three instructors pulled me down and dragged me from the tanks while I fought to get back. One of them slit both hoses, and I bent over—straining for air flying from the regulator.

I caught it in my mouth, as Scott had told me to do. I could breathe. They pulled me back again, and I heard myself yelling for help without knowing it was me. I grabbed two instructors and pushed them off. I ripped a mask from one. He grabbed my face mask and forced it straight off the bridge. Water flooded my eyes and I broke free and shot for the surface.

"Listen, mister!" one of them spat, "Get your ass back down there. There's no sympathy for buttholes like you." They pulled me back under, finished the drill. But all the life I had was gone. I'd lost. I took it all too serious.

Mitchell used to take this stuff pretty serious, too. That was what worried me. During our basic summer, when we hit the Assault Course, it almost crippled him for life. Forced to crawl through multiple obstacles, between exploding mines and shrapnel. At some stations, there were signs like, *What's your girlfriend doing right now?* Nothing you could say.

Our whole vocabulary became one word: *Kill!* Imperative, question, and reply.

Those who couldn't finish the course were taken to Cadet Ordmann, Assault Course Leader. During the academic year, Cadet Ordmann was an all-star halfback for the football team. During basic training, though, he was the last person you wanted to get to know.

Mitchell couldn't. Finish, I mean. Mitchell had acquired a slight case of lobar pneumonia during the second half of basic—the Jack's Valley field encampment. Mitchell never knew he had pneumonia, of course, and wouldn't until we were well into our fourthclass year, when he collapsed in chemistry lab and his instructor found him, face down on the desk, his hand clasped around a capillary tube.

But Mitchell knew something was wrong the day he first hit the Assault Course. When he got caught in barbed wire and couldn't get out, and it seemed that the exploding mines would eventually cover him with dirt, a team member picked him straight up from the ground by his web-belt and dragged him over to see *Cadet Ordmann.*

Cadet Ordmann was not pleased. "Hey, pretty boy," he whispered into the grimy sweat of Mitchell's face, "what's the problem here?" A bandolier of bullets crisscrossed on his fifty-six-inch chest. He stroked a grey horny toad that perched on his right shoulder. "This is my friend," Ordmann whispered. "What do you think of my friend?"

"Kill!" Mitchell screamed.

"Do you know what I do to my friends?"

"Kill!" Mitchell screamed.

And then Ordmann grabbed his pet toad, stuck it in his mouth, and bit its head off. The blood started flying. It hosed down the white shock on Mitchell's grimy face. Then Mitchell passed out.

Ordmann proceeded to slap Mitchell back into consciousness while slapping him senseless. When he came to, Ordmann ordered him to hang from the branch of a tree that hung over an open pit. "Kill!" Mitchell screamed, and then—when his arms gave out, and he fell into the pit—Ordmann yelled, "Hey, pretty boy—I want you to bury yourself!" And Mitchell did just that.

•

HEJIRA

The day of the bounce dive, I hit the water and started screaming. It was *cold!* I reached over a shoulder, checked my regulator, found it was on, and couldn't believe it. I dove deeper, trying to adjust to the cold as I sank. Some others hung near the surface where it was warmer, paddling like minnows around huge stalks of kelp that waved in the light. That was their mistake. After thirty minutes, they would still be freezing.

I found a cliff ledge and followed it down. At eighty feet, I was alone with blind fish eyes groping through dark. I watched a quick flash of silver as a moray pulled back into her den.

By the time I surfaced, I was the last to be picked up. I came over the edge to blue and orange faces, black swollen eyes, bodies shivering in blankets. It was insane. The temperature was nearly one hundred degrees that day.

Some of my companions were in shock. "A good day for puking," Scott coughed up. His face was grey.

When we hit the dock, an instructor was waiting. "All right, sweethearts. Get your tight little buns outta there. We got a run to Mexico this afternoon!"

•

This shouldn't have been just blood and guts and how much you could take, all that mako shit. But most of it was. It wasn't a game. It was real. Scott was right. I took it all too serious. Some mornings he would drag in at two or three, wake me up and tell me what I had missed. "Shoulda been there, Diamond," he'd say. "She was something else."

We'd be up by five, running toward Mexico. By six, I'd be head down in the surf, some SEAL instructor in my face. It was kind of funny, I suppose. But I still don't think it's funny. I hoped my parents would understand. It was too much. I was their only son. I figured they'd listen.

Right then, I was listening to the two closest friends I had at the Zoo. One was alive, one was dead. And they were telling me different things. One said this was all I was ever meant to do, that I should enjoy it, work hard at it, and learn to love it just the way he did, to let it all consume me. The other said this wasn't right, none of it, that I should get out now, while I could, before it was too late, before I changed forever. My parents loved me. I thought I knew that.

"There is something I have to tell you."

All my life I will wonder what he meant to say.

V

My parents had asked me to come. I had spoken to them once in the past year, and I had stopped writing, except for one note saying how tough school was, how hard it was to concentrate sometimes, how sorry I was about Mitchell, and how I was really glad they had taken the time to call *me*. And how they figured out it was time to call, I'll never know.

Not that I had ever written all that much anyway. In basic cadet training I wrote a brief postcard clearly meant to threaten or plead with my mother, Beatrice. Either she wrote me every day or I was going to quit. Period. And she did. For three years she wrote practically every day. And I almost never read what she wrote in those letters. Hell, in basic I never had time to read. I didn't have time for anything except to fulfill some dickhead upperclassman's insatiable desire to see *elbows and assholes—movemovemovemove!* But whenever Beatrice wrote about the country and the people they met outside of embassy functions, I read; whenever she stopped making observations and started observing, I listened.

That year my parents moved from Rattlesnake Station to Tehran. Colonel T-Boy Diamond, commander of the best flying wing in Air Training Command, was offered a post as second in charge and advisor to the Imperial Air Magistrate. Colonel Diamond became Brigadier General Diamond.

Beatrice took numerous precautions when they arrived in Tehran. She'd been around long enough not to be surprised by anything, and by then she was smart enough to avoid surprises. At seventeen, when I entered the academy, she and the colonel had moved seventeen times, had almost been kidnapped by terrorists in the Philippines, had suffered through typhoons in Okinawa, and had lost *all* of their household possessions in the Indian Ocean. (That happened when we left what was then Ceylon: the crane lifting our boxes slipped and dropped everything—couches, paintings, heirlooms—from the loading pallet into the water. We weren't there at the time, and the crane operator wasn't about to tell anyone. Apparently he drove over to the edge of the dock, lowered his rig, retrieved the peacefully bobbing wooden crates, and lifted them onto the ship. Ten weeks later, in Rhode Island, what was left of everything we had ever owned arrived stinking of salt and mold.)

By the time they came to the Middle East, they knew a few things. One of the most important of these was security. Beatrice had a list of over thirty-five items: entrances or exits where someone could enter a home; how many locks there were; where the closest police station was; how far to the American embassy. They looked at more than fifty places before they found a relatively cheap villa in the northern section of Tehran across the street from a Rockwell International executive and a German mining engineer, next to the Yugoslavian embassy, and three blocks south of one of the shah's palaces. Rent was only two thousand dollars a month.

And at the academy, where I was an apprentice falconer, I became drawn to Iranian myth and lore—partly because of the love their authors showed for birds of prey. One day I found a special manuscript in one of the vaults of the academy's falconry archives: papyruslike sheaves etched in Persian with gold leaf. Each page was illustrated with a visual description of the text. When I first found this manuscript, with hundreds of sheaves in this strange script of beautiful, indecipherable calligraphy, I held each thin sheaf separately to the light, like a leaf, as I moved, slowly, through its contents. I most remember a figure mounted on horseback, holding a long-winged hawk on his fist: Sásánian Khusraw Parwíz going a-hawking. The manuscript was the *Sháhnáma*, the huge 60,000-line poem that is the national epic of Persia.

It seemed a rich, distant place. From the moment when I read her first letter, I paid attention. In basic, I hid a flashlight under my pillow so I could read those small sketches of hers at night, after the last strain of the tape-recorded taps played on the loudspeakers echoing over the terrazzo. She spoke with admiration of their driver, Ghossemi, as she spelled it, who also acted as a second bodyguard behind a man named Reza, and she spoke with affection for Ghossemi's wife, daughter, and son, of how the general and she would visit them on special days, during Nouruz and sometimes on weekends. They seemed intelligent and honest, a good family, who led loving and simple lives.

I read about Isfahan, Shiraz, Susa, Bandar-e Pahlaví, Mashhad, Tabriz, and Takhte Jamshîd—the great seat of wisdom and culture, Persepolis. The academy's area studies handbooks claimed that the country was progressing, technologically and culturally, under a government of constitutional monarchy. I learned that the *sháhansháh*—which literally meant king of kings—was the second member of the Pahlaví dynasty, which took its name from the Middle Persian, and had held power since 1925. On 26 August 1941, almost two years after the nation had declared itself neutral in the world war, British and Soviet troops mutually invaded and deemed it more vital to control the country's rail routes than to respect its neutrality. That same year, Reza Shah abdicated the throne in favor of his twenty-two-year-old son, Mohammed Reza Pahlaví.

The *sháhansháh* survived numerous assassination attempts. In 1949 he was shot twice at point-blank range; his recovery was considered miraculous. He also prevented the Soviet Union from permanently occupying the Azarbayjan province, and, many said, with divine intervention (which others claimed came dressed in the guise of the Central Intelligence Agency), he challenged Josef Stalin, and won. In 1965 the Iranian Parliament conferred on him—after he survived yet another assassination attempt—the title of Aryamehr, literally "light of the Aryans." The *Sháhnáma* claimed that the royal Farr, the refulgent nimbus of fire, symbolizing God's favor, shone around the body of rulers and was recognized by beholders as a power that implied infallible greatness and fortune as long as the possessor of the Farr held the favor of the Divine Powers. The *sháhansháh* was said to possess the Farr. They called him the Shadow of the Almighty.

Sháhansháh Reza Pahlaví was a benevolent ruler, these books claimed, deeply concerned about culture and the future of his people. He wanted his country to be one of the world's great powers. In 1967 he was coronated emperor of the 2,500-year-old Iranian monarchy and claimed direct descendancy from Cyrus the Great. Immediately after placing the crown on his own head, he crowned his second wife empress and made her the first woman in Iranian history to hold such a title. He had ruled for thirty-seven years. It seemed likely that his family, holding the mysterious Farr, would rule forever.

Yet, later, when I was an upperclassman, I would pick up Sunday editions of *The New York Times* and the *International Herald Tribune,* or the *Times* of London, in the library, and find small items about clashes between nomadic Kurds and Persians, or snippets about the growing accumulation of power by the Iran National Resurgence Party, the Rastakhiz, the political arm of the shah's government. There were reports of sudden disappearances and the torture of political prisoners. I learned to recognize the name Sazeman Ettelaat va Amniyaté Keshvar—SAVAK, the secret police responsible for state security.

It's true, I always had time for her letters. Though I never told her.

∧

The act itself, like so many acts we performed at the academy, was meaningless. But it was something we *chose*, mostly because the figure of it, like some phosphorescent trace in the contrail of the atmosphere, would always survive—the sense of some internal rhythm and the dance of your feet on the rock, the feel of opposition and the wedge of your body, the truth that nothing held you in space and you were held by it. You had to use that nothingness to live.

Once you had left the rock you never left it.

They came from around the world to climb here. Sometimes, practicing in the hundred-acre rock formation named Garden of the Gods, Scott and I would just rest at the top of our pitch, for hours, watching their figures across the red rock formations, their scissoring legs holding the path of their freedom. Later, on the ground, we listened as they spoke of Él Capitán, Peru, Long's Peak—places where they could isolate themselves, be among silence. They owned huge egos and bragged among themselves. But they were shy when others were around. Hands flaked and crusty like stone, and fingers white from chalk, we would watch them rise along the invisible lines of a boulder, stretching through space as though it were nothing more than a step into absence. Scott and Mitchell and I got along with them famously.

•

I began climbing with Mitchell my doolie year (doolie—from the Greek word δούλος—slave, menial, insignificant). He picked up the mess that was the Academy Mountaineering Club, convinced people to buy us new equipment—switching from dangerous natural fiber to synthetic kernmantle ropes—created training classes for novice climbers, and taught survival, evasion, and resistance programs about how best to survive when shot down behind enemy lines, how to survive on your wits, how to avoid detection. He set up slide lectures by people who had climbed Everest, Denali, Rainier. He had shown us the vast, impossible dark, and it had pulled all of us to it.

Mitchell was with me when I bought my first shoes, French *varappé*. He made me put them on, walk out of the Mountain Chalet and test the black, inflexible rubber against the brick. He stood there, arms crossed, as he ordered me to cling, slight, pull away from the hug of the wall. He led me on my first climb, and it was the worst climb I've ever had: in winter, digging into a wall of white that did not exist, gripping the side of the face with an ice axe, believing that the crampons would hold because *they had to hold*.

During that doolie year Mitchell taught me to climb. I never became as proficient as I wanted; there was never time. There was only technique, idea, discipline, the feel of the swami belt holding your crotch tight in the sling of the rope during your first dulfer rappel. How to use vertical and angle pitons, bongs, razorhead rurps. Why it was better to use chocks on the surface instead of pitons.

When we were not climbing, we were running, always pushing ourselves. Nights, we spent hours stripping sheets of newspaper to shreds with our fingertips, feeling the burn in our forearms. And then, on the rock, knowing that burn would be the one thing to save us. It was trusting yourself, being able to move back from the rock and balance at the side of a wall and keep going up. It was tying onto a rope, bowline for leader and trail, the symmetry of two bodies—one on belay and the other climbing to find him—or clipping a carabiner to the sling of the rope and slinging the rope over a rock, holding the person beneath you, knowing he was on his way. No, it was not the act, but the act was beautiful.

At the end of our first semester of our secondclass year, Scott challenged Mitchell and me and an airman named Whitehead, who claimed he was full Iroquois, to hike Pike's Peak in winter. Two weeks later, Mitchell would fail to reach the peak of Shasta on Christmas eve—though it was a brave attempt. Solo. The wind had lifted his tent from its poles, sent it whistling down a ravine, and left Mitchell alone in the ice, waiting for light. We never made the summit of the Peak that time. I froze the right side of my foot; I still have trouble walking sometimes. Whitehead lost three toes. When we got him to the ambulance, and cut off his socks, his foot looked more like a bloated fish than what had been a man's flesh. We had been stubborn. We had refused to quit. We snowshoed through the first blizzard; pulled each other through waist-high drifts; camped in the bowl of the summit before the second wave hit.

I've hiked Pike's Peak sixteen times now; I've hiked thirty other fourteeners in the Rockies. But that night, in camp, beneath a curtain of white, sticking the deadness of my naked foot into the heat of the fire, waiting for some incredible pain to hit, I remember most that all I felt was . . . nothing.

•

After Mitchell's death, Scott took over as president of the Mountaineering Club. He had the same fever for rock that Mitchell had had. We would practice together, though we always tried to avoid climbing in Copper Canyon. The rock was not good: the sun hit the thin, inner walls of the canyon only a few hours each day, and the rock could crumble in your hands like sawdust. You had to pay attention. Outward Bound had a school there. Most days you could hear students' voices rolling up the canyon: "On Belay; Off; Climb; Climbing; Rock!" We tried to stay away from them; the last warning always drifted down to us seconds after the falling rocks whizzed past.

There was also something about that place. You could feel it. It wasn't good. Scott, because he was a firstclassman and had a car, used to drive me there—sometimes to hike; sometimes, just to get away. Most free afternoons he'd take off with Mitchell to the Garden of the Gods for another shot at the overhanging ledges of the Diamond Needle. Weekends he and I would try our skill at chimney wedges in the cracked walls of Seven Mile Canyon. And one afternoon he had wanted to test us both against a difficult bridging gap in Copper Canyon.

I had wanted to trick him, to show him up. Midway through the climb I felt him slacken on belay: he wasn't paying attention. So I unhooked from the rope and started climbing through the bridging gap freestyle. My hands on one wall and my feet on the other, in alternate moves shoving myself up the way a spider pulls up a thread. I had to move quickly. Scott was smart. He would feel the lack of resistance on belay and know something was up.

I was inside the gap, pushing myself up, my feet against the pressure of my hands on the far wall, when it happened. Scott had called for me not to look. But I heard the cry—across the canyon—and I turned, frozen in midstance. I saw the falling body, the arms twisting and circling. Like it was trying to fly. I saw the body hit the face of a wall and watched it jerk, fly up, and then fall another five hundred feet.

Suddenly the climber's rope snapped against me as Scott took up the slack. Clips and nylon rope went whizzing past, heading up the gap above my head. Then there was silence. But I knew that Scott was afraid.

"Diamond?" I heard him call. "Diamond, where are you?"
I could hear the slow panic in his voice.

"It's all right," I said. By then, I was standing on the ledge behind him, having come up and around the other face of the rock without being seen. I had wanted to make him laugh when I reached him at belay. Instead, he was furious. He tied on a carabiner brake and rappelled down to the body. He was undoing a Prussik knot when I reached him by hiking—racing more like it—down the back side.

He wanted to sling the body with him and head down to the canyon floor, to be there when the rescue squad came. But what good would it do? The thing that lay there had died long before. The sirens had rolled up from the city by the time I reached them.

The body was on a canvas rescue stretcher. We saw the sharp angles of bone pushing through its back. It had no face. They left it uncovered. There was a kid, a teenager, standing off to one side. His hands were in his pockets. He looked bored. He shrugged his shoulders when they asked him questions. He had been up there with him when he fell, a man told us. The two of them had taken LSD.

Scott grabbed my arm. I dropped my pack. He was tearing into my bicep with his fingers. "It could have been you," he said. His voice was choked, and his eyes were red. "You asshole. You fucking asshole. Keep it up, sport. Someday you'll take a Phantom right into the rock during Red Flag with a stunt like that."

He looked back to where the body was. His eyes looked like stone now. His face said nothing. Just that weird half grin started to grow. He leaned forward, and then he pushed me back. He smiled. I guess he was trying to show me that he cared.

He punched me, hard, in the stomach. I fell to my knees, and then he kicked me in the head. I was in a stream. I could hear the water on my face.

"It could have been you," he screamed.

۹

The flight from Denver to Tehran lasted twenty-seven hours. At the time, it seemed to last forever: a flight of constant humming and whine-high engines over three continents and two sunrises.

Out of Athens, I switched from Pan Am to Iran Air.

We dropped out of the clouds from an infinite height. Around me, three other passengers woke, stretching and arching the full length of their seats. Electric motors whirred. Leading edge flaps unwound. The cabin pressure gradually rose as the throttles eased back for descent, and then slowly readjusted. A voice in Farsi flooded the intercom. Lights illuminated at the sound of a soft bell, and we responded to their meanings. Seat backs, table trays, cigarettes, seat belts, humans—all in place.

We fell toward earth. Around me, the sounds of Persian rose like the chitter of birds. Outside my window, dusk lifted from the crest of the Elburz range, each peak defined, each merged into the next, surrounding the northern edge of the city. A voice announced in English that we were making the steepest airport approach on the planet. We dove from twenty-two thousand feet down to seven. It felt as though we were lifting and bobbing in air, riding a giant sled.

Off to the north-northeast, I saw a single peak looming. Huge, apart from the others, it lifted from the shores of the Caspian. It dwarfed the other tiny peaks of only fourteen thousand feet beneath it. What was most impressive was how it stood alone, a sentinel. I'd never seen anything as separate or as powerful before—how I imagined the Himalayas to be.

The peak was jagged and sharp, streaked with long, glaciated fingers of snow. Off at the western lip it became suddenly blunt, as though something had been violently ripped away—and a millennium ago, I knew from the *Sháhnáma*, something had.

We dropped out of the sky, and the peak moved to a vanishing point, sinking into the Elburz range that swallowed it. The harsh, neglecting dusk flooded the snow-tipped slopes. Still, it waited, a mountain humped like a dragon's back—home to the Simurgh, the legendary phoenix, calling, as the *Sháhnáma* had said it would:

HEJIRA

There is a lake at the mountain's summit.
The mountain's name is Damávand.

The lake is a mirror of ice.
North from the Caspian, it calls.

We touched down, slamming pavement, bounced twice into the air, and then the jet refused to fly. The weight of its sixteen-wheeled landing gear—and gravity—took control. The passengers clapped politely. Unsure if they clapped because they were happy to be home, or thankful to be alive. The thrust reversers kicked in, and we were shoved forward and then dropped gently back into our seats. The huge, spoiling air brakes slowly fell to the wing, and the plane taxied off to a side ramp.

Passengers suddenly unstrapped, stood, and ran down the aisles, laughing and shouting, opening overhead compartments, tossing blankets and magazines around the cabin.

They shoot you on Pan Am for this.

We followed the flashing, tachistoscopic lights directing us north. In the dark of the early evening, I saw workmen move off to the side as we passed—oil-rich skin, mustached, dark eyes watching us. They had been sweeping the taxiway, their brooms tight pendulums of air against the dusk around us. Now they leaned on their fragile brooms, smoking and watching, while blue tongues of cloud rose from their mouths. They pointed to one another and then back to us. Some of them held one hand to an ear, trying to muffle the sound of our whining engines. The wings of the jet, stretching beyond each edge of the taxiway, hung over sand and spare patches of grass. The rotating turbines' exhaust kicked back the dirt and pebbles that had just been swept, throwing them back onto the pavement. The hot blast of the air whipped into the men, shadows cut by the wind.

I raised my hand, but they did not see.

We nosed in toward the parking ramp. In front of us, a second group of workers, darkened by evening, swept out the space where we would park. The engines shut down. There was a slight *ping* inside the cabin, the signal that it was safe to move about. But most of the passengers interpreted differently—out of the starting gates, shoving and pushing. The roar of their voices rose and then broke. The aisles filled with bodies. They poured out of nowhere in the race to get out. As I stepped off the plane, I thanked the flight attendant. She smiled back. "Enjoy our nation," she said.

I walked across the ramp in silence, the wave of their bodies pulsing away and the distance swallowing their voices. Like fireflies, the lights of the Tehran evening twinkled and shone. Supremely, suddenly happy, I looked up into the wealth of a Maxfield Parrish sky. Something about those colors made me want to do nothing but simply stare, endlessly—the ripe, dying orange; pink tinting the edge of clouds; a sky no longer able to contain its own blueness.

I was nineteen years old. A decade before, I would have been stepping off of a plane and into the welcoming, widening death arms of Southeast Asia. But, today, I was a son coming home: uncertain of anything, but happy for being uncertain.

For the next two hours, I waited for my bags. When I found them, I spent the next thirty minutes waiting again, while customs officers searched through my worthless belongings. When one of them found a Xeroxed copy of pages from the *Sháhnáma,* he eyed me suspiciously.

"Do you know what this is?" he asked, waving the pages in front of me. The wide brim of his hat slowly arched into a tight, fisted crown. He stared at me.

"Yes. Yes, of course," I answered.

"Do you read Farsi?" he asked.

"No."

He paused, leaned into me, perhaps to check my eyes, to see if I were lying.

"Well, then," he said. "Enjoy our nation." He slapped my stamped visa against my chest, closed my bags without zipping them, and turned away.

People stared at me. Seventy-seven inches, two heads taller than anyone around me. Two hundred pounds. Someone touched my hair, bleached by the summer on Coronado Island. I wheeled around and a woman, clasping the length of her black *chádor,* covered her face, turning from me.

I headed for what I hoped was an exit: a thick wall of glass with Mondrian borders of steel.

On the other side of the wall, off to one side, a hand raised in greeting. The voice, if there was one, was silenced by glass.

Across the vast expanse of the Mehrabad International, I saw my father waving me home.

Part Two

The Shadow of God

1

Faith, I can say this now. That country no longer exists, if it ever did. None of it exists—maybe it was never there. Maybe until Shápuhr Mareta appeared and the struggle for Behesht first started, there was nothing real before.

But I remember the trip we made from Mehrabad that night. I remember the streets we passed through and the things I saw as we climbed toward our home in Shemiran. I remember now that azadi *is the word for freedom, and how what was Eisenhower Avenue became Azadi Avenue; how Shahyád Square and its grotesque tower—still intact, though peppered with a few more bullets these days—is named Azadi Square now; how Golestan, the Palace of Mirrors, the Place of Roses, would be south of what became Imam Khomeini Avenue; and the American Embassy, a place where you once could buy copies of classified documents found during the first takeover, was at the corner of the avenue of Ayatollah Taleghani—named for a man who refused to watch the rape of his own daughter by SAVAK agents, who, when he closed his eyes shut, had his eyelids burned away with cigarettes, forcing him to watch.*

And I could tell you that Beatrice, who had never allowed a gun to enter our home, had given her consent for my father to keep one in our home in Shemiran. I could tell you that when I opened the tall door of the armoire in my room that first night I found three shotguns, loaded, lined neatly side to side, at the back wall of the closet.

And here's what I want to tell you now: what it was like, that first night of the war. I suppose you could say it was a kind of miracle, a horrifying one. Old Billy Mitchell would be proud. A victory for airpower. Maybe our first.

The deadline for Behesht had passed. The Alliance for Nation-State Securities had officially notified Shápuhr Mareta that he must withdraw from the Paradise, pull back toward the Heart of the Kingdom. His special forces—the ones he named Martyrs for the Order of God—would have to leave the Zagros plateau immediately. Al-Abshár must be returned to the people who first lived there.

We didn't exactly know then that these were the conditions that had been set. Now I wonder why we didn't know.

THE SHADOW OF GOD

The only thing I remember was that after months of waiting, hours of practice and overflight and lineal mapping, we all knew it would happen soon. But we didn't know that the Alliance had delivered its ultimatum or that a deadline had passed. We weren't told.

We were just brought into a briefing room and ordered to watch this video. It lasted maybe fifteen seconds. A few words. Shápuhr Mareta seated in a corner. He looked at us. "I have finished my prayer, farangi *dogs. I know now what the one God tells me to do," he said.*

He leaned in toward the lens. His face flooded the whole aperture. We were all pretty callous, hardened folks—but I saw people actually shift back in their chairs as if he were right there, as if he could just reach out and touch them.

And then he spat into the camera. His face disappeared.

That was it. The video went blank.

"Fuckhead," I heard Troy say. Everyone heard it. She wasn't holding back.

"Suck my dick," someone else said to the black screen. But the voice didn't have the conviction that Troy's voice had. It sounded hollow and frightened. It made things worse.

"Well," said Troy as she stood up. "Won't be long now. Let's get some rest."

And then she just walked out. Turned around to the rest of us as she stopped at the door and said, "Oh, yeah. You're all dismissed. Go home."

I had taken three green ones—the sleeping kind. I can't get by without them.

Later, Troy just leaned over, shook me, and said, "It's time, Diamond. Time to fly."

I was up fast, moving so fast I could barely remember what I was supposed to be doing. My brain went faster than my body. I was thinking one or two steps ahead of where I actually was. Then it hit me. I just went blank, and looked up. Saw myself in the mirror. I looked like a ghost. That's right. I just stared and all I could think was, Where am I? And then I looked back at the face and saw my father. I am the age I most remember him at, back when I climbed Damávand. It was pretty scary, seeing that.

Preflight was fast, precise. Even without night specs, I could have done it blind. I knew where every dial, gage, screen, toggle switch, warning light, heads-up readout, radar scope, IFF selection; trim for rudder, aileron, and elevator; air dump vent, infra light set, frequency, volt, power, and ammeter; icing selector, sand shield, ultraviolet screen protection shield, kevlar shield

THE SHADOW OF GOD

and titanium plate extender, accelerometer, fuel dump, air bellows, ZSR masking type, altimeter, artificial horizon, laser-centered gyroscope, inverted rotational direction indicator and backup, ball and turn slip meter, astral tracker, sextant port, capsule launch code, escape sequence identifier, and ejection trigger were. You fight like you train.

Engine start was silent. No flares. Everything set by time sequence. The Shabahs led the pack, setting jammers and frequency pickups. Looking for active SAM sites, where they were and how to kill them. We went in on the first wave. It stretched for fifty miles, either side. Completely black.

You can't fight what you can't see, we used to say in training. That's how all war will be from now. Blind strategy, the boys with the best computers win. No forces massed across the Rubicon. No daylight charges. No fields of fire. No sequence transmissions on voice. Minimal digital transfer. We were the wave of the future. And we were ready to crush them.

My night specs showed planes as far to the left and right and behind me as I could see. The Alliance wasn't kidding around this time.

Near the edge of the Paradise, the Shabahs lifted up, hit subsonic, and climbed at eighty-six degrees until we reached the ten-mile point. It was an awesome thing, really, watching these planes lift like bats and zoom straight toward space. I saw maybe twenty all around me as I notched toward .989 Mach. Troy was on my wing.

At sixty thousand, we pushed through Mach, set our fuel reduction marks on the throttle, and started the orbit. The wave of sound pulsed by in an atmosphere of ice. The air moved in to fill the absence where our tracks were set. From that height, no one could hear us.

One turn covered the entire gulf. My scope could show me where and when and if they knew and how to stop them. My astral tracker took shots every seven-tenths of a second and kept me within three feet left or right of course. Troy and I were searching for who was radiating, trying to find if they knew we were out there. When we found them, we would pass the data link through to the nearest hunter, recommend a weapon set. Take out their eyes.

The strikes went off within thirty seconds of each other. Precise coordination. Swift, vicious, final. I saw troops on the ground running for bunkers. I saw their mouths open in shock, pointing at the darkness where they heard nothing. Until the impacts. The sky exploded. A million points of light. Seven million pounds of ordnance in thirty seconds.

I thought of my father. I thought of how it must have been for him, the wars he had fought in. It had been tougher, sure. SAMs launched at you at nine times the speed of sound, tracers dancing off the canopy like St. Elmo's fire. My father used to tell me queer, funny stories about war. About when he used to fly with Air America over the north, on Psyop missions. They would drop leaflets telling the NVA to give up, that they didn't have a chance, that the war would be over soon and better now than later to learn that Chairman Ho was full of shit. He told me he got to sit in on one of the interrogation debriefs once. He actually got to lead the interrogation.

"Did you defect because of the leaflets?" he asked.

"Yes, it was because of the leaflets that we defected," the NVA soldiers told him.

"What was it in the leaflets that made you come over?" *My father was kind of excited. This could be a Psyop breakthrough, at a time when most people thought that psychological warfare was pure crap. Winning hearts and minds, most people believed, was garbage. Bomb the fucks straight back to the Stone Age instead.*

"There was nothing in the leaflets, Colonel," they answered. "We know as well as you do that the words inside are all lies.

"No," they said. "We were just tired of being ordered to pick them up. There are just too many. Sometimes it takes all day to pick them from the trees and jungle floor. A waste of time."

You know, there was only once I remember when he told me something horrifying about war. He didn't like true war stories. He didn't like to tell them. I had asked the wrong question: "What was it like to kill someone?" *He told me to sit down, and listen. He told me that I had to understand that he had killed Americans and South Vietnamese, NVA and Vietcong. It was like that, flying ground support. Everything turned to shit in a heartbeat. People would scream on the radios for covering fire, for lay-down strikes. Nobody knew what was coming or when.*

"Just make it stop, just make it stop," *he heard somebody actually whimpering on the radio that day. And he flew in low, told the voice on the radio to just relax, that the Dragonfly Hellzapoppin was on its way.*

"Colonel Diamond, is that you, sir?" *the voice asked. You could almost hear a sigh of relief in the question.*

But he wouldn't answer, wouldn't give his position or his identity away.

THE SHADOW OF GOD

He had marked the coordinates of Zone 46A3 on the map taped to his canopy. He flew in low. He felt the tips of the rice field brushing his tip tanks. He laid down a stream of napalm for five hundred yards. Everything went quiet. The voice never called him back on the radio.

When he taxied back in at Bien Thieu, his crew chief ran out to the plane, and just kind of froze. He put his hands to his throat, as though he were choking, then bent over and vomited on the pavement. My father didn't know what was going on. Until engine shutdown, when he found the head, the face still wide-eyed and the mouth open in a perfect O, stuck in the left inlet of the Dragonfly's undercarriage.

So when I thought of my father, I thought of how different war had become. There's no term I despise more than "surgical strike," though it's true that that's the kind of cold, calculating nature of it now. Everything is distance. And the earth from this distance is small. Whole armies look like ants to my naked eye. Agony and suffering are the last imploding gleam that the scalpel reflects. How would it look reflected in the patient's eye? Some mortal flashbulb, the image fading on the blade, and then the retina.

And I thought of how my father would see me, what he would think. Dante Diamond, in the fifth decade of his life, flying a plane that was more like a missile with a man in it than anything that first lifted from the Carolina sands at Kitty Hawk a century before.

What would he think, Faith? Would he be proud of me? Or is that a stupid question? Is that the right question? Would he recognize the nervous kid who sat on the roof of their home in Tehran and tried to tell his father he didn't know what to do with his life?

I had left this life. Wanted nothing more to do with it. And a simple handdelivered message changed all that, a few words: "as of this date, you are to report . . ."

Years ago I sat in an audience at the War College and listened as Paul Tibbetts explained what it was like to drop the bomb on Hiroshima. He was twenty-eight years old, a full colonel: 6 August 1945. One flight that changed history. One day where nothing after it could be the same again.

"Dullest flight I ever took," he told us. "Never regretted a single moment . . . never lost any sleep over it. Operation Coronet would have cost us two million lives. And they deserved what they got. After all, who bombed Pearl Harbor?"

A young Japanese officer was in front of me in the auditorium. His shoulders were stiff. His face showed nothing. He held a copy of Flight of the Enola Gay in his hands.

Well, the night we bombed the Paradise wasn't the dullest for me. It was thrilling, and I was scared to death. I remember sometime after launch, when I stared with this incredible awe down the lines either side of us—this wave pulsing north—feeling my tongue playing at the base of my mouth and then realizing that a tooth had collapsed and I hadn't even felt it. I reached in, pulled it out, took some liquid solder and glued it to the canopy. I never felt a thing.

•

The Shabahs are going to help us through this war, if any weapon can. We are like the screaming archons from Mani's heavenly kingdom, the silent inhabitants of darkness who attack by night.

I know the barefoot ghost of Mani still wanders the banks of the Euphrates, constantly asking: "Do you have the courage to cry?"

People forget that Mani was hanged from the city gates in Jundishâpuhr by the Sassanid ruler, Bahram I. They remember only what Mani believed, that we are all travelers in this world who have lost our origins, who must return to the world of light. That's what I believe. That's what I think I'm doing here. I've returned to a world of counter image—the mirror image of our world. The real world is not this one. It's somewhere else. And if Mani had been there still at the Euphrates the night we bombed the Paradise, he would have asked: "Do you have the courage to understand?"

The war was over from the moment the first nosewheel of the first Shabah lifted from the runway. But the real war, the one that keeps us here forever, had just begun when the first explosion rocked the earth.

•

The Chinese say: "May you live in interesting times"—but it's meant as a curse. And we all see the same sky but we own different horizons.

Mine begins with the letter D.

٢

History of Persia—THE EMPIRE of IRAN
Area: 636,000 miles^2
Population: Well over 34,000,000; 2.7% per annum
Topography: Large central Plateaus enveloped by three sides of mountain ranges; Largest peak is Damavand, given as nearly 19,000 feet of altitude—Both a national treasure and symbol; Caspian sea ninety-two feet below the sea
Histroical Fact: The oldest established world culture; from over 2,500 years, the first rule of the Achæmenids, and the Cyrus and Darius the great.
Nationality: Because of the official shiite Islam Religion, attach great importance to propriety and to familial affectation through large family systems, and love justice as same as peace.

Dante,

This is what your father sees when he flies. Low hanging mists with the Elburz mountain peaks peeking through. The high mountain's name is Demavend.

We have your short letter. We look forward to seeing you as well.

Much Love,

your mother,

Beatrice

‎٣

What memories I have of my father, they are nearly all good ones. As if any one man could survive all that and not be legend.

"T-Boy" Diamond. Took his name from my great-grandfather, who ran his farm in Vermont for twenty years after his wife died. Lived alone. Ninety-six years old when they found him that winter morning of thirty below. By then, I've been told—a hundred times—Grandpa Therrien Boyd Diamond was blue in the face, had already lost three fingers and two toes for good, and was muttering to himself in a frozen corner about *why it was you can never get a damn thing done around here!*

Aside from his never actually being a real father, my father was great. That's unfair to say, I know. Faith and I don't have any children, so I don't have anything to measure him against. But my father was always more of an image than a man. He was always off, flying some new airplane, fighting some goddamned war. My mother had two nervous breakdowns when he was gone. Still, he never let up.

Whenever he was home, he'd take me deep-sea fishing off Long Island, camping on Cape Cod, hiking up Katahdin. Once, he took me on a wild boar hunt in Texas, taking only a compound bow and arrow along. I was five years old and spent much of that trip wedged in the high branches of any available tree—terrified, eyes clamped shut forever, while snorting angry shapes tore through scrub brush. My father stood off to one side, calmly dropping them one by one. I was a great diversion.

On our first fishing trip in Maine, I grew bored with waiting and threw my rod over the lip of the boat, thinking I'd feed the fish my line. He dove in after; he came up seconds later, ready to feed me to the gulls.

•

They also had another nickname for him—one that's passed with time. The Miracle of Bien Thieu. That's what they called him. And that's what it was. It was his second tour in Southeast Asia. He had already earned a reputation with the Wild Wolf wing, already shot down six Migs. He was flying special operations missions: psychological warfare, missions into Laos with the CIA, covert drops to guerrilla groups in the mountains, reconnaissance, ground support. He flew A-37 Dragonflys, and T-28s—a plane that was half Mustang and half something no one exactly could recall what.

That day he had taken a T-28 into Laos to extract SEAL forces trapped inside the border. If their presence were known, the international community would have a fit. It was part of Operation Jungle Jim, itself an extension of Operation Farmgate—support for insurrection forces against NVA influence. By that time, of course, the war had already grown beyond the limits of revolution or civil war. It was out of control, and special operations could put out tiny fires, but they couldn't control the blaze.

His right wingtip and most of his tail were shot off by a rocket fired from a hand-held launcher. Back in those days, those kind of launchers weren't supposed to exist.

He decided to take the plane into the jungle rather than risk manual extraction—there was just no room for a parachute to open before he hit. The trees were slamming into his cockpit. He saw his own blood on the canopy when the plane exploded.

When the SEALs found him, he had pulled himself from the wreckage and just lay there, waiting. He was still conscious. With those kind of burns over almost all his body, it was impossible to pass out. The pain was just too much.

"I remember the first boy looking at me," he told me. "A real John Wayne type. Couldn't believe I was still alive. Just turned around and barfed on the jungle floor. I admit, I must have looked pretty awful. I mean, the oxygen mask had melted to my face. My skin was gone. I was just this one great charred mess.

"When they got me to the mobile medical unit, the doctor looked down, shook his head, said without even turning away, 'He'll be dead in six hours.' When I was still alive the next morning, they medevac'ed me to Tokyo. When the plane landed, one of the nurses running the stretcher out to the air hospital took one look at me, turned around, and barfed on the ramp. When they got me to the operating room after soaking and primping and dressing me, the physician's assistant leaned over, looked at me, and barfed right there in the operating room.

"Now, remember, all this happened in, say, the space of three days. I had not seen what I looked like in that entire time. But, based on the reaction of most folks around me, I had a pretty good idea that things weren't looking up."

•

It took twenty-six months for him to recover. Doctors told him, when he arrived in Japan, that he would probably not live another month. When he was still alive, they gave him six weeks total. Then they shipped him back to a burn center in the States. Told him he would never walk again. When ten months later he was walking with a brace and then just a slight limp, they told him that he would be medically retired as a young colonel. My father informed his superiors that he would not only not retire, but that he'd be a test pilot at Edwards by the end of the year. I have a picture of him, taken five months after the day of his saying that. He's flying a Falcon. Ninety degrees pitch—straight up. He did the impossible.

He had nerves of steel. *Brass balls*—that's how they used to name somebody with guts at the Zoo. It was and had to be incredibly painful. Hours and hours of physical therapy and strain. Experts telling you you couldn't possibly do what you said you had to do. And then the skin grafts. At one point, they were even using pig flesh because it was the only thing that would take.

My mother herself had just come from a short hospital stay when it happened, in Laos. She pulled herself together long enough and expected me to be strong enough to support him. I was shocked, a little frightened, the first time I saw him. But he was still the same man. Only the myth about him grew. And we all made it through that time.

And maybe the only thing I could say that was wrong between us was that we really couldn't talk like father and son. We just never spoke. I was and will always be T-Boy Diamond's kid, and how can you live up to being that and not always fail?

It was crazy, sometimes, the way we avoided really speaking. When I was nine or ten, he decided to take me for a ride. We were living in Australia then. We used to take the Land-Rover—a 1949 edition—out for long drives in the outback. But that day was an important one. We were going to have The Talk. He was trying to tell me where I came from and how I was created.

"You see, Dante," he said, both hands fixed on the huge spoked wheel and eyes straight ahead and his face a little red, "it's something special that happens between a man and a woman."

"And they must be married," he said. "It can only happen with married people."

I was nine years old. By this time, I knew *exactly* how it happened. We'd been passing pictures of naked volleyball players around the schoolyard—those special camps where you could pretty much see everything that was going on. Roger Malone, my best friend, and I had already decided what made her a her and him a him. But, still, I wanted to act like I was paying attention. I wanted to enjoy this conversation.

"But, Dad," I asked. "How exactly do married men and women do this?"

He shifted a little. His face got a little redder. "Well," he said, "the man gives the woman his seed."

"His seed," I wondered. "You mean like a spice or something?"

"Yes, like a spice."

"How exactly does this happen?"

"Well, it's something very special."

"Is it a food? Does she eat it?"

"Not a food, really. And she can only take it at special times."

"But how does he give it to her? I mean, does he slip it to her in her steak or something?"

He changed the subject.

•

I miss him. I can still see those burn scars around his neck and under his jaw, along the lines where the pilot's mask nestles into the soft flesh.

After all these years.

3

All my life, until I got to the academy, I'd wanted to fly. I'd dreamt about the D-horizon. But when I got there, I realized that dreams got in the way of real things. I guess it was what the place was meant to do. It did a better job of convincing you not to stay than to remain. The war had just ended. People had died. We were all confused.

During SERE training—Survival, Evasion, Resistance, and Escape—which began just after our fourthclass year, Mitchell and I had completed the evasion portion of the trek. It had taken a week, traveling through the Rockies, with a map and a compass, without food and water. Eventually, after reaching the final checkpoint and the Partisans who welcomed us with open arms, we came to the inevitable, the final phase: imprisonment, interment.

We slipped through a long pass, trying to evade the enemy. We heard them moving through the trees beside us. We came to the end of a canyon, trapped. The Precambrian shadows of red rock walls looked down on us. We climbed to a small mouth in the side of the rock twenty feet above the ground. We waited.

The sun fell. We could hear movement, voices beneath. As the last of the light ignited on the back wall of the cave, I saw the imprint of fossils, left there millions of years before, glaciated cetaceans imprinted on the rock like the figure of a man's shadow entering a wall. We couldn't sleep.

Finally, a voice boomed up to us. It was time to *knock it off, the game was over*. We leaned out in the dark, called for a flashlight to help us find our way back. When we reached the earth, we were surrounded. Pushed, shoved. Black hoods thrown over heads. Blind and stumbling, tied to each other, Mitchell and I were led to the camp.

I can't tell much of what happened. It's not just that it's classified: the torture, the confinement, the noises of small animals in my tiny wooden cell, the constant blare of music—Vietnamese string instruments—the sound echoing in camp, the horrible sense of its voice, which never stopped. It's that I can't remember much of anything. I was in solitary for three days, no food, no voices, no possibility of sunlight.

THE SHADOW OF GOD

The music. All I remember is that music. Except I remember my first session with Scott Hind: the five-pointed star on his cap, the ever-ready smile. "Yankee pig scum," he would greet me. I remember how he would smile, not believing anything I said, send me off for a *correction period*, and then bring me back. He finally won, tricked me into signing a statement in which I confessed that I had wronged the peoples of Vietnam, and all the peoples of the world by murder and destruction.

All the prisoners were forced into one single camp at the end. We worked together in the yard, among the chickens and the sweat, at nothing: digging trenches, filling them with water; draining the water, filling in the trenches. Scott singled me out, grabbed Mitchell by the hair, dragged him to me, told me, "You, Yankee pig scum, will bury him." So I pushed Mitchell into a pine box shaped like a coffin. The ditch was a wound dug from the earth. In the box Mitchell could not lie the full length of his own body. He curled up like a fetal accident.

"Dig, cover; dig, cover," Scott ordered. I kept shoveling the dirt. This was a training program, this wasn't real, I kept thinking. But this was far beyond the point of sanity. I was burying my own friend, quickly, methodically, doing it as well as I knew how, doing everything I had been told.

And the music, which shifted suddenly from the harsh staccato of Vietnamese, to the soothing songs of Joan Baez, and, finally, Jane Fonda speaking from a bomb shelter in Hanoi, appalled by the crimes of her own country, America. *This must stop.*

I am a fairly peaceful person. You have to understand that. I've also always liked Baez and Fonda. They seemed intelligent and honest. I never met them. How would I know?

But, I swear, if Ms. Fonda had been standing in front of me at that instant, as I shoveled dirt onto the lip of the coffin, I would have dropped the shovel, knocked Scott to the ground, put my hands around her throat, and taken her head off.

The night General Diamond and I walked out of the terminal, I thought I had escaped, that I could forget the academy. When I had the time and if I had the courage, I'd tell my parents that I wanted to leave the Rockies, and the military, forever. My mother stood by a light blue car—the American staff car—a late model Ford. The trunk was open, waiting for my belongings.

Beatrice just stared at me. I was sure she had no idea that it was me, her son, walking with her husband. I had lost about twenty pounds in San Diego. My skin was dark. My hair was blond, almost white, from constant sun.

There was a man on the right side of the car behind her. He had turned from someone, someone he knew. He had embraced this other man and kissed him. His shirt, a dark-striped cotton of grey and black, was open to his chest. He wore a silver chain and had this huge mustache, furry and thick. The hair slicked back from his high forehead. When he saw me his frown became a grin. He snapped to attention, held one large arm to his side. He saluted me. I nodded back.

"Hi, Mom," I said to Beatrice. "Long time . . ." I bent over and gave her this kind of half-assed hug. She froze. She stood me back at shoulder's length. She put her hands on my arms and kept looking up to me.

"You're so thin—" she whispered so that no one could hear.

Yeah, it's me, Beatrice.

She told my father to help put my luggage in the car. I turned around and grabbed my duffel bag. I wasn't about to let a brigadier general stuff my garbage in his own car. The man with the mustache came up to help.

"And this," my father said, "is Ghassemi."

I shook his hand. "It is indeed a pleasure, sir," he said solemnly.

"Well, thanks, Gozameh," I said. "I've heard all these great things about you. But you don't have to call me sir. I'm just a cadet."

We got in the car, drove through the mess of the airport. We were all pretty quiet. There were questions about the flight, and San Diego, but my answers were short, polite, and didn't say anything.

We passed around a park that stood in the middle ring of traffic. It must have been a half-mile in diameter. There were four paths leading to the center: hexagons, pentagons, and squares of grass around the paved walkways. Thousands of lights hit the rising fountain beneath the monstrosity in the center of the park. It was huge, distorted: four twisted flukes of a whale rising to a single square column. The flat sharp edges of the column were cut beneath on each side by a tympanum arch.

The traffic flew by. People came around and passed us like it was the Grand Prix. Someone pulled up behind and hit our fender with the front of his car. He started flashing his high beams, honking his horn. *Well, there goes all my stuff...*

"*Ma sha' allah*," Gozameh said.

"It means the will of God," my father said. Gozameh looked back, flicked his turn signal, and slid over to the outside of the raging flow of insane drivers. The grateful man in the car behind us flew by, making gestures with his hands.

Gozameh suddenly turned his head toward me and said, "It is as God has it. Do you understand, sir?"

"Yes, but please don't call me sir. Is Gozameh okay for you?"

"Yes, yes, of course. It is a most pleasant name," he said.

"Yes it is, Gozameh."

I was looking at that poor excuse for architecture through the window. The glass was so thick—it had these extra shields almost an inch thick on the inside cabin. It was all bulletproof. The family car.

"This is Shahyád Tower," Beatrice said, pointing to the tower in the center of the park. "They are very proud of it in Iran. A young architect finished it in 1971 to celebrate the twenty-five hundredth anniversary of the Persian monarchy. If we have time, we'll take you down here one day. There is a moving-ramp museum inside. It tells all about the history of the nation."

"Kind of a strange building, though," I said.

We turned on Eisenhower Avenue and wound our way north through the traffic. It was obvious by now that the way people had driven around the tower was normal. Cars would pull into the opposite lane and come flying toward us, flashing their beams, playing chicken. Gozameh just cruised straight ahead, right on course. My parents seemed relaxed.

When we passed the American Embassy at Roosevelt and Takhte Jamshîd, my father pointed to it. There was a high wall with an iron gate out front. Spotlights from inside hit the branches of trees that leaned their arms over the street. The trees looked like shadows, white shadows of light. "Pretty big place," my father said. "A lot of acres in there."

At night the city seemed electric and alive, with thousands of lights, the noise of a great machine. People strolled along the sidewalks, slowly, enjoying themselves. Some stopped to chat with others they knew. Others leaned against the bright windows of stores, dazzled by the displays. We left the heart of the city and headed into the dark ahead of us: north, a place named Shemiran. It was, as Beatrice had called it, "lovely."

I could tell you about the house. How it was a villa behind a locked gate, with a swimming pool, and five bedrooms, and marble columns and mosaic tiles, how there were Persian toilets in the guest bathrooms and how I had no idea how to use them.

"You'll have a wonderful time here," Beatrice had said.

That first day I slept till dawn of the next day. My father had already left for work when I came down to the kitchen. Beatrice and I talked about small things, about what my plans were in the next year. She had known about Mitchell: I had told them both that day when they called me, for some strange reason, out of the blue.

They both knew that I was unhappy, but I think they also thought there would be no way I would even talk about leaving. When I tried to talk with Beatrice about it, I backed off. I couldn't speak. "Maybe some other time," I said.

"Don't worry, you'll have lots of time, time to rest."

Beatrice was always so confident, so heartbreaking. She was my mother, and sometimes she was like a little sister. She had a fit when I asked to walk through the city streets alone. I wanted to see the place. I didn't have much time. Somehow, and I'll never be quite sure how, my father convinced her to let me go.

It had begun.

ז

It was hard to sort through, those first few days. My father was gone much of the time. I spent what time I could in the mornings with Beatrice. I was, as I'd always been, uncomfortable with her.

And the way she talked about the country—she loved it and she hated it. She would call Iranians *savage, innocent, stupid, gentle people* in the same breath she would take to tell me that she wanted to learn everything she could about Persia. She would explain how at official functions everyone from the shah and the empress down to the last insignificant bureaucrat in the entourage was perfectly charming. But step out into the street, or drive a few minutes south of the city—where the people live in nothing but hovels and filth—and you'd entered a desert. Shepherds still knock at the door in the morning wanting to butcher a goat right on the porch. Children throw rocks over the wall, and scream in high lilting Farsi. Earlier that summer, they had spent a few days on the Caspian trying to relax, enjoy what they could of the desolate landscape. They had dinner one night by the water, and the maître d'hôtel thought absolutely nothing about picking his nose while serving the entrée. He had a hankering and he didn't give a damn whether they watched. "But that about says it all for Iran," Beatrice claimed. "A little rough around the edges."

The phone lines to our house were tapped—I was surprised she told me this. I doubt my father ever would have mentioned it. So it became not a question of what to say on the phone but wondering if the receiving party would ever hear what you said. You could never mention the shah. No one could. He and the government were forbidden topics. Sometimes Americans would speak of the country, but among themselves, in small, private gatherings.

Beatrice almost never let her anger come out on a phone. Sometimes a note of jeering condescension, but never an actual complaint. The week before, she had called the wife of one of my father's aides, and the background music on the line was so loud she said, "Well, it seems that SAVAK is keeping close tabs on us, what with all the strange music coming over the wires." As soon as she said this, the music stopped: only the sound of slight hissing as the long spool of recording reel unwound on the floor of the apartment from which they listened. The music stopped for several days.

She talked about attending a luncheon sponsored by the magistrate for foreign guests of the country. It was at the crumbling, decrepit Hilton: even trying to reach there by car, you took your life into your hands. That day she looked up into the chandelier, into the glaring, brilliant light of the crystals, and saw an eye returning her stare. Which just as quickly disappeared. *Here I am,* she thought, *a fifty-year-old woman, playing hide-and-seek with the secret police.*

She would veer back and forth between damnation and praise. When my father drove the Buick over the lip of a *jube*—the open ditches that carried water from the mountains—near our street, people started running from all directions to help. The rear tire had sunk into the filthy water, and she just sat there breathless and wanting to scream, angled four feet above the ground. Men opened the doors, reached up to help her down, and then pulled the car from the *jube*. They just smiled, as if it were nothing, and walked off.

And she hesitated but finally said it: she was amazed that someone hadn't tried to hurt them. General Diamond had an important job. Gozameh was probably the only reliable bodyguard and driver they had. A wonderful man: simple, intelligent, and kind. Not like that fool who used to patrol the front courtyard, who let practically everyone and his neighbor stop in for a visit, who spent most of the day making tea in his samovar or strolling the grounds with a rifle slung carelessly over one shoulder, like some proud rooster. "We only had that damned idiot for a month," she said. "Though I feel awful about what happened. Eventually, we would have fired him anyway, and should have long before things got out of hand."

She'd come home one afternoon and entered the courtyard to see him sprawled across the high branch of our apple tree. At first, she thought he was asleep. But then she saw his hand still clutched around the precious prize of the bright apple, which for him at any rate would be the choicest pick he'd ever make, the rifle had slipped from his shoulder, hit the ground, discharged one bullet that shot through his heart. She found him swinging lifeless in the orchard. She'd started screaming.

"Thank Allah or whomever for Gozameh."

She admired and trusted him. She was a New Englander, a Yankee, and that meant that somebody had to be pretty damn special to be of any worth in her eyes. She called his family "charming, and sweet." She had no doubt that he'd do anything to try and save my father if something happened.

And one afternoon I watched him show her something mysterious. It was from the Ghor'án—my parents kept the book open, set on a lectern in the center of the living room. It was beautiful, inlaid with gold and camel bone.

"Missus Diamond," he had said. "I must show you something."

He had walked to the stand and looked at the pages spread open like wings. "You have found the right passage to display." He spoke suddenly in a beautiful Arabic, or Farsi—the breath of a cooing dove.

"What does it mean?" Beatrice had asked.

"As you know, my English is not quite good—but, I could say, 'one day each soul pleads for its self.' Yes, Missus Diamond. You have chosen wisely."

And Beatrice became flustered, insisting that it was an accident, that she had just opened the book for display. There was no purpose, no direction.

"But you did choose . . . it does not matter if you knew," he said. "We call it fa'll in our tongue. It means 'destiny.' And in your religion I have heard it called something such as 'providence.'"

•

Once, before dawn, I heard her slip into my room. I pretended to be asleep. She just stood there, listening to my breath. I faced the window, turned away from her.

As if it could all come down to that: a mother steals into her son's room—the guest room—to hear him breathe, to stand there bathed in light, to know how it was to be alive. In my family, it had never been that simple, and I knew it never would. And I knew she was praying for *me*.

V

One morning before dawn my father stood at the edge of my bed, shaking me. "Dante, I want you to come with me," he said.

He was wearing a long coat, like a raincoat or a thin trench coat. He told me that there was a cup of coffee on the counter downstairs, but to be quick, we needed to be going. "Five minutes," he ordered.

I was showered, dressed, had my coffee, and on the front step of the house in four. I'd gotten slower since I'd left Colorado.

Gozameh, waiting at the car by the gate, saluted us both and opened the door of the car for my father. General Diamond moved with the swiftness and authority of someone who knew he was important, knew he had things to do, things he felt mattered.

He opened the glove compartment, pressed his finger to an electronic trigger, and the gate opened. Gozameh turned into the street, and we headed toward the city. Even then the traffic was jammed. People screaming and shouting, as a few men on bicycles were suddenly clipped by Peykans and knocked into a wall. We passed University Park, and I saw a few students, up too early for classes, walking hand in hand underneath the plane trees. Funny, I thought, this was the first time I had seen men and women actually touch each other.

"I've set up a special briefing for you, Dante," my father said. "If you really want to know this country, this is the only chance you'll get. You can walk around, see quite a bit, in fact. But not everything.

"You wear a uniform, remember," he added.

I was angry at that. *No shit, Dad.*

There was a bad traffic accident at the beginning of the business district. A car had wrapped around the face of a small truck. It was obvious that the driver inside was dead. The truck driver stood off to one side shaking his head; his truck's front end was badly beaten up. It looked like he couldn't just drive away with the damage, not to mention that there was a dead body hanging off the grille.

Gozameh chuckled slightly. He was actually laughing at this. My father looked away, impassive. "Worst goddamn drivers in the world," he mumbled to his window.

I took a chance and said it anyway, to Gozameh, *"Ma sha' allah?"*
"That's for sure, maybe," he answered with a wise-ass grin.

•

"Good morning, Cadet Diamond," said my official briefer for the morning. "On behalf of the Air Magistrate and the Military Air Advisory Group, Major General Winfield Magyar, and Brigadier General Therrien Diamond, I would like to personally welcome you to the Imperial Kingdom of Iran. I'm Major Larry Weaver, and I'll be your official information source for this briefing. I'd like to remind you that this briefing is classified Secret, and the material contained within it is nonreleasable to foreign nationals. Do you understand?"

I nodded my head. "Yes, sir," I said. *You mean, even though this isn't our country, I can't tell an Iranian that I am going to know more about this place than he will.*

Major Weaver relaxed after saying this. We were the only ones in the official briefing room of the Military Air Advisory Group, the MAAG. It was a pretty drab place, all in all: no windows, the walls had paint chips flaking off; outside the halls were plastered with framed portraits of glass and cheap metal. It didn't look any different from most of the city, which, shortly after sunrise, looked to me like a city of the dead. There was construction all over the place, spreading like a cancer.

My father had led me to his office, taken off his coat, hung it in his closet, and turned around. He was wearing his uniform, though he had been hiding it. "Security," he said. "Lots of assassinations lately."

"I'm class of '65 myself," said Major Weaver. "I've been in U-SAFE most of my career. Phantoms—best fighter we've got going these days."

"Yes, sir." I said. "Except for maybe Falcons?"

He didn't like that comment. He straightened, looked at me, slapped his briefing wand against one palm, and said, "So, how are things back in the Rockies? Keeping those new women in line?"

"Yes, sir. Most of them are pretty sharp."

He didn't like that, either.

Slide after slide shot up on the screen. He wanted me to know everything he could possibly think was important. Land size 636,000 square miles. International sovereignty of waters claimed to twelve nautical miles. A large central plateau ringed by rugged mountain ranges. Highest peak in the country was Mount Damávand, in the Elburz, 18,971 feet. Annual rainfall in slight excess of fifty inches. Total population of thirty-eight million, just shy of four million in the capital of Tehran. Mountain nomadic tribes, consisting mainly of the Kurds of Kurdistan—a fiercely private clan, which contains elements of both Sunni and Shi'a Islam, as well as active believers in Zoroastrianism. Kurds also created the religious brotherhood known as Sufis, the mystic sect of whirling dervishes and ritual poetry. Other groups included Azarbayjans, Qashqais, Lurs, Baluchis, Arabs, Turks, and Bakhtiaris. Education was basically free at primary and secondary level. His Imperial Majesty had placed a strong emphasis on university education. Although numerous students achieved undergraduate and graduate degrees outside the country, the shah had stressed continued improvement of national universities. Chief causes of infant mortality were gastrointestinal, parasitic, respiratory disease, as well as improper information reception on nutritional methods. Farsi was the official language of the nation; Arabic and Turkish were also widely spoken. The official governmental structure was a constitutional monarchy—"or, as we like to say," said Major Weaver, interrupting his own flow, "a benevolent dictatorship."

Mohammed Reza Pahlaví had held the reigns of power since his father passed down command in 1941. Rastakhiz-e-Mellat-Iran, or, the National Resurgence party, was the official political agency of the shah. Tudeh, the Communist party, was outlawed. The country itself comprised twenty-three provinces, each administered by a provincial general. There was a Supreme Court, as well as district and appeals courts, and military courts, which were a predominant feature of the overall judicial system. The nation was in its fifth year of the Fifth Development plan, aimed toward strong improvements in education, agriculture, and domestic welfare. There were thirty-six thousand miles of roads, three thousand miles of railway. Eighteen airports. More than five thousand miles of petroleum pipelines. With the assistance of the United States, Iran now possessed the most advanced telecommunications system in the Middle East. The most valuable natural resource, the center of the nation's vast wealth, obviously was oil. The official religion of the country was Shiite Islam.

"But I must remind you, Cadet Diamond," said Major Weaver, "that despite the disturbances in Qom, Tabriz, and several other places, the position of radical, revolutionary elements—those which the national media have

THE SHADOW OF GOD

termed Islamic Marxists—remains a minimal factor. Latest Central Intelligence Agency reports insist that Iran is neither a revolutionary nor prerevolutionary society. Even if such elements negative to the government were to have access to more emphatic forms of protest, they lack the military power and cohesive organization necessary to disrupt the current political system. The power of the shah, in any case, is supreme. . . ."

And so it went. On and on like all briefings. The greatest weight was given to military structure and composition of the armed forces, which, I had to admit, was pretty impressive. Aside from the largely indefinite figures about the actual size of the SAVAK organization, the army held nearly a quarter million troops, the navy, thirty thousand; and the air force, well over one hundred thousand. Troops were equipped with the latest surface-to-air missiles, several thousand tanks, nearly seven hundred combat aircraft. Despite strong opposition from Congress, the president had secured an agreement to sell seven E-3As, Air Warning and Control Systems, called AWACS, to the Iranian military forces. These aircraft, the most sophisticated monitoring platforms in the world, were used exclusively by the United States and would be seriously downgraded in cryptological and deciphering systems by the time they arrived in Iran, likely sometime after 1980.

Major Weaver knew everything about the country and thought I should, too. The last slide he showed before I started nodding off showed the breakdown of the Imperial Iranian Air Forces. Those numbers were fairly awesome. The forces were armed to the gills—they could easily control threats from Iraq, Saudi Arabia, Turkey, even the Soviet Union. They had enough firepower to squelch any local insurgencies. Naturally, I guess, my eyes zeroed in on the fighters:

	Inventory	Future Orders
F-5E	141	0
F-5F	28	0
F-14 Tomcat with Phoenix missiles	60	0
F-16 Falcon	0	160

The F-16 Falcon wasn't even on-line yet; it was going to be the hottest fighter in the world. And Phoenix missiles—you could knock anything out of the sky with those . . .

I am the eye of God.

I live, high above the upper crusts of atmosphere. Inside my jaws I withhold a man—who calls himself pilot and dreams of astronauts. Who, beneath his body, withholds all creation with a glance. I am the abomination of flight.

The perfection of all desire for escape and greed for curiosity: to see what cannot be. I can see a child scream, the button on a tweedy jacket, or two hands cross from twelve miles high. The Earth, a cross-sectioning of infrared and laser targeting on tangents, lies below me for my pleasure. The ugly surface of the planet revolves around my frame.

Here, between ionosphere and troposphere, my trailing wings, a colorless black, cast no shadow on a cloud. Here the compass rose is cast aside. I have no need for compass magnet or direction. The sun's above, then passing under. Rises by falling from humanity.

I am the abomination of God. In flight, I aim along a camera sight: the particularities of death in life. I have a purpose.

The Earth must stay exactly as it is.

9

There was another influence. Major General Winfield Magyar. Imperial Air Advisor to the shah. My father's boss, former commandant of the Zoo, and, by extension, *my* former boss.

I never really knew him that well. But his presence and what he represented were always there. He was the thing made human we all had to rebel against. When women first came to the academy, cadets started streaking naked through Mitchell Hall at the evening meal. Magyar decided to declare streaking *a sex crime,* and cadet offenders apprehended would be immediately eliminated—"terminated," as he put it.

Shortly after that threat was issued, that last semester, Mitchell and Scott and I streaked across the Air Gardens at midnight, started pounding on the huge plate glass of the cadet command post until the senior officer of the day looked up at us. He was stunned. The three of us, standing there, ski masks over our heads. We turned around and pressed our naked asses into the glass, and for a second, in the cold night air, you could see these marks like thick lip imprints.

The senior officer of the day grabbed the officer in charge, and they ran out to the command post golf cart, sabers clanging at their sides, their wheelcaps flopping like flimsy crowns. They hopped in, took after us. They never caught us. That's what it was about—at the Zoo. About rebelling, and never getting caught. About learning to fight a system that did not know how to bend. I loved it.

I loved it so much I never knew until Mitchell died that rebelling only *seemed* strong enough to make you win. The truth was, the system never changed; and if you never recognized that, you were bound to lose.

•

Brigadier General Winfield Magyar: "Remember '56," he always used to say. The only true enemy was communism. Those bastards stole his native Hungary, and he'd never forget. Sometimes when he spoke to us at Arnold Hall, he'd slam his fist into the podium, and hiss the hatred.

"Remember '56! That's why you're different, people! The enemy out there is real, and our job is to destroy them.

"If you weren't willing to do this, you wouldn't be here," he always told us. "You'd be sitting under the yum-yum tree, picking the lint out of your navel at Cream Puff U!"

General Magyar knew me because of my father. He once even took an active interest in me, but soon realized there was not much of either worth or amusement about me as a potential military officer. During basic training, he invited me to his home for the doolie dining-out—an afternoon where doolies are taken into the homes of officers and community members, given a few hours to relax, be stuffed with food till they are ready to bust, and then returned to Jack's Valley. General Magyar's home sat on a few secluded acres of land in Pine Valley. A two-storey Spanish villa, it had an impressive view of Eaglehead Mountain.

After a dinner where his wife said nearly nothing and his children *did* say nothing, he took me aside and into his study, a room specially outfitted for war paraphernalia. His father, Winfield S. Magyar the First, had been the first Allied commander to enter the underground bunker where Hitler and his command staff spent the last few days of their lives. General Magyar had taken the spoils of war as he saw fit. General Magyar the Son showed me the blade that General Magyar the Father had taken from the bunker, the personal blade of Hitler. It was a menacing piece of craftsmanship, long and delicately thin, and it gleamed with the blue sheen of its silver—not quite a saber and more than a knife, *Arbeit Macht Frei* inscribed along the edge of the blade. He opened a massive desk drawer and took from it a personal album of Hitler's favorite photographs, as if you could see the vision of a madman through a madman's eyes, the personal odyssey of war and hatred and tyranny.

General Magyar took great delight in one picture. He opened to the album's center and unfolded, and unfolded, and then unfolded again a photograph spread nearly six feet across: a massive Nazi rally taken from the rear of the crowd of eight hundred thousand perfectly uniformed, perfectly alike soldiers. At the central vanishing point, off in the far distance, the tiny figure of Hitler stood at a podium beneath a swastika, a half-mile away from the camera.

General Magyar and Colonel Diamond had formed the core of the notorious "Wild Wolf" wing, the infamous and famous ground support flying unit of early Vietnam. My father was only a recently promoted major back then, but his flying abilities were already legend. Soon he was operations officer and flying lead for the squadron commander, Magyar.

Brigadier General Magyar had earned the name of "Iron Ace" in Vietnam. Officially, it requires five enemy kills to earn the designation of fighter ace. And Magyar had indeed shot down three North Vietnamese Migs. He had also shot down an American F-4 Phantom, which ground control radar had mistakenly vectored and directed him to fire upon; as well as, in a state of trigger-happy frenzy, blowing a South Vietnamese A-37 Dragonfly across the South China Sea with a Sidewinder missile.

•

"Today, people," he told us when he left the Zoo, "marks the final time I stand before you as commandant. I'm sorry to say that only because I regret to be leaving you, regret to be leaving this academy, which for the past two decades has always produced the finest military officers, and *the* goddamned best fighter pilots the world has ever known.

"For the past three decades I have served this nation with pride, with the same pride as my father, who helped found this institution, who continued to serve this nation right up until his death. . . ."

And he ended his speech this way:

"Now . . . I leave you. Off to the Middle East. Though far away, I will never forget the mission of the academy, and the kind of men . . . and women . . . who will follow in my path. I know little of Iran. I will learn. I will think of you always. Who knows? Maybe I'll go over there and start a war. Give you something to do when you graduate.

"That is all."

A thousand uniforms rose. The general turned from the podium, descended the steps of the stage, and disappeared as his footsteps followed him into the shadows.

And I swear I heard him whisper it as he left, heard him say it just under his breath: "Remember '56."

•

Poor guy. He never got to see what happened. He never got to see Imre Nagy resurrected, never witnessed Hungary revive itself, from itself. The enemy he died believing in had vanished.

He had gone on in his career to become vice commander of the North American Air Defense Network. I heard him speak, twice, after I graduated, and each time he was able to end his speech by bringing the audience to its feet, shooting off rounds of thunderous applause, making us rise to a frenzy of patriotic fervor and attention.

At times like these it was difficult to believe the stories of how poor a wingman he had been in Vietnam—stories I never heard from my father, of course. It was not difficult, though, to believe the legend of the crew chief leaning over Magyar seated in the cockpit to check the pilot's harness and lap belt, who heard Magyar challenge him: "Ain't I the biggest, meanest son of a bitch you've ever seen?"

He died years ago: cardiac arrest. The official report states that he died at his desk, working late into the night in his office deep in the bowels of some office in Washington. I think the scandal of the arms sales in Central America, the senate hearings, and the trials, though, are what really killed him.

The unofficial report, the one I believe, the one told me by the ambulance driver—who I met in Al-Abshár when his reserve unit was called up—is the story I *really* believe. The driver had rushed the massive body to the hospital, knowing he was careening through the streets of Washington with a corpse in the back. Appearances—that's what mattered here.

He had arrived at the Watergate apartment of a pulchritudinous, Teutonic woman, who opened the front door of her home dressed in a pink negligée, crying hysterically, "He's not breathing! He's not breathing!" General Magyar lay stretched out on the floor alongside the mattress, perfectly still, assuming the position of military rest.

Dead from too much screwing. Maybe the hint of a smile still there, dying happy—the tune of Remember '56 still playing on his lips.

١٠

Call me Iqra.

I wanted to call myself Eye of God. It seemed perfect for the mission: high-altitude observation, data transfer, voice communication for the Alliance. An astronaut disc jockey. That's what I was.

But Troy Daniels, my godawful, beautiful, pain-in-the-rear flight commander, wouldn't let me. Said it was sacrilege, went against the very thing we were trying to preserve. So. My call sign is Iqra. But I say it like this: "Call me, Iqra. Let us talk. Let us know the truth of He Whose Name Must Be Without Words. Just call this number . . .

"Here there is no dark political objective. We mean to speak."

Iqra. It means to recite, to repeat. The first word spoken by the Angel Jibrail—or Gabriel—to Mohammed in the cave of Hira outside Mecca, when the prophet received the word of God. We are the angels Kafziel and Mashadber, guardians of the deaths of kings and children. Dumah, the angel of silence. Cassiel, angel of solitude and stillness.

And she is the angel Jibrail, keeper of light.

•

"You'll never be the pilot your father was, Diamond," she says. She thinks this makes me angry. It doesn't, because it's true. What makes me angry is that she could be that kind of pilot, and maybe she is already. A natural leader. She has the kind of instinct that makes people want to do what she expects from them.

"Is this the voice that launched a thousand ships?" I'll rasp poetic. "Tell me straight, Jibrail."

I love to watch her work around the flight line. I love to watch her bend and check the Shabah during preflight.

"Kick the tires. Light the fires," she'll sing.

It makes me burn. It makes me hate myself.

۱۱

A few days before, my parents had taken me to a small bazaar in Shemiran where vendors sold small carpets, copper, brass. Tennis courts, European clothes stores, the high walls of villas surrounded the bazaar. The vendors did not smile very much.

One stall, something like a hardware store, sold abaci, kettles, cookware, and something strange: long, knotted ropes tied in a bunch and attached to a handle. A vendor showed me how they were used; grabbing one handle, he flipped the ropes over his back slowly, gently, looking to me to see if I understood. I didn't. To me, it seemed he was brushing his back of flies or dust, or cleaning himself.

Later my father told me that these were called *flails*. True believers of Shi'a use them to flog themselves on Ashura, the day of mourning for the betrayal of Hussein, Ali's son and Mohammed's grandson—the day when his head left his body. The man had wanted to sell me the flails . . .

The bazaar seemed out of place in that corner of the city.

•

A humming human throng. Here, in Tehran, the market ran underneath the city for six miles, thousands of stalls, countless passageways. The constant banter of talk, conversation, laughter, argument. Some of the corridors led down a series of stairs into the ground.

Men moved in small groups along the paths of the dark street. Some would stop, jostle each other, barter with merchants; others would point to me, laugh. It was pretty obvious I was lost. Above one vendor I noticed a sign in Farsi, with English underneath:

CHLOKABABE SHAYAN
BEST IN ALL IRAN

"Hey, Mister! Is no joke—gotta try this!" someone said.

Caftans—Indian, or Pakistani—hung from high metal racks, shiny with sequins, and orange, violet, gold. Trundles of split bamboo mats. A sequence of colored plastic dispensers stacked to the roof, forty feet high. A man with a *doroshky* pulling a donkey, whipping the animal with his thin cane.

The donkey bleated, and the man kept beating. The donkey never moved.

Another man in a white, loosely wrapped turban and black robes trailing his path as he walked, seemed to follow me. I looked up to the roof, saw the light fracturing through thin, opaque panes. I turned to look at him, and the man turned away. He examined three long shelves of silver samovars. He argued with a salesman about price. As soon as I saw his eyes turn from me, I ran. For a long while.

I stopped at the mouth of the tunnel, leaned against the cold surface of stone. It stood next to a cluster of small cafés. *Chai khâneh,* I think they were called, but I could be wrong. It was quiet. Four weathered men, faces cracked in troughs from the bitter residue of smoke, dressed in four identical black jackets and white shirts, fedoras looped low over their eyes. Each cradled a turquoise nargileh between his legs, or nestled it in his lap. They took long, satisfying draws. You could hear the water bubble inside. I wondered if it was opium. It would be yellow-brown and hot as the coal of a fire's heart as you sucked down its essence through the hollow lungs of the pipe, through your lungs. As you drew on its source, the coals would bob and fizzle, and you would breathe it, deeply. You would think of poppies, or the dawn, when young children would run through fields to gather saffron in their hands and in their baskets.

The smell was sweet, acrid. A shallow wafting of cloud drew over their heads. Their eyes were soft, unfocusing. One, a small man, lifted a hand in my general direction, waved to no one in particular. They were so calm, relaxed, indifferent.

The high wail of a child. Suddenly this piercing *aayyyyyy* . . . A man pulling a lit cigarette from a young girl's face. She had squirmed and kicked, but now she sat next to him, placidly, moving up to him for protection. She was crying now, and her shoulders heaved as she held one hand to her eyes, stroking the pain. The man's arms were covered with the film of grease, swollen twice the normal size. He lifted his hand toward my eyes, his mouth whispering incoherence. *Give me something to live* . . .

"*Zendegi,*" the little girl said, reaching out to me. "*Zendegi.*"

•

A store of brass, copper, silver inlay. The likeness of the *shahbanou,* the empress, hung from a low beam. Twisted filigree and dead silence in the shop. The shopkeeper looked up from where he sat at the counter, nodded, and looked down again. Next door there were rings, jewelry, pictures of President Carter and the shah together—two good buddies. A string of bright red and yellow Christmas bulbs down through a long tunnel, which led after a hundred yards into a large, open chamber with thin openings of light in the high, vaulted roof.

Some of the stands were hidden in shadow. Every few feet, a light bulb, hanging from a wire, glared down on the items on sale. It was busy here, but the people didn't seem hurried, as if there were places to get to, of course, but not so quickly. There was the smell of roasting flesh and saffron in a bed of soft rice.

A woman, her face drawn by gravity more than by age, reached out to me. "Drink this," she said, in English. "It is curd water. Keep you healthy."

"No, thanks," I responded.

"You must," she said. "You have come to my stand for purpose, you have graced me. Your hair is blond. That will bring me luck. I will touch it. And you will drink my water."

And so I drank her water, pretending to drink far more than I did, and she touched my hair, and others gathered around me to touch me, as well. It was eerie, standing there, holding this copper cup to my lips, feeling these hands sitting me down, stroking my hair, looking into my black eyes. A merchant was polishing his wares with verdigris, and though I was too far from him to sense it, taste it, I could feel the stinging at the base of my skull, the sharp kick as its acid hit my nostrils.

Wooden doors framed by a central wooden arch. Above them other doors, sealed forever, beneath ground level. The sun faded into a cloud, and the chamber grew dark. A man selling beets, radishes, potatoes, onions, kale, cucumbers, beans, pickled vegetables; the heads of animals; the tongue of an ox; the sweet flesh, dotted by black seeds, of an open melon; the cool textures of grape, bees busy with the flesh; the long layers of flat unleavened bread brought from the open pits of a bakery early that morning; fish, eyes welling with salt, hung by their mouths from a hook, the oil of preservative thick on the scales; twisted strands of thick braided rope covering all but the smiling face of a boy as he followed beside me; deep shimmering of metal pots; the tongues of steel lined in a comb for smoothing, unknotting wool.

This is how a dervish feels before he is taken by the rapture before he knows that the end of his mind was long ago before he rises from the dwindling tunnel

THE SHADOW OF GOD

of light. Children turning pottery on circular wheels and others sat by them painting patterns and shapes on the rims of faded copper urns outside a stall, urns used for centuries by caravanserai for travelers who paused in their treks across the desert. A man bent under the weight of his load, carried a refrigerator on his back. He looked to me, smiled, and passed—accepting the burden of this world.

I saw the woman again, but she was different. Maybe it was not her. She seemed to wink at me, a secret between us. Her lips drew back to a jackal's smile, and its laugh. A high, cackling whine. She offered the root of a mandrake to me. *Source of the seed, boy, spill the seed!* But she had said nothing. She knelt on her haunches over her goods, a cluster of legumes and dry stalks.

Farther down, men in cossack hats fought with an impassive rug dealer. A crafty man, he refused to listen to their wondrous bargains, did not hear that, even though his prices were outrageous, they would be willing to sacrifice much of their precious money to please the *za'ifeh*—I kept hearing it: *za'ifeh za'ifeh*. The merchant would not listen. He raised himself on one elbow and then leaned back into the thick pile of Turkoman to enjoy the comfort of his surroundings. He turned a strand of prayer beads in his hand. His cheeks were clean-shaven, but a gruff beard flushed under his chin. He touched the cloth of his head. Stroked his beard. Looked off beyond us. Heard nothing.

You will die up there . . .

I whipped around, saw the lips and sensitive face of a woman fall through the veil of her *chádor*. She turned, walked off, and looked back once. I could not see her eyes. The *chádor* had tightened on her flanks, and I watched her move. I felt a tightening in my groin, a longing to follow her. *What had she said to me?*

"American?" a voice beside me asked. Two men sat on a long bench. One of them, his back to me, was mending a carpet. One of his eyes had no socket.

Near the top of the faded rug was a hole, a place where a figure had been, and slowly, with infinitely careful and patient birdlike hands, he was weaving the absence back into the rug. The shape of a figure, a bird perhaps, the hooked beak. It seemed to have been burned away by a flaming match, or accidental fire. The hands knotted tightly, returning the tear in the carpet's imagery. Nothing misplaced, nothing forgotten. The hands hovered over the weave, certain they could only rest when finished, when the fabric had once more become whole.

"Yes," I said to the man next to him, who, I soon learned, had exhausted the depth of his foreign vocabulary. He was friendly enough, though, as he sat on the bench next to his careful, unwavering, and indifferent companion. He wiped the grease from his plate—it smelled like a cut of fresh lamb—onto the length of his fine, shiny mustache.

And then he held up an eye, an eye that had the slotted rectangle of darkness the length of an almond—the eye of a goat—and said, *"Nazar qhorbani. Nil-e tchesm-e bad."*

He popped the eye into his mouth, smiled once, and bit down.

١٢

I stood at the steps of the cathedral. That's how I saw it: a huge, glistening cathedral, its mosaic dome interlocked with blue-and-white tile, dwindling figures that turned a thousand replicas of the sun, glancing and falling, from the sloped crest of the steep dome. There was an emblem at the crown of the roof—like an orthodox symbol, a circle with spiraling arms. And pigeons, hundreds of pigeons. Covering the tile, filling the air. Muttering, cooing, part of the dome itself. Their voices like frightened murmurs of prayer.

A cathedral.

I wanted to see it.

"Don't even think it," Beatrice had warned. "These people do not take kindly to disrespect."

I wasn't trying to be rude, nosy—nothing like that. After the rumble, the noise, and the stench of the bazaar—the mad rush of people—I had stumbled into this hidden courtyard to look up at the roof, at the pigeons. Over one wall I could see the shape of a minaret, imagine the muezzin's call to prayer moments from then. *Allah-o-Akbar,* and those few faithful remaining would come to the cathedral to kneel and pray. *La ilaha il Allah.* There is no God but Allah.

I stood under the roots of a rotting tree. Stubborn and ancient, a few severed limbs sprouted a thick cluster of leaves like grape vines near the top. A pigeon looked out from a branch, cooed down to me, and crapped on the pavement, next to me, like milky spit.

I turned at the edge of the wall. One of the long doors had swung out, and I saw pieces of metal on the door—bright, silvery, catching the light under the shadow of the arch. I walked closer, through the courtyard. By the edge of one wall, a car backfired, and I stood up, straightened. A tickle of sweat on my neck. I put my palm to my face. My hands were clammy, wet, oily.

Don't even think it . . .

Outside these walls, people were running to or from the bazaar. The city was boiling. Merchants would be happy to sell you anything. Beatrice, as usual, would be worried about me. General Diamond would be deep in the heart of some briefing.

The tiny metal figures were ringing, like voices, barely over a whisper, singing in wind. I put my foot on the bottom step. Outside these walls, the river ran in its torrent.

Don't!

They hung on the door: hundreds of faces and hands, metal, nailed, hundreds of them—like Celtic runes. An inch, sometimes two, across, *milagros,* or fetishes, fashioned out of penance to God. The arch of the eyebrows met like the wings of a child's vision of gulls, drawn into the bridge of a nose that rose from each disk. Some of the faces had mouths, formed into zeros of confusion—or supplication. Some of the faces covered the smaller, more distant figures. After staring at them long enough—and it seemed I had examined them forever—I noticed the silence. The city had vanished. I turned and looked back. No one was there.

Some of the hands reached over the tiny plates of a face. Upright fingers raised, thumbs outspread. Some of the fingers had been snapped off, so that there was only the suggestion of a hand. One of the faces had cracked, diagonally. Behind on the ancient wood of the door, there was the whisper of a shape that had once been there. And the eyes of each figure, elliptical and stretched, with one single bump of metal for each iris. I stood before them, and they questioned me, with neither interest nor praise, curiosity or understanding.

Inside I heard the sound of a low moan. I stepped closer to the threshold. I turned my head slightly, embarrassed, and frightened, that someone would find me. But the sound was hypnotic—a low whispering hum, the intimate moment when one is perfectly alone, fervent and empty before his personal god. I had intruded. I had trodden on his silence.

Shoes, neatly arranged, lined the entranceway. Most were frayed slippers, *givehs,* bound with layers of cotton and rag, or sandals shaped from the discarded refuse of clothing, old shirts and dresses, layered strips of cloth, covered with the dust of the street. Each pair, like inspection order, next to the other. I was wearing Nikes, arch-supported with foam and rubber, good for long runs by the surf, more comfortable than combat boots, more expensive than anything these worshipers could afford.

The light from the sun cut patterns through the open arch of the windows on either side of the door. Hexagonal figures of gold stretched from the door and off into the shadows. Each figure of light, perfectly arranged in a neat, ordered row, stretched and distorted, began to fray at the edges, lengthening into the dark interior.

I took off my running shoes. I wanted to see what was inside. I would be quick, very quick. I was scared, but not scared enough.

As I slipped my right shoe from the foot, it slid out of my hand and hit my left shoe on the floor. There was a soft bounce, muffled by the vast space. *Shit!*

The toe of my right shoe landed on the heel of the left.

I bent down and aligned them—as I had been taught for three years to do, dressed and correct. I turned toward the sound of the low, whispered prayer. Against one wall, in a side sanctuary—what would I call it, a sacristy?—the shadow of the broken tree leaned into the rectangle of turquoise mosaic outlined in gold. Thousands, likely millions, of pieces, each set by a hand long before I saw them. A glittering, ecstatic graffito—each figure meant to represent a prayer. I stood with the fascination of someone who does not believe religious fascination. It was beautiful. I stood, dumbly, before their symbol. It was their god, not mine.

The branches of the tree tilted, and the shadow shifted. Beneath there was another shadow: smaller, solid, perfectly still, and in it trailed the body of a man. He was on his knees, at the edge of an old Persian rug, hands at his sides. A black cap cradled his skull. His head was bent, and his chin dropped low to his chest. His feet, dark and lined like furrows, bent at odd directions from the ankles. The soles were covered with chalky white.

And I felt a little awful inside, seeing that. A man was praying, and I was spying on him. *Peeping Dante,* I thought, ashamed. It was time to get out of there.

When I turned, a man was standing behind me. I stepped back, frightened. He stood outside the frame of the nearest arched geometric window. One of the figures of light had crossed the top of his face. He was wearing a skullcap. And his face looked like a skull.

"You will be leaving—soon—on a journey," he said.

My legs iced with fear.

"I'm sorry," I blurted out. My whisper boomed in the dark chamber.

His voice had been low, soft, even, barely audible.

I *was* sorry, because I knew I was in trouble, and it would be hard working my way out of it. But I was even more sorry because I had not meant to disturb anyone or thing. Now I had ruined another man's prayer. Now I had been caught trespassing holy space. These people were strange, not very friendly, and they were Shi'as. Maniacs, murderers, terrorists. They tortured people in their idle time, in the name of religion. I should have listened to Beatrice. They're *into* violence.

That's it I'm fucked he's going to kill me.

"Usually, fellow travelers greet each other by saying, 'Salám alaikum.'"

"Yes, of course," I answered weakly. "But I'm sorry, sir. I didn't mean to bother anyone. I was just—" I stopped. I didn't know what to say. What the hell was I doing in there anyway?

"I saw you, when you took off your shoes," he said. "The toe of your right shoe touched the heel of the left. Among my people it is a belief—this means that you will soon leave on a trip, whether you care to or not.

"I am a traveler as well," he said. There, in the shadows, his voice was so soft. "I am from Kurdistan, making a pilgrimage to the Gowahr Shád Mosque in Mashhad. Do you know of this place?"

I shook my head. "No."

"It is sacred among the people of Islam," he said. "I thought you would." He pointed back to the figures on the door. "These faces, the hands, they are left by pilgrims such as myself who will travel to Mashhad, a city near Afghanistan. My home is a small village named Zhillah. It is a long journey on foot.

"I say I thought you knew, because I saw you gaze at the figures. They are brought by travelers, and left here, as an invocation to Shah Abbás, who, many centuries ago, witnessed the appearance of the Twelfth Imam, Mohammed al-Mahdi, in Kurdistan, and who then disappeared. In English one would call his absence the 'occultation.'

"But he is not dead, you understand. When the time is near, and just, he will appear again. He will bring both the peace and the end of mankind."

I thought to myself that those were strange things to wish for, at the same time. But I stood there silent, watching his face. For a few seconds, neither of us said anything.

"Do you want to see the mosque?" he asked.

Eloquently, I blurted out, "But—" I *almost* said it. I couldn't believe it. I could feel it zipping from my tongue, fed by years of garbage television and film, visions of Ali Baba slicing the Sultan and his harem up for dinner that night, or oil-hungry sheikhs who collected anything they could gather in their paws: cars, women, American cities. I almost said it: *I am an infidel.*

"Yes, of course," he answered without my saying it. "Of course, it is forbidden. But I saw the way your shoes fell. This is not an accident that you are here, and I am. Rules are always fashioned, besides, to be walked around. We Iranians are famous for that. That is why justice will always come to us, because the will of the people will always be subject to the will of Allah." I sensed he smiled then, but it was not a false smile.

"Well, *dosh*," he offered in a humored voice. "Shall we?"

As we walked, he told me to stay on his left side. He had lost the hearing in his right ear, but he did not explain why or how long ago this had happened. I didn't feel the sense of dread, or fear, that I had before. But I didn't know what to ask or tell him, except, of course, the obvious.

"You speak English very well," I said.

"Yes, well," he said, "I studied in your country. New York. Columbia." He would say a short phrase, pause in his breath, and then speak to the rhythm of our movement.

"I studied communication and agricultural planning." He paused. "It didn't help much."

We stood in the center of a massive central chamber. I stared up into the heart of the dome. The roof was cut to form an octagonal figure; at each corner, an open window framed light from the hexagons of sun that slipped across the ceiling. I could feel the traces of falling dust in the rays. We heard the cooing pigeons overhead. Above, in the central, highest point of the chamber, the roof peaked into shadow. It was architecture that became ineffable—layerings of cut stone like filigree, or honeycomb, rising in circular, geometric terraces. Staring up to it, it seemed I was lifted, pulled up into the central dark. Running strands of calligraphic symbols, etched on stone, edged the base of the roof; tiles lined the walls, outlining the figures, the absence—or the fullness—of a language I would never understand.

"This mosque is named the Imamzádeh Sáleh," he said. "I am sorry that it is not as impressive as most. But simplicity is its own beauty, I think. And where a man prays does not matter, I imagine."

He pointed to one section of the wall, near the *mithrab*: the carved, indented vault that points toward Mecca and the moon, with a small prayer rug at its mouth.

"This is some of the most beautiful of Persian scripts," he said. "Our hieratic calligraphies." He laughed. "Do not be so ashamed," he said. "The beauty of our language is that each shape melts into another. When I was learning English, and the Latinate alphabet, I became angry, for awhile. People in my village, when I was young, would curse and call your alphabet the 'square tongue of the foreigners.' Signs began appearing in English, and many would refuse to learn to read them. Some even looked away, spat on the ground."

I asked him to translate what the figures said.

"This is what the script means—from the Ghor'án," he said. "You do know the Ghor'án, don't you?"

I nodded. "Yes, of course."

"It is the holiest of books. And this is the most beautiful of songs."

> *God is the light of all heaven and all earth;*
> *the face of His Light is in the flame and the flicker*
>   *of a lamp*
>   *The lamp mirrored by glass,*
>   *the glass a glittering star*
>   *which rises from The Blessed Tree,*
> *an olive vine from neither The East nor The West*
> *whose oil eternally shines, even though no fire touches it;*
>   *Light upon Light;*
>   *God guides to His Light whom He will.*
> *God speaks to all men in symbols,*
>   *for God is the Knower of all things.*

Then he explained the meaning of other figures. He took his time. He would pause, look to me to make sure I understood, to wonder if I had a question. His arms moved gracefully, lovingly, over the walls as he spoke.

The *mahvel*, the place for the muezzin during prayer; the meaning of the raised steps of the *manbar;* the conular shape of the *kulah* at the top of the minaret—forty-seven meters high, 138 steps—from which the call to prayer was echoed.

Finally, we walked to a small courtyard.

"Take off your socks," he said. "I will hold them."

And so I did.

"Go to the pool," he said, "and wash yourself. And feed the pigeons, too. Even here, in Tehran, people grow melons, pink and sweet, because of these pigeons."

"Why won't you come?" I asked, though I was uneasy about questioning anything he said.

"I will remain here."

He moved back, farther, into the shadow of an arch.

I walked out to the terraced court. A few men strolled by, and others spoke quietly with one another at the edge of the pool. None of them looked at me. An old man stood at my side. "*Mullah,*" he said (or that was what I understood him to say), turning back to my friend inside the mosque. He lifted a small bag to my hands. Inside it were bread crumbs. And the pigeons gathered around me, swarming and hungry.

I washed my hands, face, and feet in the pool. Right hand, left hand; right foot, left foot; face. I cupped the water to my mouth. The water smelled foul. Under the surface, nothing turned. Stagnant, though the liquid was cool and cold. I leaned across the surface, and stroked a final cup to wash my hair. For a moment, I saw my own image beneath a widening circle, a tiny wave.

When I returned, he led me to the front of the mosque. He handed back my socks and my running shoes. I sensed his smile. I thanked him. I walked down the steps, turned and looked back to the entrance. He was gone.

I sat there, on the bottom step, slipping my socks on, tying my shoes, and saw a rat, oily with grease and shit, rise out of the *jube,* and, frenzied with need, scurry over the street.

And then I thought of my friend—the man at the pool had called him *mullah*—and I thought of his face. Why he would not step out to the afternoon's light.

He had no eyelids.

۱۳

By the beginning of the second week, I had grown comfortable, alone, in the city. Lost among the snaking routes of streets and busy markets, I could still find my way back to Shemiran. I had learned how to ride buses when I was too far away to walk. Sign language, a few rials in my pocket: people were willing to help. I would point north. *"Khâneh budan,"* I would say. "Home."

One afternoon I turned into a park in the central part of Tehran. Hundreds of men had gathered there, listening to a man who spoke rapidly, passionately, from a megaphone. Whatever he said had an effect—the men who listened would nod their heads, throw their arms around one another, and begin to shout.

I was probably three hundred yards away. I wouldn't go nearer. When the first of the sirens sped out of the west, I knew it was time to leave. The trucks arrived, military trucks. Soldiers in fatigues, with guns, helmets, everything familiar, poured from the back. The canvas flaps were pinned to the wall of the truck, and an army of ants began to flow. Some of the soldiers began pushing. One took the butt of his rifle and shoved it hard against the keel of another man's breast.

I ran. I ran until I couldn't breathe. I bent over: my chest heaving, my hands shaking as they rested on my thighs. I could feel the pulsing in the back of my arms. I knew I would never tell Beatrice and my father about what I had seen. I had stayed back from the crowd mostly out of fear: now I had learned, in a foolish way, that it was forbidden for groups to gather. I learned it at the dead center of attention.

The day before, I had wandered through a group of busy streets. I felt comfortable with my direction. I would follow the path of a *jube* flowing down through the Elburz. Down the end of a street, I heard a voice yell, "Hey, Yankee—do John Wayne!" He was just a kid, maybe ten years old, holding up his hands, fingers cocked. Mock combat: we drew, and, suddenly "gunned," I fell against the wall, cradling the bullet in my gut. The kid was laughing. I waved.

Off Valiahd Square, I walked by the American Embassy again. There was a line at the side entrance: the long path of men and women—studying current visa regulations, smoking, talking to one another—stretched down a full city block. They wanted to leave.

I came to a women's clothing store. I studied the items on display. Finally, I went in to look around—maybe I could stumble my way through words and pick up something for Beatrice. I was in there probably thirty seconds when a woman came up, bantering and pushing the palm of her hand against my shoulder. I just stood there smiling like an idiot. She started shoving me.

Then she grabbed my arm and dragged me to the front door. I followed, not too clear about what was going on. I thought about pushing her back.

She shoved me out the door and down the steps. She kept on cursing, or whatever it was her words meant. By that time I was surrounded. Ten people, at least. Talking, babbling, pointing at my eyes and then at a sign in the window.

"I can't read Farsi," I said to them. They wouldn't stop.

A policeman pushed his way in. By the time he'd arrived, the group of ten was now more likely twenty.

"They are telling you that you cannot enter this store," he said. Instead of looking at his face, I stared into the insignia on the high crown of his peaked cap. He held one hand over the leather band that circled his waist.

"This is a women's store—men cannot enter," he said. "I have the power to arrest you if I choose."

I was scared. Someone poked a finger in my back. No John Wayne now, I just said, "Yes, sir, I understand. I didn't know. I won't do this again."

I think he believed me. But he wasn't going to just let me go so easily. "Plus, you have broken the law by gathering a crowd," he said. "You are the cause of a problem, and I can destroy the problem by having you with me.

"It is very simple—you see? If a man hires a driver and a car, and the car becomes wreck, the fault is not the driver's. It is the fault of the man who hired the car. The driver was merely an instrument. If the man had been not present, the driver would not have wounded his machine.

"Do you know what I say?" I nodded. "Then go," he said, "just go."

I said "excuse me" to a woman. She pulled the cloth around her and echoed anger in her look. She was the only woman there, in that crowd, wearing a *chádor*. I walked quickly. I didn't want them following me.

•

THE SHADOW OF GOD

When it happened, I heard it first as a high whine, the scream of an engine. I turned and saw the car, tired of the traffic jam, whip out of its lane, and burst down the sidewalk. The bodies were pulsing off to either side. The car was getting bigger—he wasn't slowing down.

I slammed against the wall and knew that he was going to clip me. I ran. I found an alley and cut into it. The blur of the car flew past.

It was quiet. No one moved. I saw a window and a sign, in English: CURIOSITY & FACT—INIQUITIES.

I smiled—they couldn't even spell *Antiques* correctly.

Why not? I reached out for the brass knob, turned it, and went inside.

It was a bookstore. Empty. I was thankful no one had followed me. Three rows of shelves occupied the center of the room. A table at the front of the store was piled with paperbacks rising to a central cone. It looked as if the books were being set up for burning.

The walls were bare, except, of course, for the obligatory picture of the shah that hung from a white beam, almost touching the ceiling. The photograph covered the seam of a crack that ran from ceiling to floor like a fissure ready to split. At the back of the small room a curtain seemed to cover another entranceway.

Sheets of mirrored glass, lined and neatly arranged side by side ran from the back wall to halfway to the front of the room—like the mirrors a dancer would use in her studio. But the mirrors were not fixed to a surface. They were stacked against the walls, leaning slightly; if needed, they could be taken away quickly.

There was a black and white television on a wooden stand. The volume had been turned off, and the image of a cartoon flickered and danced in the dark corner. *Mister Magoo.* I heard a car hit its brakes outside—the squeal of rubber, tracing a fire of black on the street, the sound of impact, crunching metal.

The curtain pulled aside. A man stepped out, and behind him I saw a long corridor of other doorways, framed by other curtains, room after room receding into the rear.

Over his shoulder, I thought I could see the shape of another man—a man dressed like this one—in white sneakers, jeans, a sweatshirt. But the figure of the other man was moving away, his back turned to us, heading to the rear of the passageway.

"*Salám alaikum. Hál-e shomá chetowr-e?*" I said to the man, hoping the one Farsi phrase I knew might help.

"*Eh, sfacim,*" the man said. This was not a Persian phrase I had heard before.

"I have been dreaming," the man said. "A most pleasant dream."

He put his right hand to his chin and stroked his oily face. He seemed to examine me across the room. He did not look tired. He was less than six feet tall, and to me, then, he was a short man. He had thick brows and the fierce mustache of a Tehranian. Uncommonly, he had a muscled neck and shoulders under his bright red sweatshirt, with the figure of a phoenix—or maybe a griffin—rising from flame on his chest. The sweatshirt, which read, UNIVERSITY OF SIBERIA, was darkened with sweat.

"So what do you need to know of today?" he asked. "A little chaos, perhaps? The state of the country?"

He broke into a slow chortle of laughter, which echoed and built like a tiny wave gathering the force of a great wave. His voice bounced off the low ceiling and slid to the floor, skittering through the aisles of books.

"I am sorry about this *shala*, this joke," he said. "Everything thinks I am one of the filthy Iranians, you know." He walked to the television, still flickering the perils of Magoo, and reached behind.

"I am every bit the stranger you are," he said. "And you are a stranger, no?

"My name is Bogomil—one who is dear to God. Bogomil Durdanovich, from Serbia. I live here and work here, of course, but Beograd is my home—well, Vojvodina, actually, but no one know where they fuck they is. And you? You look not this people, where is *your* home?"

He took a clear bottle and two glasses from a shelf. He began to pour from the bottle. "Your hair is short—perhaps you work at the American Embassy? One of the industrial military chompleks?"

He laughed again. His English was good, but the words were off. As he spoke again, his stomach suddenly popped from under his shirt and bounced, jovially, over the lip of his pants.

Perhaps, I thought, *Bogomil is insane.*

"No, I'm just a student," I said. "Visiting my parents. They live here."

"Ah, then." He pondered my words. And then he looked at me, like a scientist studying a subject—or a specimen.

He set down the second glass and pounded one fist on the table.

"Let me see the soles of your shoes!" he exclaimed. "And drink this while we wait—they call it *'aragh*. It is vodka made from raisins."

"Funny," he said, after a slight silence, slowly crossing his eyes. "Why do idiots name a visky after a stone?"

He thrust a glass of clear liquid into my hands.

"Drink this! Damn you, man! The shoes! The shoes!"

I drank and felt the cool fire hit my stomach. He looked at the sole of a running shoe, and then said that it was "good." I put my foot down.

"So, you are a poet," he said. "I knew!" Enormously pleased, he poured himself another vodka, tossed it back, and poured a third.

"These days, you see, you are a poet if your soles are not worn," he said. "It used to be, as it was in Serbia, that if you had worn out the soles of your shoes, you were a poet. But now!" he shouted, flinging his arms to their full length, spilling the vodka to the floor. "But now! You are a poet only if you are wealthy, if your shoes have not the least sense of burden!"

He wiped his mouth with the back of his hand, poured himself another.

"Now," he said, "you are a poet if you help to rid these Persians of their wealth. This is why I am here, to help share their money. Besides, it is cheaper to live in Tehran than in Beograd, or Novi Sad. I can send what I make here back to my home, and my family will be much richer and happier without me.

"And it always better to be a poet. A bad doctor will kill people. A bad poet only bores them."

Then why, I asked my thoughts, which had become part of this conversation, *do you run a bookstore off of a small alley?*

"Because," he said, giving me a wink and the leer of a deformed smile, "I can make *a lot* of money, don't you know, man?

"Would you like to see some books—while you wait?" he asked.

I did not understand what he meant. His burble of laughter erupted again. A sliver of spit gleamed on his stubbled chin.

He ran to two sides of the room, took up four books from the shelves, and hurried back. He lay them down beside the television. "Here, look at this," he said, nodding his head. "Should not be long now . . ."

A book, once bound in leather and gold. Once, it must have been worth quite a bit. Now the face was cracked, dry. The spine was missing, replaced by three strands of tape. The title, written in an embellished Latinate script, was *Dies Irae*. The second book was in Cyrillic; according to Bogomil, it was called *The Muse Which Sings*. And the other two books were in English. They were children's books. At first, I thought they were coloring books. One was called *The Glory of Martyrdom*. The other was *Footsteps of Blood*. I looked at the pictures, and pretty quickly got the idea. A boy, brought up in a small village near Mashhad, comes to the big city, learns the truth of Islam and the holy war, helps fight the evil forces within and outside his country. His camel, even in the city, is his constant companion and guide. The boy joins with other boys and they die, gloriously, in battle, fighting an unnamed and unseen adversary. On the last page, the camel is bent over the body of his friend. The camel is smiling. His soft eyes beckon with pleasure. The boy's chest is ripped open, apparently after an explosion, and a stream of blood flows from the boy's heart down to the end of the page. I couldn't believe it. If I had been smarter, perhaps I would have said nothing.

"Should you really have these?" I asked. My question was serious. "I mean," I said, and paused only a moment before saying exactly what I meant, "won't SAVAK rip off your nuts for this?"

"Ay, *chingada! Ne* to worry, man. Nothing to worry," replied Bogomil. "I can be gone from here in jack flash."

"Besides," he added, "I can move my bookstore"—and then he winked again—"*schnell schnell!*"

There was a noise from behind the curtain, the dwindling of padded feet.

"So," beamed Bogomil, "are you ready?"

"Pardon me," I answered. "Ready for what?"

"To fuck," he cried. "My *za'ifeh*, my *kuchka*, my wench. I have a great, very old rug from Qom. Best in all Iran. You could fuck out her eyes."

What! I came here—

"No," I said. "No, thank you."

"You tell me you come here to buy books?" Bogomil cried. He looked at me disapprovingly. "Well," he said, "I can say that you can buy, and I can say that I will sell, but not cheap. Cheaper to fuck, you know."

"This here," he pointed, then tapped his finger on *Footsteps of Blood*. "This will cost one hundred American dollars: 6,218 rials. You know," he said, slapping the palm of one hand to his butt, "the ones with pictures of His Imperial Heinous?"

"No, Bogomil, thank you. This isn't what I thought it was. Maybe I should leave." I paused. *"You know?"*

"Ali," said Bogomil, shrugging his shoulders in complacence, *"jedna za drugom."*

I saw him as he spoke—standing between the mirrors on both walls. His image split off and repeated itself, thousands of fractured Bogomils emptying into the glass.

He stuck out his hand. I took it. "Well, *prijatelj—Jebem ti Boga!*" His voice was friendly and warm.

"Jebem ti Boga!" I echoed.

And I left, pleased with the sense of acquiring yet another new phrase but sorry I had learned it in a secret whorehouse.

١٤

Major General Winfield S. Magyar the Second leaned back on his heels. He sucked in his cheeks with an air of sudden consternation, a stern reflective look of both appeal and concern. He spoke without looking at the two men next to him, who looked like Arab sheikhs, or princes.

But the general—I'd recognize him from a mile away: six-feet-six, one of the few men I've ever had to look up to—physically, at any rate. He had dark, bitter eyes; it was odd to see him out of uniform. No one was in uniform since this was officially a purely social occasion. But he looked as if in his mind, he had never taken the four stars off his shoulders. The two men paid polite attention to his rambling monologue, shifting nervously as he spoke. It was obvious that Magyar was well on the way to getting shit-faced drunk.

"Good evening, General," I said. "How are you?" I put out my hand.

"*My word!* It's good to see you again . . . first name, Dan—right?"

"Yes, sir," I answered.

"Well, damn, Dan, welcome to Iran—filthy streets and camel shit. Not, of course," he said, nodding to the men beside him, "at all like *your* beautiful country!" He pronounced Iran as if it were a sentence: *I ran to the store. The day was very pleasant. I ran to get myself another drink.*

"Boy! Over here . . . now, here!" he cried. "Good, well—get me another bourbon and soda. Quick. Damn well thought I'd have to get this round myself this time."

The young waiter, a pleasant, intelligent kid about my age, bowed slightly, took the drink, and rushed off. He was dressed immaculately—black silk tie, cummerbund, fine linen draped over one arm. He cradled a silver plate in one hand.

Some of the women wore long gowns, strings of pearls, jewels, turquoise, gold. Beatrice, betraying her origins, had chosen a simple black dress with a high collar. She had a brass necklace from Afghanistan: it looked like a Georgia O'Keeffe skull, the head of a Brahman cow with lapis lazuli for the eyes. She stood in a far corner, speaking to some older men who were obviously Iranian. Dark, handsome, formal, they paid close attention. She saw me, lifted a hand and waved.

"Hell, it must be fourteen months since I left there," Magyar said. "How *is* life back in the Rockies, ol' Dan?"

I looked to the men standing with us. General Magyar had seemed to suddenly, completely dismiss them. Their faces were open and curious, interested in what I had to say about the place called Rockies.

"Well, sir," I said, "everything's OK. I just got back from a summer at 'UDT.'" I knew he would like this. "Lots of fun, sir," I said.

"No kidding," he said. "Damnation, that's got to be a tough program. What is it, two—three—percent of your class gets to go through?"

"Yes, sir," I said, "something like that. It's pretty tough, sir."

"I guess, with all the women there, the damn thing's going to really explode," he said. "Don't know many women who could make a go of Coronado."

The bourbon and soda arrived. General Magyar fired off his drink in one burst, pursed his lips, looked at me, and said, "You know, Diamond, I can say this now. Never'll go back there, anyway. But women can't fight. It's going to fuck the whole place up—the Zoo, I mean. Change the place forever, hurt the military, affect the country. Sure, I had to support it while I was there. Do what Congress told us. But now, nuh-uh, no, sir—say anything I feel like.

"What do you think, Diamond?" he asked. "You've had some time with them there—can you train them? Can you get those *cracks* into shape?"

How the fuck—I ask myself this even now—*did this guy ever get to be a general?*

"Yes, sir," I fired back, hoping to play out the minor chord of his brain. "We make them rack it back."

The General barked for one more bourbon and soda, surveyed the ballroom of the Headquarters of the Iranian Supreme Commanders, suddenly turned to the two men—who, because they were devout Muslims, were drinking nothing but water, but had listened intently during this whole exchange—and made the comment that would get him fired, sent back to Washington five days later, and basically started the downslide of his star-struck career.

"Do you know what's wrong with you people?" he demanded. He jabbed the point of his index finger into one man's nose. He swilled the ice in his still empty glass. "You smell! You *never* wash yourselves . . . Hell, you smell like the fucking desert."

•

This was the last official function I ever went to in Iran. It was quite impressive, really, this building. I've often wondered since then if it had been an official residence of one of the members of the royal family. The room we were standing in was on the east wing of a magnificent villa. Outside, the branches of the cool limbs of green willow stroked the panes of thirty-foot windows (there were eight total in this room) that overlooked the Tehran sunset. Looking out the window, of course, you would not know you were in a city. Outside, in the slight breeze, you would hear only the stirring of leaves, the creak of a thin-limbed sapling, feel only the stillness of dusk. The three fountains poured out a harmony of sound, of glissading water. The city, if there were one beyond those walls, did not exist.

The room was an interpretation of high Western architecture—an impressive and slightly bizarre translation. Most of the walls were mosaics of diamond-shaped mirrors, reflecting the light of the central cut-crystal chandelier. Hypnotic, as if the light and its hundred colored variances could flash through the crowd and enter our voices. It seemed one could not lie there, or at least not speak falsely. The conversations were mild, soothing: summers on the Caspian, the price of rugs in Isfahan. Outside, the vines pressed against the windows, touched the walls, listening. In the high corners of the ceilings, the molding suggested the influence of a baroque period. That night, before Beatrice and my father—a very different kind of general—left there, I looked up to the heart of the central chandelier, and thought I saw a hundred eyes staring back. *A great place to hide a microphone,* I thought, happy that agents of SAVAK could not hear my silence.

And I discovered other things as well, that night. I discovered that I had spent too long in this city, and had not done anything at all. I wanted to know this country. I wanted to tell my parents about Mitchell, about the academy, about me. *Two weeks is long enough for anyone.* What I discovered was that if I didn't think of it, it didn't exist—the academy, I mean. Standing in the center of a ballroom of a foreign country, it was hard to believe that I had ever been there, or that I would ever leave this place. *Two weeks is long enough for anyone.*

I was afraid. I was afraid to speak to my parents, because I had never spoken to them before. I was afraid to tell them my friend had killed himself and he had a reason I didn't understand. I was afraid to admit that it was easier to wander freely, aimlessly, through the city to watch others than to look at myself.

There is a lake at the mountain's summit. The mountain's name is Damávand. The lake is a mirror of ice. North from the Caspian, it calls.

In all the years since then, in all the books I've read and in all I've failed to remember, I've learned that it is easier to describe the architecture and the image of a room than it is to recall what would unfold inside another person's heart.

There is a lake at the mountain's summit. The mountain's name is Damávand. The lake is a mirror of ice. North from the Caspian, it calls.

It is easier to remember a building's façade than a dead friend's face. It is easier to remember restless days passing by the Marble Palace, the light green Yazd marble rising from the support of the earth; or the vast expanse of mirrored lights in Golestan Palace, the Persian rugs within its empty halls the length and breadth of a football field; or the million glittering chips of glass in rooms dedicated to the Pahlaví dynasty, a museum filled by endless corridors of absence; or the celebration of Nou Ruz Salaim. It is easier to remember being jostled by tourists as we gawk over the wealth of the Crown Jewels than to recall the face of a filthy beggar in the street, easier to describe the Place of Roses, the gardens of plane, cypress, pine; the oil paintings of the Qajars, the burnished gold of ceilings, the spiraling stone columns, the alabaster thrones of carved demons and lions than how it would feel to walk, for a few brief moments, through the filth of the adobe hovels that spread south of the city. This was not a simple version of good versus evil, right against wrong—this is not a subject in the court of memory.

This was a kingdom, by all reports, that had lasted for two and one-half millennia. No one, of course—if this was a case of wrongly used power supported by all the governments of the world—could have let such a thing happen.

There is a lake at the mountain's summit. The mountain's name is Damávand. The lake is a mirror of ice. North from the Caspian, it calls.

Yet there was one shrine I never saw, and I will never see in this life, which I will always regret—the shrine of the Imám Reza in Mashhad, the catafalque of intricate filigree, set in gold and precious metal. The government had cleared the land around the shrine of old structures—homes, the bazaars—intending to make a Western-style park, to make it a place more attractive for tourists; and so they did, running the track of the bulldozer through the site of what had existed for hundreds of years. In this case, the description of architecture is easiest of all: it is the architecture of absence.

And there was one other thing I learned. General Magyar, who, as a private citizen, would have to wait another decade—tried and sentenced for what he did in Central America—before he would ever raise the ire of other countrymen again, had been mesmerized by the intensity of light as much as I had that night. And even though I would see him grab the hips of a woman from behind, encourage other fools to follow, which they did, in starting a long, sinuous line of a rhumba there in the Grand Ballroom of the Headquarters of the Iranian Supreme Command, I think he knew that his life had changed, changed irrevocably that night.

I heard him call to me over the dance floor: "Please! Join us!"

Ineluctable: not to be avoided or overcome; inevitable. A constant. There are no accidents—I have been told this many times by many people. There is really nothing you can do.

It was ineluctable for Winfield S. Magyar the Second. It was not just the power of alcohol, it was equally the power of presence. He had had the presence of mind to say what he truly believed, and often found he could not say—until he discovered that he was able, by the simple use of his free will and words, to send himself straight to hell.

۱۰

"Do you remember reading Virgil together when you were a kid?" my father asked.

"Sure, of course. I couldn't forget that," I said. "All those voices. Kids at school think I'm really out of it when I start singing those lines," I said. I laughed a little bit.

We sat on the roof of our house. I had gone up there, alone, earlier in the afternoon to watch the mountains, to think. It was the day after the night at the Supreme Headquarters. I was pretty disgusted with a lot of things. Mostly, as always, with myself. I had been here long enough. I'd done nothing about my decisions. I knew I had to say something. I was going to ignite.

So I sat there, my butt on the cold marble tiles, looking north. The roof of our house was perfectly smooth, flat. I drifted off in the silence. I thought of the Zarathustrian tradition for burial: to bury a man in the earth would befoul earth; to feed him to the sea would befoul water; to let him rot would befoul air; a man would be taken to a high flat tower, his body presented to the sky, and the vultures, circling overhead, would feed.

My father had been standing behind me, watching, for a long while, I think. The sun had turned from us. The cast of the light was failing west. When he asked if he could sit with me, I looked over my shoulder, started to get up. I said, "Yes, sir."

He told me to stay where I was. We didn't talk, about anything, for a long time. Both of us knew that this silence had to break, what we were building toward.

He asked me about what I had seen on my walks. I said nothing about what I saw in the park, or the bookstore. I told him about the small things—the women's store. He thought it was funny: all those people gathered around me, expecting me to understand what I had done wrong. Somehow—and I may have been leading us in this direction—I started to ask about the shah, about his family, his power. He wanted to resist it, but he couldn't.

He started to open up. He talked about the power of the Imperial military.

He said that the shah's son, who was only sixteen at the time he first soloed in a T-38, was one of the best pilots the air force would have.

And then I asked General Diamond if he had ever met the shah. He was quiet. "Yes, I have," he said. "Twice. It's pretty rare, I guess, somebody at my level getting to see him. I'm a one-star, sure, but that doesn't give me much clout, in power or politics. Hell, there are world leaders in for coffee every afternoon up there."

He nodded to the palace. We could see the low roofs and the hundreds of trees surrounding the main house from where we sat.

"It was like an audience," he said. "Demitasse. Everything polite. We listened; he spoke. You know, Dante, I really believe he cares about this country." But, saying this, he suddenly ran a hand through the sparse grey of his balding scalp. I saw the hairline scars on his face, what he had taken away from two air wars, and, sadly, all that he had left on the floor of a Laotian jungle—all the handsome beauty of his youth.

"I don't think he knows everything that's going on," he said, "and I don't think that anybody's telling him. Those intelligence reports you heard about how stable this place is? They may not be on target. These Tudeh guys seem to be getting stronger.

"And religion—there's something. The riots," he said, "aren't isolated.

"Shi'a is a lot more powerful than—I don't think I should be telling you this, because we both could get into trouble, but somebody at the embassy told me that he hears the shah call the Shi'a *mullahs* 'ragheads,' that he thinks they're just a bunch of renegades. This same person told me that the embassy doesn't even have an expert in Shi'a Islam on hand. No one—can you believe that?

"It's like we're running by the feel of our guts. Well, our guts could be wrong," he said.

He gave a short sigh, looked at me and said, "Course I can tell you this up here. He nodded and turned his head to mean that he was talking about the rooftop. No microphones up here.

"You know already," he said, "that you aren't supposed to mention his name—the shah's name—in public. They call him the Shadow of God." And, he stretched his voice to a low yowl, doing his best Lamont Cranston, "Only the Shadow knows!"

I said to myself: *Maybe Black Fred does, too.*

"What was that?" he asked.

"Nothing, sir. I was just thinking of something."

And then it hit.

I had to say it. "Sir, I've got to talk to you, and you know what it's about. I feel like I'm burning, because I'm so nervous about it. I'm gonna fall all over myself, but, please, just listen—"

"All right," he said.

"It's about the academy. But mostly it's about me," I began. "I've fucked up—I'm real sorry I have to say it like that, but that's how I feel. I've fucked up my life, fucked up as your son, fucked up in uniform. I've failed so many times—" I could hear my voice crack. I knew I was going to cry. "I've failed you so many times, I don't see how you can take it.

I don't know what I'm doing with my life. Mitchell James was my roommate and my friend. But I didn't know him as well as I should have. I didn't have the heart that he had. And I came here to just wait for two weeks to tell my parents, because I was afraid—I am afraid—I'm *just . . . not . . . cut . . . out . . .* His family . . ." and I paused, trying to breathe. "His family—just wouldn't listen. So he made them hear it. And if you don't hear me—and I'm not blaming you—I think *I'm* gonna croak." *God, why had I said that?*

He let me go on, and on. I couldn't stop. "I've been lying to you all these years. I don't care if I have to spend two years enlisted. I'm just so—so damn—I don't *know . . .*

"Goddamn it!" I almost screamed it. "I've always wanted to live in your shadow, *your shadow*, and I just don't think I can do it.

"Dad—" I was sobbing. He wouldn't touch me. He wouldn't say anything. I thought he was going to explode.

After a long, long while, I wiped my face. I felt like such an asshole.

"Dante," he said after a pause that took forever. "I'm going to say something that I'll probably never say again, and I never said it before, so you better damn well listen. Because I love you, Dante. I do.

"It's hard for me to say that," he said. "Christ, your mother has followed me halfway—no, all the way—around the world and I can't tell her that I love her. Because she was always secondhand to a Mustang or a Phantom or a Dragonlady.

"And maybe I should have opened my eyes long before this, because—" He couldn't say anything. "Because if I'd said that before . . ."

I looked at him, and I couldn't believe what I saw. His eyes were full of water.

"You want to leave the academy? Fine, but it's your decision. Not mine. Not ours. Just press on," he said.

"I'm going to tell you something that even your mother doesn't know. But I'm at the end of a career now. Maybe I've just lost my feeling for it, or my guts. But we—the U.S.—don't know everything that's going on here. Some of it's pretty awful. There was a general, an Iranian, at the party last night. You didn't see him. But he saw you. He was watching you. His name is Nerezi, and officially, he works with the Air Magistrate, but, truthfully, he's also one of the highest-level liaisons for SAVAK.

"Do you know what that is?" he asked.

"Yes," I whispered.

"Well," he said, "Nerezi had me visit him one night—said he could clearly demonstrate how to persuade politically unmotivated elements. Don't ask me why he chose me—hell, maybe I used to have a reputation—but he actually had me come with him to a political 'session'—that's how he called it—like it was some kind of official state visit on my part. It was pretty bad.

"They took this kid, strapped him to a chair, and pushed a button. The kid had burn marks on his hand and his feet and his face. He couldn't open one eye. But nothing physically happened. The chair started moving toward a wall. The wall was a wall of these electric heating coils, like a toaster. The chair would make this squeaky kick, and jerk toward the wall. It moved like an inch at a time. You could feel the waves of heat from the coils. It would have taken about an hour for him to get there. But it only took him five minutes to go insane.

"Nerezi just smiled and said, 'This is how simple it can be.'

"I love my country, stupid as that may sound. But I'm not good anymore. I've missed the cut," he said. "I thought it used to be noble to be a warrior. I thought this country, our country, represented what was just and right and equal. But it's politics and money. It's bullshit. I used to believe it could be so right to be so crazy, just break all the rules. That's what a fighter pilot did . . .

"But it's over now, Dante," he said. "I have to face that."

•

And there was something else he said, something that I suppose changed everything. Something incredible. I could say that the dead have not lived long enough in memory for me to tell the truth, as I knew it. But it's even more than that. It has to be something I can see now, can finally recognize as the past. And it's true, even now, that I cannot finally remember what yesterday looked like.

Though I do remember, after a long silence, my father saying: "There is someone I think you have to meet."

۱٦

That night I slipped into the house through the kitchen entrance to the sound of my father's whispering, *"He knows what he's doing; he's been at it for three years now; Saïd said that he's found someone reliable. Gozameh has volunteered to drive."*

Beatrice said nothing. I stood back in the shadow of the hall and looked at them, together on the couch in the dark vault of our living room—my father holding her hand. *"This is something he has to do. He has to prove it to himself."*

Outside in the street, the dusk had come alive. Blaring car horns in the distance; angry shouting in Farsi; the return of laughter. Inside that room there was only the tick of the clock on the mantel. My father put his hand on my mother's shoulder. He kissed her forehead. I could see the outline of his face, the angular jaw.

Then they were still. As if waiting for something.

IV

3 August

Two eyes across a fire. Two pale, slivered almonds. Sometimes a smile, or a knowing grunt. Who was he, this Kurd who spoke no English?

He leaned toward me, touched my shoulder. He stretched out his arms to the leaves and then motioned to my sierra cup. *"More tea?"* he seemed to ask.

"Keili-koub," I said. He laughed, then slapped me hard on the back. Leaned across for tea.

This was going to be a long trip.

Part Three

Sháh-Námé

شاهنامه

١

Faith,
I could have had the bastard. Sháphur Mareta.
He Whose Name Must Be Without Words: his official title, as though even the thought of saying out loud the name he has given himself is too impossible, too unreal. Not as Jaweh, whose name was forbidden, but in the sense that all that he is is more than possible to say in words. Too awesome and too human, too real and too linked to the way of their lives. Sháphur Thraitana Zahhák Jamshîd Gayo Mareta Al-Jabal ibn Muqaffa^c. This is the name he took for himself, for his inner circle of faithful. As if he could take in all the history of the Paradise—or, as he names it, the Kingdom of Behesht—and make it true to his own. As if he could true history. Sháphur . . . placed among the gods, king of kings of Persia and of non-Persia, of celestial descent. Thraitana . . . Ferîdun, of the seed of Kayán, saviour of a people and ruler for five centuries, who, on the sacred slopes of Damávand, defeated and then chained to a wall of a cave near the summit the evil Zahhák . . . dragon of the Avesta, with snakes growing from his shoulders, who fed daily on a diet of human brain and drank his fill of souls, the Devil and the Devil's intimate. Jamshîd . . . the ancient Solomon, wise ruler and he alone of all kings who could calm the demons. Gayo Mareta . . . the Adam of Zarathustra, the first man, who dwells in the mountains, dresses in the skin of the leopard, brings the beasts into subjugation and wages war on demons. Al-Jabal . . . leader of the Cult of the Assassins, enthroned forever in the valley of death. Ibn Muqaffa^c . . . who converted to Islam from the path of Ahura Mazda and whose theology changed the Arab world.

Sháphur Mareta is how we name him. Lord and emperor, and the first man of history, the one who dressed in leopard skin. When we were all not what we have become. And this is what he wants: to unite Behesht as the one secular society on Earth, and he as its divine protector, to lead only by secular decree in the name of God.

Yes, I could have had him.
It was an accident, and seemed so impossible: Fate. Carpet bombing on the eastern edge of the front had forced the Martyrs to withdraw. They were dying

by the thousands. "Highway to Hell down there," one of the pilots chopped on the radio. He sounded happy.

And then they found their bunkers. Disappeared. Vanished like smoke. There was nothing left to kill. Ten minutes had passed, maybe, and then, in the middle of nowhere a limousine pulls up and I focus through the scope to find one single figure running from an invisible sand bunker toward the open door of this car.

The black robes like a mullah's poured off his body. I zeroed in on the face. And couldn't believe it. Shápuhr Mareta!

Where did he think he was going? There was nowhere he could run and not be found. Without taking my eyes from the scope, I reached toward the fire launch. One single directed burst and the little shit would be fried scorpion. One single twitch of my index.

And then I knew. I couldn't kill him. I couldn't do anything, even though all I had to do was look the other way, and not report it. I could broadcast over the airwaves that He Whose Name Must Be Without Words had been struck down "by the Hand of God." I could open up the talk line hours, have extended conversations past the times I normally set aside for that sort of thing. "Peoples of Behesht, do not live among the Peoples of the Lie. Call me, free of charge. Let us engage in theological debate. Let's learn the truth . . ."

But he knew I couldn't. I didn't have orders allowing me to do it.

I was furious. The Alliance claimed it had no argument with the peoples of the Paradise and therefore was not intentionally seeking to target any individual. Which meant, of course, that Shápuhr Mareta himself was safer and more free to move about than some ten-year-old cowering in a bunker, waiting for the next air strike.

Twenty miles above, I sent the hate straight back at him. I made a fist. Sometimes it takes more courage not to fire.

٢

So. It's true. I slept with her. Do you think I knew I would? God, how could I know anything? I've been here too long, too alone, too angry. I don't know what to say.

I'm sorry? I am, but if I were truly sorry or if I didn't want this to have happened, it wouldn't have. I always tell the truth. It's the ghost of my parents telling me what to do and how to be honest and when I fail at something to own up to it. God, how I hate that—how I hate telling you this. I wish I could tell you that I've been braver than I have been here, that I've only thought and done what is just and honest. I wish I could say that I knew exactly what I'm doing here, but I can't. I have been here for two years now, and I don't even know if you hear me. But I had a choice, once. I left the service, and then they took that choice away. Now I have to own up to it, to what I am. I wish I could say that when I broke down on the roof of our home in Tehran years ago as my father listened patiently, that I had taken the choice he offered me. I wish I could say that what I had done was right.

I survived, it's true. But it's no happy ending. I was the coward. I am the coward. I stayed.

•

A great pilot. She's the kind of pilot Scott would have been. And sometimes I think she's Scott's evil twin incarnate, that he's still alive.

Sometimes during data linkup and transfer—a kind of high-altitude changing of the guard—she sends me messages, little love bursts across the interface. Our wingtips touch, like we're mating, so the spool tapes are retained as backup in case one of us doesn't make it back.

go get em tiger, *she'll write.* you animal

booger the bastards, *I'll fire back.* talk hard

And that's exactly what she does. She locates the nearest telecommunication link, feeds into the source, and cancels interference. Then she announces to the people of the Kingdom that the talk lines are open. "Call me, the angel Jibrail, and tell me what is in your heart."

•

She's rude, arrogant, treats everyone like dirt. Because she is a woman, she still must ride in the back of the bus to Al-Abshár, behind the white wall that prevents male and female from mixing during the ride. I remember turning back one day to look at the traffic passing through the other lanes and saw a husband, cradling the line of his prayer beads in his hand—like a rosary—while the other hand slipped through the inch-wide partition on one side of the wall, taking the disembodied hand of his wife into his own.

But Troy respects that. "It's their custom," she says. "It's their belief." And it's her belief that everyone will have an angle, a weakness for her control. "Buttercup," she calls the women in the bazaar. The older ones who wrap their chádors tight around themselves and stare at her presence, the way she feels so at ease.

"Thank you, Buttercup. That is a beautiful carpet you have there." She's afraid of nothing. No one.

Once, months back now, a congressman tried snooping around the hangar. Trying to find something, gain some attention before the election, maybe. When she found him, just before he pulled back the door for the Shabah storage area, she warned him only once. The congressman smiled, suggested that surely she wasn't serious.

"No, sir," she said, smiling back. "I'm never serious." She put a 9mm to his ear and then explained how the bullet would ricochet through his braincase until there was basically nothing left.

"Just mush, Mister Congressman. Don't think the voters will like that, now do we?"

•

Maybe I had been asleep. I remember only total dark, and a voice.

"Hey, Diamond!" it said, like a booming echo. No emotion. No tone. I kicked my eyes open to nothing. I squirmed. I was blind!

"Diamond!"

"Where am I?"

"You're in Hell!"

And then she touched me, reached down into me. And I grabbed her by the arm, unzipped the flightsuit and my mouth was on her. Diving. I took her tongue and her breast and her hair.

Like it would never end.

SHAH-NAME

•

Sometimes I think of her with your face, Faith. Sometimes at night it is her body and your body as the same form. Sometimes, and almost always, it is both of you troubling my sleep. Or preventing it.

٣

My mother was the one who insisted on naming me Dante, after "the greatest love poet the world has known." I wonder. Somebody who writes about figures writhing in hell, up to their asses in bubbling oil, caught in a whirlwind, or scooping the goop from the back of each other's brain and then eating it, somebody who writes about that must be pretty high on love.

When I was a child, she read me the cantos from *Inferno, Purgatorio,* and *Paradisio* every night before sleep. No Mother Goose, no nursery rhymes, not even the horror of the Brothers Grimm. Dante, always Dante, a little Virgil thrown in for literary evenness:

> *Of arms and the man I sing, of the hero who first*
> *From Troy's frontier . . .*

The constant companion of my childhood. Together, Dante and Dante, we snaked our way through the nine circles of Hell, the mercy and justice of Purgatory, the final reward of Paradise.

•

For a long while, I wondered just what was wrong with Beatrice. She was so delicate and fragile. The timbre of her voice was like a song, like a bird's beautiful song. And the bones of her body were like a bird's thin wings and carriage. She could fall so easily from the sky.

Once, when she was still a teenager, she had wanted to become a nun. My father had to seek permission from the bishop of our archdiocese for their marriage. I used to think that was what had caused it all—her sickness. Her being a Catholic. That problem, though, was more likely mine. When I was at Christ the King school, Sister Mary Something-or-Other had left me with a permanent hatred of the Church. I'd had my hand raised for an infinity, pleading to use the bathroom. Finally, I couldn't take it anymore. I wet my pants. A dark stain spread across my crotch.

Sister Mary beat her combination chalkboard pointer/pummel stick into the palm of her hand like a metronome. The class was silent, staring at her, the terrified look of their eyes thanking the invisible presence of the Lord's

Mercy that it was me who was about to get it, and not them. And Sister Mary's punishment was simple. She hung me on one of the hooks at the back of the cloakroom door, telling me that, for my penance, I should hang there for as long as necessary to *contemplate the death of Christ.* Those things happen. But I never forgot. And I never understood, until years later, how that was not the cause of Beatrice's pain. Back then, in Alabama, I remember coming home one day to find her sitting in the television room. The sound was off, but there were figures pouring through the black and grey on the screen. She just sat there—staring through the glass to our yard. The vines, the honeysuckle were still alive. She seemed to follow every lifting and stirring. I called her, and she did nothing.

I touched her, gave a slight shove, and even then, when she turned and saw, before the slow recognition of her son pulsed behind her eyes, I wondered if she would ever know me. Poor Beatrice. Poor, goddamned Beatrice.

A few weeks after that, I ran from class, burst through the double doors into the schoolyard while my classmates screamed in joy that the *nigger lover* had been shot in Dallas. I ran toward Beatrice from a great, long distance; the closer I approached her, the larger she grew and the slower my steps. Her face was twisted, and her tears were like glass. I thought to myself, then, that *she isn't going to make it; she's not well, and she's not going to survive living in this place where no one's sane.*

Even at six I realized not everything was normal in a world of black and white and red and blue. Even at six I learned to forget the terror I once felt in my room in that house in that country. At six there are too many things your mind can create. We lived near the state penitentiary. The whole time we were there, there were two, maybe three breakouts. That was bad enough. I used to move against the wall, in my sleep, folding myself into myself, hugging the corner of darkness. I thought that because I'd always been a pretty nasty kid, the maniac outside the window would know it, would pay me back for it. Trying to sleep, or waking from a dream, I'd hear footsteps down the hall that led to my bedroom. The footsteps started at the far end of the hall, grew louder as they approached my bedroom. And then they stopped. Once I even heard the sound of padded feet at the edge of my bed.

I used to think, turning my face away, squeezing my eyelids tight together, that I could see this hand on the outside door, turning the handle, coming inside. I could see the knife in the hand, the glint of its steel in the light. I could feel the hot echo of my breath against the wall, my face scrunched up, trying not to breathe.

Just do it. Just stick the knife in my back and kill me. Don't let me be this frightened.

For years after this, I used to have this dream, every six months or so, that these shapes—things that were cloaked and hooded, grey peaked things like ears above a face without features, no eyes, no mouth—were ripping into me, tearing my chest out. I always died in those dreams.

Years later I heard that others claimed there is a feeling at the moment of death, but I'd felt it back then—a lifting, a weightless burden, a rising to look back at the mess of what once was my body. The dreams stopped for me during basic training at the Zoo. I used to laugh about it, explain it all away by saying that at the Zoo you don't have time to dream.

But that year these *things* started happening. I had completed my apprenticeship, become a licensed falconer. The first bird I could ever call my own was a grey gyrfalcon. I named him Greystroke—chosen, I thought, because it seemed to fit so well, and because it was a way to call back all those Edgar Rice Burroughs novels I used to sneak into bed with every night in Australia. A flashlight, me, and Greystroke, Lord of the Apes.

It wasn't until well after that winter morning I opened Greystroke's chamber to see his still body lying on the window perch, his eyes that had caved in and surrendered their light, that I realized I had named the source of my own bird's death. It was supposed to be Grey*stoke*—Tarzan—Lord of the Apes. Greystroke's face was turned to the view of the Front Range of the Rockies; the hooked edge of his beak had slipped through the notched bars of his window.

But back then, my sophomore year, this hadn't happened yet. We were best friends—Greystroke and I—and Mitchell, basically, had to put up with all the falcon shit and feathers in our room or find himself another roommate. Mitchell loved Greystroke, though. Not as much as I did, of course—that wasn't possible. But Mitchell, sitting in the stands, would be mesmerized at how I flew my great, grey gyr during halftime at football games, how Greystroke fell from the high roof of the sky to seize the swinging lure at two hundred miles an hour.

One afternoon, Greystroke perched on the edge of my headboard. He slept, hooded. I was trying to sleep, too, but couldn't: academics, as usual, were killing me. Finally, I fell into a doze, but woke when I heard the shake of Greystroke rousing himself. I opened my eyes to the blur of falcon dandruff and white down, which landed on the grey of my blanket, required always to be spotless.

I heard the sound of footsteps.

It was a cloudless day, but our room grew dark. There was a shadow. The shape of a door opening behind me and the figure of a man stepping into that door, his body lengthening as it carried into the afternoon light. One morning, at dawn, the sun barely up, I saw the same thing happen again. Greystroke cacked, shook his feathers. I finally had to speak with Mitchell about this, even if he thought I was nuts. Instead, Mitchell looked relieved. He had seen the same shadow.

The Zoo, I thought, not even half-believing it, is haunted.

•

If Sigmund Freud had been a member of the family, he would have told me that all my fears could trace their origins to Beatrice. That I loved and hated her, obsessed about her, desired her, and that she made me feel true fear. Bullshit. The truth is that Beatrice was ill. She had an illness. And she fought it, as best she knew how, for all those years. It took courage. I know that now.

At the Zoo, of course, no male cadet could handle women. We could not handle female cadets, most of all. I remember when Ursula Friedman, a well-known feminist/speaker/author addressed the cadet wing. She was sharp, nasty, and aggressive. And something else, something I had never seen before: a lesbian. *A faggot, a chump, a crack*—that's what most male cadets said about her after that night. Maybe because she was there to anger us. And maybe, because of Scott Hind, she lost. We could go on believing the easy things about how women are to be treated, how men behave.

I was a thirdclassman when Ursula came to the Academy. The first class of women to enter our school was the class behind ours. We were the class of '79; to use the stupid phrase, the Last Class with Balls. Ursula knew that, and knew she could press the button that would make us all go crazy. Why do I say us? Perhaps I *was* angry, but I don't remember it. She fascinated me. Five feet—grey shoulder-length hair; glasses so thick they made her eyes swell up like an owl's. And she was a regular spitfire. The female cadets in the audience were all doolies. They had to shut up. They had to listen to all the comments of the men in the audience. They had to take it.

Ursula had come as part of a symposium on women in the international arena. But her lecture had nothing to do with international corporations or the business world. It was about the academy. She laid it on. The men in the audience had to face facts: that women were more intelligent, yet had been screwed by men of every known society on the face of the earth; that housewives no longer had orgasms waxing the kitchen floor; that it was a good thing the powers of this country had decided to allow women to enter military academies before the courts forced a decision. She talked about the brutality, and the violence of men. She said that at the academy, men masturbated at least five times a week.

A hand shot up from the audience. There were probably five hundred people in that auditorium—students from all over the country had come for this event. The other women, the ones who were not doolies, could sit there in that room and agree or echo or argue among the other students about what was being said. Only the doolies had to shut up. And then Ursula actually recognized that hand.

"Yes," she said, "what is it?"

"Pardon me, ma'am. I don't mean to interrupt," the voice answered.

It was Scott Hind. That bastard interrogator. Mitchell and I looked to each other, rolled our eyes. Why did we have the luck to be sent into Goshawk with this loophead?

"But I just have one question," he said. "You claim that cadets, on the average, *master*—baait"—when he said this he stretched out the word for as long as he could in that west Texas twang—"like, um, what was it—five times a week?"

"Yes. That's right," she said. I slid low in my seat and waited.

"Well," Scott said, turning his back on her and facing the audience, "goddamn it . . ." And then he flung out his arms—"What I want to know is *who the hell* is bringing down the average?"

It was pretty funny. The room exploded. Ursula was hit by the recoil and never recovered. But I felt sorry for her, too. She was trying to piss us off, sure. But she also had something to say.

•

I was afraid of women. One whore, probably older than my grandmother, in La Paz—that's all I knew. And when the first class of women came in, I knew we would antagonize them any way we could. It wasn't intentional. It *was* intentional. Streaking. Verbal abuse. Worse.

Scott and I, though we became friends, never agreed about women. He believed you married *your* woman, you slept with her, she had your kids and cleaned your house, you worshiped her, but you also took time out for the boys; and she waited for you while you flew your combat missions during conflicts. He was pissed, really pissed, when women were admitted. It was that simple, those three words: *Women can't fight.* They had no business at a place that was supposed to be all about war.

That year Mitchell and I and all the other sophomores had the job of training the doolies, all of them. I first began to wonder then about how you act toward women. A lot of them were tough. They had to be. I saw a lot more men cry at the tables in Mitchell Hall. I took a lot of evil pleasure in seeing a man cry. "Look in my eyes," I used to say, "go ahead and cry your goddamned heart out, but look in my fuckin' eyes!"

Even now, I don't see how they could have made it, at the Zoo. There were rumors of awful things, too. Like rape—women shoved against a shower wall by shapes with wool caps pulled over their faces, taken and abused. They were only rumors, and rumors, like the one about a ghost in Goshawk squadron, were never really believed all that much. But when I was Goshawk first sergeant, I was called in for an emergency meeting with the commandant about continuing incidents against women cadets. A woman had received a gift-wrapped box, a shoe box. Inside was a mound of human shit. It wasn't fair, to get this kind of treatment. The men only had to put up with being slapped against a wall, screamed at, double-timed in place with a rifle while doing the manual of arms, giving the discipline quote. For women, it wasn't right to be singled out, dumped on, hated. They had to be crazy to come there in the first place. If they survived the place, they could survive anything.

But women, after all, were *things,* not people. One day, outside one of my classes, I heard a cadet talking about how he had gotten laid that weekend, how great it was, how he had *really fucked her brains out.* Fuck out her brains—I can't believe that even now.

And maybe I remember best how one doolie handled herself during a meal in Mitchell Hall. "Hey, smack," the table commandant had said. You couldn't call them *cracks*—it was disrespectful and good for thirty tours with your rifle out on the drill pad—but you knew that's what men wanted to call them. "What's the waiter's name?" You had to know all this garbage. You had to know who the idiot waiter was because your life depended on it, because you were going to fly a *weapon system* one day.

"Sir!" she barked. "The waiter's name is Mr. Gomez!"

"Hey, crack," the waiter fired back. "The name's Archileta, asshole."

She handed in her plate and then ate shit. But she didn't break. She took all the abuse, answered all their idiot trivia questions, kept her cool. And that doolie never forgot, either. Her name was Troy Daniels.

Now, she's my boss. I've slept with her. I thought I'd fallen in love with her. I thought I had lost my own wife.

But she solved all that in a second. The day after, when I watched her during preflight. She whipped around, furious.

"Get moving, sport," she said. "We got work to do." And then she added, "I don't like you dicking around."

Like I was nothing.

•

I'm glad she wasn't there. We were fascinated, amazed, appalled. We stepped off the bus and waited inside a small shop while the faithful gathered for the final call to prayer that day in Al-Abshár. It was Friday, the time of common worship. The muezzin's song, *"Allah-o-Akbar,"* rang from the high minarets. A bent, arthritic old man, wielding a clublike stick, had gathered his robes and chased us—the infidels—from the purity of the streets.

Outside in the huge square, they knelt toward Mecca. A throng of perfect silence. This single mass of men, spreading their rugs, kneeling on the lip of rich wool. At first a few kneeling together, and then hundreds pouring into the square, all of them hypnotized, in rapture, hierophany. They knelt with a common discipline, neat, even, ordered. None of them spoke. They stood as one common person, bowed seven times, straightened, and then fell to their knees, prostrate before God. They rose, then fell to their knees again.

But then the prayer ended, the men rose, kissed one another, and the babble of human commotion began. The streets returned to life. We left the store and were caught in the mad flood of bodies; chattering, excited voices, guiding us through turns and down long alleyways until I had no idea where I was. By the time we arrived wherever we were, there was a huge crowd. Seeing us, they smiled—a kind of parting of teeth and a yipping snort of expectorant laughter—pushed some others aside and propelled us to the forefront of the crowd. People stood around us, chattering. I kept hearing them say, "*Chop-chop.*"

The first punishments were tolerable. They were repulsive, of course, and uncomfortable, but I knew of these things, the eye for an eye rule of order. A man was convicted of stealing—his arm was placed over a long block of wood and his hand was cut off. A man was found guilty of drinking, and he was strapped to a pole and whipped eighty-eight times with the equivalent of a cat-o'-nine-tails.

And then a woman, her hands and feet bound, a knotted white scarf over her mouth, was *rolled* into the square. A section of the crowd moved like a wave, parting, and opened a space through which came a truck loaded with boulders. Next to me someone butted my arm, gave me a leering smile, and offered the symbol of obscene pleasure—the middle finger of one hand sliding through the zero, formed with thumb and index finger of the other.

She was going to be stoned. Even if this was the end of the twentieth century, even if technology had provided swift and sure delivery of punishment in the form of a dump truck, it was impossible to accept what I was watching. I heard her screams, muffled by cloth. The truck slammed into reverse and backed up to her. The bed lifted, tilted diagonally away from the frame. The rear gate unhinged. The rocks covered her body.

There was a sound of sudden cheering, but I hardly noticed the noise. I saw her body, squirming to avoid the fall, pushed, jabbed, crushed. After the last rock had dribbled onto the messy pile, a man—a doctor, I assume—ran out to her, leaned over the body, checked for a pulse, listened for the sound of a heartbeat. I understood when he lifted his head to call out that *she was not dead.* I understood when the hurling bulk of another man carried the massive weight of a rock—God, it must have weighed over a hundred pounds—to her still body, lifted it above his head, and let it drop on the shell of her head.

Out of ceremony, like a fool, the doctor kneeled over her again. *She is dead.* A roar from the crowd. There was nothing I learned, nothing to believe. I saw it, though. How there is nothing one human—especially a man—will not do to another.

•

So do I pity Beatrice? I did once. But not now. Now I love her. She survived.

ع

Gozameh's wife, Sakina, was beautiful. She sat on the floor, away from him. Her traditional skirt was alive in fuchsia and purple. Her blouse glistened with gold thread. A string of gold coins around her neck. A thin scarf, like a veil, covered her head.

As we spoke, she nodded and pulled at the warps of the tiny loom. It seemed like a horizontal version of the Navajo looms I had seen as a child. She paid attention, quietly, to everything that was said. But her hands wandered. Her hands had a different kind of attention all their own. They danced and wandered over the wool. Patterns, flowing arabesques and flowers, turquoise and vermillion came to bloom in the wool beneath her fingers, as if she were weaving her life with a kind of private joy.

Later Gozameh would show me the carpets she had created.

"They are different than those you would find in Isfahan or Shiraz, perhaps," he said. "But they are truer, as well."

I did not ask him what he meant.

His daughter and son were polite, asked me questions about the Rockies. How did I like my visit thus far? Would I visit the Caspian? What had I seen and what most interested me? Suddenly animated, I turned to Gozameh and asked if he thought the shah had advanced the rights of women. That's not exactly how I phrased it, I suppose.

"But what I really want to know," I asked, "is if you think your daughter will secure a profession? To help her country, I mean."

Gozameh paused, for just a moment, and then responded. "Both my daughter and son are exceptional students, Master Dante. They will do as God wills it, and as God finds their paths."

•

Later Beatrice told me that she and the general had been very proud of how I'd acted that night. My one mistake was that I had mentioned the shah. That one mistake aside, I had a wonderful time. Dinner was lamb—kebab—and saffron rice. Eggs whipped into tomatoes and aubergines. Tea leaves, with water drawn from a bright, boiling samovar. Baklavá, and *sohan* from Qom.

When we left that night, I bowed low to them. Gozameh smiled.

"The peace of God be with you," he said.

"*Sáyeh ye shomá kam, nashavád,*" I answered. May your shadow never grow less.

They were a remarkable family. They were happy.

◐

We stood by a glass case in the central corridor of the Imperial Armed Forces Officers' Club. A uniform, stained with the black of old blood, was on display inside the case. You could see where the bullets had hit the shah then, in 1949—how the mystical Farr had saved him. A man pretending to be a photographer had entered a meeting. He'd held the gun in the shell of his camera. There had been five attempts on the shah's life; he survived them all. During the last several years, he had allowed only foreigners to visit official state functions or celebrations.

My father walked off, and I followed to catch up. We climbed a second flight of stairs, and then turned down three empty hallways. Still, beside him, this easy unfamiliarity. Our heels in stride, the echoes clicking cadence. Until the night before, I felt I had never spoken with him, honestly, about what was wrong—with me, with him, with us. He had treated me no differently that morning, it's true. Gozameh had driven us here; we stood from the open doors, and walked off. There's always been this incredible *purpose* in the way my father walks. Thirty years is a long time, and my father carried all those scars, all the years of service that lay beneath the rank.

Under the proscenium arch, two guards stood together, smoking. Two others stood at the entrance. Seeing him, the general, they all stood straight, saluted. My father answered them, saluted, flashed a recognizing smile. I passed a friendly nod. They did not respond.

•

General Saïd Sadeghian, president of the Iranian Mountaineering Federation, sat behind a dark, flat desk of mahogany. Seams of inlaid pearl ran around the edges. The desk looked like the deck of an aircraft carrier, or a helicopter landing pad. Aside from the cup of demitasse the general was sipping from, the only things that touched the wood were mountaineering maps, spread out like plans for war.

"So, Mister Diamond," said the general, "tell me all you know of Damávand."

He was a short man, and rather fat. His face, even with the thin suggestion of a mustache, was brutal.

"Well, sir, not really all that much," I said. "Eighty kilometers northeast, Tehran to Pol-e-moon. Altitude 5,672 meters. At its summit, the mouth of an extinct volcano, there is a frozen lake of ice. Numerous solfataras . . . sulphur releases are common."

"I see you are indeed your father's son," he said. "You have a good recall."

"Thank you, sir," I said. I was embarrassed. I sipped from my coffee, which tasted half like mud and half like Pennzoil. "I've just had to learn a lot of facts lately."

"Well then," he said, "here is the fact you might enjoy. The relations between Iran, or Persia, as it was then, and your country go back over 130 years. Eighteen hundred and forty-nine, something like that. In the time of Nasir Al-Din Shah. And then, of course, the first sale of—what should I call them"—the general stroked his face, and smiled, "military arms?"

"What?" my father said. He beat me to the punch.

"Yes, yes," he said. "A report, I have it here." He stood and pulled a leatherbound book from the top of a shelf and slipped it across to me. "About the sale of Zemboureks for use in battle," he said. "It is written by your secretary of wars, the man who became your president, a Mister Jefferson Davis. He was your president, was he not?"

My father was silent. "I guess you could say that," I answered.

I put down the coffee and flipped through the book. The title was A Report by the Secretary of War, Jefferson Davis, *Communicating in Compliance with a Resolution of the Senate of February 2, 1857, Information Respecting The Purchase of Camels and Dromedaries for The Purposes of Military Transportation.* There were etchings of Bactrian and Arabian camels. The interest, specifically, was in Zemboureks.

I opened to the first two pages. Letters and reports concerning the expedition, signed by Davis:

10 MAY, 1855
ASSIGNED TO SPECIAL DUTY IN CONNEXION WITH THE APPROPRIATION FOR IMPORTING CAMELS FOR ARMY TRANSPORTATION AND OTHER MILITARY ASSIGNMENTS, YOU WILL PROCEED DIRECTLY TO PERSIA, AND THERE MAKE SUCH INVESTIGATIONS . . .

13 AUGUST, 1855
THE CAMEL HAS BEEN USED IN TUSCANY FOR OVER TWO HUNDRED YEARS,

AND HAS INCREASED AND MULTIPLIED FROM A FEW THAT WERE BROUGHT FROM THE UPPER PART OF EGYPT. THE GRAND DUKE MAKES THE OUTSTANDING CLAIM THAT ONE ZEMBOUREK WILL DO THE WORK OF ONE THOUSAND HORSES.

I looked up.

"So you see," said General Sadeghian, "we were the first ones to sell *you* a weapon system."

"Yes, sir."

"Some more coffee, Mister Diamond?"

The stuff wasn't all that bad, really. But I was getting nervous, uncertain about him. "Yes, sir, if that's all right." I swirled the oily mud inside the porcelain crater of my cup.

General Sadeghian studied a piece of paper on his desk. Without even looking up, he raised his right hand and snapped his fingers. The door flew open and a guard rushed in, rifle swinging from his shoulder. He snapped his heels, fired a salute, and barked something in Farsi. *How could anyone hear those fingers in the hallway?*

"More coffee—*now!*" The general spoke in English, for my benefit, I'm sure. My father's Farsi was pretty solid. I'd heard him speak it with Gozameh. General Sadeghian looked up, smiling.

"Before we speak of your trip," he said, "I am going to ask you to do something, Mister Diamond. It is an ancient Persian custom, so do not think it is strange. I want you to open this book and show me what page you will come to."

He rose from his desk, reached for a small book that had been lying next to the Jefferson Davis report on the shelf, and, instead of just sliding the book across to me, he walked to me. I took it. My father kept silent.

"I am going to say something, Mister Diamond, and I want you to repeat what I say in Farsi. Do you understand?"

"Yes, sir."

"Do not think of it as foolish. Even I take these things seriously. My country is a land of wisdom, but a useless wisdom. We have given the world the rose, the pomegranate, the most beautiful carpets. And our poetry—through our poetry we have expressed ourselves. What we have given the world makes no one's life easier, but we have embellished life. I live by these words, and someone else, someone you will soon meet, insists that I do this.

"*Goush-esh ceda midé.*" The general paused. He stood above me, and I thought that maybe I should be standing as well.

"This means," he said, "that his ears are ringing."

Whose ears?

"This book is a book of poems, *divans*. It is written by our greatest poet, Hafez. You will come to a page, and we will see what it means. But you must repeat what I say exactly—I will speak slowly."

And so, slowly, I took these words from the haunted air and said them as he said them:

"*Ya hadje Hafez Shirazi—toh Shirazi mán Shirazi—toh kachef-é Harraz-i-mán taleb-e yek fali.*"

"Open the book. And show me what you find."

I did. The page was near the center. The spine of the book cracked as I opened it. The black words meant nothing. He reached for the book and I handed it back, keeping the page open for him to see. His face rose in delight. "Wonderful," he said, "Mister Diamond. This is what I expected of you— one of the most beautiful of ghazelles. I will have no problems translating this, since, as you can hear, my English is quite excellent."

But instead of telling us what the words meant, he lit a cigarette and walked to the light of the window behind his desk. He turned his back to us and enjoyed his tobacco. I heard a man scream, far off—a clear, articulated pain from somewhere down the corridor. I looked to my father in hope that he felt as queasy about this as I did. My father's eyes said nothing. So I sank back into the black leather of my chair, put my arms on the rests, and didn't move. The coffee arrived, and as the soldier bowed slightly after he placed the tiny cups on the table, I wanted to thank him. But I didn't know how. The soldier was gone.

"You cannot leave on Thursday, Mister Diamond," he said. "This presage is very accurate. Will this cause you any problems, General?"

"No, Saïd," my father said. "Dante will leave when the plans have all been made, when everyone is ready. I have no intention of rushing things." While my father spoke, the general kept his back to us. *Turn around, you fuck— you can't treat him like that.*

He lifted the book to his face and stubbed out the cigarette with his other hand. Then he spoke in English, clearly, as if he had long known what I would find, as if he were singing the lines:

> *Lie down, beneath the flowing stream*
> *and see Life pass, and know*
> *That of the world's impossibilities*
> *one sign would be enough for us.*

"This really is quite beautiful, Mister Diamond," the general said. "Very nice—very, very nice."

He put the book back on the shelf and turned to us. When he removed his glasses, I saw one of his eyes quivering. He started to rub it.

"His name," he said, "is Asadollah, and he is a Kurdish mountaineer. I have never met him, but you can trust that he has been specially chosen. Many of my colleagues think quite highly of your father, Mister Diamond. You can trust that Asadollah is the best that one could find in such a time. He is dependable, strong. No one, I believe, knows how old he is. But he knows these mountains.

"And," the general guffawed at saying this, "he speaks no English. You will find other ways to get along."

As he spoke, the general put his fingers to the topographic map, tracing the wandering ascent, the trills and rises, like streams, or veins, which split toward each far corner of the map. His voice grew animated. He spoke of climbing Mount Whitney in California, a peak four thousand feet lower in elevation than Damávand. He had found many *technical pleasures* in Whitney.

The normal path to Damávand followed a sheepherder's trail to an elevation of thirteen thousand feet. From there you could hike to the Mountaineering Federation shelter. The next day you could achieve the summit. No technical expertise was necessary. On the normal trail.

"But," and he smiled when he said this, "everyone would want to know the true composition of Mister Diamond." Asadollah had suggested a path that wound its way up by a conical twist. He called it the Circle up to Heaven.

He said that he would soon contact me with all arrangements and suggested that I be ready to leave quickly. Finally, he asked if we had any questions. And I had one.

"General Sadeghian, sir," I said. "This has nothing to do with Damávand, but perhaps it does.

"You said that Hafez was the greatest Persian poet? Well, sir, correct me if I'm wrong, but isn't Ferdausí the greatest of all your poets?"

He looked shocked. He had been standing all this time, and now he sat. "Tell me what you know," he said.

"Well," I said, "I wish I could tell you more. I mean I studied the *Sháhnáma* back in the U.S., and I've been trying to read it here. I've got a pretty good English translation. Born in Tus, near Mashhad, eight hundred years ago. It took him thirty-five years to write it. Sixty thousand lines. But what I want to ask has to do with the legends about Prometheus, and Ferîdun."

"This is really wonderful." The general was beaming. "You come to climb our mountain, and you study our legends as a way to prepare. Perhaps, Mister Diamond, you are a real Persian. There is indeed a great deal to tell you. Especially of Damávand. Your question about Prometheus is true—it comes from the defeat of Zahhák by Jamshîd."

And the general began, leaning back into his chair and crossing his fingers on his chest, telling a story, as if this could be one of the many he could tell:

"Many centuries before his inevitable defeat, Zahhák was tricked by the devil into murdering his own father. Out of Zahhák's shoulders two black serpents grew, and thus he could only feast on human brains. He grew in power until he became the equal of Jamshîd, and he killed the king—

"You wonder why I know so much of this?" he asked. "Every man in Iran knows the *Sháh-Námé*, Mister Diamond. It is the Epic of the Kings.

"And every man knows that Ferîdun the Brave crucified Zahhák on the summit of Damávand, tearing his heart out and letting the life's blood weep to the earth. And that Zahhák's heart returns to its body, and the birds of the sky devour him each day."

"Ferîdun, who was no angel,"—I spoke it slowly, wanting him to know that I cared about this, even if I seemed pompous—"was not made of musk and verdigris. By truth and doing what seemed right, he came to ecstasy."

And then General Sadeghian spoke the same verse back to me, as Ferdausí wrote it:

> *Farídún-i-farrukh farishta na-búd:*
> *Zi mushk ú zi 'anbar sarishta na-búd.*
> *Bi-dád ú dahish yáft án níkú'í:*
> *Tú dád ú dahish kun: Farídún tú'í!*

He began clapping, slapping his palms on the desk. I turned red. My father was smiling.

"Absolutely *excellent,* Mister Diamond," he said. "Because of this, I must show you one last thing."

•

There were some men in uniform at the edge of the room, clustered at tables and drinking tea. They were on a platform looking down at the dance floor. There, men, stripped to the waist and wearing things like cotton skirts with tartan plaids, were dancing. They carried chains in their arms, and moved slowly to a beating drum. One man would grab hold of another and knock him to the ground.

It was called *zúrkháneh,* the house of strength, as the general translated it, and it had existed since the time of Darius the Great. It matched physical exercise with the discipline of dance and the moral purity of Islam. Even here, in this building that was meant as a retreat for commissioned officers, soliders would practice their skills against each other, as they chanted passages from the *Sháhnáma;* sometimes they faced off, in single contests, with wooden clubs and iron bows. We felt the slap of a man landing on the floor, the breath shoved from his lungs. His victor stood over him. The drum kept beating.

Wild.

ר

During the two days before I left, Gozameh fluttered over me like a worried nursemaid, like I was going to give birth to a kid or something. He made arrangements to obtain an extra staff car for my father. And even though he didn't have the power to do it, he ordered Reza, my father's official bodyguard, to take over the driving of my father so that Gozameh could help me prepare. Reza obeyed.

He was excited about the trip. He wanted to make sure that all my preparations were sufficient to take me to the summit. I don't know how, but he persuaded a local policeman to come with us on our shopping sprees, so the man would watch our goods while we went inside new stores to see what else I needed. The morning we picked him up on the corner, the man hopped in the front with Gozameh—Gozameh had refused to let me sit up there with him. He'd even threatened to throw the keys in a *jube* if I persisted.

The policeman turned back to me, smiling away. He tipped his cap. "*Salâm*," I said.

"Hello-how-are-you-I-am-fine-thank-you-very-much!" he answered, giving the range of his entire English vocabulary in the space of two seconds.

Gozameh and I spent most of our time at the morale and welfare recreation complex. It was an official agency that supplied gear and information to American government employees and their families—setting up trips, providing maps, ways to get to know the country. We rented a fairly hefty backpack, laced with orange canvas, a mesh buckle for the shoulders and waist. It had a strong metal frame. I picked up a long knife, rope, pitons, carabiners, a sturdy hammer-axe, sierra cups, water bottles, compass, silverware, a butane stove that could fit in the pack's side pocket, fuel, iodine tablets, first-aid kit, waterproof matches, a reflecting mirror, and flares—though I didn't know why I needed these.

I pushed the flaming canisters across the table to the attendant, and Gozameh grabbed and pulled them back, saying, "But you must!"

Beatrice had given me fifty dollars to go wild on supplies with. Because I couldn't rent hiking boots, and I hadn't brought any with me, I picked out a pair that looked solid—leather, with metal eyelets and red laces. They cost twenty dollars. The equipment rental was less than five.

In the American Embassy commissary, I selected as few food supplies as I thought necessary. The commissary's prices were pretty high, at least for me: six bucks for a scrawny stalk of carrots. They had two packages of dried food, and I bought them both: scrambled eggs and "country-red" potatoes. Gozameh loaded the cart with canned cherries and olives. I knew I would never use these canned goods; they weighed too much, they took up too much space, and the food itself was too heavy to burn off quickly hiking. But he insisted, and then picked out a small can opener from the shelves, saying that I had to have fruits, and canned fruits were my best guarantee of freshness. All the weight of these cans, I told him—I'd never make it to the shelter. "But you must!" he cried.

He snatched a graham cracker pie crust and, giggling like a child, declared, "Look! You pour out cherries and make a pie! That's for sure, maybe!"

•

That last morning, we waited in line at the bakery at Rheobab Street. The bread was baked in a hole dug from the earth. The hole was three yards across. The walls were sealed with hard clay. At the bottom of the pit, the flame of a coal fire baked the flat, unleavened sheets. The heat was intense. If a woman was unfaithful to her husband, Gozameh told me, he had the right to throw her in this fire. Young boys would reach across the heat with poles to get the fresh bread from the flat surface of stone. They threw it to a handler who then threw it to the counter where the order was made final. Gozameh took thick sheets of the thin bread and stuffed them in my backpack. He saved one, which he tore in the street outside. He gave half to me.

Yes, I did think of communion as we stood there in the early sunrise of Tehran, in the quiet stillness of a world that had not yet woken, not yet quickened and come alive. I stood there, munching away. He was my friend, Gozameh.

•

I still have those boots. The leather is cracked from age. And I never knew then how little I knew of him, and how much he had been willing to give. Now: now it is too far away and long past any good to hold his life inside me.

•

"Arab, Mister Dante," he said, "may be the voice of Allah, but Persian is the music of the angels."

We waited at the corner. Gozameh placed his hand on my shoulder; he was really starting to like me.

"My friend, Mister Dante—do you know Sohrab? You *must* know Sohrab Sepheri, the poet."

And he started to sing these lines, and apologized for his awful English that he gave as his translation. But the words were wonderful. Everybody quoting poetry almost every waking second—what a country.

> *I must pack my bags*
> *Leave only room for clothes of solitude*
> *I must head for the epic tree*
> *And enter the wordless enormity*

I heard the frail bleat of a bicycle horn. A motorbike—it looked like a training cycle with a poor excuse for an engine—sped down the street, squeezing off its nasal honk. The rider was playing chicken, like an idiot, daring all the Peykans to clear out because he was coming through. There was a hooded falcon on the back of his bike, perched on the lip of a wicker basket. The falcon leaned and twisted like a gyro as her insane driver fought against the impossible downstream current.

An old man, bent with age, stooped from the shoulders, began weaving through cars as he walked across the street. He was probably no more than five feet tall. His neck, back, and legs were thick with muscle—you could see that immediately. He walked like a goat.

The motorbike headed straight for the old man. The driver screamed something in Farsi. The white-haired old man stopped and faced the driver. He just stood there, derision and scorn playing on his lips. He looked the driver over, puzzled at first, and then dismissed the presence bearing down on him. I wondered if this guy was just going to reach out and slap the rider to the ground.

The rider must have sensed that too, because just as suddenly he veered the handlebars and went around, still yelling, shaking his fist as he sputtered by. The old man turned and traced his path straight to us. He knew me; we knew him. Brown eyes, white mustache, trace of stubble on his chin.

"*Salám alaikum,*" I said, hoping this time I'd get it right. "*Hál-e shomá chetowr-e?*"

I stuck out my hand. He looked at my eyes, as though trying to see if he could trust me. The rawhide face cracked into a grin. He took my hand. "Damávand," was all he said.

∧

4 August
My hands are shaking. Already the weather is bad. The sun will set soon. I don't know where to go. At least I'm alive.

Clouds roll off the peak and down the edge of the glacier. The dragon coming out of his lair. Soft, boiling clouds roll up the ice wall.

I stand at the edge of a cirque. The ledge I have to cross is less than ten inches wide. One side is rock face. The other is hundreds of feet down. Nothing.

Straight ahead a rock overhangs. My leg starts to shake. My back screams at the pack's weight. I'm afraid and don't know what to do. My fingers are ice. Numb.

I slip under the rock and inch along. An hour maybe, and I'm off the ledge. I turn up and find a ridge of snow, follow its rise and fall as it arcs with the frozen glacier. The way is hard now, even worse than before. The sun will be gone soon, and I'll be here alone. Wondering what happened.

Briefly, I have this fantasy—the one I used to have when I was a kid. The people who find you after you're dead. What will they say when they find *me?*

Who was he? Why did he die here? So close to the path? So far from the summit? Why do you think he was alone? Why does his face look like that? Hey, let's take his wallet! Let's check his pack . . .

I come to another rock wall and stare at it, unbelieving. To have come so far, to have survived the peak and its illusions, and just to die here. Like a dog. A *farangi* dog. I feel myself slipping. I don't know how to move. My feet don't want to move. Hands and legs and knees shake. I take the ledge. I can only hope.

Take the last edge. Straight on. Almost vertical. The snow is bad, but the hard rock is even worse. A stone lifts from my heel and sings down the glacier. I'm almost there. The clouds move in. Zahhák is breathing. I can hear him. I need sleep. I know it. I'm tired and angry. And frightened.

Part Four

The *Ghazal* of Memory

You must recall these Days of God as you have and you must not forget them. It is these days which build the human. It is these days when our young ones left the places of entertainment and entered the battlefield. These are the Divine Days. These days awoke our people.

—Ayatullah Rouhullah Khomeini,
Address at the Faiziyeh School in
Qom, to commemorate the one-year
anniversary of the seventeenth of
Sharivar, the day called Black Friday.

1

Faith, there's something else I never told you. When we were roommates at the academy, Scott Hind claimed he knew the exact moment when he would die. The exact date. 24 April 1980.

He'd describe the faces of the other seven who would die with him. Sometimes, just after waking, he could even give names: The aircraft commander, a captain, Shuttleworth; the navigator is Harvey; there's a Marine sergeant, H. Smith . . ." Sometimes he could name the letters of the alphabet of all the crew, the crew of a helicopter and a cargo plane. Initials. The dead letters of their names.

I used to laugh at this. "That's impossible," I'd say. He never told me where it would happen. Just the date, just the sense that he had no doubt of its certainty. He was a quiet guy—Scott. Stocky, with a frame rolling with muscle, the human equivalent of a bulldog. I first met him during SERE—he was my interrogator when I was taken captive, and then Mitchell and I transferred into Goshawk. We went through Hummingbirds together.

He grew up, as I did, following his father all over the world. But his father was a senior NCO in the army. Career enlisted—three tours in Vietnam, a cluster of medals—and a fair share of Purple Hearts. Scott had always wanted to go to the academy. It was his dream. He wanted to be a pilot. I pictured him as chief of staff one day. It sounds dumb now, I know—but if you knew him.

Three days before leaving on that Christmas break, Scott walked up behind me as we were lining up to march to the evening meal. I knew it was him, even before I turned.

"I'm going to be your roommate next semester, Diamond."

"What are you talking about? If he decides to stay, Mitchell said that he would room with me again."

"I think Mitchell will be leaving. We're going to be roommates."

We were friends by then, had even started rock climbing together, with Mitchell. I was spending part of Christmas break with his family at his home. But it was a weird time to bring this up. And when Mitchell came down to see us during that vacation, I never asked him. I knew he wanted to leave. I didn't want to push him.

And that spring break, when Mitchell came back, he was really bad. Scotland and Germany were great, but he had to go back to Washington to tell his family—that is, confront his father—that he was leaving the academy. I knew it hadn't gone well. But I wouldn't ask him. I thought I had problems of my own.

Three nights after we came back from spring break, the spring of '78, Mitchell was dead. I saw him standing in the dark and never paid attention. Our room was cleaned and scraped and poked and inspected by special agents, and after I refused to return home because I saw no real reason to ruin the rest of the year, the AOC called me into his office. He asked me if I was sure of my decision about not taking time off. I said yes.

And then Scott stepped in. Roommates. And one morning before dawn, I saw Scott already dressed and already walking for the door when the knock came. The cadet-in-charge of quarters told him that he had a phone call. He mumbled, "Yeah, I know." And then, seeing I was awake, he closed the door and turned to me, and said, "Look, the call is about an accident. A hunting accident. I already know about it. My father's dead."

This really happened. Everything is true. Scott had seen the gun go off, seen the shell explode in his father's face, and then had seen through his father's eyes: the hunting boots around the body, everything fading to red. He had dreamed this. Black Fred had helped him dream this.

Later I thought to myself, and then, hell, I told him, that he sounded a little looped, that this was something that could hurt him, seriously. He would say no, no, Black Fred would never hurt him.

When he was a kid, he said, he was in the car with his mother. He was dreaming. The shadow of Black Fred slipped into the front seat between them. He touched Scott on the shoulder, told him to look; his mother was going to kill them. Scott came out of the dream—in time to shout to his mother to look out, just as their '59 Chevrolet began to veer from the face of flat rock on the high mountain road. She had fallen asleep at the wheel.

Other things would happen. The time he woke to say that Luckett, the school quarterback, had been killed in a car accident at that very moment, and the little surprise we had when we learned the truth the next morning. The way he'd turned to me and said "I'll be your roommate next semester,"

THE GHAZAL OF MEMORY

even before Mitchell had died, even before I considered that Mitchell would ever leave the academy, even before that final postcard, which arrived two weeks after his death.

And then his final restlessness, the final thing he came to accept. He came out of that first dream screaming, and whimpering. I could hear him. I could hear him whisper it:

24 April 1980.

And I began having dreams, where I was inside a freezing crevasse, blind, until a door opened above me. I saw the figure of Mitchell, hugging the light, coming for me. One night I woke from the dream again: Mitchell, dead those past few weeks, opening the oubliette of light, descending on me, like a hawk with talons. I cried out and came straight out of sleep. I sat up. There was a shadow in the room, pulling away from my bed.

"Just forget it, D," Scott had said. "Just go back to sleep."

And as I lay there in the dark I heard him say this, thinking that I couldn't hear: "He'll be leaving soon, anyway."

Yes, I know exactly why I never told you this, Faith, though I'm not sure why I'm telling you now.

•

Except tonight, I saw myself, clearly, the image of my fishbowl helmet reflected on the canopy, the reflecting gold of my visor reflecting my image on the glass. I saw myself carried off in opposite directions—an astronaut's outline repeated, infinitely, across distance—and studied how the helmet locked into my SDB 10100101-T suit, how the pressure-vent valve and food-access port and the emergency-release latch suggested there was something under the visor, something in that helmet that lived, that breathed, that knew about the world it saw.

What did I look like? Like an angel—in gleaming white and gold and steel. My "protective assembly," all twenty-seven pounds of it: a helmet fastened to restraint assembly, pressure suit, coveralls and bladder bag, capstan and face and body radiation barriers, survival kit.

Frank Stewart told me once that on his last space walk, back when there used to be a shuttle, he had turned his jet pack away from the ship and away from the earth to look out, completely alone, toward the universe. There was nothing between him and the rest of forever. He lasted almost fifteen seconds before he whipped back around to his crew and the craft and the lights, and the earth sailing beneath him. "But in those few seconds when I just looked out toward 'It,'" he said, "I was living the most beautiful and most horrifying moments of my existence."

And tonight when I saw myself, it was not my visor or the image of my visor that startled me. It was what I saw reflected in it: the dark curve of the earth, the spread of the whole horizon dropping away, and the sense that I had fallen, finally, into space, forever. I took a hard breath, seeing that, then seeing how my sudden physiological change was monitored on the digital ergonomic scale, the same machine that drains the nitrogen from my blood, keeps me breathing pure oxygen, makes sure I'm still alive.

And to make sure I was alive, I thought of the past and of the stories of the past, of what had brought me to this place so many miles above the earth. Memory can make the dead speak. And what would they say, if only the dead could survive?

٢

The Falconer
The Ancient Sport of Falconry is still Practised in Scotland

    D,

       Long time no see or hear, eh? What's it been, a week? I am spending the first days of leave here in Scotland and England. I've met a girl named Alice. She works at a hotel near Drumnadrochit. I've kind of committed myself. Be home in a few days. Bet my parents will shit when they hear I'm leaving!

       Maybe this will reach the Academy after school starts and you'll never read this...

                                              So long.

                                            Mitchell

THE GHAZAL OF MEMORY

The Holy Kaabah of Mecca represents the source of all Islamic artistic expression. At its Eastern corners stands the sacred meteorite known as the Black Stone. The whole is covered by a silk canopy, the **Kishwah,** exquisitely embroidered in gold with the words and teachings of the Faith.

Dante,

Your father and I were able to take a short trip away. We had always wanted to visit Saudi. As non-believers in THE FAITH, we were not really able to enter the city. There is even a sign on the highway, which reads CHRISTIAN BYPASS. But it's really fascinating!

Much love,

your mother,

Beatrice

THE GHAZAL OF MEMORY

ΡΟΔΟΣ: κόκκινη ελαφίνα   —   φάρος

Dante,
The Colossus of Rhodes stood here at the entrance to the harbor at Rhodes—one of the "Seven Ancient Wonders of the World." It was destroyed by an earthquake.
How are you? We haven't heard from you in ages.

Much love,
your parents

THE GHAZAL OF MEMORY

The five lakes of Band-i-Amir rising in tiers at 3,000 m. altitude, are bound with each other by cascades, frozen in winter, changing this natural wonder into a mineral, fairy land, unreal society.
Original phot. printed for Hamidzadah, Kabul Afghanistan

Dante,

The scenery here is spectacular! We'll be traveling in the Hindu Kush mountains today and tomorrow. Your father keeps saying it's a storybook.

Thought you would like this stamp—Mohammed Daoud is the president of the country. Seems to be popular.

Much love,

your mother,

Beatrice

٣

The dark face of my son. Slowly, he raised his hand, returning my call. It seemed—to me at least—that he was going to turn then, break for the exit, take the next available plane heading west.

"He's waving good-bye," I heard myself saying.

But he walked through the doors and down the length of the customs corridor. And then he stopped, his head cocked and turned toward the glass. He was sizing me up, checking me out, probing my face for something, someone he could recognize.

And then he moved on.

There's always been something strange about Dante. I remember, back in Australia, this little kid who'd crawl into the front seat of our '49 Rover—hell, he could barely get over the running boards—and suddenly sit beside me, suddenly rise to my height, trying to figure me out, talking like we were equals, not father and son.

He'd lost weight, I thought. He looked like a stick: thin, brittle, and fragile. Sunburnt. And blond! My God, his hair is blond. Beatrice won't recognize him. The T-shirt was rolled back on each side to his shoulders; muscle stretched like wire. The veins on his forearms stood out. His teeth, what with the dark burn he had gotten, were incredibly white. He looked awful.

"Hello, Dante," I offered.

"Hi ya," he smiled back, and without breaking his rhythm, "sir."

He stuck out his hand, then suddenly reached down to hug me. He was a big kid, and throwing my arms around him wasn't so easy. But, just for a second, I held him tight. I kissed him just as suddenly on the cheek. And he reeled back from that. Suspicious of anyone—even himself. Something, I knew, I passed down to him.

I'm not very good with words. I've never had to be. Every act, every thing, every move I've made in this long haul of a career has never had to depend on how well or how true I expressed myself. It doesn't make a damn bit of difference.

There is never time to say what I mean. Beatrice has known me long enough to accept that. I broke her because of it. Once, she tried to change me, but I couldn't change. She became a part of it. She had a gift with thought, once—but, now that we've both been at this business so long, I think she's lost it, too—the grace to say what you believe. You just live out your days, live as wisely or as well as you have to.

So I said nothing to Dante. There was a lot I could have burst out with. I didn't.

We walked through Mehrabad. He stayed close to me, his giant's frame brushing my shoulder sometimes. For a moment, I could have closed my eyes, could have thought this is years ago—we're back in Australia—we are a family.

I knew he had come to tell me he was leaving. I knew it. I wouldn't try to argue. Growing up to be just like me.

Funny, what I thought of then. When he was three, maybe four years old, when we had just come to Maine, we got this phone call from Fides at the General Store. Dante had run, completely naked, from our house—over a mile away. He just popped into the store, tearing down the aisles. We found Fides running back toward our house, carrying Dante wrapped in butcher paper.

•

Something happened up on that mountain. He never told us. But after he came back he never mentioned leaving again. He was quiet, kept to himself. When he graduated, went on to pilot training, eventually took over his own crew, he seemed more sure of his choices, and more determined.

Things just unwound over there about the time he came. Six months before, a neighbor—he worked for Rockwell—was found in the side alley. His throat slit—no, gashed really—like some massive claw had clutched down on his neck, then ripped it away. Some "Yankees Suck" type of slogan pinned to his chest.

And the day while driving to work, they surrounded my car. Black wool, or maybe nylon, masks on their heads. AK-47s in their arms. "Get out and die." And I thought, *this is it, it's all over. There've been a couple of times like that in my life.*

But Ghassemi smashed his foot to the gas, and got us both out alive.

Two years from that night Dante stepped off the plane, I flew back into Mehrabad, carrying a briefcase with three and a half million dollars in cash inside to pay for the release of our people in Qom and Isfahan. The damn

THE GHAZAL OF MEMORY

driver kept on stopping every thirty minutes for tea. In Qom he wanted to watch the demonstration. People were going nuts, burning flags and screaming. Khomeini just stood above it—calm and furious at the same time. It felt strange then, returning. I was the only American I saw. Most of the other Americans were holed up in the embassy as hostages. That was the day when Perot's plan to spring his troops from the Tehran prison finally worked out. I've read of how it was a carefully orchestrated breakout. The truth was that prisoners were tired of not being fed, and finally rioted. The Americans took that as their chance, and they ran. And they made it to the border.

Ten years ago Beatrice and I were in Kabul the day the Soviets rolled in. Lately, during the past decade, we're always in the wrong place almost too late to get out. Morocco, Seoul. I was at Quatif, too, when they took over the mosque and started throwing bodies down the front steps. Company business.

But we were just tourists that day in Kabul. We had left the confusion and mess of Tehran and walked straight into a goddamned hornet's nest. We'd been up through the Khyber Pass that morning, at the Pakistani border. We were climbing up through a high mountain route to see some Buddhist sanctuaries where monks had worked these massive bas-reliefs on the rock centuries before. There were these huge, and I mean Goliath-sized, figures of the Buddha—staring frozen-eyed over the valley, each figure meant to protect those below. Each face was different, but each was the same—hard, unforgiving, wanting to comprehend everything and not very pleased with what it found. Probably over a hundred of these things, cast in the rock, waiting, watching. The people who sculpted that army of saviors are all gone. Those figures will last forever.

It's a beautiful place, Afghanistan. Cut off by high peaks and rocks, arid topography, narrow paths, it's carved out the people who tried to survive. It's a place where you can walk out of a village and really believe it's a thousand years gone from the time you're living in.

Their Farsi is simple, direct. Beatrice and I had no trouble getting around. We spent a few days in bazaars, shopping for rugs. Their work was strong, direct. Some of those rugs, even now, I can just hold in my hand, feel how incredibly tight the weave and the strength is. It was different from what we found in Isfahan or Nain, but, in its own way, just as impressive. There's hundreds of knots in a square inch. Someone could spend years making this rug that costs almost nothing. Scary, that. All your life passes by, and you don't remember most of it. You spend each day thinking about how to get through, how to act and be as good as you can. But you hold one of these rugs in your hand: you hold someone's life. You start to remember.

We were a small group. Most of us came out of Tehran. There were some Aramco people from Saudi. A few of the officers who worked for me at the Magistrate. We pretty much kept to ourselves. We were free to roam on our own. But that day, we were plowing down from the Khyber Pass in this old, coughing bus, smelling of diesel, dust. Our driver would sing to himself, laugh sometimes. But he'd never smile, not when you spoke to him directly.

Near the city, he slowed up, stopped. His mouth opened. He was smarter than the rest of us. His eyes widened, and he just went into shock. He opened the door of the bus, started to yell something I couldn't understand, and just disappeared. He ran down the steps, out the door, and vanished.

Some of the people saw the tanks, and like bozos, started snapping pictures of these squat ugly machines with huge barrels and tracks pounding past. When their tracks rolled down the dirt road, they kicked up dust demons. They were carrying a storm with them. I saw the red stars off the turrets. Soldiers marching behind. They'd been going for hours, you could tell that: shoulders hunched, heads bent to the weight of their packs. Each carried a rifle, muzzles pointing out and away.

It's funny. I'd been in the air force almost three decades and I'd never seen one of these bastards before, not face to face. The thing that impressed me the most were their faces. Their faces were stone. Even then, seeing them enter Kabul, most of us didn't realize. We thought it was some kind of show of force, a warning to the Afghanis that if they didn't get their act straightened out, they sure as hell could.

Then the jets came. High and behind the tanks, a chorus of engines falling out of the sun, high and behind the rotating turrets. When the planes started strafing the streets, I really got scared. I thought it was all over, again. And this time, after all those years, Beatrice was there with me. It was a funny feeling to think that we were going to die there in the streets of that country, in the back of that stinking bus, our arms round each other. So many times I thought I would die in an airplane, and now it was going to be some other airplane that killed us together.

Fortunately, they weren't too damned smart. They came in from a steep

THE GHAZAL OF MEMORY

pitch—SU-7s—one lead pilot and then wingmen trailing his wake, and then started firing. But the stupid idiots had their flaps down—guess I should be grateful for that. Their noses may have been pointing at the ground, but their angle of attack was pointing practically at the horizon. Most of their bullets went wild, hitting buildings, pinging off walls. Later, this kid came on the bus—hell, he looked about sixteen—and started screaming at us in Russian. He didn't have to explain because we had a pretty fair idea what he was talking about. He motioned us off. He was flinging one arm in the air, pointing. But as we marched off, I bent down and picked up one of those shells that hadn't ignited. We still have it, Beatrice and me—this long, bright, thin little missile that never went off.

We had been staying in a hotel in the center of town, right next to the palace. We heard the shots when the president was killed, as if fired from outside the front door. Later, an interpreter told us he had committed suicide.

We stayed in the lobby most of that night. Just sat on the marble and waited. If you had to relieve yourself, you just went in a corner. Surrounded by guards. Outside, in the street, they were still fighting. Shells blew a hole through the wall in the building across from us.

Near dawn, we were loaded onto a troop bus and shipped out of the city. We stayed in this whitewashed barn, slept with the burros in the hay. Most of us they left alone. On the second day I was taken into a small hut and questioned for a few hours. It wasn't tough. It wasn't all that pleasant, I mean, but they didn't start shouting or kicking, or stick live wires on my genitals. They asked a few direct questions, then trailed off the subject, then came to those same questions again. The interpreter claimed I was a CIA stooge. I really started smiling at that, almost busted up laughing. For a while, I think I was so tired I couldn't stop laughing, I felt sure they would cart me off, because they thought I was some kind of idiot lunatic. But I answered their questions the same way each time.

One of the kids in our group—she looked about Dante's age—was taken in, too. I would have been shocked if I hadn't known. Back in the hotel, she'd pulled me aside that first night, don't ask me why—maybe because of my rank—and actually told me she was an operative, as if she were confessing to me, as if I was supposed to forgive her.

She didn't stay very long when they took her in. She came back red-faced *and still crying. After awhile, I guess they figured she was too nervous for that kind of work. Maybe they just felt sorry for her. Hell, who knows? They just let her go.*

Sometimes I think how crazy it is. If those idiot pilots hadn't dropped their flaps and screwed up their bullets' trajectories, they would have scissored the bus and cut us in half.

It's small things like that I'll always be grateful for. Dead reckoning, we used to call it. If you know where you are, you can't see where you're going.

•

These days I spend a lot of time flying. I don't have to. In fact, I'm not supposed to. But it's one of the things I do and I truly love. When I think of all those I helped to destroy, or destroyed, maybe it's the only thing I ever loved. I left the military a long time ago. I've never regretted it. After the shah left, things went fast. Everyone knows about it. No one understands it.

It's funny, too, thinking about what happened in Tehran—happened so quickly when it came—by the time we realized it was for real it was already over. Sometimes you think we'd learn to act quicker—as a country, I mean— learn to act a hell of a lot sharper in these predicaments. But we don't. We act like this damn fool who scratches his damn head in wonder after it all turns to shit, and keeps asking, "What happened?"

I liked the shah. He was a good man, intelligent, articulate. He wanted strength for his country and respect from the world. But he wanted power, too, and we let him believe he could have it. When he started to force and to push, to claim that he had the final right to his rule, he was suddenly helpless. For over a year, he listened to practically everything Magyar said. That was a dumb thing to do. Magyar wasn't too smart. Everything he said or tried to instigate was something that came from the mad angels singing in his head. No one else heard them, thank God. But Mohammed Reza Pahlaví listened to the singer speaking in tongues. If you push hard enough, something has to give. What fell first was Magyar, who got fired for abuse of position, then was shipped off to a retirement job at NORAD where he could spend most of his non-decision-making days on the golf course. Magyar's in big trouble these days. He's spending a lot of time up in Washington trying to save himself from prison after his escapades in Central America on the behalf, he claims, of resistance fighters.

But, back then, the shah had suddenly stopped trusting Americans; he ignored the advice of the Magistrate. He was a good man, but he did some strange things. I knew how he used the SAVAK to interrogate prisoners, which groups he picked out to crush, how he kept tabs on advisers. Hell, everyone became so paranoid. It all came crashing down—I've always wondered if we had decided we'd had enough of the nonsense and decided to invite, and help, Khomeini in any way possible. But that's just a guess on my part.

That was a long time ago. I don't think about it much, because it no longer matters; not to me, not to Beatrice. After I left the military, which was right after we hightailed out of Iran, I got a job with defense contracts overseas. We've stayed overseas since then. Once, a few years ago, we thought of returning to the States, but who knows? Maybe we'll never go back.

I heard from Dante the other day. He's doing well; that is, about as well as I suppose he could. He's always seemed best with being slightly unsure, dissatisfied with anything or anyone. He writes to us, sometimes. That's fairly significant, I suppose. In Vermont. Some semesters, he teaches. Mostly, he and Faith live up by Jefferson Pass and keep to themselves. He tells me he was right to finally leave the service when he did. I don't know . . . it was his choice.

•

These days, wherever we go, I make sure the contract deals specifically with planes. Though it's illegal as hell, I wouldn't be taking these jobs if they didn't include bennies like flying a jet. Sometimes—actually pretty often—I'll slap on a G suit, hop in an F-5, and leave. I remember most in Morocco, how sometimes I'd grab a test pilot and we'd fly formation over the desert, this huge sprawling emptiness, lift our noses to pop over a telephone wire, and then glide back down to the dirt. Sometimes storms would rise up like hurricanes off at the edge of the horizon. I'd tap an afterburner and climb at sixty degrees of pitch to watch the storm and the swirling sand from above, watch it swallow the desert. I'd head for the sun and the stars and the empty universe.

I was happiest then.

Once, back in Bien Thieu, something happened that I'd be happier if I could forget. I came back from ground support strike with some poor sod's head stuck in the undercarriage just aft of an intake. The look on what used to be his face scared the shit out of me. Sometimes I still see this poor bastard's face. He must have seen me coming. He must have run. He looked too scared to have been just sticking his head up from a rice paddy and just had it clipped off. He knew what hit him.

I used to be a good fighter pilot. Probably the best. Now I'm just a good pilot. Something changed that day. Something went away.

ج

Saturday afternoon
16 December 77
Hotel Shah Abbas, Isfahan

Dante,

Waiting and hoping that Ghossemi will bring me some mail. Your father left for Stuttgart, Germany 3 days ago—very suddenly. He went so quickly that he didn't even have orders. He's due back at Mehrabad in the morning. He's been gone a lot. I don't like it here alone but ALSO in the morning it has been very SNOWY and dreary—day after day. He left in a bad snowstorm!

The roof has been shoveled three times already back home, at 1,000 rials (14 dollars) each time. There is no garbage pick-up when it snows. All the garbage men go out and shovel roofs instead. They walk up and down the street SHOUTING that they are available & carrying something that looks like a wooden oar or a paddle. Looks like they're going boating. It has been very COLD also. "Paroo! PAROO MIZANIM!" they shout.

Dad was deeply disappointed that he did not get to see you when he was in Washington. He works so *hard*, Dante, and never gets time off. We should just pray that he keeps safe.

Bingo!! 2 letters from Grandma, one from Auntie Margaret, one from General Truong (you remember him, don't you? he was an Air Force commander in Vietnam). Ghossemi is such a nice guy.

I have adjusted very well here, Dante. Some people really DISLIKE it. If you could come see us, I think you would understand. I run "hot & cold" depending on what is happening. I'm not terribly unhappy in Iran but I'd come home in a FLASH! Please do keep your Father in your prayers. It is not very *safe* for him here—if it is for *any* of the Senior Officers. Due to a string of suspicious incidents—such as what happened to our poor neighbor, the Rockwell employee—which are reported, he's authorized to carry a gun and has been issued a pistol.

THE GHAZAL OF MEMORY

10:30 P.M.

A few days ago, the police came to our landlady one night to tell us that they had a car under surveillance. They told us to stay inside and lock all the doors. There were 4 policemen outside. Later there were more like 20 plus Army types (anti-terrorist committee). They have *the car*—(false registration/license plates) They LOST the people. When they tried to stop it they exchanged gunfire. CIA was there when Dad left in the a.m. Four policemen briefed Reza & Ghossemi. The police have told us NEVER to leave our car outside in case they might put a bomb in it. We have been careless in that department. We have begun to check it over each time. We had TOP SECRET material in the house at the time. I won't permit that to happen again.

Ghossemi is going to the airport to get Dad in the a.m. I'm sorry you haven't really heard much about Reza, your father's official bodyguard. (Ghossemi is really only the driver—but he does so MUCH more!) He's really super. He and Ghossemi are friends. I have complete confidence in them. When Dad is with them he is in good hands. Occasionally they have a day off and some of the other drivers are bad. And the guards are useless!!

It is snowing AGAIN. Most days it is so cloudy overcast I cannot even see the mountains. Even here, in Isfahan, there's nothing to see beyond the window! A freak of nature—so much snow at this time of the year.

Good luck on your grades—how do you think you did? I had a lot of trouble with Engineering as well . . . Do you take after me in that department?

Don't neglect your *friends* at the Academy. You know, if you chose to— and if you had the time—we'd be happy to have you stay with us. We *all need* people.

Lots of love,

your Mother,

Beatrice

○

May 78

Dante,

Was good to hear from you. When you are here this summer—and we expect you will be—you'll get to know our friend Ghassemi very well. I think it would be appropriate if you wrote to him before your arrival to introduce yourself. His full name is:

BABAK GHASSEMI NEHLAD

Perhaps it would be proper to send him something? Like a saber plaque? If you do, mail it by the end of June, before you leave for San Diego. It takes about 10 days to get here.

I'm rushing to get this letter in the outgoing mail.

Your father

Muhammed Zaman, Iranian, 17th Century
A Blue Iris   1663–64
Opaque Watercolors on Paper: Sheet, 13 1/8 x 8 3/8 inches;
image 7 1/2 x 4 3/8 inches
The University of Teheran Museum 78.27

My very dear friend

Mr. Dante,

I look forward to meet you. Your mum and dad are very fine people. It is very pleasure to know them.

Welcome to my country.

Your Friend

Ghasemi Nehlad

٦

I am a simple man. I think myself a simple man. Each day, night, dawn or dusk, I kneel toward Mecca and pray that I will remain so. When I hear the muezzin's call, Allah-o-Akbar—I do not mean the call to prayer from the minaret, I mean the voice inside—I kneel and pray for this. Though it is not a simple thing.

I live in a land where this will not be rewarded. I have often thought myself confused about the world around, what lies outside this country. I am faithful of Islam, of course. There is no other path to follow. But I have questioned, asked myself silently, what has become of my kingdom. I do not question the Emperor. He is a great man. He has taken from the path of frozen history to make a great land, as great as the ancient kingdom. We are the new Persia.

It is said, in the wisdom of Zarathustra, in the Yasna songs of the Avesta scriptures, that we are the Peoples of Righteousness. All others who do not follow us, those who kneel in line to worship Mithra, are the Peoples of the Lie. We live, according to law, to honor Allah: this is the law of my life. But, in the way I live it, it must be to guide the good examples and proper paths of Ahura Mazdah and his six attendant deities: Vohu Manah, Asha Vahista, Khshathra Vairya, Spenta Armaiti, Haurvatat, and Ameretat. They represent, in order: good thought, righteousness, divine kingdom, pious devotion, salvation, immortality. This is the struggle between fire and earth, the powers of light against the bridge of separation. When Saoshyant returns, when all the dead will rise to face their final reward or punishment, the way we have lived will be the measure of fate.

I believe and do not believe this. To be faithful of Islam, I must forget such words. Though it has filled the history of my land for as far back as time stretches. There is, I think, some wisdom in this. It is wise to have a set of inner rules, a faithful light which will burn against the sense of how the day strikes and people live. To say it simply, I must not believe everything I am told. Or not told.

I am ordered to protect General Diamond with my life. He is here, as I am, to serve the kingdom and the Emperor. I do not mind this. I have come to know him well, these past years, and come to love him as a friend and fellow *servant. To say, in the rank of men, that he is a greater man than I is no revelation. But the strength of his greatness does not lie in the weight he wears upon his shoulders, the single silver star which spans a width of blue.*

He is a great man because he is a good man. I have thought him quite different from the others. From Magyar, who I do not trust, to my own commanding countrymen, like Nerezi or Sadeghian. I am told to watch him, and to protect his family as well. I am not told perhaps that, even though he is here to serve, it can be equally true that he is among the Peoples of the Lie. In the end, when sides are counted, the draw may turn against him. I do not know this truly, but I feel it. When I am called to report on his activities: what he and his wife do regular, what progress of the past has been which I must reveal by week, how his habits are, who he sees outside his office, where he goes, and what has he ever said to me, I wonder who it is who is meant to be trusted.

I do not question this. It is not my place. But my greatest sin—or my least—is to know that I have not told all which I know. I have not told how I have felt sometimes, driving and speaking privately with General Diamond, that I am conversing with a normal man, a peaceful man. When I cannot see the uniform, I do not believe I am here to protect a military officer.

I do not tell of how his wife seems to me what I have heard named in their tongue the strange bird. She seems to like me, but seems as well to fear this country. She is like a stem of glass willing to snap. I do not think Iran has caused all of this. And she becomes worse. Her smile lingers less on her lips, and appears less frequent. She does not enjoy the official functions, as they call them—they seem like rather parties to me—to which I sometimes take them. She does not mingle with the other women. She keeps to herself, and that is a dangerous thing.

And the son, the one who arrived a few days gone now, I do not know what to make. He is too quiet. That could be to his honor; that could be because he is stupid. Though I laugh when I consider this and do not think it long. Nothing like a fool would spring from the general's and his wife's union.

I have been informed that he too is a military man. Yet he is very young. The age of most of our soldiers, rather than officers. I do not know what to make. When I drove him with the General to the office yesterday, I watched in the mirror as he stole glances at his father's clothes. As though he were with a stranger. When I drove to the airport, and saw him striding from the terminal, I snapped to attention as he saw us, raised my hand in salute. He saw this, he too began to raise his arm, then looked to us and dropped it back again. He smiled.

All the way to the house, he stared through the window. He is too quiet. Too quiet. The most common thing he says is "Thank you." Surely he must speak more than this. Perhaps he thinks he cannot trust me. This may be wise. Perhaps I do not trust him yet. Only today he began to call me Ghasemi instead of Sir.

Something happened, shortly before he came, in which I sense connected with him. I cannot explain this truly. He does not know of it. I do not think he will ever be told. The General did not tell his wife. And I, for other suspicions, never told it in my report. I have my reasons, as well. They are people I live to protect. I have no wish to bring them harm. Now, among me, I do not know where trust lies.

We traveled a back route through the upper section of the city. The General had met with Reza Shah earlier that morning. It was the second time the General had seen him. General Diamond is not the highest-ranking officer of the Air Magistrate. General Magyar most often meets with the Emperor to take long, private counsels. But General Diamond had been asked personally to the palace. He seemed excited at the chance. We never speak together of the Shah—such talk is not permitted. But I often hear him, in conversation with members of his office, speak and speak high.

The General was in conference less than an hour. We left the palace and headed north, taking the route which wound up through the city to top the base of the Elburz. I had thought of taking him immediately down to the administration offices in the central city as soon as the gates of the palace swung open, and we pulled away from the royal residence. But the General asked that we drive away from the city.

"Let's take our time here, Gozameh," he said. "I'm in no real rush to get back."

We climbed high and above the city. We looked down from a summit. We could see the university and the city park as they bent into the plain of urban view. I felt disappointed: I have lived here all my life and so rarely get a chance to see the city of my birth from such a height. It is my own fault. Laziness.

As we rose above the last residential section, the General said, "That's

OK." I turned the car, and we fell down through residential streets and winding alleys. We passed through the richer, private section of the city. Many foreigners lived there, but many wealthy Iranians also. The streets were quiet. Some of the streets were muddy with jubes overflooded. Refuse and ungathered trash blocked some ditches and water flowed across some streets to the opposite jube. The high walls of each residence blocked many of the houses from our view. I thought of the many beautiful gardens hidden from sight, the blooming roses and careful tenderness given to each blossom by hands we would not see, the peace of the courtyards and the private shelter given each person who lived inside those walls. I have often wished the same for my own family.

Twice we passed a butcher with his patient and attendant herd of sheep following close behind. This was rare privilege. I had offered Mrs. Diamond my advice whenever such butchers came to our door. Nothing is more fresh than a hand-picked lamb slaughtered at your doorstep. Lately, she has trusted this task entirely to me. I argue, of course, over price—that is the expected thing—and watch closely.

I thought something strange then. As we drove, mostly in silence, I looked down the path of a long tunnel which the sunlight wished to break above the walls. But the walls rose higher and the light was blocked. It grew darker, though I remember it was a faultless blue of day. And then it happened.

A black car, a German Opel—I remember that too—shot out from the corner of a blind intersection and blocked our path. I opened my mouth to curse them and saw two men wearing hoods jump from the backseat of the car. It was a hot day. But the sweat was cold on my face. I turned and threw my arm behind. I screamed at the General to lie down on the floor. As I shoved the machine into its reverse, the tires wheeled against the pavement and screamed. As one bullet pierced the rear window, I saw our path behind us blocked by yet another black car. There were figures running toward us, raising Kalishnikovs. They headed for us, aiming to fire. It is God's will, I thought, that I will not die among these dogs. I pressed the accelerator as far as it would drive itself into the floor of the boards of the car. We flew in reverse toward the car behind. The two running figures paused but had no time to move. When we struck them, they rose in the air on separate sides of the street. One was lifted and slapped against the wall of a home. The other slumped over the edge of a jube. We smashed against the car and crushed the driver's door. I heard the metal crumple. It looked like a wave bending on itself. I never saw the driver.

The dust swirled. For one moment, everything was quiet. The air grew clear, and thus I saw the figures in front of us, perhaps thirty to forty metres away, stunned and unbelieving. Then one of them screamed. But I did not hear him. I was beyond hearing. Their bullets cut into the window, and the glass splintered. Crinkled, impossible to see through. I shifted the transmission forward, pressed one foot on the brake, one foot back down on the accelerator, and drove my head between the steering wheel to stare at the instrument controls. I was beyond seeing. I released the brake: I remember the sound of our tires as our massive weight shot straight ahead. I never saw the impact, but it was sharp and sudden, and as we hit I knew that we were going to live. Our car did not stop, did not even slow, but surged ahead through the street. As we passed through the hood of the black Opel, after the sudden crush of it, I pulled up from the dashboard, and I thought I saw the car behind us in the mirror, how it snapped from front to back and smashed into a wall, pinning one of the men in what had been the engine.

After the General asked if I was well, he did not speak for a long while. Finally, he said something which I thought at first strange, but now I think I clearly understand. "We must tell no one of this," he said.

When I brought the car to the official mechanic, I reported that we were hit by a rockslide on the northwest section of the city on a road that had been closed that very day. Damage to the windshield had been so severe I had peeled away the twisted glass, as a snake does his skin, and left it at the scene of the accident. No one questioned me further. And no one asked about the several punctures in the front and rear section of the car.

•

I have thought myself often a happy man. I have a wife and two children I love. Even among the faithful, though, I see through those who are insolent and uncontent. They are the overwhelming force in this world. They are what will consume us all. In the courtyards of the wealthy, there is a blindness to the insolence and anger and poverty of the weak. No one seeks to help them, even to see them. And so as no one is blind, no one will as surely die. In the market, in the street, in the bazaar, there are those who scream and bicker, cry out without ears for their hearing that their time has come and they will not willingly drag themselves to the cemetery without witness. The newspapers claim that all is well. They report a country of peace and bliss, but it is not this nation. It is not this city. I have seen men who can no longer bear their burdens in silence. And I have thought how those men who would kill me were part of something larger they could not comprehend, as though they were the instrument, the anvil upon which all discord and vengeance will be struck, willing to sacrifice themselves so that all troubles will cease, so that the true sense of their faith will reveal itself in martyrdom.

Perhaps there is no such thing as a happy man. Perhaps, in a time like this, happiness itself is an impossibility of the real. I do not know. Sometimes I wonder if it is better to be blind, to live at ease with one's family and daily cares, to be at peace, to move as effortlessly as a grove of cedars stirred by wind. But then I know that it is a lie. I cannot place myself among the kingdom of the Peoples of the Lie. La ilaha il Allah.

V

Faith, it's true. Instead of heading to Corpus Christi that Christmas vacation, we drove straight south to Mexico. Mitchell, after his failed attempt to scale Shasta, had driven straight from California, and when he got to Scott's house, he told us both, "Let's just go. Somewhere. Let's just drive." We ended up in a town named La Paz. Scott said that's where we had to stop.

"Boys," he said, "we are gonna have us one good time."

The first day we wandered through the street, the one street of town. We looked in the markets, talked to a few storekeepers. It was a pretty dead place, the wrong time of year. There weren't many tourists. "Why," I kept asking myself, "are we here?"

The old woman, hunched and squatting, rocked a little and hummed as she bounced, lightly, against the wall. Her face was the texture of cracked clay. She saw us looking at her and stuck out her hand, pleading.

I turned away. She had exposed one breast, and pressed the withered dug of it to the baby she held. She was trying to feed it—she had nothing to give. That baby couldn't have been hers.

We walked down the street, and then Scott asked me how much money I had. "Enough, enough to get by."

"Good," he mumbled, and he turned around. As he walked off, I stood there kicking the dirt with Mitchell.

"What kind of guy is this?" Mitchell seemed to ask the air. "Is he crazy or just completely weird?" I saw Scott bend down and look in the old woman's eyes. He squatted so that she wouldn't have to look up. She held out her hand, and he put everything he had into it.

"Here. Take this," he said, "and don't be afraid."

                                Λ

                                            New Year's Eve, Year *2537*
                                            Tehran, 20 March 1978
Dante,
   Sal-e No-barak! Happy New Year!
   NouRuz has lost its novelty this year. It's been a bit of a drag and an expense—at a time when we don't have time to wrap gifts, visit, send greetings, et cetera. Gifts or money are given to everyone who serves you in any way regularly. It will be well over $200 this year. Well in excess.

   Later . . . *NouRuz* proved to be "catching" after all. Something for the *asheali* (garbagemen), the policemen, Hajar, Moussa, Ghassemi & Reza & families—a basket of gifts sent downstairs. Like Christmas!!!!
   The sound of children (next door) playing with toys downstairs. Laughter & happy talk. Families visiting. Bright spring days. Therrien & I decided to indulge ourselves. It's been such a strain lately. A *big* misunderstanding.
   We took a 4 day vacation in Tehran. I've wondered what it would be like to be a tourist. The first day we headed for the bazaar in the southern part of the city. We couldn't get to the bazaar because His Imperial Majesty was down at Golestan Palace for Sal-e ceremonies. There were hundreds of police, 4 or 5 on every corner & in between. Truckloads of police at scattered points. Roads blocked off. Just like when we were in Cairo after the riots. I'm just as glad we didn't get to the bazaar. There has been unrest in the city & rumors of danger to foreign women. The bazaar is never completely safe.
   We went to the Plasca Bldg., which has a shopping arcade. Even after all this time, it is uncomfortable. People stare down south. It's especially risky carrying a camera. We talked to a very nice young man—a real artist—& bought some things. He works in KHATAM, camel bone inlaid work.
   We spotted some velvet dresses with *morvarid* trim.
   It was unreal! No sizes!! They must have opened 30 or 40 packages, a mountain of dresses and blouses, that they measured against each other.

THE GHAZAL OF MEMORY

Things at the bottom of the pile were really CRUSHED velvet. I finally bought a blouse. Can you imagine a $70 black velvet gold trim dress with NO size, a purple zipper (sometimes) or a zipper that wouldn't stay closed. Only in Iran!!!

Back to Manuchehri St. where we left the car. "Come In! Come In! It does not cost anything to look!!" I don't like to be pressured. We came home really beat! But happy!

Next day. Trip to SCS to open safe for secret info for Magyar. Outing to Chinese restaurant for lunch. Trip to Museum of Contemporary Art. Brand new. Interesting. Trip to Khalil Galleries (brand new)—some rare archeological treasures. Priced Pahlavi Coins & settings Saltanatabad. Home early. Beat!!!

Thurs. a.m.—Therrien worked early. Haircuts. Lunch at O'Club. Went to Marble Palace downtown. *NouRuz*. Closed. Walked around beautiful grounds & gardens. Took a short trip from *Travels with a Persian*. Evieh Village—like stepping into another century. Less than 5 minutes from Hotel Evieh the expressway. Saw National University of Iran—quite impressive. Drove into another small valley & village. Incredible. Afraid to take pictures. Obviously no garbage pickups in *either place*. A Mountain of TRASH in center of village. Told it is the same way in resort areas. The glamour, tourist spots?

Went to Tajrish Bazaar. Smell of ROT hits you first. Don't dare take pictures. Bought tiny tea glasses & saucers & spoons (very Iranian). Got outfits for the nieces & nephews. Man had his clothing on a table & hung on pegs on brick wall. We could buy something soiled & snagged for the girls or get something too big, which we did.

Children playing soccer in alleys. Huge tongues & fish heads for sale. Rotting fruits & tomatoes. Beggars with their hands out. Being pushed & shoved by the crowd. Home early & tired again.

Friday—Therrien had short trip to Magyar's house. Time change. We lost an hour. Trip to Moses's to inspect carpets from Mashhad. Brunch at Skytop Restaurant—lavish buffet, linen tablecloth & napkins, panoramic view of the city, including the valley & village we had visited the day before. A trip to Negarestan Museum (new)—Persian art.

Driving to Archeological Museum, a traffic policeman pulled us over on an empty street. We thought it was a security check. Apparently we'd come out the wrong way out of a one-way street. As we were driving away & the policeman walked back to the intersection we heard a THUD—and 4 or 5 cars stopped in the other lane behind us, (other side) I half glanced over my shoulder—just another accident in Tehran. Therrien looked in the rear view mirror, saw shoes fly up in the air and come down in the street. There was no sound of crunching metal when we thought about it. Just a THUD. Therrien says if you hit hard enough to knock your shoes off— you're dead.

Feeling sick, we headed north and went to Niavaran Park. The forsythia & hyacinth & daffodils are blooming. Iranian families were strolling & children playing on the swings & seesaws. Little girls running down the hillside with their *chádors* flipping in the breeze. We hate *chádors* on children.

Therrien said an Air Force major hit & killed an *asheali* over the weekend. I've been expecting it to happen. They collect at night now & they just leave their carts down the middle of the street and they wear dark clothing. Sad.

Tehran is drab & colorless as far as actual COLOR is concerned, but it is a lovely, colorful, interesting place. We missed the picture of 2 policemen kissing on each cheek & then on the lips (a common sight) in the park. Or the 2 Men crossing the street holding hands (a common sight) or the 12-year-old boy holding 2 brothers by the hand crossing the road (a terribly uncommon sight)—children are usually terribly careless about cars here.

We leave for Afghanistan soon. We're holding up under lots of pressure. We need a vacation—Kabul should be just the ticket.

with much love,
your mother,
Beatrice

9

Thank God or Allah or whomever for Ghossemi. We were so lucky to have him. He truly seems to care about both of us. And his family is so lovely, and sweet. I've no doubt that he'd do anything to try and save Therrien if something happened. It was natural that Ghossemi would be the one who volunteered to drive Dante north for the hike.

It was difficult enough for my husband and my son to persuade me that this hike was something even halfway worthwhile. Particularly with all these horrible things in Tabriz, and rumors of more government shenanigans to start around the country. But Dante was always running off and doing absolutely incredibly bizarre things.

When we moved here, I wanted to learn about Persia. It seemed romantic, mysterious. I thought, like a fool, we would be living like royalty, enjoying all of the best in this possible world. But our experience certainly doesn't show it. Oh, Therrien never complains. I think that's what really irritates me about him the most: he can take the worst of any situation and not think there's anything wrong. He'll listen to my honest questions, things I've really thought through; he'll nod his head gravely, his dark eyes will draw close, his brow will look sewn together, but I know he's not listening.

I still can't believe I let him leave. I'll spend the next week worrying, thinking and asking why I let him go, and what if something happens to him. When he found out about Demavend, his eyes lit with this wild excitement, as if hiking the path up to his summit was something he had to do, even though I have no doubt, despite his claims, that he'd even heard of the mountain before arriving here nearly two weeks ago.

•

When Magyar first arrived here, he told Therrien that Dante is among the highest-ranking cadets—militarily—in his class. He's shown the officer cadre that he can lead, command. Dante, according to Magyar, was just super.

This summer he was in charge of ten cadets sent down to San Diego to train for underwater demolition. I don't know how he does it. I never knew he was so—how do I say it?—military minded? He seemed, to Therrien and me at least, so completely averse to everything about the markings of a uniform. Discipline?—completely apathetic.

When Therrien was at Bien Thieu, he was even hostile. What we are doing there is wrong, he'd say. How could he change so in just a few years?

Therrien, of course, thinks this is wonderful. That's natural for a father. Sometimes I think he's reliving the beginnings of his own career through the life of his son—though neither of us would ever tell Dante that. My husband never had the benefit of an academy education, which, in the circles we move in, is roughly equivalent to what Ivy League beginnings are in the spreading circles of the larger pond. Magyar claims that you can tell the fiber of a man even when he's only eighteen: You can know what kind of things he could handle, how he'll be under stress, how he works with people, how well—this the unsaid all-important item—he can kill people with a jet and how he will or will not feel behind the act. You can tell, Magyar says, what he'll be like three decades down the line. I saw Therrien nod solemnly in agreement.

There's something really repulsive in this: the idea that you can—and I'll use the disgusting term here—"groom" someone for the wreath of leadership. But Therrien truly believes this. As much as he wants to separate himself from all this military nonsense, he can't. Under the exterior—scars he'll carry forever—under the boyish grin of his, he's the same mold as everybody else. Here we are, falling into the last part of this idiotic century, finding or not finding ourselves following the folly of the past two centuries.

Therrien has made his own way in our career. I say our because it's every bit my career as much as it is his. When it's time for him to handle emergencies, to go off to war, I'm the one who's had to struggle, raise a family, make the right decisions. This career has almost broken me; someone with less wit and disinterest would say it has broken me.

At times I would feel my eyes cloud. Almost as though I were blind. Therrien will try to hold me up; my fingers will rip at him.

•

When I told Dante how proud his father was when we learned that he would accept the appointment to the academy, he shrugged me off and looked away. He wouldn't look at me.

It's true, though. Therrien was ready to bust with pride when he learned about Dante's tender of appointment. He wouldn't tell Dante this. He would never tell Dante. I can't say why or even know why. Just his personality, quiet and stubborn refusal to accept any emotion. More than once, that refusal has come close to costing our marriage.

Perhaps it's because Therrien and Dante are so alike.

Therrien finished school after Dante was born in Vermont. But Therrien, all his life, was getting into trouble. Just like Dante, he'd had plenty of chances. Years ago, while he was a premed student at BU, he got his last warning after he was caught painting the statue of John Harvard the deep tonal of his own school colors. His roommate, Theophilos, also a medical student, was known for his fear of cats. Therrien thought he'd cure that fear by stealing several dozen cats' eyes from the biology department and plopping them down in Theophilos's sock drawer. Theophilos, without saying anything, went white and hit the floor shortly after he began dressing for dinner that night. Later, that same week, Therrien baked a small cake as an apology. He'd laced the cake with a chemical used for laboratory tests, which, when taken with food, turned your urine blue.

Finally, Therrien burnt his last straw. Inside the B of the BU—the letters doused on the field with gasoline and then lit at the first hint of security guards—in Harvard football stadium. As soon as the first tongue of flame burst into the night air, Therrien knew he was trapped. And he just waited. And then it was all over: the end of a medical career.

And the beginning of a military one. He seemed happy, though. Unlike his father or father's father or father's father's father, he never really wanted to be a doctor. He just wanted to fly. And now the air force was the only option left.

Sometimes—no, almost always—I am glad Dante is at the Academy. They seem to have finally straightened him out.

When he was a child, in Maine, he would run around the schoolyard during recess, screaming that this was the best part of the day anyway, so why bother to come back inside? Here he was, in the first grade—the first grade, mind you!—and he was a delinquent. Most of each day was spent in the principal's office. Heron Island was a small place. We were isolated. Therrien worked out of a remote radar site and flew regular alert missions out of the north. For the first two years, before he was old enough to attend school, Dante spent much of his time in the woods surrounding our house. He'd always return with wild stories of creatures and strangers he met there.

I've wondered, too, what it was I could have done, what kind of awful sin I had committed, to have given birth to such a child. As a kid he was just completely wild. He was the wildest, most incredibly rebellious child I've ever known.

I remember picking up the phone in the kitchen to learn that my son was in the emergency room with a bad head injury. He was six years old. When we arrived and found him sitting quietly by the school nurse, he smiled up at us, even looked relieved. His head was bandaged with thick gauze, his left cheek bleeding from a long gash down the length of his face. One of his classmates had cut into his skin with a shard of glass.

Dante, we learned through the nurse—why do we always have to learn these things from other people?—was the leader of a youth gang. His band of little thugs had tussled with a rival group during recess, and the result landed Dante in the hospital. Hearing this, I broke into a kind of nervous laughter. The children in these roving bands were the sons of farmers or paperworkers in the mill. This was a small town in remote Maine. This wasn't New York or Boston. For a while, I'd thought that they were a bad influence on him. I came to realize, painful as it was, that he was the bad influence on them.

His forehead looked like a massive pregnant sore: purple and incredibly swollen. The doctor kept shaking his head. He said that Dante would be lucky if he had only severe migraines for the rest of his life. But after the huge awful swelling died down, and for a while it seemed as though it never would, Dante never even had headaches. That's one thing I can say about Dante. Despite all the trouble he's gotten himself into, he always manages to survive. He always recovers. He's lucky that way.

A week later—a Wednesday—the principal called and asked Therrien and me to come to school immediately. I wasn't particularly responsive. Dante was in the principal's office nearly every day, and the school's intimidation sessions didn't seem to be having much effect. But the principal sounded exhausted, and said "Please, Mrs. Diamond, this is serious."

Dante seems to have grown tired of having to continually fight for control of the schoolyard. So he and his band of merry little men had decided to attack his rival at the place where he thought it would hurt most: at his home. The boy's house was across the field from the school, through a short path in the trees. There was a small cemetery back there, too, and the principal complained that he had seen Dante taking naps on top of the gravestones.

THE GHAZAL OF MEMORY

So Therrien and I rushed over to school just in time to witness the sheriff of Heron Island dragging Dante into the office by the scruff of his collar, shouting, "I'm going to arrest this little brat, I'm gonna do it, I tell ya!"

Dante, at noon recess that day, had found his way to get even. He and his loyal gang of delinquents had attacked the home of his rival. The boy, of course, wasn't home. He was probably back in the schoolyard, skulking around, looking to fight. But the boy's mother was home. She leaned out her living room window, screaming "Stop!" The thugs didn't listen. They emptied their pockets of the golf ball–size stones they had collected and whipped them against the house. They broke every window of the two-story home, every one but the one the woman, pleading and crying, had been leaning out of.

Dante looked helpless and lost when the sheriff brought him in.

His hands were clasped in a pair of handcuffs that didn't do much, because during the course of the next hour he slipped out of them and held them in his lap, and no one, except for me, I think, even noticed he'd taken them off.

We thought that it would be best to get him away from the school. He needed a good Catholic upbringing, and it was obvious that the example Therrien and I had tried to set wasn't strong enough. So, the next year, we sent him to Christ the King when we moved to Alabama. The sisters were stern, scrupulous. They knew how to stress a strong parochial education, and knew how to stop youth and restlessness from interfering with the aims of schooling. They had no qualms about whipping children; some days Dante would come home with his knuckles still bleeding. I should have been sharper. I should have seen that if a child gets whipped so often, the lesson is apparently not being received. But I didn't perceive anything until this little boy, who still is a little boy to me now—even though he's nearly six and a half feet, and weighs over two hundred pounds—came home during the middle of the day in the second semester of the second grade and declared himself an atheist. I nearly fainted. And if Therrien hadn't been there (which, fortunately, he was—for one of the few times in our marriage), I think I would have come completely apart. Little boys in the second grade aren't supposed to even know what the word "atheist" means. And then when he issued an obscene remark—and how he learned that I've still no idea—in class to Sister Mary, he was expelled.

Whenever we moved, and we were always moving, Dante would get into serious trouble.

How many times would I pick up a phone from the wall to learn of yet another awful thing my son had done? It's funny, but I never once dreaded picking up that phone: I always thought that Dante would have learned, would never do something so terrible again. Equal parts optimist and fool: that's how I best define myself as mother.

When we moved to Australia, I thought Dante would ease up a bit. There were a few incidents. Minor for Dante, outrageous for most children. His best friend was Roger Malone, whose father was a liaison from the Royal Air Force. Both of them, the Yank and the Brit, were outcasts, and it was only natural that they would grow close. But Roger suffered worse than my son. British by birth, the other kids hated him from the moment he arrived.

Once, Dante gave up his sight for a time because of friendship. He'd tried to defend Roger during a soccer match. The field was a favorite grazing spot for the cows that roamed the grounds. Dante was pushed face down into a pile of cow dung, and his face mashed into the center of the flop. (It wasn't uncommon for some of these cows to poke an inquisitive head through the open window of a classroom while class was in session.) With their soft eyes and cuds, they probably watched that day as a ring of small boys mashed my son's face into the dirt. The boys were all dressed in ties and shorts, their school jackets draped over a fence. Some of the young girls, in blue and gray checks, their hair tied in a bow at the back, probably stood at the edge of the field and cheered.

Dante was blind for three days. The worst case of conjunctivitis I've seen. The membrane covering his eye was swollen, rimed with pus.

Soon after that both Roger and Dante were expelled from the local Cub Scouts pack. During a local outing, they had tried to "help" another scout who they'd heard writhing in pain outside his tent one morning. The poor kid had found the ugly sign of a tick buried in his crotch. He was crying, half out of horror I'm sure. Dante and Roger suggested dressing the wounded area with kerosene. When this failed to coax the thing from its nest, Dante took the head of a barely extinguished match to the parasite's backside. The boy's crotch exploded in flame.

Dante said he was only trying to help. His reasons were innocent. Most of my parenting life, I've believed that his reasons were innocent: he just wasn't smart enough, or he never took the time beforehand to consider the consequences of where his sometimes good intentions led. I suggested, on this particular occasion, that he should know exactly what he was doing before *offering help.* Dante nodded solemnly. He obviously never took my advice.

And then, after a few days had passed, Dante and Roger wheeled a cart full of watermelons through the yards of the neighborhood. They had found a wild patch of them, each the size of a grapefruit, in a dense section of bush. Roger had suggested that these melons would make an excellent marmalade; it would be an act of good faith for the two "aliens" to graciously distribute the fruits to all neighbors and friends. The act itself was gracious.

When Therrien came home that day and learned what Dante had done, he was angry, really angry. "Those things are poisonous! If someone cuts into one of those and takes a bite, he's dead!" We spent much of that evening scouring the neighborhood trying to recover their murderous gifts. Roger and Dante obediently trailed behind us. They apologized to each household, cradling the refused melons in their arms and then loaded the fruit back into the bed of their wagon. The melons jostled and bounced their way down the street; sometimes, a few fell off and hit the gutter, exposing the ripe, pink, sweet flesh. What few of those he could take, Dante would bend to gently place back on the wagon. By the end of that evening, the wagon was so full Therrien made Dante carry the extra burden in his arms while Roger pulled the full cartload beside him. Quiet and resigned, he'd sometimes stumble and drop a few—though I'm not sure it was on purpose—reach down, re-form his pyramid, and run to catch up with his father, whose sad shaking head carried his disbelief as we followed a path under the light of the Southern Cross.

•

My most vivid, perhaps even happy, memory of Dante is from his tenth year. We had spent two weeks on a sheep ranch in New South Wales. A working ranch as well as a spot for a real family vacation. It was probably the best vacation we've had. We were living in the real outback, spending our days on hikes and picnics, following trails in the arid one-hundred-degree heat. At dusk we would watch kangaroos stampede, or see koalas cling to the high limbs of eucalyptus.

And shearing work—Dante, knee-deep in wool, loving it, digging his hands deep into the mess of it. The wool was loaded like hay bales and brought out to the waiting trucks. The station workers moved with incredible efficiency, almost gracefully, gently lifting the fur from the body. The hair curled like tongues, lifting, falling to the unseen floor.

At night we would gather at a huge rectangular boarding-style table. Everyone: workers, the station owner, his wife and children, visiting families. It was a wonderful time. Like a sense of communion, really. We'd laugh and talk, listen to wild tales of the outback. After dinner most nights there would be slides of places like Ayers Rock or Perth or Tasmania, even the Great Barrier Reef one evening.

That was one of the happiest times in our lives, I think. Therrien and I were having a difficult time of it in our marriage. His flying was going well. But, as a fighter pilot, his flying had to go well. Otherwise you wouldn't stay alive. He loved the Vampyre and the Mirage. But he was always a Yank, always under stress. He would keep the pressure bottled inside and release it at the strangest, most inappropriate times, this sudden lashing fury, which I couldn't understand. He thought he was expected to perform better than anyone else. He believed he could. That kind of pressure, I know, destroyed many of our friends. And then there was Southeast Asia. Australian troops were leaving in larger and larger numbers. Droves of them. Who had ever heard of SEATO before? Therrien thought that when we got back to the States, it wouldn't be long before he was heading over there.

I felt myself the foreigner when I was in Australia. True, they spoke English, but it wasn't a language I knew. Australians were hardheaded and independent. They might seem, on the surface, friendly and warm. But I was alone there. Therrien's attempts at understanding this almost always came off as a basic indifference. Plus the fact that he was almost always gone on alert. Exercises. Tactical maneuvers. I'd spent all our years together raising our child. I was tired. I couldn't keep raising him by myself. The March of Folly was marching on.

That time at the station was a reprieve. A chance to know each other. Wife and husband, mother, a sense of our son. I remember, one day, an outing on horseback. A four-, maybe five-hour trip. At the end of the fourth hour, Dante's horse broke free and cantered off over a wide, flat plain. Dante's voice was a muffled cry for help. The horse disappeared in a thick wood—about as thick a forest as I've seen in that part of the country. I saw him lean into the saddle, stretching out for the bridle; terrified, holding on for all he was worth. The wind whipping the mane.

Therrien broke from our group and chased after him. Some of the other workers followed close behind. But Dante was gone. Vanished. I was frantic.

By the time we got back to the station, the owner had promised to take all of his four-wheel-drive Jeeps out immediately to search for him. "Not to worry—we'll find 'im!" As he was saying this, some of the hands were unstrapping the saddles, and loosening the bits of our mounts. In one huge stampede, the horses turned and bounded down toward a large pond several hundred yards away. Their flanks were foamy with salt and sweat. They plunged into the pond for a midday bath.

And just as suddenly as they hit the water, the shape of a tan palomino flared down from the trees, straddled by the bouncing figure of the rider. Without bothering to pause, both horse and rider leapt for the pond. The splash was tremendous, like a cannonball from a high dive. Dante fell off the horse, laughing and screaming. The water frothed and churned. Wet manes, tossing heads, glistening bodies. The bobbing form of my son in their midst; there was his clear, high laughter and his shouts as he splashed water over the other horses or threw his arms around the strong neck of his own horse, as if he wanted to be, as if he could be, one of them, forever.

•

I've often wondered about the right way to tell a story. We begin here, proceed along smoothly with flair, have a tidy ending, and then it's over. You begin with a memory, knowing how memory is a distortion, and then try to recount the days that have numbered and fallen. Most of them are gone. If I thought of the directions in our lives that led us to this place, I'd be astounded: misplaced ideas and tangents, the notions of purpose spinning wildly off. It becomes a difficult, uncomfortable thing.

It seems funny to me now. Because I do have trouble remembering. Some time after my first or second "breakdown" (and what exactly is that supposed to mean?—there's no gentler term to use—disassociation? nervous disorder?) a doctor told me that the way to begin again was to remember. I never thought it would be this difficult.

In some ways I had no choice. I had a boy to take care of, a husband who was never home, a home that was always a strange and new place we would always be leaving from. I think now of what I could, would do differently. I have nothing to offer.

Now I sit in the huge vault of our living room in this Tehran villa and stare at nothing. The clock ticks on the mantel. The only life is the sound of chimes. Time moves, but I am not a part of it. Sometimes I put on a false face, try to act bravely in my letters to Dante. When Therrien comes home in the evening *he'll step silently onto the landing, climb the few steps to this room, flick on a tableside lamp to watch me. Even then, I can see from his face, with that look of rare distraction, how worried he is.*

Always I'll ask him to turn off the light. And he will do it. We will sit in the dark opposite each other.

There is something happening in his life apart from me. Something that he will not tell me. I don't mean supporting a mistress, nonsense like that. There is something happening in his work and he will not tell me. Something evil, corrupt. And it burns him, eats away at him.

I see the outline of his face, the angular cheek and jaw, the line of his somehow beautiful scars. It isn't real. His hand on mine.

•

When Dante came out of the airport terminal that night, I didn't recognize him. The first shock I noticed was his blond hair—it was almost white! Much thinner than I'd ever seen him. He was a giant next to his father, or next to anyone else for that matter. Maybe to compensate for how completely apart from the others he stood, he stooped from the shoulders, rolled his hunched frame forward. It didn't change a thing. Except to make him look older, aged.

But he stayed close to his father, as though he were hiding under a wing. His face was emotionless. His head kept turning to look at people and sounds. He stared at one young woman who ran through the airport and jumped into her boyfriend's arms. Her lips were a fiery red. Black stockings, skirt so tight it looked like her rear was going to explode. The whole number. Totally tasteless. Why do mothers think this at just about the worst time? Why do I think this? I know he hadn't seen me yet. In one way I recognized the sensation of his twisting head immediately: beyond the wonder of his own sexuality, beyond that—he was entering a new universe, one we are never prepared for. Mehrabad was only the entrance.

He is my son. He will always be my son. Even here, standing like strangers, separated by the expanse of terminal, he is the child who dropped out of the Maine woods, full of stories and creatures torn from his wild ideas. He is the one always getting into trouble, for all the wrong reasons. I started to cry. As if I had already lost him.

To me, Dante will always be that little boy.

"Hi, Mom," he said. He was smiling, but he was equally distant and *formal. I'll bet he probably calls a squad to attention during drill practice in the same tone.*

He reached down to hug me, and his arms engulfed me. I felt like a rag doll in those arms, as if there were enough strength to snap me in half. This will always amaze me. I hugged him back and stopped crying.

"Welcome home, Dante," was all I said. Then Dante turned to Ghossemi, who waited by the trunk of the car to load the two bags of luggage. "Hello. My name is Dante. I've heard a lot of great things about you, Ghossemi." I was thrilled when I heard him say this. Even if Dante never wrote, almost did nothing to keep in touch with his own family, he knew about Ghossemi.

Ghossemi smiled broadly and with pleasure. Instead of taking the proffered hand, he snapped to attention. Completely serious, Ghossemi's hand flew to his temple in a sharp salute. *I thought I was going to die. Great! I began looking around. It's bad enough people know Therrien's in the military. But my son! If anyone sees this, if anyone is watching, our lives are in danger.*

Inside the car he was quiet for most of the ride home. We passed Aryamehr Monument, and he seemed very impressed. The sight of the city at night is lovely. And deadly. The traffic is murderous. No one pays attention to traffic lights—considered advisories only—or street lanes. At night you see none of this. We turned up Eisenhower Avenue and headed north of the city. Home.

He slept for eighteen hours. When he woke, he was restless, even nervous. He wanted to talk privately to me about his year at the Academy—I could sense that—but he kept on backing off, cutting himself off, saying maybe some other time. I wasn't going to push him. We took him to the usual sights: Golestan Palace, University Park, the Imperial Vault—the crown jewels. We were invited to an embassy function, and I thought it would be good for him to see General Magyar again.

But he was never comfortable. When he asked our permission to walk through the streets by himself, I immediately said no. But Therrien insisted it would be fine. Dante was just a young college kid; no one had any reason to bother him. And so we let him. He would come home some afternoons excited and full of talk about what he had seen that day.

It was Therrien's idea for Dante to climb that mountain. I knew that Dante had learned to rock climb in Colorado, and he had told us a bit of his experiences climbing and hiking in the Rockies. I was afraid this trip would *be dangerous. Things have been restless here—even with all the quiet in the papers, you can sense it, feel it. Especially since that awful thing in Tabriz . . . But Therrien, once again, assured me that it would be fine. "It's a once-in-a-lifetime chance, Beatrice," became a refrain with him.*

General Sadeghian, president of the Iranian Mountaineering Federation, had found a reliable, safe guide for the trip. There need be nothing to worry about.

The morning before he left, I tiptoed into his room. The light was pouring down from the Elburz. It was just after dawn. I stood over his bed. Just stood there, listening to my son's breath. He was facing the window, turned away.

He didn't wake. He turned slightly, and rolled over. I stepped back into the shadow of the armoire. On his night stand, there was a Xeroxed copy of some pages written in English and Persian script. The title at the top of one page said something about the shah.

Now that he's been gone for two days, I have been wanting to ask him what that manuscript was. When I went into his room later that morning, I couldn't find it. I know I was just snooping around, but I was pretending even to myself then that I was just going in to pick things up a bit.

He had left his room in perfect order, as if he had never been there. When I opened the drawer of his nightstand, I found his passport, face down.

And I've started to worry again.

۱۰

Tehran, 17 August 1978

Dante,

A short while ago—this is a horrible thing—some people were locked in a theater, a movie theater, and they were burned. 400 people! Now the awful rumor going around is that it was SAVAK who did it, but, of course, you'd never see that accusation in the papers or television. The riots are spreading in Isfahan, Shiraz, Ahvaz, Ahlabad, everywhere.

While you were gone, with Asadollah, the shah spoke out against the horrible events. He had called for free elections last June, more leaning to Western democracy. It seemed to work then, weeks ago. It was so quiet. And now it seems worse than your father and I have ever seen it.

We have been told not to worry, that this is a minor unrest. But though we had no idea what would happen in Kabul, we know what could explode in Tehran. This is our home, we live here, we have many good friends. The MAAG command has said not to worry about potential risk to dependents. This is all an "internal conflict." I want you to know, though, that we have seriously discussed the option of my leaving for Athens or Frankfurt, until things calm down or until there is some more permanent solution.

I am not comfortable with this idea. But I am not comfortable with the idea of just sitting on a time bomb and waiting for something to go off! We will do what WE feel is right, including the decision to start sending household goods back, preparing to leave for good.

Your father has not said anything to me, but I think he has seriously considered coming to the end of his career in the military. He was very disappointed in the way things ended up here—with General Magyar. I think he knew this was coming and just wouldn't tell me. He's a very quiet man, your father. If he decides to quit, I'll be happy. Thirty years is a long time. I'm sure that he will have few problems finding a position with an overseas firm, since that's what he seems to enjoy most. Perhaps we'll just quit for good and buy ourselves that dairy farm in Vermont we always talk about—wouldn't THAT be something! Set a few black & whites up on the hill!

THE GHAZAL OF MEMORY

Your father loves you and I do as well. Already we miss having you around here, even having you with us during all the tension and uncertainty.

with much love,

your mother,
Beatrice

11

30 January 1979

Dante,

This has to be a quick note—have to get it out before the mail run tonight. First, I want to tell you not to worry. Last, I want to say that it's all over here—nothing more can be done. It's obvious now that the shah won't be coming back, not any time soon. I read in *Stars & Stripes* today that it's for sure, Khomeini, I mean, coming here tomorrow. The people are going wild. From my window in the study, I can see much of the city—on fire. This is worse than "Black Friday" back in September. They were burning the city in protest then. Now I think these idiots are going to really let it all go—they're delirious that the ayatollah's coming. The flames are just outrageous. The fools may torch this whole town!

I want to tell you not to worry, and here I am describing Tehran on fire . . . I'm sorry. Distracted lately. Pissed off. There could have been a lot we could have done to help here. No one paid attention. Just sat on our butts and pulled the draw chain. And that asshole Andrew Young—have you heard about this—calling Khomeini a "saint"! Unbelievable!

It's really strange, Dante. Within a month after you left here, it all turned off. Gone. The White Revolution. The Great Civilization. Magyar getting fired. That idiocy in Jaleh Square. None of us were smart enough to see it.

We've—the U.S., I mean—had connections here. But we're total strangers. Total, complete strangers. Wonder how many other countries are going to roll over and play possum when the time comes. We'll shrug it off, say we didn't know. Do you remember General Sadeghian? Asking if Jeff Davis was the president? And those dancing soldiers? God, I thought I would bust a kidney I was ready to laugh so bad that day!

Your mother is fine. I haven't seen her since Hellenikon and Christmas, but we're in touch mostly every day. She's much safer there. Letters, phone calls from the comm post at MAAG headquarters. I don't want you to worry. I knew things were bad, when you were here in August, but I'd no idea they'd go insane like this. In a way I'm kind of happy we were ignorant of it. Probably never would have let you climb that mountain—now you'll never regret you did. Your mother tells me to tell you that she's OK. Don't worry. Especially about me. Been in a lot rougher spots than this.

Just so damn angry I could piss blood! We've done irrepairable—is this a word, don't even have a dictionary with me!—damage. We seemed to care only about selling tow missiles, and sidewinders, Cobras, Phantoms, Falcons, Tomcats. Hell, this country was starving, and we watched the shah spend all his bucks on making bigger, bigger, bigger.

I really respected him, still do. But he was a bit of a fool. He really loved this country, never spent a dime on riot control. Thought his people loved him here, too. Course he never took time out to see what they really needed, things like houses, food. I can't blame him for being so blind—this city is one of the filthiest in the world, but inside those walls, those high walls of every house that line every street, those beautiful courtyards, those peaceful homes. Step inside those walls and you're in one of the most beautiful places on earth. Did I ever tell you that the rose came from Persia? Always know your people, Dante. Know them & pay attention & care about them. If this sounds like a lecture it's because it is: you won't be worth anything as an officer if you just do your job as best you can—you've got to care about your people, Dante.

This has got to be one of the most rambling letters I've written in years. I'm frayed out, tired. I'm not living at home anymore, can't go back anymore. Don't worry about the stuff, household goods I mean. Most of it was shipped out in October when it became pretty obvious that the smoke wasn't gonna just clear away the debris. All the rugs are gone & in the mail. Some of 'em will probably be stolen by customs. We'll get some, finally. What's left in the house doesn't matter now.

I want you to understand why & how this happened, Dante, though I don't think it will ever be too obvious to anyone, & whether or not you read the papers or magazines doesn't matter because mostly those are reporters who don't know a goddamned thing. You know the story of Noah, the Ark? (Obvious question.) Well, that's how it happened here. Tehran as Mt. Ararat, the few of us Americans clinging to the rudder of the sinking, overloaded boat. The only difference here is that the forty days keeps happening over, & over, & over, & over again. Tehran, Isfahan, Shiraz, Zahedan, Babol, Mashhad, Yazd, Qom. It started in Qom. January, I think

THE GHAZAL OF MEMORY

it was, *Etela'at* wrote this piece about Khomeini, saying he was an outsider, a stranger, a—Allah forbid—foreigner. His grandfather came from India, it was obvious he was working with Communists. Well, the people in Qom didn't think that was too cute. Qom is Khomeini's hometown and it's where he started calling for the shah to go way back in '63. The people gathered on the streets at dusk, to talk about this article, to read it to the others who couldn't read. The people just wanted to talk, just talk. The police had a fit. I don't know if you remember now, but that day you told me about when the policeman started shoving you outside the women's store, when all those people were standing around watching? Well it's because it's forbidden to gather in public, just like it was forbidden, used to be anyway—to say the shah's name in public, or use words like *oppressive, madness, fall, instability, screw, dark, flat on your feet, withered, all dried up, insane, outrageous, parched, quicksand, something's wrong here, something's got to give, wallow in it, blind, dumb, deaf*—what we in the States would just simply call *snafu*. The people just wanted to talk. The police didn't know how to handle it. They opened fire on them from the rooftops.

They wrapped the bodies in white sheets, put them on the biers on the square. People started crying. Wailing. Then it's silent. Forty days of mourning. Forty days later, relatives, family, friends gather to commemorate the dead ones. People get angry. Crowds of them. & explode. They go crazy. And then it spreads. Tabriz, that was the worst. They had a rally for the shah—300,000 there. Screaming. Shouting. Didn't do much good. In September, just after you left—did I mention this before?—people gathered in a place here in Tehran called Jaleh Square. They fired on them from helicopters! Can you believe that? Bodies all over the place—children dipping their schoolbooks in blood—there's this incredible fascination with blood—and running screaming through the streets. I saw a tape—they'd never show this on the television—a man trapped in the center of the square; he was in a wheelchair, couldn't get out because of the bodies in place, he kept turning and turning in a circle. Three snipers on three different roofs just took their time: one cross hair for his head, one for his gut, one for his heart. When they were done, they just left him there.

Do you know what xenophobia is, Dante? It's a fear of foreigners, of strangers, of what's different, outside. All our lives Beatrice and I have taught you never to do that, to be open to other worlds, other ways of seeing. That's what knowledge, education mean. They didn't learn that here. The newspaper *Kayhan* kept on insisting that the Ayatollah was wrong, that these riots were caused by "spoiled children," "Islamic Marxists." After a while the people just stopped listening. All of them: students, businessmen, bazaaris, religious groups, Tudeh. The pressure was bound to snap. I heard a few days ago that the Ayatollah would make phone calls from Paris, they would record his calls, and broadcast this cassette tape through speakers & minarets all over the cities & villages. A phone call, can you believe that? Last month they marched to Shahyad Aryamehr Monument—do you remember that place? Two million of them! They're calling it Freedom Square now. A bomb went off in a school bus last month in Isfahan—American kids, no one hurt. Larry Weaver, the one who briefed you about the country at MAAG, was shot last week. He'll be OK, but it was pretty scary. That's what upsets me the most. We just let it go. We just let it all go.

They could have done so much here. We could have. The general who came in from NATO? Talked a lot, consoled a lot, did nothing. Told the Iranian generals, the CIA, hell, probably even the President, there was nothing to worry about. Alexander Haig, the boss up at NATO, has called it quits forever, official resignation, because of this business. In the past two months, three different generals from Supreme Command Headquarters asked me if I wanted to sell some of our household goods, since it was true, wasn't it, that we'd all be leaving soon?

Guess this wasn't such a short note . . .

Did you ever wonder what it looked like, Dante, when crazy Nero torched Rome? It looked like this, with the sky lit up with gold, & when the Imam touches down at Mehrabad tomorrow, there may be nothing left.

We'll be home soon.

Your father

۱۲

He told me that the guide had been chosen with care. Everything was prepared. That is surely in God's hands now, as it has always been.

I do not know what to make of him, the son of the Diamond. Sitting there, that day in my office at the Imperial Officers' Club, straight as a black rod, quoting poetry in the same breath as his knowledge of aircraft—and mountains.

Perhaps he will live. He knew the Sháh-Námé.

۱۳

In my country, many centuries ago, the king named Solomon drew together the five hundred spirits of magic we call the jinn from his kingdom. The king ordered these spirits to be banished from his land. Thus, in exile, they fled to the mountains of Zagros. The adjenne took with them five hundred virgins from Europe as their brides and came to settle in the place we call as Kurdistan. And we are called the children of the jinn.

He should have known. This mountain is filled with all the adjenne, peris, the devil and his daughters. *You can see their foul yellow breath, and smell the stench of their mischief, rising from the caves. This is a peak too sacred to ascend. You will reach the top, but not the summit. Why do you strike me? Why do you strike me?* Tchera mi-zeni mano?

Last night, I bowed and prayed for him. I do not want this to happen. I knelt before the flame, murmuring it over and over again, bismi'llah-o 'rrahmané 'rahim, la hawla wa la qovvata illa billah. *I know and knew its power working. I felt their presence, the unrest of their sleep. The candles burned to keep them off. He did not understand my words, but he surely knew when I told him to still beneath the walking dagger's path. I prayed that night. I did not sleep. I spread the rice. I said the words.*

I damn myself for having family in that city. It is a long walk from our country. Why did they have to leave? This boy I should call a man, he did not understand with his square tongue; but he listened to me. He trusted me. He did not drink the water. I gave him tea and sugar and watched him piss all his water out.

How long will this torment burn in me? It was never in my hands. He wanted to share life and I spit on it. He was young, and strong; he thought he could keep the path beside me. But no man—or thing—has ever touched the prints of my feet before the wind erased them.

Nerezi has said: if he stumbles, to let him fall. If he falls, to let him die. Let the son of the she-bitch die.

Part Five

Kooh Damávand

کوه دماوند

1 August

They had not been getting along, Gozameh and Asadollah. Fighting for attention, they passed through periods of angry banter and then silence. Asadollah would cross his arms, lean back in the seat, sometimes tap his knuckles on the bulletproof pane, wink at me, and grin. Gozameh would grip down on the wheel, grind his jaw, stare straight ahead. Sometimes he would point to something in the distance, and tell me, "Master Dante," that I should look. And I was happy to look at the beautiful, unreal land.

We had stood on the street corner that morning, and Gozameh had told me twice that I should not trust this man—I should let him prove his trust to me. I had told Gozameh that I had trusted only a few people in my life, and I said that I knew that that did not sound like a good thing to say. My mother and father had raised me to be honest, and to expect that honesty in others, and when it did not happen, to be very unforgiving. "But I trust you, Gozameh; I will always trust you." He smiled at that.

General Sadeghian had told me Asadollah was a good, strong guide. I watched him as he looked out the window of the car. He was old, only this morning, back in Tehran. But already he was changing. He was more relaxed; his grin was less strained, appeared less often, no longer forced. His body had lengthened, if that's possible; his legs uncurled to their full length and rested on the floor. His face beamed as we curved through the high passes. I thought: *he's coming home, to the mountains. He's happy now.*

No, they had not gotten along during the drive from Tehran—no short jaunt to the mountains. The road, though it was smooth asphalt, wound up through the Elburz like a snake, following the contours of least resistance. It had not been an easy highway to build. I was embarrassed to think it then, but I wondered—had foreign engineers been imported to build even this? We passed the ski resort of Ab-Ali. Gozameh had pointed it out with pride. *This is where the foreigners come to enjoy the mountains of Iran.*

There was a bulldozer working at the entrance to the resort. The Caterpillar's jaws dug into the hard earth, churning up rocks and black dirt. I saw the chair lifts, sloping down into the basin of a valley. *The Alps of Iran. The place where all the world comes to jet set.* I smiled at that, and Gozameh smiled back. Asadollah stared out the window as we passed, and said nothing. He shook his head slightly as Gozameh spoke.

Funny, I thought—it was the reason I smiled—I read about this place before I came here; I studied it. But it wasn't until the day I dropped from twenty thousand feet over Mehrabad that I even realized this country had so many mountains—stark, imposing mountains. I had thought of Iran as a land of unrelenting desert, arid plains, of poverty and incredible wealth, domes and palaces where the emperor and his family strolled the gardens every evening among the nightingales.

I thought of how we would look from the air, from a great distance— our sky blue Ford twisting up the mountain pass toward the village where we would begin our hike toward Damávand. I had only seen that mountain once—from the air and from a distance. I imagined the sprawling plateaus of rock and desert; the clefts of canyons falling to the earth; the still streams and rivers. I imagined the reign of mountains rising out of nothing, like a sacred place, a citadel of height. And the single cone of Damávand rising out of that—extinct volcano, a peak frozen in snow and ice.

Asadollah sat in the backseat beside me. Every few minutes he would motion to something he thought I should know. He was doing his best to teach me Farsi, and I was a fairly poor student. Gozameh, both eyes on the road ahead, would listen intently, and then interpret what was being said. *Gardaneh*—Asadollah would say, pointing to a break in the fissure of rock before us. "It is this saddle," Gozameh would offer.

And then I saw it, perfectly. I thought of the saddle of a horse. And long after we had disappeared from it, I could see it: the saddle of a mountain, the depression in the ridge of stone.

We were following the course of a river. The water flowed over sharp boulders. There were trees, too. I was surprised to see them. *"Rudkháneh,"* Asadollah would slap my arm, point, and say.

"He means a river, doesn't he?" I asked Gozameh.

"Yes, he is correct," Gozameh answered. "This is a river-stream."

I didn't really care if I could follow all the words. It was the sound of their voices, and the sound was a kind of wonder. I looked at the landscape fanning beneath us. This could be anywhere: the high Sierras, the Collegiate peaks. It didn't *look* that different from the Rockies.

KOOH DAMAVAND

If I ignored the huts, and the people on the roadside, I could say that I had never left America. But then came the sound of their voices, their soft tongues, and I thought it was only a matter of interpretation. This was how you made a country, a culture, a language. *Maybe, Diamond, it's not all that tough. You're just trying to make it that.* And then came the flood of voices, and hands; their arguments.

Asadollah grabbed my backpack and began going through my supplies. "He is fulfilled that you have brought the rope, and these pee-tongs," Gozameh said. "He will find a strong face for you to scale during your climb. But you have brought too many clothes. You will not need them." Gozameh turned and yelled something to Asadollah.

"Do not do this, I am telling him not to do this."

Asadollah had pulled all my clothes from the pack and stuffed them on the window ledge behind him. He was using my pants and shirts and underwear to block out the sun. He nudged me and then leaned and tucked his nose into his armpit. He grinned. It was better to smell the stench of one's own sweat, he seemed to say, better to use the excess to block out the sun. Beatrice, who had always worried about the least things in her life, and who, I had to admit, knew the least about rock climbing and hiking, had insisted that I take as many articles of clothing as I could fit, or stuff inside.

He pointed to my jeans, meaning that they would be the only pants I'd need. He took one sweater, heavy with wool, put it aside. He grabbed a pair of socks, one change of underwear, and a T-shirt. He placed them in the space of the seat between us. He pulled his own pack from the floor, a knitted wool rucksack. The straps for his shoulders were worn, frayed with use. He opened it, nodding his head for me to look inside. There was almost nothing in there. There were no clothes. And then, seeing that I understood what he had wanted me to see, he closed the flap.

What he wanted me to see was that we were going to travel very lightly together. And, after a week of packing and hiking, both of us were going to smell very ripe.

He was upset when he found the canned goods at the bottom of my bag. He pulled a can of cherries out. Groaned, curled his lips, rolled his eyes. He said something, and whatever he said ignited Gozameh. Gozameh lifted both hands from the wheel, turned and threw his arms into the backseat. *First he's going to strangle Asadollah; and second, as he's killing him with patience and infinite attention, we are going to depart the road, fall off this cliff, and plummet to our deaths.*

Asadollah became equally vicious in his argument. He shook his right hand. The palm of it was open. His voice was hard and certain. He took his open palm and pressed it to his stomach. He pressed hard into the wall of his flesh. Gozameh turned back to the wheel. When Asadollah found the graham cracker crust, he pulled it out and flung it into the front where it landed by Gozameh's thigh. He said something curt. Gozameh winced.

Asadollah returned to his window, Gozameh to his wheel. After a while, Gozameh spoke. "I am sorry, Master Dante, I am in fault. This man, this guide, he has spoken the truth. You cannot take all this food. You do not need it. The cans are much too heavy, and the fruits within too rich. He tells me that he will not let you eat for twenty hours before the summit. The food within your stomach will blow up"—and saying this he pressed the palm of his own hand to his soft stomach—"as you rise in air. You will be very ill with richness."

"I am sorry, Master Dante. I want you to be well."

•

The road had twisted and unfurled like a tongue. The day was cool compared to what I had experienced in Tehran. The temperature was in the low nineties. Gozameh drove with the air conditioner on. Asadollah did not object. He did not try to open his window; he knew what the shields meant.

We came to a flat, thin valley. There was a river, and I murmured *"rudkhâneh,"* and Gozameh said, "quite so." Plane trees lined the edge of flowing water. The valley was green, and I was surprised to see it. The pass we had descended from was filled with clumps of snow, and fracturings of rock and dirt.

"*Kooh*," Asadollah said. He sat up, pointing, slapping my thigh. "*Kooh Damávand!*"

It rose out of the distance—long veins of white scalloping its face. The south ridge looked as if part of it were missing, had flung itself into the air during an eruption.

There is no other way to say it. I was enthralled.

•

We drove to the village of Damávand. It was a popular place for the wealthy of Tehran to reside in leisure, Gozameh said. The village was simple, and there were a few small adobe houses off to the side of the road as we climbed toward a small structure that stood above the road. We were still inside the fertile valley; with the windows closed, I could only imagine the whispering of the leaves, the sound of their green faces flickering like aspens in light. We drove through a wooded ravine, crossed a bridge over a stream, and started to climb.

The building itself was an octagon. It stood on a flat plateau, and it seemed, to me, that the plateau had been built to support the shrine. I was sure that it was a shrine. "The tomb of Shaykh Sheblí," Gozameh said, answering my question. A tenth-century man of mystics and governor of Damávand. The octagonal shapes represented his powers. The tower was a mirror, as Gozameh explained it, of the twin towers of the tomb at Kharraqan.

Gozameh told me that we must do one thing before we arrived at Pol-e-moon. He stopped the car, walked to open my door, and I got out. I walked beside him to the tower. I thought that Asadollah had waited behind, but when I turned one face of the octagon, trailing Gozameh, I saw Asadollah, standing there. He held a book, reverently, in his hands. He kissed the book. "Do as we do," Gozameh said.

We walked together, circling the tower. Three times. I was between the two men, and each arm was linked with the arm of another. Asadollah to my right; Gozameh, my left. "He is going to say a *talqin*," Gozameh offered, "a *do'a-ye talqin*." He did not explain what that meant.

As we circled, I thought of oxen turning the grindstone of a mill. But the tower was still. On our fourth circle, we stopped halfway around, across from the point where we had started.

"He will say the *do'a* now."

Gozameh moved away, and Asadollah turned to face me. He motioned me to bend slightly. "This is the Ghor'án," Gozameh said. He said it so softly it was like a whisper. "This is the holiest of books."

I bent, and Asadollah whispered something in my ear. I didn't understand. I only felt the rhythm and heat. Then, when he was finished, he took one of my arms and pulled me up. He stretched to his full height, placed the book on my head, whispered another invocation, took the book away, and kissed me three times; each time, the bristle of his lips landed on an opposite cheek.

And then Gozameh stepped forward, placed his palms on my shoulders, and kissed me in the same way.

"You must be strong, Master Dante," he said. "You must be perfect. I think I need to say you must be pure. But the meaning of the two—how you call the shades—I am afraid, they are in doubt."

•

My introduction to the village of Pol-e-moon began with one image: a naked child atop a fire engine–red picnic table. He was pointing to a woman. The woman pulled her *chádor* tight against herself and turned from the rest of us. She wept in violent sobs. Each time the child pointed he screamed, and she shook, harder.

Gozameh stood and walked over to them. He was concerned, but he also wanted to keep away. The child stood on the table, waving the naked flesh of his sex to the people in the restaurant. The uproar grew.

A man, apparently the husband of the offended woman, ran from the counter at the far end of the room. He grabbed a smaller, darker man, apparently the father of the boy, and they came to fists.

When one fist slammed into the other's face, there was the soft thud and the crack of a tooth or a bone. Blood ran from one ear of the smaller man. The sweat stood out on his cheeks.

The child just wouldn't shut up. He began suddenly to take on the wail of a banshee, and reached down to his genitals, pulling, hard, as if trying to rip them away. The skin of his pubis was like wax—glistening and milky white. He pointed at the man who was crushing his father.

The man pulled a knife. Gozameh, who stood off to the side, yelled something. A wave of men ran over and pulled them apart. I saw the knife in his hands. The crowd swarmed over them, and his arm flew up, the knife flashed, and suddenly there was a cluster of hands reaching for the blade.

Then it was over. Everyone returned to their picnic tables and their meals. The woman who had been crying ran outside to find her husband, who had disappeared in the crowd. The naked child ran after her.

While this was happening, Asadollah grunted and slurped his way through his meal. He looked up once, and then sank his head back to his plate. He was disinterested, unconcerned; this had nothing to do with him. His plate of *joojeh kabob,* the chicken piled on the wealth of buttered rice, the flat sheets of *nán* to sop the grease with—these were important. Especially since I was paying.

I wondered how often he ate, even a simple meal like this. He looked healthy and strong. He had bright, shifting eyes; I thought I could trust him. He smiled a lot, and he looked at me when he did. *"Keili-koub,"* he would point to his food and say. I smiled back. *"Joojeh kabob?"* I asked, wondering if that was what he meant. He laughed, gripped my shoulder. His hands were like a vice.

By the time Gozameh had returned, Asadollah had gone for his second plate of kebab. It was good stuff; he was hungry. He listened as Gozameh spoke, as if he understood what was being said.

"It is a sad thing, what has happened," said Gozameh. "Not necessary."

"Well, what exactly *did* happen?" I asked. The restaurant was quiet, save for the buzzing of voices, the scraping of plates.

"I have spoken with the driver of the bus," Gozameh replied. "He is a cousin of—ah, and what do we have here?"

He broke off his sentence and smiled. I turned and saw a child standing beside me at the table. She placed the flat of her palm on my thigh. She held a glass in her hand. I thought she was begging, that she wanted me to buy her something to drink.

"She is bringing you this, Master Dante. It is a drink called *doogh.*"

"Please, you must take it," he said. "It is very good fortune when a stranger, especially a child, brings you water of the earth. It means that there is no expectation of return of thanks, but that you will return on your travels in goodness."

"Goodness?"

"Good health, good health," he said.

"And how do I say thank you?" I asked.

"Just say it."

So I turned, leaned over, and looked at her. Her eyes were jet dark. Her face said nothing. "Thank you," I said. "Welcome," she said in reply. She smiled and then began laughing. She ran off.

"Keili-koub," Asadollah exclaimed.

"Is this something you eat, Gozameh? You know I wish I could say something intelligent to him."

Gozameh erupted in laughter. "No, no, not all. Not to eat, but to be. It means great, fantastic. How would you say—A-OK? He, your guide, is happy because the girl brought you the yogurt water."

"Keili-koub," said Asadollah, smiling.

"*Keili-koub,*" I said. He slapped the table, wiped the grease from his lips with the back of one hand.

I turned back to Gozameh, filled suddenly with exhilaration and new confidence. This trip, I knew it now, was going to be unlike anything I had ever known. Suddenly excited, I said, "Gozameh, I feel good about this—I mean this whole trip—except for what happened over there." I moved my head back to where the fight had been. "Which was?" I raised my eyebrows.

"Ah, yes, well," Gozameh stammered. "It seems the child is not only young but confused. He has said a bad thing. And the husband of the woman is most upset."

"What did the child say?"

Gozameh was embarrassed. He didn't want to tell me. Finally, he offered, "The child claimed that this man did not have the member—the instrument, you know . . ."

"The member?"

"Yes. Well, I suppose one does call it 'a' and not 'the.'" Gozameh stood from the table and pointed to his crotch. "Do you understand?"

"You mean a penis, don't you? And how did the child know that?"

He was really red. "Yes, this is what I mean. A pee-nus. The child claimed that the husband did not have a pee-nus, and that his woman was possessor of such . . . I do not know how he could know of such a secret. It was, I think, a bad joke. She is most upset."

"I guess so."

•

We had to say good-bye. I felt badly. I had grown close to Gozameh the past few days. He had shown concern for me. I was the foreigner, and he had been the first of that country to care for me. I knew that he could not stay; my father needed him.

I thought of calling Beatrice to tell her that I was all right. I likely had enough rials to call back to Tehran. Gozameh could help me, tell me what I should do. But I did nothing.

We stood outside in the dust and sun. A small bus had pulled up to the side of the restaurant. The man who had been attacked in the restaurant lay on a makeshift stretcher of canvas tied to two thin branches. A small crowd hovered over him. Another man leaned over him, pressing a cloth into the blood of his wound. He'd been stabbed after all.

KOOH DAMAVAND

I thought, at first, that he was unconscious. But he moaned when the other man pressed his stomach too closely. His eyes were closed.

A third man, probably the bus driver, began moving his arms in tight circles, shouting in an excited frenzy. He seemed to be telling the others to lift the victim, and they did. One arm fell from the victim's side and trailed in the dirt as the stretcher rose. The men who moved him were patient and concerned. But they could not move the stretcher up and through the door of the bus without having to tilt it; and if they did that, the knifed man would fall. The man who had tried to staunch the flow of blood with the bundle of cloth bent over the stretcher and gathered the victim in his arms and carried him up the steps. The diesel backfired into life, and the tires loosed a few stones in the rutted path. They drove off.

Asadollah had hardly paid attention. He kicked his heels at the ground, spoke quietly with Gozameh, and finally, turning to face the knoll of hills that rose above us, he opened his arms and spread his palms—trying to encompass the perfection of it all.

Gozameh had wanted to wait. He said that there could be something he could do to help the knifed man. But, equally, I think he wanted to stay with me. He looked very sad. He would not look in my eyes when I spoke to him.

Finally, he asked that I walk to the car with him. I put out my hand. He ignored it and threw his arms around me. He gave a tight squeeze and then kissed me on the cheek.

"Be well with your guide, Master Dante," he said. "You will learn to speak."

Before closing the door of the car, he said something else: *"Mordeh nabashi. Zendeh bashi."*

I did not know what he meant. I saw him then, with his sad dark eyes behind the bullet-proof window, and thought of how I had learned about these people's history and culture and still knew next to nothing about them as people. And as he drove off, I thought of how I did not even know the words, in his tongue, the music of the angels, for thank you.

٢

Asadollah wanted to hike. After a few minutes of silence, he uncrossed his arms, grunted, pointed to my pack, and strode off. The restaurant was empty. A few chickens nosed through the dirt, or pecked at my feet. I strapped my chest and waist buckles. Feeling the weight of the pack, I was glad that he had intervened in the car. My pack was still heavy. I grinned—Beatrice would be even more worried when Gozameh drove up to the house with the last of my underwear still lining the window ledge.

I turned and gave one last look. It was a small place, broken and rundown. The stucco had fallen from the wall in hundreds of places. *A year from now, will this even be here? Or will it last another century?*

I followed Asadollah through a small courtyard in the back. He walked with determination, a sense of direction. Places to get to. He never once turned to see if I were coming after him.

•

I've always wondered what exactly happens when you hike into the mountains, to a new place. And with a new companion, the equation becomes even more uncertain. I never say all that much. Walking, feeling the rhythm and the burden, I match my walk to the stride of another. I am, naturally, a slow hiker, the way I am naturally a slow reader—I like to mull over the enjoyment, forgetting I exist for awhile. Walking with others, I match their pace so that I can forget them as well, so that we do not have to speak, so that we can disappear. Now I was in a situation where I could not speak at all.

•

We had been walking for several hours. The sun was soon going to set. We were in a canyon, following a road that wound through the pass. Several trucks had passed, and the drivers had leaned out and seemed to ask Asadollah if we needed a lift. He always shook his head no.

We reached a small plateau before entering the canyon glade. The view of the valley beneath us was stark: pastures and grazing land for sheep, a few cattle. When we had driven through it, it had been green, fertile. Now it all looked burned, too much used, too many times, and could never return what it had once offered up. I saw the shapes of small peaks rising over the valley, and behind, the edge of the desert stretching all the way south to the Strait of Hormuz. The peaks were barren sentinels rising straight from the valley floor. The light had touched their faces, and they glowed in stone. At the edge of sight, where the last of the peaks melted, the few trees that grew had become dots, a hazy blur, small points of distant black.

We entered the canyon, and the cliffs rose sharply on either side. The sun cut through to the high edges of the walls, but we walked in shadow. It was cooler here, and I was glad. A dark grass grew sparsely at the edge of the road; small tufts of it rose out of the dirt every few yards. The walls of the canyon were fractured into millions of lined veins. The light rarely touched this place during the day. It was bad rock to climb on—it would crumble in your hands.

We came to a small cleft in the canyon. A single tree grew there, its bark rippled like hickory. A few people stood under the tree, waiting. A woman was striking her daughter with a bag, and the daughter was screaming, tired of insult. She kicked her mother in the side, spilling their groceries—a few pomegranates and nuts, a bag of herbs like tea.

A man, unsteady on his legs, stood over a bush, pissing. Asadollah looked away as we walked past him. In the lap of the tree, another dark-faced man squatted on his haunches and stared at me. We climbed behind and above them, following the thin suggestion of a trail. Asadollah walked slower, seeming to think about something that troubled him.

We stopped at the mouth of a small cave. I figured we would spend the night there. I wasn't too happy. The mouth in the rock stank of urine and shit. But the smell seemed to lift as we picked our way through stone, deeper into the rock. There was only a single cast of light that shone at the entrance. I felt the breath of air coming from deeper inside, which meant that there was probably another way out.

He knelt, opened his rucksack, and pulled out a small rug. He looked up to me and said it so quietly it sounded like an apology: *Ma sha'allah.* He didn't have to tell me. I respected him for it, and I was uncomfortable because of it, but with his prayers, maybe, I would have more of a chance to rest as we climbed. I walked out of the cave, took off my pack and waited for him. I heard the murmur of his voice. It didn't bother me, that sound. I'd been told that the faithful prayed five times a day, but, since we were on a journey, perhaps he would stop more often—at every shrine or place where he thought he could express devotion.

I picked up some pebbles and threw them off the ledge. The people who had been waiting were still there, three hundred yards away, a hundred yards below us. I wondered why I would have to rest that much during this hike. He walked quickly, it was true, and I did not like to do that. But, still, I was in the best shape of my life: one hundred push-ups, four hundred sit-ups, a twenty-mile jaunt to Tijuana. That was all behind but still inside me.

Asadollah grabbed the pack and tilted it toward me. He shrugged. It was time to go. We walked back to the tree and a yellow pickup stopped almost immediately: a tiny, beat-up Chevrolet, with LUV decaled on the side.

None of the waiting people moved. Asadollah walked to the cab and leaned over to speak with the driver, then stood up and waved me over. I walked to the bed of the truck and stood there. The pickup was filled with green watermelons; some of them had split. The seeds and fresh juice dribbled through the gateless rear.

There were two men in back. One sat on top of the melons with his knees drawn to his chest. He watched the other man intently, refused to look at me. The other man lay the full length of his short frame on the other melons. It wasn't comfortable.

They didn't seem like Iranians I had seen in Tehran. They dressed like Arabs. Both wore *ghuthrahs:* a double ring of black cord holding their headcloths to their foreheads. The man with his knees drawn wore a dark cotton *thawb,* and it flowed down to his sandaled feet. The man beside was wrapped in a heavy wool burnoose; in the heat of the day, it must have been unbearable. Somehow, knowing I was there, the man rose slightly, to one elbow. He looked at me.

He was an old man. His beard was tired and grey. His flesh sank into the hollowness below the eyes. He whispered something to his companion—perhaps his son—who paused and reached down to the trail of the old man's burnoose and pulled it up to show me: two smashed legs, swollen, ready to burst, purple with infection. I smelled the blood and the stench of his pain. I gagged.

Does anything normal ever happen to people around here?

Asadollah opened the door of the cab and motioned for me to get in. I was surprised when he did not slip in beside me. Instead, he walked to the bed of the truck and apparently told the young man to get out. The driver grinned at me, and then sang in this high whistling call: "Yankee?"

You bet, dude . . .

The cab of his LUV was lined with fringes of tiny pom-poms, pink and orange. A pair of black-and-white furry dice hung from the rearview mirror. I looked back at Asadollah, who smiled at me. He leaned over the old man, whispered something. The driver slammed the truck into gear, and the gears ground until they found a place to engage. One tire slammed against a boulder. The truck glanced off it, and we were off.

I saw the man in the long cotton robe standing off to one side. He was looking at the ground, and his headcloth masked his face. But as we drove off, he looked up and the desperation flashed. He shouted and ran after us. The driver ignored him. He downshifted and pressed his foot to the pedal. We rose up the path. The pom-poms were quivering.

.

٣

Once a Catholic, always Catholic. You stop believing in it long before, all of it; the only thing you don't stop believing is that you're going to go to hell for your loss of faith. Recently, whenever I tried to explain my thoughts to others, they had no idea what I was saying—they'd look at me as if I were insane. Maybe it was why I loved hiking so much: the silence, the circles rolling from the tangents of thought. I could walk for hours, tasting a single idea, rolling it over and over, twisting and shaping it. I had been thinking about something Saint Francis once said, that God must be praised for having created both thirst and water. Thank God for pain and sorrow, too.

I had been thirsty; I wanted to drink from my water bottle. A few minutes later, I felt guilty with how I had lost all faith in religion. Asadollah refused to let me rest. I was getting dry, dehydrated, and I knew it. I motioned to him, then looked to a rock, and moved both palms down saying that I wanted to stop.

He shook his head and walked forward. One hand waving—we had to go. Finally, after the path turned from the trail where the yellow pickup had dropped us, I understood.

He called it a *ghanát,* and pointing to his tongue and then mine, wanted me to say it. *"Ghanát,"* I repeated. He nodded, pleased.

It was a basin of stone, cut from the rock wall. A pipe carried the runoff of the mountain springs from higher elevations. Asadollah reached into my pack, grabbed both of my water bottles, and opened them. He poured their contents in the dirt. He took one bottle in each hand and plunged them both into the water. Bubbles of air popped to the surface. Then he capped each bottle and placed them back in with the rest of my supplies. I thought of Lourdes, of miracles and cures; but I was still going to the damned because I stopped believing.

•

Most of the homes in the village were adobe. Many of them had no glass in the windows, and a few had no doors. It was a hot day, but I thought of how it would be, here, in winter. You'd have to be tough to survive. A small girl saw us as we hiked into the cluster of homes. She called out, and people came out of their doors to talk to each other. Children ran to Asadollah. He smiled, patted their heads with the tenderness of a father. Some of them gathered around me, pulling my pack or slapping my thigh. Some put up their hands, and I took a few loose rial notes from my pocket and gave them away to them.

We came to a larger building with a cement porch on all four sides. The overhanging blue metal roof sloped over the porch, and several white columns supported a central arch. The building stood at the edge of a cliff and looked toward the long valley we had climbed above that day. Unlike the other homes, there was a tall gate that ran around the perimeter. Flowers, like bougainvillea or hollyhock, climbed the trellis of the metal bars. The flowers were in bloom.

The sign at the gate was written in Farsi and English: IRANIAN MOUNTAINEERING FEDERATION. The man who stood at the entrance, who I later saw was cook/caretaker/gardener, waved welcomes to us. *"Khoub hasti? Jur hasti?"* he asked, and Asadollah shook his head vigorously, bowed, and replied, *"Salamat bashi."*

The man was fairly heavy; he had not, it seemed, climbed Damávand in a few years. He was bald and had a thin mustache. I looked away when I saw it—I did not want to ruin his hospitality—but as I shook his hand, I saw that he was a harelip. He took us inside. The walls were ten to twelve feet high, painted tan; the frames of the doorways were a clean white. He brought us sheets, pointed to his watch and then brought a hand to his mouth to let me know when dinner would be ready. Then he brought me to the porch to tell me that, if I wanted to, I could cook for myself there.

Asadollah shrugged his shoulders when I tried to ask him if he would be sleeping in the same room with me. He put his hand on the door, opened it, and motioned me inside. He did not follow. Three bunk beds, nine beds in all. Two men lay on lower berths. They were asleep, and I slipped my pack and supplies as quietly as I could from my shoulders. I leaned the metal frame against the wall, in the opposite corner from their gear, some of which looked pretty serious. Their bags were thick down, could easily take subzero. Thick-soled hiking boots; gators; crampons.

One of the men gasped in sleep. I froze. One of his feet was bound in faded gauze.

The other man stirred, rolled over to peer at me. Rubbing his eyes, he mumbled, *"Wie gehts?"*

"Mir gut. Und Sie?" I replied.

"Wir sind sehr müde..." He said it with an edge of weariness, exhaustion.

He was Swiss, and his German was softer than the harsh language I had learned at the academy. And it soon became apparent that my knowledge of it couldn't sustain a conversation. We switched to English.

They had ascended the eastern face. They had made some technical climbs and decided to spend the night at the summit, to camp on the ridge overlooking the ice lake: to sleep at the summit. The temperature had dropped, and the wind kicked in. As he spoke, I wondered how acclimated they had become before and during the ascent. Snoozing at nineteen thousand feet might not be too good for your body. He claimed that his thermometer registered twenty below, and that pressure changes caused wild fluctuations in his altimeter.

His companion had suffered *erfrierung*—frostbite.

"He will lose his foot, most likely." And then he paused, for emphasis: "You will like this mountain, Damávand."

The comment pissed me off. *If you were dumb enough to stay up there while he was losing the feeling of his toes, why should I listen to a damn thing you say?* Thinking that, I felt the twinge in my own foot. I did not want frostbite a second time.

•

After dinner, I sat on the terrace and looked down the length of the long valley. The sun had mellowed; the peaks glowed pink and gold. The trail of a highway twisted into the cleft between two rocks. At the edge of the cluster of houses beneath the cliff, a thin line of cypress and short evergreens had begun to sprout. Some of the houses had thatched roofs. And it was strange to see telephone poles, the threads of wire, or a few television antennas.

The peaks were born in the shifting of the earth, long before us. The clefts and crevices rose out of shallow and then sharply rising V's. I studied the map General Sadeghian had given me. On one side of the Federation's imperial symbol, the name was written in Farsi— کوه دماوند , and on the other side I read: DAMAVAND. There was a glossary, a guide to "populated places," a summary of most known trails. I touched the words as I read the names of the mountains that surrounded me: *Kooh-e Zirehvar*,

KOOH DAMAVAND

Halzam Lahrak, Kooh-e Seyah Riz, Malakabad, Ab-e Garm, Kooh-e Rangraz, Kooh-e Hamahsoom, Neyak, Esteleh Sarrang, Kooh-e Nemak Kuhshar, Kooh-e Kanizur, Kooh-e Kerd Pileh.

Night fell. There was a full moon. Light splintered down. Somewhere in that darkness behind me was the mountain I no longer had to name. Two soldiers walked down a path that ran by the terrace. One of them embraced the other briefly, and then they returned to holding hands. I was getting used to seeing that, between men. I couldn't imagine that at the academy.

The academy—another country, long ago.

That night we slept in the village named Reeneh.

ع

2 August

The touch of his hand on my shoulder took me from the dark. I opened my eyes to the shadow of his face. He said nothing. Seeing I was awake, he turned and slipped out the door. I had been dreaming. It was only the feeling I remembered. It was about something violent and strange. I woke, suddenly, and knew that it was gone.

I dressed quickly, taking my clothes from under my sheets—another survival trick I had learned. To sleep naked and to keep your clothes with you. To sleep with them, but not wear them: the clothes would insulate you as you stood in the cold provinces of air. I searched in the dark for my gear and supplies, cursing myself for having forgotten a flashlight. But everything was there: rope, pack, the touch of my food.

Outside, Asadollah had built a fire on the terrace. He gathered a few twigs, shaped them into the tight weave of a cone. The fire started to crackle and blaze. He held a metal pot over the flame. He nodded and smiled when he first saw me, said, "morning" in Farsi, and I said, "morning," in return. I wanted to ask him to say it again. But how could I?

He was not wearing any gloves. The heat of the fire, as it brought the water to boil, would also flow into his hands. The heat would be intense. But he didn't notice, it didn't bother him. I stared in amazement, certain he would suddenly cry out and fling the boiling pot against the wall.

Dawn was just beginning to suggest itself. Thick mist rose from the valley and echoed in the hills around us. He put out one hand, showing me the splendor: *"Keili-koub."*

•

When we left, a few minutes later, he did something strange. He checked my pack to make sure it fitted, turned me around, and took my hand. He made both of us walk *backward* down the path to the gate. He seemed relieved after that. We walked through the quiet of Reeneh. No one moved.

Later, the sun rose beyond the clouds, without penetrating, and it became clear that it would be a long while before the mist would lift. I liked that. The air was deadened, muffled. I would not see what was up ahead. I would have to trust Asadollah. Sometimes I would look ahead to the edge of a ravine, and it seemed that the mist, rising from beneath the walls and curling up the face, was rising from nothing. It seemed the path dropped into air.

•

We were being followed. Two boys riding a donkey. They had trailed us from the village, I think. Asadollah had known they were behind us long before I picked up the soft thud of hooves in the dirt. Finally, he turned, crossed his arms disapprovingly, and clucked his tongue. "*Hin,*" he said, nodding his head toward the boys, "*hin, hin . . .*"

I have fantastic eyes—I can see two and a half times the distance of normal vision. Maybe it was because he knew what the sound meant; maybe because his eyes were even better than mine—but Asadollah did not seem surprised when they lifted out of the fog and came up to us. "*Saá,*" he said, and the donkey stopped. No one said anything. Asadollah waited. I shifted the weight of my pack. *I could use some water . . .*

"*Hay-loo,*" one of the boys sang. "Howdy," I said in reply, giving my best Yankee note of warmth and friendliness.

They looked like twins. Their hair was curly and dark, combed down the middle of the crown. Long eyebrows; full faces. Unlike me, they had known it was going to be a cold day. They wore ski sweaters, the design of running antelope pursuing each other in the woods. One of the boys had wrapped a scarf around his throat. The donkey wore a single wool blanket on her back, the figures of birds and trees woven in its design.

"Picture," one of them said. I looked to Asadollah, and he nodded that it would be fine if I wanted to stop. I leaned over, slipped the weight of my pack from me. I found the camera my father had lent me in a side pocket and wondered if I needed to use the flash. They smiled as I walked around them, snapping their harmony. The donkey bent to chew on a tuft of grass.

I thought they would want money, but when I offered them a few rials, they looked to each other and shook their heads. They turned the donkey, kicked her in the side and headed back down. When I turned to ask Asadollah if he wanted his picture taken, I understood his refusal. He turned, and his body melted in the fog. I stuffed the camera in a pocket, pulled on my sweater, and went after him. My pack was heavier than his; he didn't understand that. I was in better shape than he was; perhaps that would make the difference.

I caught up to him at the sound of the first shouts from below us. They were strange, insistent voices—a chorus of men, military men. It was the morning calisthenics in the compound somewhere below us. They may have been performing the exercise of *zúrkháneh*. I thought of the two soldiers I had seen the night before; they were down there, I was sure—stretching and yelling.

We had entered the rise into the ancient Damáreh glacial field—one of the eight faces that rose to the eight ridges of Damávand—but I could not see what it looked like. The voices of soldiers lifted to us and mingled with the muffled step of our boots. We hiked above the valley. I heard the air carried in a voice of wind. A rock, dislodged, followed into white. I had left my passport in my room at Shemiran.

Intentionally. Beatrice and my father would never know. I was trying to forget—maybe you could say *erase*—myself. If I were caught without it, here, alone on this mountain—if anyone wanted to question me—I'd be in serious trouble.

Asadollah began humming. I followed next to him, our steaming breath metered by his humming song. The mist thickened, and we entered.

•

We lay in a field of poppies. The sun was high in the atmosphere. I closed my eyes, felt the soft grass around my head. The call of a bird. The flowers, past their season, tilted in the breeze. Orange faces with black centered hearts.

Asadollah shrugged *no* when I tried to pull my water bottle from the pack. He was making tea, and I was going to drink it. He must have thought it had some magical powers. He wouldn't touch water and stayed away from streams. He squatted on his haunches over a fire, holding the burning metal in his asbestos palms.

Maybe I would stay—at the academy . . . It didn't seem such a big choice after all. Funny, I fell into going to school there, used to tell people that the judge had said either jail or the academy, and I had said jail, and the judge had said, sorry the jail's all full. I had changed, and I had been changed; I might not know how to live in the outside world. I still wanted to fly; I wanted to see the earth from the D-horizon.

I don't know why I was thinking it: they were different things. They were cruel, didn't teach me anything. The first came from a gym class, a boxing class. The instructor, who was also the baseball coach, had ranted at us that boxing meant determining the moral fiber of a warrior, the way that being a good golfer meant that you were going to go far in your career because you spent all of your free time on the green, with your boss, making important decisions. I hated boxing the way I hated golf. I hated watching the blood spurt from my face and paint my partner's gloves seconds after we started sparring; I hated feeling my nose explode in agony. The coach knew that. He'd take me out on the mat and explain to everyone what a woman I was, how I'd never be worth a shit as an officer. And then one day he grabbed two volunteers whom he wanted to clearly demonstrate how you go at it: viciously and with hatred. They laid into each other, fists pounding a stomach or slapping a jaw. The smaller student, who had the longer reach as well, had the clear advantage. It was no real surprise, then, when it happened: the hard crack of a solid hit, and the sound of a body hitting the blue mat. I turned away. And then I turned back because there was this perfect silence. Everyone, including the student who had fallen and then picked himself up; including the instructor; stared, reverently, at the mat where he had fallen. Lying there was a perfect round turd.

And those letters, the ones that girlfriends sent you from home, telling you that they never wanted to see you again, that she'd found somebody else, somebody better. And the way people would mope around the squadron for days, talking about how it felt like they were going blind—they were so angry or moody or quiet. Then, after awhile, they would pin the letter to the squadron bulletin board, and people would make comments and corrections and belittle her, and then someone would send the letter back to her. The day Scott got a letter from a girl he thought he loved, that's the way he said it. There was a picture—you could see her smile at the edge of the frame—she had opened her palm, and in the center of her palm was this big, thick, anonymous cock. She had written on the back, *"Who needs you when I can have this?"* Scott had sent the picture to her mother. "Let's see if the bitch gets any more of *that* for awhile," he said.

A shadow leaned over my eyes. I opened them and saw Asadollah bending down. Tea was ready.

○

Asadollah had taken a lamp from the wall, struck a blind match, and turned up the pressure for light to point to where he wanted me to sleep. I was exhausted.

I had not brought a watch along with me, but I knew that we had started the day shortly after five and that we'd hiked for well over an hour after darkness. The day had turned from mist to intense heat. As we walked, the circles of sweat under our armpits grew until they joined the swaths of wet heat on our backs and on our chests. We rested twice during fourteen hours of walking. Asadollah let me scramble the freeze-dried eggs and the "country-red" potatoes. The food was heavy with salt. I pretended to go behind a rock to piss, and I sucked down half a bottle of water.

There were no running streams. When I came back to him, he offered another cup of tea. I told him no, but he was so insistent I had to take it.

The taste was bitter and hot. The sun grew more intense as we climbed into the sky. I unzipped a pocket, pulled a twist-stick of sunblock out. I spread it on my hands and then over my face and neck. Asadollah looked puzzled. I passed the stick to him, and showed him how to twist the cylinder from the bottom, how the stiff waxy paste would rise. He took some of it, spread it on his hand, and tasted it. He smeared it on his mouth. I think he thought it was lipstick.

I started laughing, and he laughed in response.

He was a handsome man, still. Those intense, glowing eyes and the white hair cropped back to his skull. His skin had turned to leather in the sun. You could see the deep furrows of an honest face, see the lines where the set of his wide, grinning smile fell into place.

•

He put one finger to his lips, held the lantern up, and pointed to the place where I would sleep. He twisted the pressure knob, and the light went out. I saw his shape at the entrance, vanishing into night and the shivering stars. Blindly, I dropped my pack to the stone floor. I unstrapped the sleeping bag, unrolled it. I kicked my boots off. I crawled inside, too tired to take off my clothes. I slept, immediately.

KOOH DAMAVAND

I woke—a few hours later, I suppose. The stars were no different, their axis of rotation fixed. I'd had a dream: I was hovering over the city, and then I flew through the French doors off the balcony of our house. I just held there, in the air above the bed where Beatrice and my father slept. Without knowing why, I had whispered to them, asking forgiveness.

ו

3 August

I woke to a woman's breast—to see the image swim before me. *Where am I? Who is she? What have I done?*

A hole, like a cornice, had been cut in the central arch at the roof of the cave. A braid of light broke through and emptied down on us. I could see her face. She was smiling. She said something to me, and I said nothing. I tried to offer up a feeble greeting. She brought the infant, wrapped in a thin blanket, to her breast. The child sucked at her warmth.

She had been lying next to me, watching me and holding her baby as I slept. It was a strange feeling: I thought he had taken me to a primitive cave to spend the night, and here I woke in someone's home.

The mother called out a soft command to the shadows. A boy, who had been sitting on a chair in a dark recess of the room, stood up, walked to her, and knelt down. She whispered to him.

He giggled, a high nervous whisper of air. Then he stood and half-ran to the boiling water of the samovar. He opened the core to check the heat inside the chimney. A short puff of steam flew out as he lifted the brass cover. He turned the spigot, and the water fell into the cup of leaves. He took five cubes of sugar and dropped them in the cup and brought it to me.

I sat up, drawing my arms around my bent knees. Somewhere else, I knew, I might have been embarrassed to wake beside a woman and her new child. But it was innocent: nothing to be afraid of. I sipped my tea. As she rose to speak to the boy, the wide folds of her dress, like petticoats, flared out behind her. The cloth of her dress shimmered like satin, and the patterned sequins on the cloth caught the light.

We sat on a Persian rug, worn with use and age. I had not remembered spreading my sleeping bag across it in the night. I remembered only the cold stone and the hard answer of its face. This was their life. They didn't have much: a Bombay chest, small table, a few chairs, a samovar. It was the first time I had entered a place in Iran and not seen a picture of the shah looking down from some high perch.

When the boy had knelt to me, I said my rousing *Keili-koub* to him.

KOOH DAMAVAND

"*Keili-koub?*" The way he answered had the rising tone of a question. He began laughing, and his mother laughed as well. She was young; she could have been younger than me. "*Keili-koub,*" they sang to each other.

At the entrance to the cave—a form cut by nature—the figure of a man appeared. He blocked what little light there was behind him. Asadollah. He stepped in, bending his head to avoid the rock, and walked down a few steps to the one chamber of the house. As he crossed through the braid of light from the roof, I saw that his eyes were on me.

It became a litany between them: he bowed slightly, and the woman who now stood before him, bowed, and sang out her response.

"*Mordeh nabashi.*"
"*Jur hasti?*"
"*Hané cheeze koub. Koub hasti?*"
"*Salamat bashi.*"
"*Zendeh bashi.*"
"*Sáyeh ye shomá kam, nashé.*"

Asadollah carried a pouch or a sack under his arm. I stood, walked to him, bowed evenly. He grinned. He offered the sack up to me, and I knew what it was: the stomach of a cow, or a goat. The lining at edges had been sewn with a thick needle. The woman motioned me to the long wooden platform, which I guessed was their dining table. Asadollah took a knife from his rucksack, and with infinite care cut several cords of the lining. The thin white yogurt spilled into the cups she had set out for us. I walked back to my pack to take some bread for all of us. The woman stopped me.

I looked to Asadollah, and he nodded his head to say that, yes, I was in their home, their guest, and both of us would live by their hospitality. The boy brought us flat sheets of bread, bubbles of uneven heat rising in the sheets, still warm. Asadollah and I knelt at the dark wooden platform and ate. The woman and the boy moved away from us and sat together across the chamber from us in the dark. They said nothing. The baby burped and then started cooing.

Later, I stepped outside and saw two men—swarthy and wearing thick-wooled sheepskin vests. The older of the two flashed his eyes on me and then went back to his work. It was a seesaw device: they stood on opposite sides of a forked wooden frame, swinging the sealed stomach of an animal, making yogurt.

•

I suppose it was not a cave, because light could touch almost all the faces of the rock inside. I walked down through a long meadow of wild grasses. I turned and looked back. The men were still working. The entrance to their house had been shaped from a crack in the boulder that leaned over them. It was probably twenty feet high and then sloped to a high peak of at least fifty feet. Their home was in a corner of the rock. There were a few other holes in the rock where people could live, but it was obvious they lived alone. And I was standing in their meadow.

I found a stream and washed myself. I drank the water, greedily. I was sorry that I had not brought my pack along to fill my bottles. I had remembered to take the camera, though. I sat in the grass and focused on Damávand above us. But it was also no longer above us, because we were now on Damávand—at ten to eleven thousand feet of altitude.

I played with the zoom of the lens, bringing the peak into and then out of focus. I shot for the snow tips at the summit, and then brought the whole shape of the volcano back into my field of vision.

We had started on the southern front, and, based on the sun, it seemed that we had already circled to the west of the peak. I had seen a path, once, yesterday. But Asadollah had turned from it as if it were not there. It looked like a good path, winding through rocks and rising to the southern slope of the mountain.

I was glad to have this time. I had to admit it: I was exhausted. It wasn't just the altitude. The Rockies had helped me adjust long before. It was Asadollah—he could have been sixty years old, and sometimes he looked as if he were twice that age. But he could backpack better than any human I had ever seen. His pace was quick, and as our first day lengthened, he had actually quickened our pace. He made it more difficult. If the choice were between the gentle rise of a pasture or an outcropping of rocks, he went for the rocks. He motioned for me to show him what I knew of bouldering, and I would drop my back and lift myself to the face. He crossed his arms and watched. I didn't have climbing shoes. I was wearing new hiking boots, which should have been broken in long before I started the hike. But I didn't have time, and already I felt my feet blistering, knew they were bleeding. I clung to the rock and lifted myself away, searching for balance. *It isn't over yet, Diamond; you're not there . . .*

KOOH DAMAVAND

I heard the clang of her bell first—a calf, with beautiful, soft eyes, and twitching tongue. A turquoise ribbon circled her neck, and a triangular brass bell hung from it. I brought the camera to my eyes and focused. I watched her image flood the frame—it was going to be a great picture. Her face became two eyes and a nose, and then just a nose, and then just her ripe tongue in the light as she licked the flat glass of my lens.

I pulled the camera back, and she moved in—started working on my face.

V

My mother had given me the words as a child: *Caminante, no hay camino. Se hace camino al andar.*

"This is what poetry means, Dante," she had said. "When you say the words so many times they no longer have meaning. When you understand the words so well, you no longer hear them. The words become pure sound.

"Walker," Beatrice would sing to me, "there is no path. You make your path in the walk."

And in the dirt. The way it flakes and crumbles in my step, the way the grass snakes its way through barren space. It was the way I would always remember this country, by looking down: the dirt and fractured pebbles of Iran. I had lived for it for almost twenty years, and it had waited twenty hundred million years for me to get there.

As we hiked, Asadollah hummed to himself. He shifted the weight of his rucksack, and bounced along, smiling—immensely happy. It was not music he was giving me: it was more like the fugue of words, twisted and shaped. Sometimes, he would run up the face of a steep slope and sit and wait—for my slow, plodding arrival. "Ah-ha!" he would sing out and then rush off. I wondered if he were impatient to get rid of me, to reach the summit and go home. But I don't think so. Mountain goat, or satyr, he lived for movement.

And as he climbed into the air, he seemed to tire less. The lines of sweat vanished from his clothes. His brow was shiny and clean, while bright beads of water poured into my eyes and stained my sunglasses. We crossed the threads of streams running from the glacial fields, and I would want to stop, to drink and to rest. He would shrug and motion for me to follow. I was wearing myself out, and he knew it. He offered to carry my pack, and I refused. Stubborn pride, the belief that I could survive anything. The old man was not going to destroy the young.

The sky was darker here; we were closer to the sky, purple at the edges, black above. The light burned through my skin. My arms were singing red. I offered him more sunstick, and he still did not understand what it was. He grinned as I spread it on my hands, neck, face. We heard the wind cross on the rocks above us—the eclogue of a mountain's elevation. We stepped into the atmosphere. The forgetting and the remembering, the pulse of our legs and movement, the wave of repetition, rhythm breathing climbing rising the natural abstract, sweat, the earth beneath us revolving us: the hike was carrying us, higher, through the motion of the season, the year unfolding, the specific congruence of form ruining all sense of direction. Just take it and follow.

•

It was what you carried in you: to walk lightly and step surely; to take the source of breath deep in your lungs and balance all gravity in the pit of the stomach—the place where the thing they used to call the soul lived; to see by walking, to climb above the ledges and the rocks flying from your path and down the moraine. To take the air in your heart, and rise. *Walker. Walker. Walker.*

˄

We stopped for our second serving of tea for the day. Asadollah pointed to a rock where he wanted me to sit, and then took a few twigs and his pot from his sack and started working on a fire. I had offered to use my stove to boil water. He shook his head no. He was getting good at that.

I squatted on my haunches next to him. Grinned at the serious expression on his face. At that moment, hot water and a few leaves in our sierra cups were the only things that mattered. I didn't like tea, but I had become accustomed to it. Though even as the heat grew less severe as we climbed, the warmth of tea and the sugar weren't welcome. I had to let go of my own water more and more. I had stopped to piss at least thirty times that day.

We had crossed the western slope, and we were climbing toward the federation shelter at fifteen thousand feet. We would spend the night there. I expected on the day after that, the day we would reach the summit, that we would come to the peak from the northern face—the place of the glaciers. I was sorry I had not thought about taking crampons. But then, Asadollah didn't have any either. He carried twigs, matches, a prayer rug, and a book.

At this altitude, which was 13,000 or 13,500 feet, the water began to bubble almost as soon as the heat of the flame reached up through metal. Still, it took some time to boil. I watched his face. He knew I was watching him, but it did not seem to bother him. His life was simple, but it made sense. I had tried too much, perhaps, thought too much about all that was wrong. I wondered if we could ever call each other friends, or if that idea even meant anything to him.

That time I went with Scott to visit his family in Texas—Christmas vacation. His father was a strong personality, and he cared about his family. Because I was a cadet, and he was only senior enlisted, he called me "sir"; and because he had been in the army for over three decades, I called him "sir." It went back and forth like that for awhile. His mother laughed a lot. Scott had a younger sister. She did all the things that you were supposed to do in school, and seemed happy with that. Before dinner, they held each other's hands and prayed. I closed my eyes and pretended. Squirmed a little.

KOOH DAMAVAND

I had read a poem once by a man named William Matthews in the academy library. There were two lines at the end about how family life is easy: you just push off into heartbreak and go on your nerve. I looked up from the page and would not look at how my hands were shaking. It was so fucking obvious. It wasn't just families, and happiness, all that garbage. It didn't have to be so goddamned hard.

A bird skittered by our campfire. But it wasn't any bird; it was a bird that didn't belong there. A sandpiper. I looked to Asadollah in surprise, and his response was only mild interest. He brought the cup to his lips.

•

We came to a shrine at the center of a cluster of looming red granite boulders. If you didn't know it was there, you would never see it. But Asadollah had meant to bring me. It looked like a gazebo. The thatched roof rose in the figure of a cone. There was no door. The windows were open. The square of the floor, eight feet across, was concrete.

In the center of the floor, an iron grille covered the shape of a hand pressed into cement. Asadollah knelt, kissed the grille, and pulled his rug from his pack. I stepped out of the shrine to wait. I wanted to say the words to him, what I'd learned when I first began studying this place called Persia. But I did not know if he would understand.

Perhaps he would think I was ridiculing him. I didn't even know if the words were Farsi: *"Besmellah-o-arrahmané, arrahim."* "In the name of God, the merciful, the compassionate."

He stood and knelt, stood and knelt again. He was facing southwest, away from the face of the mountain, facing toward Mecca, and I heard the purr of his words. Below us, the clouds had covered the valleys and the plateaus. All I saw were peaks that ran forever, their sharp fissures and shadows playing in the clefts like layers of black flesh folded back on themselves. The blanket of white had covered the world.

•

We reached the shelter near dusk. It was built in the form of a naval Quonset hut. Rippled sheets of corrugated metal curved down to form the walls. There were two windows at the front, and a rotting wood door swung back against a broken hinge. The wind had died hours before. It was still.

Inside we found the planks for four wooden bunks, and a table low enough to kneel at. I unstrapped my sleeping bag and spread it out along a frame near the back of the hut, against the curve of the wall. The hut itself rested on a flat ledge.

The clouds had cleared. I could see a hundred miles. Twenty yards beneath the shelter someone, long before, had built an outhouse with a Turkish thunder-hole inside. I wandered over, though I had no intention of using it.

When I opened the door, the stench made me reel. The inside door was littered with graffiti. Two of the sayings, carved with a penknife in English, were very strange: "Art is long. Life is short. Art is Life. long is short." And the other, "If anybody calls for me, and says that she's someone other than my wife, tell her that I've already left. I am not here."

Altitude does strange things to people.

We sat on the ledge. For the first time since we had started the trip, he let me use my stove. Matches flicked at the tongue of fuel, and the stove sputtered into life. I started to boil water. But when I reached in my pack, to see what kind of dinner I could make, Asadollah gripped my forearm and shook his head.

He took my hand, pressed it into the rock of his stomach wall, and then pushed it off. Air—rising—the food would swell inside me, and I would be sick. I nodded, but I realized, too, that with nothing in me I would be weak during the final climb.

He fed me herbs and a few leaves, which, when I tasted them, exploded a sharp bitterness in my mouth. He dropped a bouillon cube in my sierra cup and poured the water in after it. It was smooth, liquid heat. I swore to myself that when I got off this mountain I would never drink tea again. The sky turned to gold and then to blood and then to black. The stars appeared, because they had never left.

•

I don't remember leaving the fire we had built. The last thing I saw was the corkscrew of smoke lifting into darkness. I woke inside the hut because of the crack of his voice. He was warning me. I froze.

And when I felt it on my chest, the awful stretching legs, like antennae, I stopped breathing. The hair on my arms was rising, and in the idiocy of the moment, I was suddenly thankful that I had none on my chest. I had not zipped my bag to its full length. The top of it had been pulled back. I was naked.

KOOH DAMAVAND

It was a scorpion. Huge. The body was four or five inches long; it glowed with a pink luminescence. I couldn't see the tail, only imagined the sharp piece of its plunging stinger in my skin. I had never seen one this large. And it wasn't just walking along in a straight path. It knew what I was: it was testing me. It walked a few centimeters and then paused, and then after an infinity moved again. There was the awful itch of its legs, hundreds of them. Finally, it disappeared. I heard it *leap* from the bed and climb the curved metal wall. *We're at fifteen thousand feet—there are no scorpions here!*

When I tried to get up from the bed to find it, and kill it, Asadollah—who had been kneeling on the floor before three lit candles—grabbed me and shook his head. He pushed me back to the pallet and kept on repeating something. Soon I was asleep. I woke three times. Each time, I saw Asadollah circling the room as if he were praying to all four corners of the earth. He would kneel before the candles and then rise and walk, and then fall to his knees. I don't think he slept that night.

The third time I woke, his voice had grown distant. I felt the slow rise, the slow fall. He was repeating a phrase over and over. He blew out two candles and prayed to the single light. I was falling back.

He looked enough like God to satisfy me.

9

4 August

I stood in the light of dawn and let the clear air fill my lungs. This was the day I had been waiting for. I was going to make it.

I turned and looked at the huge boulders above me. Beyond that was the false summit: it looked like the peak, but the real crest of Damávand rose above it. Pliny, I read once, had called the path of the ancient caravans the way of the thousand steps; but, for me, the path to paradise, the word that had come from the Persian root *perdows,* required 999,000 more.

•

Asadollah had disappeared. But, shortly after sunrise, he returned from a high cluster of stones and jumped down the worn path to meet me. His heels kicked into earth as he half-ran, half-hopped. The path he came from was the normal hike to the summit: there were some sharp rises, but it didn't look difficult. I knew that we would not take that path.

He built a fire. We drank tea and shared a single cup of bouillon. We started off minutes after that. The rocks rose sharply on several routes, and the surest one was not going to be easy to find.

It was strange, I thought, as we started off. He couldn't be collecting twigs up here, where nothing grew. When he had opened his pack in the car, the contents were almost empty. But he always had this inexhaustible supply—he piled the tiny limbs onto a roaring fire, and he squatted beside it, holding the metal pot, humming away.

And as we started to hike, he opened his tightly clenched fist and threw a cluster of rice kernels down on the path behind us.

•

All that day we climbed. The pace was quick, and I was uncomfortable with it. But I wanted to make the summit before dark, wanted to prove to him that I could keep the path beside him. He did not stop to rest, ever. When I found a pace that matched his, he increased it. My breath was coming hard, and though I was wearing only my T-shirt I was sweating like mad. He didn't seem to notice. *Go, go, go, Diamond.*

He was tough. He avoided the rock croppings as we circled from the west to the northern face. We entered the first ice field, and I fell behind. He waited once for me. It was the last time. I fell and winced in pain as my elbow slapped into rock beneath a thin film of ice. I pulled my combination hammer-axe from my pack, ready to use it if I fell again, hoping it would stop me if I slid down the slope.

The snow was getting deeper. It didn't bother him. He kept moving, and I strained to match his pulse and rhythm. I felt as though I were back in Coronado, pressing to catch the dwindling pack on a five-mile jaunt. I knew there'd be a Hummingbird instructor who would pop from behind a boulder, force me head-down into the surf and lean over, screaming, giving me my morning lecture.

The landscape held three colors: the high blue of the sky; the white of the snow and the white clouds, pillowed shapes beneath and rising to us, tumbling from the wind and pull of earth; the black of the smaller peaks sprouting in the distance, dark crevasses and glacial clefts, couloirs, the slopes of *Esteleh Sarrang* and *Gardaneh-Ye Mazyar*. Like outstretched hands, the water flowing from the melts was cooled by the shelter of boulders.

We cut diagonally across the third ice field, rising quickly. When the snow was deep enough to touch midthigh, Asadollah turned back to me and plunged through the wet blanket. He unfastened my rope and tied us together. The knot he made was unlike anything I'd seen. I said to him, in English, "Let's rest. I'm starting to really get tired. I might get sick."

He grunted.

I offered him the axe—if he fell, he could dig into the ice with it; otherwise, he might keep sliding all the way down until he hit a ravine and went whistling off in the fall to his death. And he would take me with him.

He shook his head. He wouldn't accept it.

My lungs screamed for oxygen. The altitude didn't seem to affect him at all. He started humming. *Gentlemen, remember your* personal *hypoxia symptoms!* I thought my heart was going to rip right through my chest and plop down in the snow. My head was stinging, light. I *was* light.

Waist-deep, we locked hands and pulled ourselves through snow. Sometimes the snow was less thick and we could walk, rather than push through it. When I slipped, he tugged the rope—more like he was leading a disobedient dog than a climbing companion.

Once, the snow even reached to my chest.

•

It would take no more than two pitches. A few hundred feet. After that the summit would be a short hike. It would all be over. The glacier had poured around both sides of the wall of stone. It flowed down on us like a blue waterfall. I could see the final crest now. The wind was stirring there, kicking up tiny crystals of snow and blowing them off the mountain, the swirling figures of ghosts.

He was telling me to uncoil the rope. I took off my pack, and he slipped some carabiners from it and clipped them to his belt—a frayed cord of twined sisal. He dropped the pitons in his rucksack, took the hammer, tied himself on, and did not wait to check me. He started climbing. By the time I checked myself, he had hammered seven pitons in the rock. I looked up. He was moving away at an incredible pace. He knew what he was doing.

I wasn't sure if what I was going to do was a very good idea. I didn't have the security of stiff-soled climbing shoes, and though the shoes probably didn't matter, the Vibram of my boots wasn't going to help. I'd never climbed with a full hiking pack before. My head was aching; the veins in my temple pulsed.

There were several overhanging ledges we should avoid; a few fissures we could negotiate. Most of it didn't look terribly difficult—5.7 or 5.8. But so high.

It was a clear day. I was impatient to be on the rock. I felt like throwing up. Maybe, I thought, movement would help forget my sickness. Sometimes the snow would drift from the rock above us, and the crystals shivered down to me staring up at them.

Near the end of the first pitch I saw Asadollah do something impossible. He was moving toward the most difficult part of the face, setting the pitons in places where, even on a normal day, I'd think more than twice about going for. I saw him reach the underbelly of a massive overhang. I thought he would go around it, climb to the ledge, and set up the belay. But he didn't do that. He just scrunched up under the rock—clinging to it. The overhang jutted out from the wall, a facet of stone, or cut diamond.

He reached straight across the overhang. Hanging there, in nothing, only his fingers touching the surface. I saw his legs arch from beneath him as he looped under the rock, and then over, flew up to the ledge and disappeared. Maybe a spider could have done that. But no human.

•

He was not a very good lead. He would call out sometimes, but since neither of us understood the other, it didn't matter much. Sometimes he would tug, sharply, on the rope, as if trying to feel if I were still there. I almost fell, several times, because of that. He never left slack.

I had to make a choice before I reached the overhang. The face was difficult to the right, but I could follow my own path on the left. I came off the rope. I stepped across a thin ledge and inched up through a rising incline to the overhang. Somehow, he had known I would do that. He sat there, coiling the rope, as I reached him. His legs, splayed in front of him, stretched out to a boulder. I was breathing and sweating, and he did not notice.

He started the second pitch.

•

I was in a chimney, concentrating on the pressure of my body against the rock. I had slipped twice, and my arms were bleeding from cuts. I wondered if I had broken a rib. *Push against it, balance.* I thought of it with such focus that I never noticed that the rope was looping beneath me.

It was coiling down into space. Puzzled, I reached up to the line above me and tugged it: I wanted him to know that I was coming. His belay wasn't finished.

The line came whipping down. The full length of it, slapping my face and my body. I braced for it, saw it coming. Pressed my pack against one wall and pushed the flat soles of my boots against the opposite rock. My quadriceps flared and howled, on fire. When the rope hit me, hot tears rolled from my eyes.

What the fuck is he doing? I was so angry, I screamed, "Shithead!" up through the roof, and the only reply was booming echoes. I knew I had to control the anger, to use it to get me out of this mess. And when I looked up, I noticed that he had erased the path, that he had never made a path. There were no pitons in the rock above me. He had the hammer. I was alone.

I found a ledge, coiled the rope, tied it to my pack, and started up. It wasn't so bad—I was gasping for air, and my arms and legs were quivering—but I had focus. I had a voice that told me I had only one direction. It was stronger than the voice that said *don't think about the scream; don't think about the falling body.*

When I reached him at the flat top of the rock, tea was almost ready. He held the metal pot in both his hands as he squatted by the fire. He smiled when he saw me, glad I had finally arrived.

"Hey, dipshit, whatta you think you're doing," I spat at him. He smiled.

It was useless. I sat by the ledge, pouting.

What was wrong with this guy? He took a sierra cup from my pack and brought me tea. He put one hand on my shoulder and gave a tight squeeze. The tea was awful; the acid hit my stomach like fire on a surface of oil. I wanted to go to my pack, dig out the water bottle, and drink it, all of it, what little there was.

I started coughing. *Air, just a little air.*

Asadollah stood up, mumbled something, and then started up. The peak was three hundred yards away, and he was heading for it. I splashed the tea against a boulder, stood, and hobbled to my pack. I began to strap on, and called for him to wait. And then I bent over, dropped the pack; felt the dry heave of vomit. But I had nothing inside to give.

He couldn't beat me, not now, not so close. The distance between us was an unreeling line—lengthening, melting. The figure of him, vanishing.

"Don't leave me!" I screamed. "You asshole! You fucking asshole. Why are you doing this?"

When I fell, I looked up for the last time to see him raise his left arm high into the air as he walked. He was waving good-bye.

۱۰

They were up there, the black shapes. Maybe they were vultures: the long fingers of their wings circling in thermaled air. Waiting. And blindly, from sleep, I heard how they were not vultures. Their cries had the slow moan of a banshee. They were familiars of the Simurgh—the great bird of the dark who lived in the core of Damávand, the possessor of wisdom, knower of all things.

•

I lay there, feeling it seize me. I reached for the Velcro seal on the inner pocket of my pack, digging my elbows into dirt and stone, slipping through blood. My fingers, shaking—a quivering I could no longer control. How I watched them, disinterested, amazed: they no longer belonged to me. I would never use them to snap the O-ring.

Slowly, forever . . . I hit the rubber cap and pushed it back. It was taking me now. I pulled the tab on the lead of the ring and lifted the canister into the air. Red smoke jetted from the flame.

I knew that God, though she or he did not exist, would be the only entity to see that burning.

Part Six

Zabán

زبان

۱

Often, I cannot clearly see that mountain, Faith. In Farsi, you pronounce it "kooh," like the coo of a mourning dove. The long slanting vowels fall from the tongue. Some nights, at altitude, I imagine it, there, in the dark, asleep. To the west, north, and south the armies push across the landscape, lobbing artillery rounds in the place they last saw their opponent or at the spot where they would next expect him to be—a savage guessing, the dead reckoning of war. And sometimes at altitude I look through the right sensor and see it: the ice fields, the mouth of the volcano, the place where I fell and dreamed. Though I am more like God now, looking far down on a puny landscape and the puny humans who want to ruin it. It's not the same. It's not the same as when I stood in the shade of a plane tree four centuries old at the edge of a stream, with Asadollah at my side, and looked up to the image of Damávand as the looming peak it is and knew that it would be the last time I would be able to view it from that height. And when the image is transformed, when I can clearly see, it is not a mountain at all. It is an image of faces, a place, a time I lost. Forever.

They say the Ayatullah Khomeini is dead, that his country will live in turmoil and anger. But his image will never fade. Perhaps, one day. But it is the face of the man himself: the fierce, implacable eyes; the unwavering stare. The man who rose from the obscurity of Qom to puzzle and terrify the world. The white beard, black robes, quivering brow, the quick dart of his eyes. The face that never moved. The eternal ascetic, a prisoner, some would say, in the courtyard of his medresh, seated against a wall, beneath glowing minarets and perfect mosaics of turquoise, blue, a sea of green. The world had come to visit him.

It is the source from which that other man, the man who named himself Citizen of the World, Defender of the Order, the First Man, Lord of all Creation took nourishment—the country of illusion. Radicals, outcasts, mystics; faith, prophesy, exaltation. It is where all roads unwound, all points of attitude erased, all lines become impossible; where the pilgrims—screaming children, Sufis, chádor-wrapped women, the diseased and dying, the lame— kneel and chant, read from the Ghor'án, kiss the marble columns, touch gold and enamel, lift their children to the cold façade of silver, the tomb of the Imam himself, circling, invoking his divine spirit within. It is as Mani preached: all men came from darkness.

Agha umad—*the Master has returned.*

They say he has passed away, but there are no pictures from his youth. For all we know, he may well be eleven hundred years old. He never perished. He vanished into the caves under the great mosque in Samarra. If he were not always alive, the world would not live. When the Awaited One returns, all will be well and right and as it should. And then the world will end.

Perhaps he is dead. Perhaps he has never died. When I think of Damávand, I do not see a mountain. I see a place, an image of so many people, ideas, and misunderstandings that the image, finally, no longer is visible. If only the dead could survive.

When the bodies line the streets and rise in answer to the muezzin's call to prayer, and the city fountains—Isfahan, Shiraz, Tabriz—will flow with dye from Persian tapestries, boil with the sacrifice like a mouth speaking blood, where, deep in the guts of each cell a prisoner will survive who will not forget . . . Agha umad. *How long before each face becomes a voice wrapped around a scream, each tongue about to speak? How many lives were wasted in those years?*

٢

I was blind. Standing. *Christ,* I kept thinking, *I've lost my eyes.* The cold. And the stench of sulfur. *Don't be afraid, don't be afraid. Say it like a prayer.*

My legs were shaking. Reached down to touch them. I felt nothing. My kneecap quivering in my palm. Reached out and touched. The rock, the surface of it. The feel of stone, the voice of its skin. Sleep. I needed sleep.

Where am I? Why don't I have a flashlight?

And the silence. Couldn't hear my heart. Feel its pounding. And the blood in my ears, torrent of a flood. Pouring of blood from my ears. The sound of wind far below. The cool whisper of breath—there could be a way out of this.

Drop to all fours. Spread myself out, prone, searching with fingers. Maybe, somewhere, there was light. Then I could see, when my eyes grew used to the dimness. Then I could see my way out. Put my hand in front of my face. Wiggle my fingers. Feel the dangling of tendons in front of me. Nothing.

Out to the full spread of the flat rock I lay on. Swinging arms in a circle. Left hand slaps the nylon of the pack. *God, thank you—the sense of touch. It never felt so good.*

There was a stove in there, could light a fire; could see again. Reach for the pack, draw it to me; hug it like a child, never let it leave again. Feel the sleeping bag strapped to the frame of metal. The line of rope on the back. Moving fingers, searching the body. Clink of the pitons.

Rip the bag open to the contents. Matches, stove. I wanted light.

And then froze. The pack was empty. What was happening? Whose sick fucking joke was this? The pack was empty!

I shook it. Shook it like a broken doll. The buckles clinked on the rock. The flimsy orange—God, why couldn't I see the orange?—flapped on the frame. I spread out my arms again, flapping and swinging. *Where are they?*—everything I needed. I lay my face on the cold stone. *You're screwed, matey. This is it. You're not going anywhere from here.*

I thought about Beatrice and my father. Would they ever find me, ever know what had happened? How that stupid bastard ran me into the earth until I couldn't breathe and then he dumped me. I could see their faces. I remembered them. And I could see stars, and I knew they weren't there. I kicked with my legs, to feel out space. Some kind of crazy breaststroke. My legs pounding the rock. A piece of rock slipped from the smash of my boot. Hear how long before it hit bottom as it flew off. Knew it was falling through space.

One thousand one, one thousand two, one . . . The rock whistled down and never hit. That's impossible. *It has to hit somewhere. It has to hit where the wind was coming from, and the sulfur. It can't be that deep.* I found another rock and threw it out, into the dark. Felt its flight and fall through gravity.

Then nothing. No sound.

I was on a ledge. I knew that now. I had to get off. I looked up. The stars again. But the stars weren't. They were the singing behind the pulse of my eyes. They were my desperate need to see.

I thought of the night three months before when Scott and I had climbed Barr Trail to camp at eleven thousand feet. There had been a rumor of a local Sasquatch going around—they say he lives in the wilderness area. We laughed about it, didn't believe it all that much. The locals, the ones who had seen them—since they all claimed it was not just one but a family of Sasquatch—they had named it Stinky. Whenever one of them came up to a house in Green Mountain Falls, you could smell its stench, the awful, panting breath, the rot of its skin. We hiked up to the Erdrich experimental station. It had ceased functioning years before. All that was left now were split concrete slabs, the foundations of buildings. There was a stream, and we camped by it. All night long I heard its gurgle, the coo of running water. We didn't have a tent; we slept in our bags.

The thing that tripped over me let out a scream. It was Stinky, I knew it: Stinky had come to rip our hearts out. And Stinky could speak: "Hey, dude! I thought you were a damn log!"

Saved by the word. Scott slipped the gun back into his pack. I knew he had gone for it. I knew that he would do that, the first thing, straight out of sleep: the hand darting for the pistol he said he had to carry when he was in the wilderness, and the gun I told him he was stupid to have—you could trust people, finally. "You're wrong," Scott had said. "When you're out there, alone, people can hurt you, people can do awful things, and no one will find out about it."

God, Scott. You were right.

•

I came out of the fog. I shook my head. The blurring trickles of light sliding like filaments. Still, nothing. White flashes burst in my eyes. Pulsing and fading in my head. My arms were shaking, the cold sweat. Blind dark in my sockets. Triceps quivering. I couldn't breathe. I threw up.

Nothing. Dry heaves. And then the coursing of blood over my chest. The feeling that I was going to lose it all. I was going to puke—to puke myself out, like when we went to Rockefeller Center when I was a kid. In the radio studio they showed you how they did all those tricks, how when they played the show about the chicken heart that ate Chicago, they could make it seem so real—this fifty-foot muscle pounding down the street, crushing cars and baby carriages—that you would believe it, you would believe it so much, you'd piss yourself, leaning into the radio, terrified, not wanting to miss anything. And the man who turned inside out: the way they took the rubber glove and squeezed, pulled it to its full length and then opened it out; they showed us how they did it, but when I heard it on the radio I knew that *a man* was turning inside out. That was what was going to happen to me, losing everything until there was nothing, not even my eyes. And what did they matter now? I couldn't see.

I had to get out of there. I knew that now. I had to sleep. My head was killing me. I was vomiting away all the water I needed to live, couldn't stop. It was happening. I was dying.

Rope in. There's nothing up there. Take a rock—here, this pebble biting my thigh. Shoot it into the roof, to hear if there's a roof. Hear it slap: eight, ten feet above. And then fall, clip the ledge, and tumble back to the infinity below.

I could abseil—is that what they called it? Lay your pitons in and double the line, get to another ledge, slide the rope back down, and keep going; hell, I could go rappel all the way down to Tehran! But what if the pitons weren't strong enough for that? Of course they were! What if there were no ledges beneath me? Nothing.

I was alive. I had to stop vomiting. I had to sit up from the pool of the mess of what I couldn't see. Lean against the rock. Think of what to do. Descend: get down to the wind and the stench of sulfur. It was the only way out. I could make it. I knew that now. I was alive. My hand touched the wall and it felt good, the cold. It felt good to think that if I ever caught that bastard Asadollah, I would squeeze his fucking head off. My fingernails scratched on stone. I made a fist. Why had he made me drink all that tea?

He'd kept pointing to his stomach, whenever I even thought about water. Even if I tried to hurt him, he probably wouldn't feel it. I thought he liked me. Maybe he wasn't a man.

Why?

I had to sleep. I couldn't move yet. I could breathe. I wasn't on the summit, that's for sure. I could breathe here. I could take the air into me, relish it, let it fill. And I had to stop throwing up. If I didn't I would die. I knew that. All the black around me. I would sleep. But I would get ready before I did. I reached into a side pocket and found a single carabiner. I reached out; my hands skittered across the ledge. I found a rock, heavy and dense.

I set the head of a piton into the wall: I could drive it in with the rock, even if I couldn't see it. I knew the rock would smash my hand holding the piton while I stumbled in black. I knew that it wouldn't hurt when it hit my fingers. It didn't. I heard the echoes of a voice below, and leaning into the space off the ledge, I listened. It was harsh, panicked: the frenzy of canine panting. And then I knew. I was listening to myself!

Keep it straight, pal—just cool it. Going in with the odds against you. I started laughing at that. *Oh, T-Boy . . . if you only knew. Spent my life trying to get rid of your image, finally believed I could do it, and came up here to kill myself. Sorry, Dad. Thought I could make it . . .*

There was the echo of insane laughter and the echo of pounding rock. It was in. I slipped blind up the rock and tugged my finger through the eye in the head. Put my feet in the rock and pulled against the piton. Nothing. It was going to hold. Going to hold under the strain. I could make it. Work.

I slipped a carabiner onto the piton and started to tie in. *What am I doing? This isn't how to do it. I don't know how to do it!* I went blank with the terror of it. I wasn't that good a climber; I'd never seen this done before; I'd have to guess it. *Get it straight, Diamond. Know everything.* If I clipped on—that meant I could climb up or down, but always come to the same place. But I wasn't coming back.

I'd just have to guess. *You fool—why didn't you ever learn this?* I'd just have to believe I'd do it. I'd rather die in the fall than rot on the ledge. I leaned against the wall, grabbing my stomach. The acid was burning through me. I couldn't breathe again. Gasping, I knew it was going to come: the hard swallowing, the burning. *Don't think about it. Don't let it happen. It's going to kill you.*

Swearing, silently, cursing God and all the universe and all the poor idiots who fell into it. *They're going to go on without you, Dante; they're going to blow each other all into oblivion, pal, and you won't be there to see the balloon go up. Always missing.* Laughing. The gasp for breath. It was my throat now; I could feel it. *Don't think about it.* My esophagus was closing: I had to let it come. I had to breathe.

And then I heaved, again and again. My head was splitting open. I held it in my hands, and I slammed my fists into my thighs. *It had to stop, it had to stop*—I was screaming it. The pain was crushing me. I had to sleep.

I had to stay awake. I couldn't let this happen to me. *Gentlemen, remember your* personal *hypoxia symptoms!* Fingers turning blue, head going to explode. Wish I could see my fingers. This horse. She's running in the corral. Her saddle is shaking, and she's nervous. She jumps the rail. A voice, saying, *Show me.* The voice of my mother—though I can't see her—saying, *He is free now.* And my father, asking, *Where is my son? He should have been back by now. We can't stay at this sheep station forever.* Slipping between, the shape of a room. The three mirrors. We are strangers before you, sojourners, and our days are on earth as a shadow, none abiding. The waters frozen. The dolphin in clear blue. Two mallards side by side on glass. She was young. She took my hand. And we stood before the fracturing of mirrors. The burn.

I had to keep awake. I lay and stared at the black roof above. There, there it is: you can't reach it, but you know it's there. My hands under my head were a pillow: I closed my eyes.

The night he found us on that trail. He was really screaming. We all laughed about it. He didn't know a damn thing about hiking. He didn't know that you shouldn't walk up an old trail in the dark and think that the half-moon was all the guide you'd need. When he stumbled into our camp by the stream, he didn't have anything with him: no pack, no compass, no water. We let him stay with us. *We thought you were Stinky, at first.* I gave him my bag. I couldn't sleep anyway. I'd make us all breakfast in the morning, and we'd all drink from the stream. He had been in Kathmandu. He loved it—eighteen months of wandering through the Himalayas. I didn't believe it at first, but I did later. He was too simple, and too foolish—I mean, he was wearing sneakers and said he always wore sneakers when he hiked. He was telling the truth.

At dawn I sat on a boulder and fed a chipmunk from my hand. The light slipped through thin Ponderosa pines. I heard the birds. And that night they lay side by side: Scott and the boy from Kathmandu, the tight hood of the mummy bags wrapped around their faces. I listened to them dreaming. And off there, off to the west—that's Cheyenne Mountain. People live and work inside that mountain now. The watchers: the ones who'll see the missiles flying even though it'll already be too late, flying at twenty-seven Mach, they'll hit velocity and zoom for the stars. They'll call the president: *six minutes, sir; six minutes before they hit the earth and we all ignite.* Six minutes. Lean over, kiss your sleeping wife good-bye, take the dog out. Don't forget the morning paper. Step out on the porch, look across the lawn to Pennsylvania Avenue, and say good-bye to all of it. Watch those stars.

The stars. I looked up into the night and saw them, all of them: some of them dead a thousand years, a million years—could that be possible? They shivered in the cool ascent of altitude. And some of them, some of them were moving: speeding across the night in patient arcs. Satellites. I watched clear air and looked up into the void where every tenth star above was a running satellite. This whole country's going to explode, and you run off to go hike a mountain! Idyllic, lovely. It's because they couldn't stop, they couldn't stop you. *Take a good look around. This is the place you wanted: and you've circled down to the very pit of it.* The cold circle.

Live in his image. You're gonna go far, kiddo, before you fall. Before the wax melts. This is the cone, the place of the volcano. *Look at the puff of air in your breath: look at it rise and join the clouds. Look at it roll across the mirror of the frozen lake*: four hundred metres across, one hundred metres below. *Look at your breath, stretching out, mirrored in the ice.* From the *Pay attention to that.* town of Bedrock *Watch it. Hold on.* a place right out of history *Because you won't come back if you don't. Those mountains?* Sunny day washing the clouds away! *Just above the cloud deck there? That's the Elburz—east and west. Bandar-e Pahlavi; Shahsavaar; Baabol.* Yabba, dabba, doo *Those people over there—in Turkestan—the ones waving? They can see you, those little kids. And the parents*—well, they're sending off congratulations. Let's go with the family down the street *Look at 'em yell in Azarbayjan!* Look, look who stands on Damávand! *He's up folks, yup.* Here we go—off to the Land of Grow. *But not of his own free will. It took me to come get him.* Sunny day chasing the clouds away. *Good thing you can't see what he looks like: all the blond shag of hair and his face thin as a skull; puke all over his front.*

Start breathing, Diamond, or you won't make it. Take some water from your pack and wipe your front. Yabba, dabba *What kind of beast did Beatrice raise? you with your anomaly-haunted life.* On our way to where the air is sweet. *The freak of circumstance and Goshawk Squadron. All you need is the faith that you'll survive, Diamond.* We'll have a doo time, dabba doo time *That simple that easy.* Can you tell me how, tell me how, tell me how *The faith that this is all leading somewhere. When you fall, you will not feel your own weight. When you rise, your feet will never touch the earth.*

At death, you break up: the bits that were you start speeding away from one another forever with no one to see. We'll have a gay old time! It's only oblivion, true: Everthing's A-OK *we had it before, but then it was going to end, and was all the time merging* to bring to bloom *Friendly neighbors say* the million-petalled flower *that's where we'll be!* of being here. *Can you tell me how to get, how to get to*

life's true face is the skull.

To look up in the black where you lay on the ledge. This is the place where you had traveled to all your life.

Had I ever left this? Had I always known? I mumbled the lyrics of a song I remembered; but when I got to the part about *running on empty, running blind,* I was frightened. The sound of my own voice frightened me. I was going to die. I had to accept that. *Remember, remember.* The word is a place we prove real by dying in it. Who had said that?

And then my skin iced. The hair on my forearms stood up—no, shot out like *live wires.* There was a door above me, a trap door, and it was opening. There was light. And there was a figure, descending: coming for me. The figure of Mitchell, his shape and his voice that I had been hearing in sleep. I should have known. Should have done something about it. All my life I had been traveling to this single pinprick of nothing. Should have known. And a voice. *Tchera mi-zeni mano?* This is it.

٣

This is what I remember, Faith. And now it's time . . .

We sat on the roof of our house. We sat in the dusk, watching the shadow of light flooding the slopes of the Elburz, watching the darkness float down from the peaks and embrace us, embrace all of Tehran in a shadow of calm. Against the edge of one mountain, we watched a hawk glide in a smooth, arcing ellipse, forward and back in our field of view. A fulcrum of patience, waiting, searching for prey to slip from their cover and become game.

"They took this kid, strapped him to a chair, and pushed a button. The kid had burn marks on his hand and his feet and his face. He couldn't open one eye.

"But nothing physically happened. The chair started moving toward a wall. The wall was a wall of these electric heating coils, like a toaster. The chair would make this squeaky kick, and jerk toward the wall. It moved like an inch at a time. You could feel the waves of heat from the coils. It would have taken about an hour for him to get there.

"But it took him only five minutes to go insane. Nerezi just smiled and said, 'This is how simple it can be.'"

My father had paused, took in a sharp breath. "I used to believe it could be so right to be so crazy," *he said.* "Break all the rules. That's what a fighter pilot did . . . But it's over now, Dante," *he said.* "I have to face that."

Then like an idiot, or maybe a madman, he chuckled—I mean, after a story like that.

He had this half-grin.

"Do you remember a few months ago, in Colorado, this plane that flew over during a formation?"

"Yes, sir," *I said.* "It was amazing—we never saw anything like that. They never got him. I heard that Richards—you know, the commandant who took over after Magyar left?—was furious, bitching about it for months because they never caught the guy who did it."

Straight down from Eaglehead, like an incoming warhead. Straight over the terrazzo. No markings, wings swept, cockpit cut like a diamond, a plane accelerating so fast we seemed pulled back from it. One hundred feet off the deck and heading straight for the north dormitory. This huge WHAP! and the figure of absence where his plane had been, and the sound of his engine rushing in behind his trailing wake.

"Well," he said, "the reason they never got him is because he flew out of the Nevada desert and cruised along the deck until he hit the academy. Then he hit the burners and zoomed on down.

"And this plane, which is so dangerous and wild—this flying wing—that will probably not see production for another twenty years—and can go three thousand miles without refueling.

"And the reason they never got him," he said, "was because I was the pilot." I could tell by his face that he wasn't lying.

"I knew that you wanted to see me when I came out to Washington, so I made damn sure that if I couldn't see you, you could see me."

I thought of how as a little kid, in Australia, we'd all stood out in the schoolyard on ANZAC day, lined up in parade formation in our black and white and green school uniforms and sang in memory of those who'd died half a world away and half a century before, trying to remember something I knew barely anything about. Then I thought of that day in Colorado, seeing that plane pop through the horizon and disappear . . .

"Ho Chi Minh said it, once: 'The poet should know how to lead the attack.' Do you understand what that means?" he asked.

"No, not really."

"Well, maybe one day you will."

•

I think he was right. And if I could say that I remember the story he told on the roof of our house, all those years back now, I remember as well the image I saw looking down from the sky that day on Damávand—because in some way I had become part of the sky—looking down at the shape of my own body, frozen in sleep, just beneath the lip of the summit.

I knew then, though who knows how, that I was not going to die, that I would live, in the way my dreams kept living even after my body had collapsed. What I was seeing was not the moment of death, but the sense of being willing to live, to live through it, survive. I saw the shape of my father's plane, one wing of colorless black, tracing a course through the lake of ice, the mouth of the volcano. I saw the clouds above as ghosts of the Paradise: Jamshîd, Zahhák, Rostram, Sohrab, Ferîdun, all of them, rising, into the air.

I saw my own breath drift from my body and rise toward the summit of ice. And out of the fog of my breath, my body took form and I could see my legs rise, with purpose and confidence. I saw Beatrice and Scott and Mitchell reaching out to hold on as I pushed through a field of snow, waist-deep and cold. They reached out in turn and pulled me to them and then each pointed toward the sky, to where Saturn hung in its orbit. "Go," they each said wordlessly. And I would move, legs lifting in silence, only the upward schuss of my form, like skis, pulsing through snow, through a field of shadows, glacial, shifting.

And there at the final base of the summit, a steep rising talus of granite that came to a face of perpendicular rock, I saw my father reaching out to hold on to me. The two of us rising together, heaving and breathing, and then pausing to rest, to look out from the snow and the ice, to look out toward the future, the wilderness and the course of a blue river, a hundred miles away, snaking its way to the sea, to an ocean that covered the world. Perhaps we said something then, about how the world looked different now, from that height, how it made sense, the way a story can make sense of our pasts, or an image make sense of a life. How I wanted him to be there with me, for our hands to be joined as we stepped up to the plateau of the summit, to touch the presence of altitude, and, together, peer over the lip of the rim to the sudden mirror of sky. I wanted to tell him that here, this is your hand in mine, *and both of our hands are bleeding together from the sharp cuts of the rock, and neither of us can be sure whose blood is his own now, the way I could never be sure the lines cut in the path of my palms were ever mine, were ever anything more than the course of a history that flowed like words, like lines, like rivers.* Here is my past; here, my future. Here is my death, the line I will never uncover, the line that will uncover me.

Here is my hand, *easier to cut off and discard than erase the history it tells of sources, connections, our stories.* Here is the story *I would have to be able to tell one day, how my father and I stepped from the summit and into the air, and kept rising, into the light, and into the darkness. Nothing to hold us as we passed beyond heaven. And he would have to believe me when I told him, one day, because you have to believe your own history.* It's all I have.

ع

I woke. Began to vomit blood. The blood turned to water. I lay with my face pressed to earth and then rose like a sphinx on both elbows—my forearms straight ahead. Inside my head the howl of effort and the scream for air had numbed beyond sense. Half-asleep, half-dead, I had to get out of there.

I pushed myself from the ground and looked back. My pack was open and helpless fifty feet behind. I could see where my knees had hit the dirt, and where my thighs and my upper body had made a path like a snake's as I dragged myself along.

The burnt canister was at my feet. I must have run and stumbled, carrying the white torch. And I could remember the dream—or the illusion of it. I knew that this was real now. I knew who I was. I looked up. It was there. I'd rather die than not see it. Even if I did die, no one would know. One day they would find me, asleep at the summit.

•

I opened my throat to cry out, but no sound came. Only the puff of my lungs shoving a note of white breath, lifting and joining with the mist rising from snow and from the lake's frozen mirror. The jagged circle of the cone: a quarter-mile across, hundreds of feet below. I knelt and then spread myself perpendicular to the edge, looking to it, my fingers hugging the lip of the rock—the clouds reflected and rolling in the fractured blue nilas.

And then above me, the cool ascent of breath heading for the impossible, dark sky. It was what Mitchell had shown me, or what the dream of the figure of Mitchell had tried to keep me from.

I went to my pack for the camera. As I reached for the flap of orange nylon, I saw my fingers and forearms trembling. I would have to be quick. Looping a strap over one shoulder, I circled the cone of the lake. It was beautiful. No other word could replace what I saw. I brought the camera up and flooded the shutter with the last images of film. The side of the metal housing around the frame was dented and chipped. The lens was not scratched.

•

We had climbed from the northern face. It was the longest route to the summit, and the most difficult. To escape, I would have to find the quickest path down. I could not stumble back through angling uncertainty. I was conscious now, dehydrated and broken, but I was standing. A minute later?

I took off my sunglasses, placed them in a case and then zipped them in the side pocket of my pack. The light was intense, reflecting the snow—blinding. But I could not lose those glasses during the fall. And this would not take long . . .

I stood at the edge of the eastern face and mapped out a way in my head through the glacial cut of ice and scree. The tiny rocks looked like the rocks of a stone beach, places where the waves grind stones into pebbles, smoothing their bodies with salt. I put my arms through the straps of my pack and jumped down. It would have to be a dance of falling, the way a child on a sled would feel the kiss of snow and flash of speed, thinking he could move so fast he could lift off the ground and fly out of himself.

I wished that I had the ice axe with me now. I knew this feeling; I had practiced it. The day Mitchell and I had crawled on our knees to Audubon Peak. We lay there, exhausted, our faces in snow—staring at each other. Mitchell had reached out his hand, felt something, and dug out two candy bars: Snickers, Three Musketeers. It was a miracle, we knew it. We laughed between gasps for breath. Lying on our backs we looked up to the atmosphere, devouring the mush of frozen chocolate with the snow we crammed into our mouths. The sun was behind the summit, and we were two hundred feet away. The concave bowl of the peak had sleeved us in shadow. We stuffed the wrappers in our pockets and we were off. When we reached the top, we found a different world. There were probably thirty people there, oohing and aahing, pointing to the distance, mulling around the snack bar. The grease of boiled hot dogs and hot chocolate hung in the atmosphere. It had been easy for them: they had taken the cog railway to the roof of the earth; they could snap a few pictures, mention to each other how the altitude was so thin, and then they'd be gone. We asked a woman to take our picture, Mitchell and I together, and she backed off, frightened. We must have looked horrible—our clothes dripping with snow, our faces frenzied with sweat. When I asked her again, *please*—she took the camera, told us to *smile, or at least try,* snapped the photo, hurriedly returned the camera, and then turned and walked from us. And when Mitchell and I jumped from the roof of the summit, we ran through the scree slope—skipping and hopping to timberline, pretending that our boots were skis and that we knew what we were doing.

And I fell through the glacier, remembering and pretending. I felt the pulse of my body and my feet, the jostle of my gear in my pack. I was moving quickly; I told myself that I would not fall, and the only way not to fall would be not to think about falling. And I thought of the night, the last trip Mitchell and I had made together. We had skied cross-country to the remote peaks outside Leadville. I thought then that it was a way of saying good-bye to Mitchell, in case he had really decided this time to leave the academy. We set up camp at eleven thousand feet; the first night it dropped to ten below, and we huddled close for each other's warmth. His bag was thinner with down than mine. I heard the bridges of his teeth chattering. He said nothing.

Other than nights when we dragged ourselves back into the tent, we spent the entire weekend on skis. The second night we strapped on head lanterns and strode off for an outing. The moon was full, and we saw that we did not need our own light. We switched off the lanterns. It was a strange, unreal wonder: hearing the kick of our bodies in the rhythm and the glide, the pulse of our fog. We sailed down through woods sometimes knee-deep in powder, and we herringboned up through the rises. We came to a steep, smooth slope. Mitchell said that we should try to downhill. He knew how to telemark, and I had never even downhilled before. "It's easy," he said. "Just follow me. Bend and balance, shift your weight, stretch, and drive."

And he pushed off, and I stood there at the crest, watching him fall. I followed him. And I didn't get very far: I hit the first mogul and was in the air. I saw myself as an ostrich; I knew it was coming. I flipped over, saw my skis pass in the light, as my head impacted the soft snow, sank into a plush white.

And I knew it was coming now when my foot misstepped on a rock that slipped from the ice. I fell on my side where my rib was already throbbing. I yelped in pain, tumbling, farther and farther through the ice field. It would have to be luck now that saved me. I couldn't brake.

My pack opened, and pieces of equipment began racing my broken body down the slope. The camera hit a slick of ice that my body missed and went skittering past. I saw the back of it open, pieces of glass shatter as it flew off the edge—to splatter on rock two thousand feet below.

•

Despite all the mistakes I had made, I was alive. It was near dusk. I sat on a flat ledge, sorting things out. Most of my equipment was gone—the rope, food, the camera, knife. The few pitons and carabiners, because I had zipped them in a side pocket, were intact. I did not need them.

I had one flare left. One sierra cup. One empty water bottle. A signal mirror. I dipped the water bottle in snow and pressed it under my thin, ripped T-shirt to the flesh of my stomach. It would melt, eventually. The snow was a hard cold but did not hurt. I took a handful of white powder and forced it to my mouth. It would be all I could have, despite my raging thirst. Eating snow for water would bring hypothermia. I'd had enough problems that day.

"What should I do?" I asked myself abstractly. I was speaking aloud: asking the question, tasting it, probing for an answer. Yes, I was in a bit of a spot. My Kurdish sherpa had dumped me; I had no passport; I did not speak Farsi. I would walk into the police station below Reeneh, put up my hands and surrender, to speak the only words I knew of their language: *stream; mountain; saddle; river; A-OK* . . .

But what else could I do? Make my problems someone else's, let them deal with another dumb American? I ran my fingers through the grease of my hair. Sighed.

I turned over the signal mirror in my hands, like a talisman. I saw how a tiny vein ran through the glass in one corner. I held the mirror to my face and almost screamed: All the blood vessels in the sclera of my eye had burst. There was almost no white, only thousands of ruptured threads, splintered in blood. And at the center of it, luminous: the black iris.

I reached for my sunglasses, put them on, and sighed again. *Hell—does anything normal ever happen to me?* Long after the sun had set, I leaned against a rock and propped my pack on my thighs. I drank the melted water. I breathed the air. It was fine here. I'd have no problems. Only fourteen, maybe sixteen thousand feet. It was growing dark, and my eyes grew to the light.

I rolled out my faithful sleeping bag, stripped, and slipped inside. I lay on my back, arms crossed under my head, and watched the night brilliant with stars. *The music of the spheres sent from the empyrean,* Pliny called it, *a voice beyond all hearing.*

Because of the altitude, the stars did not flicker. Their light was a constant beam, and the rays of that light shivered down to me. There were no satellites.

◊

5 August

I had rolled up the sleeping bag and strapped it to the frame when I first heard the voice. I thought it was a trick . . . I had not heard the sound of another human for a long while.

But the voice kept coming, booming from somewhere above. And when I realized whose voice it was, I was frantic. I thought about running. I thought about violence. I decided just to stay calm and take all the help I could get. I pulled my final flare from the pack, ripped off the O-ring and shot the smoke into the slight wind. I shouted. The red flame hissed and sparks danced off the face of the rock I had spent the night by.

When he found me he was in a kind of reverie. He ran: threw his arms around me, and started slapping me. *"Keili-koub, Keili-koub,"* he wouldn't stop with that garbage.

I thought I was going to be angry, but I wasn't. I was glad to see him, too. He started checking my cuts, feeling for breaks and damage. As if I were a horse.

I winced when he touched my rib. He looked into my bloody eyes and grunted. He went to his rucksack and pulled one of *my* water bottles out. He made me drink. All of it.

•

We hiked, slowly and carefully, that day. We rested, often. Asadollah hovered over me like a worried wet nurse. He knew that I was hurting. When the water from my bottles was gone, he gave me all of his. We paused at streams when we could find them. "Drink," he motioned to me, bending over the water. "Drink."

He knelt beside me at the edge of the still, trickling water. I looked at him from the mirror of liquid, and he looked down to my face. We saw each other first as reflections I could say, but what I saw you would not believe. They call it the veronica.

He knelt and I waited. I studied the wool of his rug and finally recognized—it was called a *nain,* named after the village where it was made. Beatrice had shown me one, in our home. The tight weave and the colors made it among the most valuable of Persian carpets. I watched him as he prayed. How could a man give so much of his life for the invisible? How could I ever understand this man who'd pushed me until I broke and then cared for me now like a wounded son?

Maybe the people of this country knew something about themselves that we, the *farangi,* couldn't understand. Maybe they knew that there was evil inside everyone, and you just had to accept that, maybe even be thankful for it, the way you thank the day for being day, or the sun for having light. I would never know.

I smiled. I heard the soft whisper of Asadollah's prayer and then my father's voice. "Press on," he would say. Beatrice would, too. "Press on with your life."

When he had finished he knelt in the silence. It was still. We heard the trickle of water, running, beneath the melting snow.

•

We came out of a series of switchbacks from a steep ravine. The voice of a man called to us. We waited. He hobbled up, trailing the tether of his donkey behind. She looked tired. Her blanket was heavy with dust. The two men greeted in the ritual I had seen performed in the cave. Asadollah turned to me, motioned with his head toward the donkey. I shook my head no. He took my arm, pulled me to her side, and slipped the pack from my shoulders. "You *must,*" he was surely saying to me.

I rode for several hours. Sometimes I nodded into sleep. She snorted, stopped for dry clumps of grass. Together we followed behind the two men, stopping and then moving up to them, ranging freely. They did not notice. They were caught in the babble of speech.

Later, the man stopped and I climbed down from the donkey. I bowed slightly to him, and he smiled and returned my gesture. He turned and took the tether in his hands, and walked away—to the south, back to Reeneh. We did not follow him. Instead, we trailed as straight as we could down into the dusk, watching the dark slip over the path that took us back into the world.

٦

6 August

I lay in a stream that pooled into a basin. My arms drew out to their full length, and I held my legs together—a deadman's float. The water was cold. It was the first time I had washed since beginning the climb. I stopped, immediately, when I saw the basin. I was sweating like a fiend.

I called to Asadollah, and he looked back to me, puzzled. My pack hit the ground, and I ripped the clothes from my body and jumped bare-ass into the water. "*Cheshmeh,*" I called out to him. "Spring." He nodded and did not reply. He turned away when I stood up, naked, splashing water at him. Perhaps it was because the dark hairs of my crotch conflicted with the blond of my scalp. Perhaps it was the cuts and bruises that littered my white flesh. He would not bathe. He looked embarrassed.

I lay there, thinking of it, feeling my arms float away from me, both of them heading for opposite shores:

Today is the holiest of days: the day of the Transfiguration, the day Christ ascended the mountain. Thirty-three years before today, before I came to surface in this moving water, one bomb ignited over all Hiroshima. This was the day one man became a single particle of light. This was the day the world began our dwindling toward silence.

•

A black hump on the roadside. Under the innocence of her *chádor,* the claw of a hand pushed up as we passed by. I looked away. Frightened, misunderstanding. *Is this how you will come to spend the end of your days, woman?*

I walked ahead, quickening my step. And I thought of Scott. I turned back, to see Asadollah emptying his pockets of everything he had and bending to her open palm.

•

We walked along the highway for three hours. The dust from the cars zipping by clotted our pores. Dark pockets of dirt took hold in Asadollah's snow white hair. The stark canyon walls on both sides of the road broke, finally, into *darreh* farms and wide pastures. Sometimes a car would swerve to pass us, beep, yell something back to us, but never stop. I wondered how long it would take to reach Tehran by foot.

It was worse when the buses flew past: the dust would kick up and trail after in the dwindling wake. Rocks would splinter on our legs. My pack felt like it was molded to me now, a throb of dull pain I had to carry with me.

Finally, a bus slowed. It was a frightening sight: broken windows, roof piled incredibly high with luggage and furniture and even livestock, passengers leaning from the windows—the kind of bus that stopped for anyone. The door creaked open, and a boy leaned out. *Where to?* I suppose that's what he yelled at us, sixty metres down the road from him. *"Tehrán!"* Asadollah called.

We boarded, and I took a few notes from my pocket and the boy took from my hand what he needed for our fare. He motioned me toward the back. The bus was full. There were two seats. One was next to a woman wearing a white babushka with a flowered print. She stared at me as I walked down the aisle. I was two heads taller than anyone. My hair was a strange color. I went for the seat at the very back of the bus. Asadollah sat beside her, greeting her and asking her permission before he sat.

I stripped my pack, sighed, and swallowed hard. The ripeness of my own stench was no worse than that of my fellow companions. The heat was close to one hundred degrees outside, but no one but me seemed bothered by that. The wind licked at the curls of the driver's hair, slipping the smoke from his cigarette out to the highway. Plastic flowers, shaped like roses, lined his windshield. Above his head, a torn, faded *Playboy* centerfold.

It was a green Mercedes diesel. There were thirty-three of us on board. I counted. Everyone, in turn, looked back to stare at me. No one let his eyes leave me before someone else took over the watch. A few men turned bright blue prayer beads in their hands, muttering to themselves as they leaned into the aisle to check me out. The engine backfired. As we entered a tunnel, Asadollah uncrossed his arms, began the hum of his song. I should have known by now—if there were a way out of this, it was up to me to find it. I thought about pretending to be asleep. But even before we broke out of the long dark and into the light, I could feel their eyes.

We stopped at a small café. I slipped a few rials into his palm, and he went inside. I pointed to where I would be sitting. It was a grove of plane trees and poplar. I leaned against the trunk of a massive plane tree, and closed my eyes to feel the rush of branches stirring, and the trickle of the water of the stream that flowed beside me down to the rushing river. I slept, and dreamt that above me the branches of the ancient plane tree were opening, reaching toward the sky, pulling away from the weight of their own past. I heard the call of a bird: distended, muted.

•

Asadollah put his hand on my shoulder. He presented a plate of mulberries, cracked wheat kernels, a few slices of melon and cucumber, a pomegranate. He passed me a small Coca-Cola bottle; the brand was written in Farsi script. I sipped at it, and then almost threw up. The taste was horrible. I spit it on the ground. He gave me the *doogh* he had bought for himself, and I nodded, sorry that I still did not know how to thank him. I let the cool yogurt flood my throat.

We ate. He broke open the pomegranate and showed me how to squeeze the juice into my mouth. When we had finished, he was quiet. He looked at me with an expression half filled by sorrow and half by joy. He reached into his rucksack. And he made me stand.

He placed the *Ghor'án* on my head, said the words he had said six days earlier. And he said something else, something Gozameh had said.

"*Mordeh nabashi. Zendeh bashi.*"

He took my face in his hands and pulled me down. He kissed me. As he started to turn, I did something that shocked him. I loomed above him and took his face in my hands. This little man, who was eighteen inches shorter than me. He looked at me quizzically. Dark tentacles of sweat poured into his collar. I bent over and kissed him back. I took his lips to mine. The harsh salt dripped through the white bristles of his mustache.

May you never grow tired. May you live forever.

And then we faced the peak of Damávand. Somehow I knew it, then: this would be the last time in my life I would ever see that mountain from that height. He clasped his hand over my fingers and placed them to my forehead, lips, and heart. This, I would come to learn, for one who is faithful of Islam, is how you say farewell.

•

The horn of the bus was blaring: it was time to leave. I was the last one on. I looked at their faces. They were all in the same seats they had taken before. The woman in the babushka stood up and pointed to my assigned seat in the back. *Thank you, ma'am.*

As soon I sat, the engine coughed and we were off. *Please stop looking at me—I'm not all that bad.* I spoke to the reflection of my window. I could hear the prayer beads clicking in their hands. And the sound of a paper bag, shaking. I looked at a man, who was twisting like a gyro as the bus wound up through a pass. We made a hard turn, and he gripped at the rail of the seat in front of me as the bus swung in its tracks. He was shaking the bag again. It was full of small, brown apples. I shook my head no.

Everyone was looking at me, everyone, I noticed, except Asadollah. The bag shook for a third time, and so I nodded my head in thanks, reached in and picked the smallest apple I could find. No one moved. Once again, the bag shook.

So I bit into the apple. A few people started clapping. *Yes,* I thought to myself as I started a silent laugh, *it is amazing that Americans eat apples.*

The man smiled, turned to the two men in front of me and gave them their choices. He worked his way toward the front of the bus. Everyone ate. Even Asadollah, who would not look back to me. But I knew he was smiling.

And the woman beside him, flashing the flowers of her babushka as she turned, holding a finger to her lips, and whispering—in a voice louder than the strength of our moving: *"Zabán!"*

Open your life, stranger. So we can't speak, I thought for the last time. Maybe we'll never speak. Hell, at least we can still smile. And we all sat there, heading for home. Munching on fruit, surrendering our mouths to the sweet juice of the apple. I stared out the window, then turned to their faces. Asadollah crossed his arms and blew out a soft sigh of contentment. He nodded his head.

Whatever the test had been, I had survived. Survived to witness the sound of our groaning climb into the cleft of a high mountain pass. The engine grumbled and churned. And I knew that we would climb, together, into the distance, and that we were bound to fall, one day, fall into the dream of blue sky.

Yes. I said it, even then. I loved them. If I lived among them for a thousand years, I'd never be any closer to understanding. But that day, that afternoon, I loved them as honestly as any boy falling backwards into manhood could. *Mordeh nabashi. Zendeh bashi.*

Part Seven

Dead Reckonings

*One day each soul
will plead for itself*

—the Ghor'án

*Farídún-i-farrukh farishta na-búd:
Zi mushk ú zi 'anbar sarishta na-búd.
Bi-dád ú dahish ráft án níkú'í:
Tú dád ú dahish kun: Farídún tú'í!*

—Shah-Námé

1

Faith, here—I am alive. I can say that. For days—weeks—I lay in this half-suspended state. Half-real; half-dreaming. Dreaming of you, dreaming that you would always forgive me. That you would always understand. Dreaming of voices, the memory of light.

A ZSU 396 had taken my wing off. A clean burst through the exhaust port and up through the leading flaps. I saw it, not believing it—watching the black broken sail crumble in the slipstream. The mean chord was interrupted, and the plane bucked. Pitched up and then left. The wing snapped. Fell away.

The escape sequence identifier launched the capsule as soon as I ran the checklist. How many times, I thought, had I known this would happen? How many times had I been there before? Reach up—wind the clock before you kill the fire—Relax . . .

But the priority sequence did something I never bargained for. Figuring launch trajectory, winds aloft, predicted impact, and slant target range along the return flight—where I was the target—it was clear through dead reckoning that I was excess baggage. The tapes, or me. There had been no time for transmission relay. There were no backups.

One of us wasn't going to make it back. The computer was clear. Operator termination—*the letters formed by digits flashed across the heads up display.*

I was shot out over the gulf. Seat pack, pressure suit, and zero chance. Ten minutes' worth of oxygen. I fell. Pressure breathing. Scared. The blur of space. I looked up at the stars and wondered if this would be the last thing I'd remember. The Great Bear rearing. Orion drawing his bow toward the infinite.

I hit terminal velocity. Arched my back and flew toward earth and the ocean that covered the world—they blossomed beneath me like a net.

"Diamond," I heard Troy call out on the radio. How could I answer? "Time to die, now. Time to die."

"Blesséd be," I swear I heard her say it—but what can I really *remember? "Blesséd be his name. Praise the sacrifice of Igra, the great angel has fallen."*

Strange to hear this, I thought. Strange to hear Troy's voice—the angel Jibrail. She's passing through the stars. She's talking about me.

My oxygen bled off. And still I fell. At ten thousand mean sea level feet, the chute deployed. I lived. Unconscious, but conscious dreaming.

Three days later, they found me face down in the water. Still asleep. Still alive. The helmet and the pressure seals all intact. Later, someone told me I looked happy. They asked if I could remember anything.

Yes, I do remember. I remember how I fell—descending with the angels until the dawn.

•

While I was in the hospital, I found out. It's true . . . though I don't know if anyone has released the information or unlocked the satellite relays. But I believe it now. I saw the tape.

Shápuhr Mareta is dead. Consumed by the crowd. They swallowed him. His dark political objective was truthfully revealed. "Peoples of Behesht, believe me," he proclaimed, "believe Mohammed al-Mahdi!" He spread his arms in joy. "The occultation is at an end. I have come to reveal myself."

The crowds went quiet. Dead still. And a voice, huge, rolling, booming out of everywhere and out of nowhere: "He is not the Imam . . . the Imam would not reveal himself thus."

And that was it. The crowd threw up its arms as well, and rushed toward him. The guards surrounding the platform melted in the wave. Shápuhr Mareta was frozen—still filled with joy. And horror, when he saw it was real, that it was going to end. For him.

It was over, that simply and that quickly. All those years of pain and agony. Over in a single sentence, a single word.

It's something about the place—the purity of the faithful, the fervor that threatened and yet never seized the world—that consumed most the unknown and the faceless. The sudden burst of light, the bodies falling through black provinces of altitude; Kurds dying in droves because they refused to accept the truth that they did not have a home; Baha'i, persecuted long enough to only meet their end; the bomb masked as a cassette recorder inside the mosque; how, at night in the capital, after the revolution, you could hear the aftermath of summary trials and conclusions—a single bullet's report in the dark; and in the morning, you would see their faces on the newsprint—you could walk the boulevards and buy the postcards of the faces of those tortured by the Martyrs, but you could not know who would die and when.

It was over.

DEAD RECKONINGS

And when I saw the tape, I thought I would be coming home. But it's not that simple. The aftershocks wear on. A new war rages. Why—I can hear the Alliance pondering this right now—won't these people behave? How can we have democracy when they won't do what we want them to do?

But they have won, I think. The Paradise is theirs. They had suffered for the faith of their one God, and they have won.

Perhaps it's true. Perhaps the Imam who has never died still looks on now, nodding his approval.

•

Years ago, when I climbed Damávand, I thought I understood. But it changed. Strategies are all decided on the other side of the world. And they are played out here on the desert floor. There is nothing valid anymore in the idea of the single human.

Sure, we believed it. We believed Thoreau and all the other fool romantics when they took off for the wilderness. They forgot the other world out there, the other humans who needed us. It was the dream of the failed man.

"We will come together in Behesht," Shápuhr Mareta had said. Maybe he's right. Maybe the Alliance understands that without knowing yet.

While I was in the military—the first time—there were thirty-nine revolutions in the world. None of them survived. And I thought I left active duty for the same reasons I decided to remain at the academy after climbing Damávand. I thought there was no epiphany, no revelation. But I was wrong. For each act there was a thought preceding it: one said, you must leave; the other, you must stay. I have been woven into this—subject to the court of memory—like a certain part of all of us that lives outside of time.

And when they called me back, there was no choice. I came.

•

You know I have always loved flying. The sense of height, distance. Nothing to do with systems or sophistication. Nothing to do with speed. It has to do with grace. Yes, that's what it is—grace. From that first morning in pilot training—when I broke the sound barrier and the plane arced through forty thousand feet, I knew, looking outside the cockpit, that Zeno was right: I was frozen in space. Perfectly still. I was a dot, insignificant, fragile, streaming high above the surface of another planet, another earth.

In the space between is a curtain of memory. The awe of flying through the aurora at night, thirty thousand feet above the polar ice cap, watching the phosphorescent arms of grey and green hover on the skin of our ship. The whispers of light that said you do not belong to this earth.

Memories of ten-thousand-foot-takeoff rolls, with nearly two hundred thousand pounds of fuel on board. Or crossing the ocean so many times I seemed to think myself an eighteen-wheel trucker of the airwaves. Losing cabin pressure over Iceland, watching the cockpit flood with the cold, intense rush of air; falling to the runway beneath us.

One morning we streamed over a glacier north of Alaska: no other presence for hundreds of miles in any direction. The sun peeked over the horizon, fell and then rose again. It seemed we were flying away from the light even as we streamed toward it. The blue veins of ice splintered off in all directions.

We all heard the voice on the radio. Disembodied, so perfectly crisp and correct in its pronunciation. A British version of our language. Proper, trim, precise. "Pardon me, could you provide magnetic heading?" I looked back to the navigator, thought he'd been playing a joke. But, puzzled, he was looking to me for direction. And then we heard the voice again, barely whispered, slicing through the Guard emergency frequency—"Pardon me, could you provide magnetic heading?" I heard my copilot's voice on the radio. "Oh my Gawd . . . Look!" She jerked her arm over her shoulder, and I leaned to where she was pointing.

I remember the four of us, crunching our faces to the window watching the silver, cigar-shaped plane, its huge dimensions, flying formation beside us. And their faces were pressed to glass watching us. The counter-rotating propellers blurred in the soft haze of dawn. The red star on the tail gleamed in the light.

It was a Tupolev-95 Bear Bomber. The pilot was speaking, explaining that they had picked us out from the ice and landscape clutter on their radar—and I thought to myself: their radar is not supposed to be that accurate. *They had flown as quickly as possible to intercept us.*

Their course systems had failed. Their radar screen had faded only minutes before, and now the screen was completely blank. They could not distinguish the huge ice floes from recognizable landscape features. And no map, no matter how detailed, could help the naked eye out of that wilderness. No compass, no direction. Lost.

The impossible chance that we had flown by in that ethereal blue and white space and had painted our shape on the sweeping arc of their scope. The con-

trast of our visible silver body against the white had saved them. They would have wandered aimlessly until their fuel no longer fed their engines. They would have vanished.

We took them as close as feasible to a remote airfield off the northern coast. My navigator gave them accurate coördinates on the radio, winds aloft, the best magnetic course to follow, corrected headings for variation and drift. Near Soviet airspace, we broke right, reversing our course and heading back out over the waters. A few minutes after that, we picked up an intercept Mig heading toward us from the southwest. We asked our newly departed friends for help relaying a radio signal. The fighter disappeared immediately. We thanked them, wished them safely to their destination. We hoped we would not have to meet again.

•

Years ago, eight months into pilot training, I walked into the squadron common room after a mission. A television had been brought in from the education center and set up on a table. A few crews, instructors and students, crowded around it. The president's image filled the screen.

His face looked desperate, and his voice was coarse. He had difficulty breathing. He was making an announcement. On the early dawn of that day, in the Iranian desert, some 130 special operations forces, army rangers, logistics support personnel, and Farsi translators, as well as 50 pilots and aircrew members, were forced to abort the attempted rescue of fifty-three American hostages from the embassy in Tehran.

While the evacuation was in progress, a helicopter, low-level maneuvering, sliced through the frame of a top-secret MC-130 during a freak sandstorm. Both aircraft burst into flames.

All eight men aboard the craft died.

The plan was ambitious. Six C-130s were to lift off from a location in Egypt with men, fuel, and equipment. They would land at a secret airfield named Desert One. There six Stallion seacopters from the aircraft carrier Nimitz, on call in the Arabian Sea, would join them. The copters would fly to a mountain hideout near Tehran. Clustered in vans, the rescue team would drive to the city, seize the embassy, eliminate the guards, free the hostages, and extract the chargé d'affaires, Bruce Laingen, from the Foreign Affairs Ministry.

If the rescue team encountered resistance, C-130s overhead would control any possible insult with airborne Gatling guns—with rapid-fire delivery up to seventeen thousand rounds per minute.

But no one counted on the storm. No one counted on failure.

24 April 1980.

The president was apologizing for the failure of "this humanitarian mission. . . . To the best of our present knowledge, all crew members on the scene of the incident have died." My friend and roommate was among them.

He died in that desert, and the wind erased his existence. The sand buried his corpse. It was pulled out of the ground and displayed, what little was left, in the street outside of what was once the American Embassy. He was sent home.

Years ago, I sat on a bus heading for home. And a little babushkaed woman had placed a finger to her lips. Everyone smiled. Her mouth opened, and her tongue touched the breath of one digit. Everything I knew was erased.

"Zabán," she had said. I thought she was telling me the word for quiet, the time to pay attention and listen—the way a mother would tell her child to listen for something important, something she was about to say. But no one said anything.

And then I thought she was telling me the word for tongue, and in time I knew that is what she had meant. She had given me the word for language. The impossible gulf we could not narrow between us. Still, we had been able to speak. She had told me of language, and the failures of language.

I thought I understood.

Years ago.

Now most of those I knew then are dead. Asadollah disappeared after I left. Like most Kurds, he was hit hardest by revolution, by a nation that would never recognize his nation. I suppose he fell back to the hills, and was found, and was killed. But I'll never know.

Gozameh, though. He had to flee. The northwest routes out of the country were cut off, and the Soviet borders to the north didn't provide much temptation. So they traveled overland and only got as far as Qom before they were stopped. Why Qom—of all places? It was not the shortest route west. There had to be a reason. Hearing the story of his death, years later, I couldn't stop asking that question. Why Qom? Police pulled them over, asked where they were going, weren't satisfied enough with his explanation, pulled him away from the car and fired. He fell into the dirt. His wife started screaming. His daughter and son stood frozen by the door of their car. One moment their father was standing, and talking loudly, shaking his arms and his hands. And then he was nowhere.

I know that my father owed Gozameh his life. The day that Gozameh saved my father from assassination was a favor due in return. When my father flew into Mehrabad, after the fall, he drove through the city trying to find Gozameh. His Farsi was good enough that he could get by, and no one had stopped him. But he found nothing that day. When he reached Gozameh's family in Paris, he found the truth.

Gozameh had been followed, for a long while, because he worked for my father—because he worked for Americans. When the family moved west out of Tehran, they were not alone.

I will never understand.

•

Do you remember, Faith, when we first met? I think I loved you even before you spoke your first word. I was so nervous leaning across the table in that seminar. You were so beautiful.

I just stuck out my hand and said, "My name is Dante Diamond and it's a pleasure to know you." And it is, Faith, and it will always be. And I will never forget.

I will never forget the days before I left. Now I am no longer afraid to speak of them, to speak of you. That must mean something. Something good, Faith.

How the light there on Jefferson Pass could make me stop breathing. A wash of pure gold over the house and the hills. I would really stop breathing. The light would flare for a second, and then be gone.

I will never forget the nights. The time at dusk we reached the peak of Mount Memphremagog. We dropped our packs and spread our sleeping bags in an outcropping of rocks beneath the crest, and waited for dark.

And later that night, the shower of bright meteors fell: the dark flare of their tails leaving their thin paths of light, fading but unwilling to fade, the afterglow of their absence, how there was another glistening at the heart of that burning, an infinite half-life, another luminous trail in the dark, the gloam of a path our eyes could not see.

Lying together, I heard the sound of your breath in sleep. I held you and would never let go. I looked up and saw it—the D-horizon, the place in the ionosphere where once only the great reconnaissance planes, trailing wings of colorless black, could rise to: the place where their roving eyes would look down and check all in balance, make sure that everything must stay as it is: the place where they first discovered radio waves reflected back to earth could make it possible to speak, without connection, across distance.

I thought of Damávand. I saw the place, and the people, flare and fade into one another. A lake of ice, circled by the descending cone of snow and rock, a glacier that had saved my life. Beatrice and my father—they had loved me, in their way.

And I saw our bodies—your body and mine, Faith—in the dark shape of two animals, pushing the sheets of crumpled water out ahead, hugging the shore.

When I woke near dawn, there were two shapes lying beside us: a doe and her fawn. The doe lifted her head, testing the air—and then seemed to relax. She bent down to nibble the earth, chewing and watching me, calmly considering us. The fawn would mimic her action—nuzzling her side, testing the pine from a low-lying branch.

•

I am happier now—if I can say this—to know my parents never lived to see this war. I am happy to know they returned and settled, there, in Vermont. That they lived, and survived, and died with grace.

And this is true. It happened. I dreamed it, though I don't remember if it happened in the fall or in the sleep that happened afterward. It was so real I could touch him. I was in the mist and he was beside me. It wasn't cold. Just this billowing cloud as we walked up the path to our house. We stood by the porch and my father looked at it, for a long while. "You've done fine work here, son," my father said. "We are proud of both of you. But remember," he said, "and pay attention—what you should look for in the world is not just for what you want to know, but for more than you want to know, and more than you can know."

And then he turned and walked into our house. He turned the knob of the kitchen and then looked back at me. "We'll keep the porch light on for you, Dante," he said.

I don't know what this means, Faith. But when I thought of this just now, I started crying. And when I dreamt it . . .

It was a dream. I don't think my father could have ever said something like that. But in a dream, things like that can happen. You can make people real.

DEAD RECKONINGS

You can tell the truth. You can see that memories can save you. You can see how your father lived his life in the words he could never speak. You can make the dead alive.

•

Here. The magnetic compass turns aside. The sun rises by falling south. Fly by the stars. Follow what each instrument predicts. Dead reckoning, we call it. Where even the earth flies out of an artificial horizon.

I am the Shabah over Paradise, the ghost haunted by its past. Here is the angel Jibrail, keeper of light. She sprinkles stars across the land with the sound of her voice, or a word. Here is Izrail, angel of death, who holds your soul flapping like a headless falcon in his hand and points in the direction of a yawning grave. The Pit of Wailing and the bitter Zagghume, the tree of Hell. Here is Eden and the pit of Tartarus. Here is Cerberus snarling like the wounded beast he is. The king of Hades with his bride at his side. The fields of Illyrium. The lamp burning in the branches of the olive tree. The shadow of the self inside the body, the moon rising from the sun. And here is the traveler, Charon, bent and wicked with age, waiting for your passage at the river. Patient, he can wait forever. We the living speak through the dead. And the dead condemn us with their silence.

We will die from being human. Dead men conversing with dead men.

Years ago, I touched this landscape. Tonight the angel of fate sits in heaven, unwinding the string of memory from a spindle—the genius, or demon, twisting the past to what I remember.

If I remember that moment, so long ago, if I remember it truly, it is because it is trued of distortion—like the echo of words in Satie's Gymnopédies, *or the song of Asadollah, and I am all the more happy to know that, here, in the silence, I can only remember the words—*

Bismi'llah-o 'rrahmané 'rahim
la hawla wa la qovvata illa billah

Now as I think back to the afternoon I never left, I see faces and figures whose names I will never remember. Their names were never important.

Those who lived on Damávand will be like legends to me. Those who shared a simple bus ride through a mountain pass were part of the most mystical journey I will ever take. A woman raising her finger to her tongue, the slight cry of "Zabán!" Asadollah smiling his inscrutable smile under his blossom-

ing mustache, looking back to me finally, and then out the window. The old men, turned in their seats and watching me. Everyone watching, as if I were learning their secret.

We were rising through clefts in a canyon, and falling again, following a way that turned back toward Tehran, tracing our way by a river that flowed down into the waters that cover the earth. Zeno was right: frozen in time, following a series of moments. Still. If only the dead could survive.

Now I think back to that day I never left. Together we lean and twist in our seats, lulled by the floating roar of the diesel. We follow the twisting path south from Damávand, which looms over my shoulder and always behind me, snaking our ineluctable path by the path of a river. I can't help but whisper it, like a poem or a prayer, or pure concentration: We're moving; we're flowing—*hearing the pulse of the engine, and our indecipherable thoughts. Down into the unknowing, unmeasured space where one language shares the silence with another.*

•

There could be other stories, yes. Other languages. And they would all be true. And if there were one night when I could say it all could end, it would be this night. Now. But it must begin and it must never end. It must run on, like time and like the spool of memory, and it must be everywhere and it must be nowhere. It must flare in one tiny exclamation point of light that my hand impresses on the page. One explanation, understanding, life. Here, this one.

Author's Note

The voices in *Diamond's Compass* speak in many tongues, from Arabic and Farsi to the technical language of engineers and pilots. They do not always agree on spellings and style. For example, *Sháhnáma* is the generally accepted English spelling of Ferdausi's monumental poem of 60,000 lines, *The Epic of the Kings*; a more phonetically correct spelling, however, would be *Sháh-Námé* or *Sháh-Námeh*; it appears here in all three forms, depending on who is speaking. As certain words and phrases will be unfamiliar, I have included a glossary of some of the more confusing terms, which appears after this note.

The first draft of this novel began in Colorado and ended, a decade later, in Braşov, Romania. First, I owe thanks to William Carpenter and Babak Ebrahimian who advised me on an early draft, written as a poem of 1,728 lines titled "Tellurion," and to Julie Agoos for her help with an early prose draft. Paul Jones and Jon Eller helped proof, edit, and give the right advice when the end was near. Thanks as well to Louis and Robert Rubin, who provided support when others questioned the idea for the book. Friends and mentors all.

The epigraph for this work is from *The Go-Between*, by L. P. Hartley (Alfred A. Knopf, 1954). The *Sháhnáma* epigraph for "Dead Reckonings" is from *A Literary History of Persia, Volume I* (University of Cambridge Press, 1964). The poem quoted in "Zaban" is "The Old Fools," by Philip Larkin, from *High Windows* (Farrar, Strauss, and Giroux, 1974). The quoted translation from the *Ghor'án* is XXIV, 35. The translation from Farsi of the poem "The Call," by Sohráb Sephéri, in *"Sháh-Námé,"* is mine. In one of the addresses to Faith, I have freely adapted a line from William Matthews's poem, "The Scalpel"; in the final address to Faith, I have adapted a line from one of Eudora Welty's letters to Diarmuid Russell.

There were a number of books that influenced the writing of this work. Two, in particular, were Ryszard Kapuscinski's *Szachinszach* and Taghi Modarressi's *The Pilgrim's Rules of Etiquette*. Many of the specific technical facts and geographic information come from *Iran: A Country Study* (American University, 1978).

AUTHOR'S NOTE

Finally, I owe thanks to the MacDowell Colony for time and space and Schelling studio.

—P. H. Liotta

Glossary

Abseil. German: the swift descent from a steep cliff via a rope secured at the summit.

Adjenne. Genie (plural of the Arab djinn).

Aga umad. The master has returned.

Al Abshár. A title neither Persian nor Arab, but, if it were to exist, would mean something such as "the waterfall."

Allah-o-Akbar. "God is great."

Aryamehr. "Light of the Aryan race."

Behesht. Heaven; paradise.

Belay. Providing security to another climber based on proper friction, position, and anchor.

Besmellah-o-arrahmane, arrahmané, arrahim, la hawla wa la qovvat illa billah. A rough translation of this might be, "In the name of God, the compassionate, the merciful, there is no truth or strength but in God." In Iran, every prayer, public announcement, parliamentary proceeding, official speech, and academic lecture begins, as does each *sura* of the *Ghor'án,* with the sacred Arabic invocation of *Besmellah-o-arrahmane, arrahmané, arrahim* . . .

Bong. Pitons with angles greater than 1½", of steel or aluminum, and full of holes to reduce weight.

Cack. The harsh, staccato banter of a falcon used as a warning or fear response.

GLOSSARY

Caminante, no hay camino. Se hace camino camino al andar. From the poetry of Antonio Machado: "Walker, there is no path. You make your path in the walk."

Carabiner. Shaped like huge safety pin to connect rope and piton.

Chádor. Hindustani: *chádar;* rectangular cloth used as a full-length shawl.

Chai kháneh. Tea-house.

Chenár. Plane tree.

Chesmeh. Spring.

Chingada. Spanish obscenity.

Chock. Used in place of a piton with the advantage of being easily removed from the rock.

Darreh. Literally, "cliff," although a more accurate use means "mountain valley," or, "valley between two mountains."

Divan. Poems used for divination collected in alphabetical order of the final letters of end-rhymes.

Do' a-ye talqin. Roughly translates as "the circle of blessing," although "circle of the self-induced spell" is closer to its real meaning.

Doroshky. Russian: *drozhki;* low, four-wheeled carriage.

Dosh. Roughly translates as, "My man."

Dulfer. French: classic rappel method, with one hand on the rope used for braking and the other for balance.

Eh, sfacim. Italian obscenity.

En sha' allah. "If God wills."

GLOSSARY

Fáll/fáli. Literally, "a presage"; a method of determining fate through either *fáll-e nohod* or divination through the consulting of poetic works; the subject reads the first poem (*fáll*) and then a second poem (*sahid*) as witness to foretelling future events.

Farangi. Foreign; European; Western.

Farídún-i-farrukh farishta na-búd:/ Zi mushk ú zi 'anbar sarishta na-búd./ Bi-dád ú dahish ráft án níkú 'í:/ Tú dád ú dahish kun: Farídún tú 'í. "Ferîdun, who was no angel, was not made of musk and ambergris, but, by truth and doing what seemed right, came to ecstasy."

Flail. Whip used by flagellants.

Gage. The technical use of "gauge."

Gardaneh. Mountain pass.

Ghanát. Underground water channels.

Ghazal. A flexible lyric form, also spelled ghasel, or ghazelle, that appears in Persian and Arabic literature. Usually it means a group of couplets, sometimes unrhymed; it is also employed in long poems such as the *Sháh-náma*.

Ghuthrah. Kaffiyeh, the headdress of the desert Arab.

Goush-esh ceda midé. "His ears are ringing." Used when speaking of someone who is absent. If the right ear rings, a friend is speaking of you; if the left rings, an enemy speaks.

Hále shomá chetowr-e. "How are you?"

Hané cheeze koub. "Everything is fine."

Hejira. The "hijra," or flight, of Mohammed from Mecca in A.D. 622; the first day of the Mohammedan calendar of A.H.—"after the Hejira."

GLOSSARY

Hypoxia. Oxygen deprivation; altitude sickness.

Jebem ti Boga. Serbian obscenity; literally, "I fuck your God."

Jedna za drugom. Serbian: "one or the other"; "it doesn't matter."

Jinn. Genie.

Jube. A natural irrigation, water, and sewage channel alongside streets in Tehran.

Jur Hasti? Salutation, roughly as "Are you together, in one piece, well?"

Keili-koub. "Very good; A-OK; fantastic."

Kernmantle. Climbing ropes with an outer sheath surrounding long inner filaments; it slides with less friction than traditional hemp rope over the rock surface.

Kháneh budan. To be home.

Khatam. Inlaid camel bone.

Khoub hasti? "Are you well?"

Kooh. Mountain.

Kuchka. Serbian: bitch.

La ilaha il Allah. Literally, "there is no God but God," though a more accurate sense of these words might be "your life is in the hands of God."

Mani. Born in Baghdad of Persian parents and founder of the Manichean Gnostic sect (216–276) that maintained a theologic dualism that the body and matter are comprised of darkness while the soul originates from and strives to liberate itself toward light.

Ma sha' allah. "What God wills."

GLOSSARY

Milagros. Spanish: miracle, amulet.

Mir gut. Und Sie? German: "I'm well. And you?"

Mithra. Persian God of light and truth.

Mohhammed al-Mahdi. Certain Shi'a sects believe that Mohhammed al-Mahdi, who disappeared as a child centuries ago, has never died and still waits to manifest himself.

Mordeh Nabashi. "May you never grow tired."

Morvarid. Pearl.

Nargileh. Hookah, from the Persian root for "coconut," the original material of the tobacco bowl.

Nazar-qorbani. Literally, "eye of the sacrificed animal."

Nil-e tchesm-e bad. Amulet, used most often for children, as magic against the evil eye; a black line drawn with the image of a roasted wild rue seed on the face.

Paroo! Paroo Mizanim! "Shovels! We shovel!"

Peri. Mischievous fairy.

Piton. Spike with a ring (or rings) at one end that is driven into the rock face during a climb and to which the rope is secured.

Prijatelj. Serbian: friend.

Prusik knot. Provides the climber greater flexibility to slide the knot freely up or down the rope, taking the weight off the climber's waist; helps the climber avoid suffocation during an emergency.

Qajar. Persian dynasty that reigned from the late 1700s until the 1920s.

GLOSSARY

Rappel. French: to recall; the descent from the rock face by rope.

Rudkháneh. River.

Rurp. Realized-Ultimate-Reality-Piton, invented by Yvon Chouinard.

Salám aleîkum. "Peace be upon thee."

Salamat bashi. "May you know health, well-being, salvation."

Sáyeh ye shomá kam, nashé. Informal use of *Sáyeh ye shomá kam, nashavád:* "May your shadow never grow less."

Sazeman Ettelaat na Amniyaté Késhvar (SAVAK). Organization for Information and the Security of the Country.

Shabah. Arabic; ghost.

Sháhansháh. King of kings.

Simurgh. The legendary Phoenix that lives on the slopes of Damávand.

Sohan. Caramel-like sweet made of pistachio and honey; the two most famous varieties come from Isfahan and Qom.

Tchera mi-zeni mano. "Why do you strike me?" Legend claims that Zahhák still lives—with the devil and his daughters—deep within the caverns of the high slopes of Damávand and so few should climb to the summit. When a stone is thrown into his cavern, a voice issues back, *Tchera mi-zeni mano?*

Thawb. The dress of the desert Arab, similar to the djellaba.

Umma. The community of Islamic believers bound by religion rather than allegiance to nation-state.

Varappé. French climbing shoes with rubber along the sides, toe, and heel for adhesion to the rock.

GLOSSARY

Wir sind sehr müde. German: "We are very tired."

Ya hadje Hafez Shirazi—toh Shirazi mán Shirazi—toh kachef-é Harraz-i— mán taleb-e yek fáli. "Master Hafez of Shiraz, we are both from Shiraz. You can discover each mystery, and I, I ask for a presage."

Zabán. Language.

Za 'ifeh. Farsi obscenity for whore.

Zendeh Bashi. "May you live forever."

Zurkháneh. "House of strength"; the exercise of dance and discipline to the recitation of *The Epic of the Kings*.